Bodie Gone

By Bill Hyde

I0561912

First Fiction Series

SANTA FE

Sunstone books may be purchased for educational, business, or sales promotional use. For information please write: Special Markets Department, Sunstone Press, P.O. Box 2321, Santa Fe, New Mexico 87504-2321.

Library of Congress Cataloging-in-Publication Data:
Hyde, Bill, 1934–
    Bodie gone / by Bill Hyde.-1st ed.
      p.cm
      ISBN: 978-0-86534-317-9 (hardcover) ISBN: 978-1-63293-136-8 (softcover)
        1. Women journalists-Fiction.   2. Gold mines and mining-
Fiction. 3. California, Northern-Fiction. 4. Gold miners-Fiction.
  5. Time travel-Fiction.

PS3558. Y354 B63 2001
813'.6-dc21   00-054745

Published by   SUNSTONE PRESS
                Post Office Box 2321
                Santa Fe, NM 87504-2321 / USA
                (505) 988-4418 / orders only (800) 243-5644
                FAX (505) 988-1025
                www.sunstonepress.com

"O wad some Pow'r the giftie gie us
To see oursels as others see us!"
                    —Robert Burns, *To a Louse*

"Not he is great who can alter matter,
but he who can alter my mind."
        —Ralph Waldo Emerson, *The American Scholar*

Acknowledgements

I WANT TO THANK MY WONDERFUL wife, and best friend, Ann, for her patience and help as I struggled with this novel. Without her encouragement, and assistance correcting and inputting *Bodie Gone*, I could not have completed the story. My daughters, Ann and Mary Kay, were also great resources: Ann gave me positive motivation and Mary Kay got the first draft of the transcript on a computer disc and showed me how to master my laptop.

I also want to thank my mother and father, Anne and Herschel, who provided educational opportunity and inspiration.

I am also grateful for the final review and critique of the galleys by Richard Doss, Ph.D., retired Professor of Philosophy and Religious Studies, Orange Coast College. His corrections and suggestions were invaluable.

Prologue

ON JUNE 10, 1995, I FOUND MYSELF—
Frances "Tip" DeQuill, affluent housewife, mother, and sometimes newspaper/
magazine writer—in jail. The clink was located in a remote, high, mountain-
valley community in northern California called Bridgeport. I had been
investigating a perplexing night sighting in the valley on June 9th. The awesome
and mysterious vision was followed the next day by the unique appearance of
a group of strangely dressed persons walking out of the gold and silver yielding
Bodie Mountains towards the old mining camp of Lee Vining.

My story marches back in history to the mother-lode days of the mid-
1800s and forward to 1995, interlocking the adventure and mystery of the Old
West with gold, love, lust, murder and the supernatural. It chronicles the stories
of people, both good and evil characters, Tex Garland, John de la Roche, Juan
and Pedro Olivera, Sean McCarthy, Betty Jane Allen, Nellie Moore and Daly
Storm, who made their way to Bodie seeking riches, revenge or adventure only
to find the bizarre. I call my story "Bodie Gone" and I wrote it while being
hunted.

1

IT WAS FRIDAY, JUNE 9TH WHEN I WAS taking my usual after dinner stroll with my mother, Joan DeQuill, along the dirt road connecting the McCarthy Ranch in the valley to the paved highway running between Bridgeport and several nearby lakes. We were on vacation; a time for horseback riding, hiking, fishing and relaxing at a location we had frequented several times each year since I was a child. Since early youth I had listened to Linda, a direct descendant of the founder of the ranch, and her cowhands tell tales about the wonders of this place.

The McCarthy Ranch was homesteaded in the early 1860s by an engineer from Boston named Sean McCarthy who disappeared one night in 1882 from the gold camp in Bodie. His family retained the property and they left fresh flowers on his grave each September. They raised cattle, sheep, Morgan horses, llamas, pigs and assorted vegetables. The animals grazed in the tall valley grass during the summer months and were trailed to lower ground for the frigid winter season.

When vacation cowboying became popular they had started taking in dudes to help cover their costs and in the summer the ranch house had a regular weekly cast of occasional cowboys and cowgirls. At the center of the property the old ranch house, set among the poplars, oaks and pines, served as the central headquarters for the owners, the kitchen and dining room for the guests, and a conversation piece for those who happened by. Scattered around the ranch house were a number of cabins that housed the dudes in modest comfort.

The Bridgeport Valley, once a high desert plain, populated by sagebrush, jackrabbits and rattlesnakes, had been transformed in the 1860s by Sean McCarthy's irrigation plan and leadership. A prospector himself, Sean had seized the opportunity to find his kind of gold in another way. Hiring Chinese laborers who had been laid off by the Central Pacific Railroad, he, and others, built irrigation ditches, siphoning off water from the many creeks, rivers, springs and lakes that spot the landscape. They cleared the sage, logged the timber, built a sawmill to provide lumber for sluice boxes, damns, mine shafts, wagons and buildings. He bought the land for twenty-five dollars per homestead, built the ranch house, fenced the property and began the difficult task of raising livestock in this harsh environment.

I had been to the ranch many times but I never ceased to marvel at the sunset behind the awesome peaks of the Saw-Tooth Mountains towering above the ranch house to the west. The valley lay at six thousand five hundred feet above sea level but a half-day on horseback would find one nooning at eleven thousand. The scenery in the high country could be matched in only a very few places in the world; steep sheer cliffs cut by ancient glaciers and icy cold mountain waters produced a myriad of hues, gray, blue, brown, white, black, green and red.

The upper Buckeye Canyon, above the roughs, is a place of unbelievable beauty and vivid color, I thought. It's the perfect location to view the hard metamorphic and igneous rocks that hold the mountains in place against the forces of nature. Those same rocks produce a rich, red, rust-like soil that is perfect for planting. Timber, magnificent stands of pine, oak, ash, poplar, cottonwood, birch, juniper, fir and hemlock trees spring from the rich earth to decorate the eastern slopes and valleys of the Sierra Nevada Mountains. Many of the timber stands have been previously logged—trees cut down in the prime of their lives. Some of the trees had re-grown out of the stumps of the presumed dead, others had re-seeded themselves. New forests were standing tall and fresh. This countryside is surely a place to make God proud and human beings reverent, I thought.

The winter of 1994/1995 produced the heaviest snowfalls since 1861, leaving the speckled black and white granite, black basalt and more colorful rocks buried under a thick blanket of white. At sundown it always cooled quickly; the wind invariably swept down off the mountains with a rip.

This evening, however, was different. The wind had a sharper bite than usual and it possessed a strange, inexplicable thickness, producing a feeling which seemed to come from inside my soul, something like what my mother said she felt when she heard a particularly well delivered sermon from a truly captivating minister. The feeling, its grip, seemed to demand silence— an unusual state for me.

Mother was strolling along the gravel road pulling her tan button-down sweater closer to her body, which was beginning to show the signs of her advancing years. Those first twenty went so slowly, the next fifty, so very fast. Where had the last years gone? She thought, and where would the next lead?

Mother was of less than average height and build, with small bones and a wiry frame. Her *coiffure* kept every strand of her blond hair tightly in place. She had a thin and wise looking face. Her blue eyes contained a depth worn in by wisdom and a spark charged by curiosity. She was a graduate of UCLA where she had studied French, become an avid reader, and was well traveled. She was viewed by most as fortunate. When cornered, or otherwise disposed to express her true opinions, she was honest to a fault and devoutly religious. She had granitic, rock like views on moral righteousness stemming from her Lutheran youth. She held similarly definite ideas about personal behavior and justice. She was sure, always sure, that she knew the important values of life, confident that she could see the truth, finding that truth in her church's description of God's will. While she sometimes decried ideas that did not square with correctness as she saw it, she was wise enough to recognize that not everyone felt as she did. And, she had the ability to be charming, a wise hostess when business or social circumstances called for *savoir-faire*. She knew how to ask the right questions, to get people to talk about themselves. She was particularly adept at getting "little folks," gardeners, maids, dressmakers and the like to feel comfortable in her company.

After my "troubled years" I recognized that my mother was smart— very wise actually—and like most intelligent people, she hid her true self from most others. However, when pressed to speak her mind or teaching family values, she knew right from wrong. In the eyes of family members, the little folks and other people who embraced a conservative Lutheran philosophy, she was considered to be saint-like. She had a good social conscience and always provided help and comfort to those in need. As her years advanced, she communicated mostly with her pastor and to those family members that were close-by and bound to her by the magnetism of her will.

Mother's tan cotton dress swung briskly as she made her way over the ground, arthritis paining, but not slowing her step. Stoic! Yes, she was truly a stoic. Never conceding to physical discomfort, never complaining, never allowing some physical malady to disrupt her lifestyle. She was strong as a horse, both physically and in spirit.

I noticed her glancing over at me and I wondered how she saw me? She must know that I am a typical product of the 1960s. Long blond hair, leftist ideals, smoking, Jesus shoes, a failed early marriage and other symbols of my revolt filled youth had given way in recent time to the more traditional values and benefits available to the well-to-do. Know thy self, I thought in recognition of the fact that I had taken to some excesses, vestiges from my troubled youth. Yes, I was smoking, drinking, using too much purple eye shadow and still relying on some of the ideas expressed by Joan Baez, The Kingston Trio, The Beatles, The Monkeys and other musicians of my time. These things are part of me, I thought. I have experienced total immersion in the spirit of my generation and the solution will never fully wash off.

I hoped my mother was pleased that the difficult years were behind me and I knew that she respected my degrees from both Stanford and Vanderbilt. To be sure, I was the consummate academic, reading everything while laboring primarily as a housewife. I had made a modest attempt at paying work as a stringer, writing occasional articles for mostly low-circulation "horsey" magazines. A few of my stories had perked some interest at the *Los Angeles Times* and found space on the interior pages of that old established newspaper. Once a brief of my article about the wanton slaughter of older horses had been picked up by Reuter News Service and received worldwide circulation.

My interest in writing caused some close friends to call me "Tip," and I decided to use Tip DeQuill as a pen name. In fact, in a manner consistent with the spirit of a liberated California lady, I continued to use my maiden last name after marriage. Brodrick, my husband, is a successful surgeon and unlike most of the women from my era, I am not required to work. I have time to care for our two girls, Francesca and Paula, ages fifteen and twelve, ride twice a week at the stable located near our Pasadena home and play golf or go swimming when I please. It's not a bad life, not bad, really, I thought.

I looked over at my mother. When I was seventeen the measuring stick on the doorframe proved I was three inches taller. I liked being taller and I liked being thin, almost anorexic. Oh, I'm not anorexic. No one in our family is that skinny and it would still be okay if I lost a few more pounds. Hell, we modern ladies would kill to look like one of those fashion models. Those bastards that peddle health diets are trying to get us all to look like sticks. They got me, hell they always get me.

I may be taller than Mom physically but I'm not bigger in spirit. I have never been able to manage her strong will. I wonder what I will be like when I am her age and I wonder what I will look like, I thought. My sharp featured face is already becoming lined, aged somewhat early by the unrestricted lifestyle of those from the generation Viet Nam. Regular, irresponsible smoking must be accelerating my decline, stripping me of the good things nature had bestowed. I should stop, end the bad habit, but I can't. Hooked. I have been hooked by the masters of deceit who run the big tobacco companies. It's "them" again. In this case it was a bunch of men who had the bravado to swear to the United States Congress that nicotine was not addictive and that there was no proof that it was medically harmful. What bull! Everyone knows better, but once you are hooked you are stuck.

Mom and Dad have been great, patient, willing to encourage and advise, able to deal with my bad times, my smoking and sometimes drinking too much. They have taught me a lot, I thought, as I strolled along. Oh sure, I know they talk more and better than they listen, but so do most people from their generation. So do I, when I get the chance. Their way forced me to listen and to develop, to some extent, the skill of using my ears, attending to others' stories. However, there is more to being a good listener than just hearing. My mom has tried to teach me how to draw people out, and capture their secrets. She does that very well, herself. It's been a game and it's been fun for her for many years. I've tried, but never really mastered the technique. It's an art form,

I think. I can't be like her. I'm a person from another time—a product of a different set of struggles.

"They will be lighting the campfire soon and I am looking forward to roasting marshmallows on a stick," I said.

"I wonder if they will remember to bring the song books," said Joan, "I never remember the words, except that one about the Bridgeport jail:

Oh, fare you well to liberty,
For all our foolish pranks,
We long shall be imprisoned,
Within the Bridgeport tanks."

Light from the brightest stars began to pierce the azure twilight. The high desert, even on a moonless night like tonight, is brightened by the sharp clear beauty of the stars. You see them better up here because their luminescence is unobstructed by man's pollutants—smog and other stuff humans create and shove up into the sky leaving it hanging over their major cities. The stars were always there, watching, shining only at night, like the eyes of the nocturnal hunter. Since the very beginnings of recorded history man has watched the jewels of heaven and dreamed, dreamed and wondered about the mysteries of the universe.

God knows, I thought, the things that fly around up there can be both spectacular and scary. They pique one's imagination. Maybe that's why almost everyone studies the horoscope every day. Everyone knows about their sign, their zodiac sign, well almost everyone. I'm Cancer, born under the sign of the Crab. The heavenly bodies were positioned in Crab-like manner when I came into the world. Did their configuration and the pulls and tugs of their gravity help shape my being? Cancer-people are emotional. They have huge highs and lows. If I were a bowler, I wouldn't have any spares, only strikes and gutter balls. My horoscope says that my emotional energy produces either all good or all bad. I can set down deep roots, unify family and build a consensus with people who have common goals but I can also be provocative, self-serving and intolerant.

Astrology is a science, or pseudo-science, that has been mystifying mankind for a hell of a long time. Does the position of the heavenly bodies at the time of one's birth help shape the personality? Does tonight's position of the objects in the heavens have some control over what will happen to me, to my mother, to others? Can the movement and configuration of those same objects be used to foretell the future? Who knows?

I can't see most of them yet, but the stars will all be up there for all of us to look at in a few minutes. Pegasus, the Winged Horse, will be flying westward in the autumn sky with the comet tonight. But, what about other things that might be up there somewhere? Is heaven a place in the sky? Is hell? Is it God's home? If so, which God? Zeus, Aphrodite, Odin, Brahma, Buddha, Vishnu, Shiva, Jehovah, Christ, Allah? Is there a Valhalla, a great hall, somewhere in the universe which houses warriors who were honorably killed in battle? Do other people live up there in the far beyond, humans like us? Is there something else that may some day swoop down out of the blackness of space? A being that can travel at the speed of light or faster and live with the black holes, intergalactic dust, meteors, asteroids, shooting stars and cosmic rays? Are such beings trying to communicate with us now, using the strange radio signals that come regularly flying out of space toward earth? What kinds of Gods, what kinds of peoples, what kinds of things live in the universe? Can they, or it, see us? Are we being hunted? Gad, that's a frightful thought. No one wants to be pursued.

It's twilight, I thought. A time when people's thoughts begin to focus on the approach of night, the supernatural and the mysterious things that live in the universe. It's also the time when pilots at sea use the stars to locate their place on the earth's waters.

Sean McCarthy had been a ship's navigator for a short time during his diverse, early years. His sextant, a mechanical device, used to "shoot the stars" and determine the ship's location at sea, hung in the ranch-house dining room, a family treasure. Modern mariners aboard the newer ships use a variety of electronic gadgetry to find the vessel's position at sea, but many smaller ships and those under sail still rely on the stars and a sextant. Thinking to myself, I wondered, almost outloud. What kind of device do space travelers, if there are such beings, use to find their way among the stars? And if they come, will we be their prey, their victims or their curiosities? I wanted to talk about the strangers who might be bumping around in the universe but, I kept quiet. The thickness of the night demanded silence. It didn't matter, such thoughts, expressed to Mom, would go unanswered, or worse, receive a retort, something like, "Oh don't be so silly!"

The shadows gave way to dark faster in this high country than one expects and as the chill grew deeper, I pulled the zipper up tight to my chin on the blue windbreaker I wore over a denim shirt. My Levis were warm and tight, well broken to the saddle.

What was it, I thought, while holding my breath. A blanket of thickness, stillness, blackness and tenseness rolled across the valley, covering everything in its path and stealing normality. We felt it, sensed it, but didn't understand it. The thickness created a feeling similar to that preceding a tornado, a mid-western thunderstorm or an earthquake. Stillness, tenseness and blackness were conditions foretelling the unusual, or the dangerous. Whatever it was penetrated our space like the invisible mass of a ghost feeling his way through a graveyard.

The cattle on both sides of the road stopped grazing, and those in the east pasture who were chasing a coyote halted, then turned in unison, correlated like a well trained dance team, to face northeast. Even the large bull rose from his mound of dirt, joining the dance. The llamas that had been teasing the thoroughbred horse in the south pasture also came to a precision stop. The ears and noses of all the animals went up in the tradition of frightened prey, earthbound players in a drama—frozen—a snap shot in history.

"Lord a' mighty," said Joan who was looking high to the northeast. I wheeled right and there it was—the phantom—moving fast. A single, silvery mass. Like an old fashioned fireball with a tail trailing to one side. It had no clear definition, yet we could see it halting, starting again, moving rapidly, left, right, down, closer, still closer—very close—fast overhead, turning south then unexpectedly dividing into four like a string of pearls.

Dipping down below the horizon to the south, somewhere near Bodie, then back, this time as three. Looping, circling, turning, swooping down again and then back as four. Turning north, rising one after the other at slightly different speeds, shooting upward like roman candles, disappearing into that small space in the sky that brings us the "sun-gazing" comets. No sound, no blast of air, four flying objects simply departing—vanishing—sucking the thick blanket of tenseness with them.

"Lord a mighty," said Joan again, her face ashen. "Is it the devil himself?" What was it that had suddenly sprung, like a phantom, from the nothingness?

Normality would return to the valley, but not quickly. First the hum and clatter of the insects gradually came back and could be heard over the whoosh of the breeze in the grass. The animals were still unsettled and they ran back and fourth or circled without any obvious purpose. They would not revert to eating, playing and loafing for a long time. The chill was still alive in their bones and in mine. I was shivering. My pulse must be a hundred, at least, I thought, as my heart pounded out a firm, fast rhythm in my chest. Afraid, excited and bewildered, that's how I felt. What had happened? What had we seen and felt? Was there a meaning or a purpose to the encounter?

We hurried back to the ranch filled with stories about the phantom but none of the other guests or hands has seen or experienced anything. They were all standing around the big fire roasting marshmallows on long sticks. The bright light, color, warmth, and crackle of the fire capturing the other guests' full attention. "Sounds like good stuff for Superman," someone said laughingly to Joan. "Call Ghostbusters," came from one of the ranch hands as the chuckling spread. Mother handled the joshing fairly well until someone whispered, "Think they got into the spirits tonight!"

Angry and rejected, both Mother and I retreated into silence, ridicule producing timidity even among the bold. We left early, the chorus from The Red River Valley, hanging in the crisp air. "From this valley they say you are going . . . ."

2

IT WAS SATURDAY NIGHT, APRIL 20, 1880, and Tex Garland was with his rowdy friends at Allen's Ice House drinking and listening, as he had many times before, to yarns about gold and the west being spun by cowboys who mostly had stayed east of the Pecos River. Tex was bored and, unlike the others, he had a burn to go and see for himself. In fact, it was more than a burn, it was a boiling caldron of need, a compulsion, driving him to prospect.

Talk of gold heated his blood, made his heart pound, seared his soul, and the beer and whiskey he had consumed heightened the blaze. As much as he loved being a Texan, he wanted out of Houston where the summer was hot and humid and his clothes stuck to his body like wet cheesecloth. In the summertime, Houston was a miserable, bug-infested swamp where high temperature and high humidity persisted even into the night. It had contributed to his saddle sores, itchy crotch, and the brown fungus that had grown in his extra pair of boots.

Born to the saddle, Tex could ride, shoot and hunt with the best of his friends, but he was fed up; the cycle of adventure had gone out of those activities. As a youth he loved to ride, breaking his first horse at age eleven. He would bet strangers that he could slowly mount his saddled horse from the ground and from the side without securing the cinch. Mounting a horse without a tightly fastened saddle girth is not a trick but it requires an accomplished horseman. Tex could do it every time. When he was only sixteen, he wagered he could stay ten seconds on a bull and won. He had driven cattle on the Chisholm Trail, rounded up strays, cut out those needing branding and cared for the new born.

He would always be fascinated by the challenge of working cattle but some of the adventure it provided had worn off. He was looking for new worlds to conquer. Cowboying also recently cost him his best friend, leaving a scar that needed time to heal.

Rod Taylor had been a good guy, strong rider and genuine pal. His life came to a premature end when he was fenced by a mustang and broke his neck. In some ways his sudden loss had caused Tex to change. It was a subtle change that his conscious mind hardly recognized. He stopped thinking like a child or an Indian. He was no longer focused entirely on the "now." The death of his friend caused Tex to start contemplating his future and to reflect on what he wanted to become, where he wanted to go, how he wanted to live. He didn't know it, but his thoughts about the future were a sign that he was growing up, becoming an adult. Contemplating the future wasn't easy. Maybe, that's what the Apache said. Maybe filled up the future.

You can't be a cowboy forever, he thought, not realizing that the cowboy in some men lives forever.

He knew that gold fields, like people, had life-cycles, born by prospectors find, matured by the rush of seekers, shrunk by the news of the next bonanza and dying as the ore ran out. The bright spark that lighted the gold rush fire in California was flashed at Sutter's Mill in 1848, thirty-two years ago. There had been gold, silver, other minerals, even diamonds found on the western slopes of the Sierra Nevada Mountains with its beautiful, high, snow capped, peaks, clear cold creeks and tall trees. The color was fast being exhausted in that area, the cycle too far advanced for Tex to experience. Later discoveries on the eastside of the Sierras offered more promise. Tex's eyes flashed when one of the storytellers mentioned Bodie. It was a big find, one with more promise than Virginia City, according to some. Ten thousand people were reportedly scratching about on a huge series of mountains that rose to over ten thousand feet above sea level, bigger mountains than Tex could imagine. *Veda Madre* was the term used to describe the bonanza by one of the Mexican *Vaqueros*. Tex wanted to get there before the Bodie's life ran out.

Bodie, thought Tex. It's hope, a dream, a challenge. But, how many fulfill the dream?

The tall Texan with broad shoulders and the thin, bony, body of a young cowpuncher, shifted on his barstool, ordered another beer and considered, in his steady, unruffled Texas manner, his future. Systematically, he was coming to a decision, one that would radically change his life, leading him much further down the trail of the unknown than he possibly could have imagined.

He ran his big right hand through his long, brownish-blond hair, focused his clear, blue eyes and set his square jaw before slowly saying. "I'm goin' to Bodie. Goin' 'fore it's gone." The palaver stopped, heads turned, and a hush fell over the icehouse. "You-all hear me now. I'm goin' to see the elephant!" Everyone in the place knew that Tex was not given to aimless conversation; in fact, he said very little but what he said stuck. He was an open, honest, no nonsense cowpuncher, a product of the South and the times.

When he said something, he could be counted on to speak his mind. He owned up to his mistakes but never apologized. His word was good and a handshake sealed a bargain. The brief utterance had committed him, pledged him to a future where dry desert and cold mountain winds would clear up his itches and fungus, but many other adventures, mostly unexpected, would greet him. For, like most western folklore, the stories of gold left out the harsh truth.

It was late June 1880, when Tex mounted his five-year old mare, Moonshine, and drifted out of Houston toward San Antonio where some forty years earlier, one hundred and eighty-seven men had defended the Alamo against a force of over five thousand Mexicans. His head felt big, bigger than a fat buffalo. He had stayed up until dawn and drunk too much beer. His icehouse-gang had sent him off in style and their last words hung in his mind, "You-all come back now—both you and Moonshine—ya hear."

Would he, would he ever come back? He asked himself.

Moonshine was a mixed breed, her lineage partly from some heavy draft family of horses possibly of Belgian descent and partly from wild appaloosa, a wild western breed, probably lost in the area by the early Spanish soldiers and explorers. Roan coloring, black and white spots of an appaloosa and the broad, tall, powerful look of a load-pulling horse made her unique among the cow ponies. Standing fifteen hands high, bigger than the regular cutting horses, she had the stamina and range to carry a big man like Tex combined with the quickness and agility to handle cattle.

Moonshine was born at three in the morning in an open field when the moon was high and full. The afterbirth glistening in the moonlight inspired the name. Or was it the Kentucky sour mash used to fortify Tex and the others acting as midwives? Or was it the white spot on the mare's chest? No one could remember exactly why she was called Moonshine but what did it matter. The birth was a memorable experience for Tex. It marked the start of a fresh lifecycle and the beginning of a strong, close comradeship between man and horse. In a sense, Tex was restarting both of their life cycles now, changing them from cow punching to prospecting.

He knew that some things cycled, starting over and over. A drop of rain fell to earth, joined a young mountain creek, grew to become a great river which traveled to the ocean where it evaporated, joined the clouds, only to fall again to earth, restarting the cycle. Did people come back, recycle as humans or something else? Did folks go on forever in another life, a world of spirits and souls? What would the world be like without cycles—no births, no deaths, those living continuing on forever? His mind was full of the thoughts of a lone rider at the start of a long journey. His questions were impossible to answer without faith.

Tex and Moonshine drifted west from the flat swamp-like country around Houston with its tall sugar-pines, water oaks, live oaks and cypress acting as homes for squirrels, tree roaches, mosquitoes, ticks, lizards, birds of many types and other animal life. The horse and rider moved in easy harmony out of the wet, sponge-like Houston atmosphere into San Antonio's oak-spotted, rolling hill country where the air became dryer but the heat persisted. The trail was well to the north of Baffin Bay, Texas, the post Civil War slave trading beach on the Gulf of Mexico, where his friends, the Caldwell family, had been sold into slavery. Patty Caldwell had been a friend in school. She was one of those older girls who helped young men get through the difficult years of early adolescence. She, her mother, father and younger brother were picked off the road going south toward Corpus Christi by a marauding group of toughs who traded anything and anyone for money. Soldiers picked up their trail but it was too late to save them. Slavery continued to be practiced, the Emancipation Proclamation didn't stop it, the Civil War didn't end it, there was profit in it, money, gold, that was all that was needed to keep it happening. The fact that it was illegal didn't prevent white men, Indians and Mexicans from taking captives in the United States for years after the Civil War ended. The most prized captives were young, "fresh" women, pretty females who were valuable for sale into prostitution. What a horrible thing to happen to his pal, Patty, thought Tex. I wish I could somehow find her, help her.

Tex rode into San Antonio, sitting tall on his saddle. Slung on his right side was his Civilian Colt.44, with a four and one half-inch barrel and a black rubber grip. He had a Winchester of the same caliber, allowing him to carry only one type of cartridge. His kit included three shirts, his extra boots and three hundred forty-two dollars and thirteen cents.

Tex had studied San Antonio while in school. His work on the Texas trail rides had provided the opportunity for him to visit the city previously and to listen to other cowpunchers talk about the town. San Antonio had become the "Cowboy Capital of the Southwest" in the late 1860s, after the civil war when cattle that had been concentrated in south Texas needed to be driven somewhere so that they could be sold and transported to the large hungry eastern markets. Jesse Chisholm, a half-breed Cherokee Indian, opened the northern part of a trail from the Oklahoma Indian Territory to Abilene, Kansas. The trail, named the Chisholm, was extended south to Texas where it branched out like the roots of a tree, with each root positioned to accept cattle driven from a wide variety of coastal, central, and border locations including Houston, Brownsville, San Antonio, Austin, Del Rio and Laredo. Longhorns, gathered into great herds, were driven north to the railroad at Abilene for shipment. Most of the cattle that came up from the south passed through San Antonio.

When Tex was nine years old, he made his first trail drive up the Chisholm with his father and a huge, mixed herd. He, his father, and two cowhands brought three hundred head from Houston to a spot on the trail northeast of Austin where they joined up with Charles Goodnight, a trail-boss, leading a much a larger group. Tex had several chores: to assist the cook by fetching firewood and water, gathering onions, cleaning dishes and to help with the young calves, particularly those born trailside and orphaned. The dogies, baby calves, sometimes got lost or just couldn't keep up and Tex always felt sorry for them. He would first try to mother them up and when that wasn't possible he would seek out an agreeable foster mother. Once, he fed a very small, young dogie milk from the finger of an old glove for weeks to keep it alive.

One night while washing dishes, Old Blue, the lead cow with a bell tied around her neck, stopped for a handout. Blue favored most things humans ate but she was partial to fresh vegetables and sugar. Tex had heard Goodnight say that the lead cow was more valuable than half a dozen cow-punches so he was generous, providing carrots, leftovers and sugar to the wise, lonely beast who refused to mix with the other cows. Blue would be the only member of the herd who would not be sold, returning to lead another drive.

Each day as they formed up, Old Blue took the head and the others followed, each almost always taking the same position in the herd. Tex hadn't thought much about leadership and he didn't realize that the old cow was a kind of teacher. Showing him the importance of staying out in front of the herd. Conveying the loneliness of leadership. How alone, he thought. How solitary is the role of the one in charge.

He saw other leaders in action on his first drive. Charles Goodnight was an experienced trail boss. He was rough, outspoken and given to fits of temper. The men followed him and did what he told them to do because he was right most of the time and because they feared him. On the other hand, the point rider, John Dursh, was quiet, a listener. However, he was clearly the best rider and cowhand Tex had ever seen. Dursh set an example and he got other cowpunchers to follow his lead without saying much of anything. The other cowhands respected him and a steady look was usually enough to get what he wanted. When he did speak, they listened.

Tex began to take note of such things that summer and every summer thereafter as he trailed on the Chisholm, honing his skills as a cowhand and unconsciously developing his motivational abilities. He had an easy, natural style that was well suited for leadership. Eventually, Tex found himself in a lead role, riding the point of a huge herd, glued to his horse like a tick on a dog's ear.

That's when he first began to feel lonely. His experience and intellect helped him form a philosophy, a set of beliefs, that each person had his own view of reality. Some folks saw the bright side of life, responding to quiet leadership. They were generally self-motivated, easy to encourage by reward, challenge or acclaim, while others lived under the dark blanket of fear and ugliness, responding affirmatively to little short of a powerful command, strong arm or swift kick. Dursh used a quiet, forceful style. Goodnight ranted and raved, using fear and intimidation to lead. Both men were solitary figures with strength. Tex determined that the best leader would be one who could see each man's view of reality and lead accordingly, encouraging some while bashing others.

He rode a number of times with an Apache Scout called Red Hand. The Indian had been with the cavalry before becoming a trail scout. Red Hand kept to himself. He said very little and often sat alone by the fire for hours. A lump, thought Tex, a silent lump, hiding under a blanket. What does he think about? Why doesn't he join in? What makes him hunch over next to the fire like that? What does he think about us?

One day, when it was dry and hot and Red Hand was having trouble finding a water hole, he killed a lizard and placed it belly up in the sun.

Tex said, "What are you up to Red Hand?"

He grunted and said something in Apache that he knew Tex would not understand. Tex had heard plenty of stories about Chiricahuas in Houston and on the trail and he remembered some of their superstitions.

Tex said, "Red Hand, reckon you're not gonna tell me what your up to lessin' I do somethin' to get your attention. I'm gonna ketch me an owl, Red Hand, hear me, a big owl. I'm gonna put him in your bed roll some dark night soon!"

As soon as Tex said it he knew that it had been a mistake, a bad error, one that could be fatal. He had used bad judgment by trying to prod a man that could only be handled by encouragement. The look Red Hand gave Tex was full of hatred. It was more than enough to get Tex to recognize his mistake and want to change his approach. It wasn't in his nature to apologize but he needed to make things right. However, the Indian responded before Tex had time to correct his error.

Red Hand said, "Coyote told my people, killing lizard or rattler, putting it belly up to sun, can bring rain. No work, all time, but sometime, maybe. Man with owl worse that rattler. Needs be belly up!"

Tex knew that Red Hand was in a temper, and he knew that he was responsible. But Tex didn't fully understand why. Why had the mention of an owl gotten him so riled? Owls were harmless creatures. They said, hoot, hoot, hoot at night but who cared. He told me what I wanted to know but he is now an enemy. I kicked him into telling when I should have stroked him, he thought.

For sure Tex needed to say somethin', somethin' fittin', somethin' that would get him off the prod. "Pshaw, Red Hand," Tex said. "I was only funnin'. You are a chief, a chief among Apaches. I was funnin', didn't mean to be chidin' you. If I wronged you with owl talk, I'll make it up, pay you back by protecting you from the owl spirits. If you see one, hear one hoot or learn of one, just tell me, and I will kill it for you."

The Indian's expression changed and there was a sense of relaxation. He nodded, moved away, seeking his own council, but Tex knew that a run-in had been avoided.

Not long after the owl incident, Red Hand began telling Tex Chiricahua stories, Apache folklore, often revealed by animals.

"They call me Red Hand 'cause when I very young I pointed to sky one night and just then bolt of lightning struck a tree—big oak—near our *wickiup*. Lightning is arrow shot down to earth by Thunder People. We hide our red things, no ride painted ponies when it's 'round. The power seeks red. They say my hand called it down. I made an amulet from the lightning burned tree bark, an amulet to protect me from its power. It hangs here, 'round my neck all time. Some my people think I talk with lightning, have influence over it. They call me *di-yin*. Many others think I *Shaman*, witch doctor, able to cure those struck by Thunder People arrow. I think lightning come without help from me. But I no tell my people I have no power."

Late one afternoon, they were camped on the Brazos River and several of the cowhands went fishing with the cook. It wasn't long before they had a good string of catfish for supper. Strangely, Red Hand would have none of it, and later that evening he told Tex why.

"Long time ago, they say, many our people very sick, hot with fever. *Di-yins* took them to sweat bath, then river. When they came out of river, they all die. The dead Indians were spotted, just like fish in river. Spirits of bad women in fish killed them. Fish no good to eat," he said.

Strange fish story, Tex thought to himself. It wasn't the last bit of Apache wisdom that the Indian would offer that was inspired by food.

Several days later, the cook made trail stew using a number of rabbits shot in the afternoon. That night, Red Hand told Tex, "Long time ago, they say, Coyote went chasing jackrabbits to eat. Rabbit went into stump hole and when Coyote reached in, jackrabbit grabbed his paw, held it fast, shouted for grandmother to get knife and cut it off. Coyote began howling, begging for paw. Finally jackrabbit agreed to let him have it if he would go away and bother him no more. Coyote agreed, left and never returned. Apache tricks are many," he said. "We have tricks, also power. Power come from *enemies-against power*, strength from spirits. Strength help us surprise, fool, defeat our enemies."

After that, it seemed to Tex that Red Hand had a Coyote story for almost any situation. The myths, like fairy tales, came with other colorful characters: Tip Beetle, Turkey, Lizard, Vulva Woman, Prairie Dog Woman, Bear, Snake and many others, each story delivering some message, some form of Chiricahua wisdom. *Coyotero* was the word used by some people for Apache. Tex surmised that the word grew out of the Coyote stories.

Tex grew to like Red Hand, began to understand Apache life and customs, began to appreciate that all red men were not bad, a revelation contrary to the teachings of his youth. They prized family, courage, dignity and generosity, wise standards for any people. Very close continuous family relationships were the main fiber of their society. Relatives lived in clusters, close together, relying on each other for food, clothing, support and defense. Everyone within the cluster took some responsibility for the teaching and development of the children, often accomplishing results through story telling which, Tex learned, could be used as a powerful way of motivating, communicating and cleverly directing others actions.

Red Hand taught me a lot of things, things I plan to use on this ride, Tex thought.

At the time Tex rode into San Antonio, it was no longer necessary for the cattle to make the long march to Abilene. The advancing railroads were now in place at Fort Worth, Texas, and new rails were being laid all across the Lone Star State. Trains, thought Tex, would be the easy way for folks to travel. I could ride the rails but what about Moonshine? Well, I suppose they would take her too but it would cost a bundle for us to both go west that way.

Tex knew that the Chisholm Trail was nearing the end of its life cycle. It had been born out of economic necessity and it had matured in spite of monstrous hardships. There had been Indian attacks, road agents, desperadoes, bone-chilling winter storms, throat parching blazing summers, grasshopper invasions and rattlesnakes. A success in its time, its usefulness was declining as the steam engines advanced, bringing with them new holding pens, stockyards, slaughter houses, meat packing facilities and refrigerated cars. Other, newer trails had been built west of the Chisholm to famous places like Dodge City but they, too, were destined to become obsolete, giving way to mankind's machines.

San Antonio was more than a cattle town. Its roots lay with an early Spanish settlement and the Mission of San Antonia de Valero. It became central to American history and fundamental to the existence of Texas as a state with the battle at the Alamo. When he was a kid Tex had played a game called "The Fort" with his friends. He always took the part of Jim Bowie, Jim Travis or Davie Crockett and took up a defensive position behind a tall rock wall. Tex and his friends popped their heads up and down firing imaginary guns at an imaginary enemy.

They never could find anyone who would play the part of Antonio Lopez de Santa Anna and his troop of five thousand Mexican men. In the game, the Texas kids were outnumbered by more than twenty-five to one but they still managed to hold the fort for twelve days. The end was always the same. The kids died bravely after being overrun. Tex was proud of the men who fought for his liberty at the Alamo and when he played the game he felt as though he was actually there, fighting with brave comrades. At such times, he had wanted to be a warrior, doing battle for his family and fellow Texans. The brutality of the engagement was lost on his youthful mind that was caught up with the delirium of the event.

San Antonio's nineteen thousand residents spoke more Spanish than English and many followed the teachings of the Catholic Church. They were shielded against periodic raids by Apache and Comanche Indians, a serious problem in the past, by Fort Sam Houston. The fort was rapidly becoming obsolete as more and more of the red men were corralled on reservations.

As the hub for early cattle movement, San Antonio had developed and continued to maintain the sinful characteristics of other trail towns, including sporting houses, saloons with gambling and opium dens attracting card sharks, con men, gunfighters and other bad men and women of all types. The drover, John Dursh, didn't talk much, but Tex remembered him saying, "San Antonio, now that's a town—got the best whores out west. Rosie, she's my number one. Big tits, round and soft, nice brown nipples, and an ass, what an ass, a real bouncer." Soldiers from the fort joined trail riders in keeping Rosie and the other mostly dark-haired ladies of the night active and solvent. Tex knew that a person seeking sin or adventure could find it anytime day or night in San Antonio.

Rosie, he thought. Might just look Rosie up tonight. She works at a place called Vaudeville, he recalled.

Tex had ridden there straight away without taking the side trip his buddies suggested to La Grange which boasted "The Chicken Ranch," the best little whorehouse in Texas. La Grange was out of the way and he had no time to waste. Besides, San Antonio had plenty of sporting ladies. He was dry, hot and ready for some fun.

He ambled into one of the first saloons he saw. It was owned by a short man with a goat-like beard, mustache, deep set eyes, strong, large brows, small nose and a belly so fat he could only button the top of his waist coat. In fact, Roy Bean looked like a weathered, flat-nosed Mexican goat. He wore the sombrero, vest, long sleeved shirt and leather boots with the typical Hispanic flavor favored by many cowpunchers in the southwest. Roy was a survivor, a bright, creative scoundrel with a bully's instincts and the guile to bend folks to his will. He had been in and out of trouble, jails and bordellos all his life and he had once played the lead role at a hanging. It left him with a very stiff neck. Roy would talk to anyone who would listen about southern California, the beautiful black-haired *señorita* he had trifled with many times in the rear of his San Gabriel saloon, the duels he had fought and won, and the high staked poker games in which he triumphed.

He allowed as how, "Che'tin' at cards was a hangin' offence, if ketched." Spinning yarns while watering drinks and short changing drunks was how Roy survived.

Bean took a liking to Tex because the boy was heading west to find gold and adventure. When Tex asked about the change owed him from his beer order Roy said, "Why son, that's fur the Jersey Lilly", he continued, bragging on about the most beautiful woman in the world, born on the Isle of Jersey, the British actress, mistress of the Prince of Wales, Lilly Langtry. Roy said, "I'm bringing her out west one day, by gobs, I will." His ardor was so sincere that Tex chose to forget his change. Tex never knew that Roy was destined to become the notorious Judge Roy Bean of Langtry, Texas, who would live on the Rio Grande and become the "only law west of the Pecos" while dispensing his version of justice from his saloon, the "Jersey Lilly."

Roy told Tex about the trail he had taken between San Diego and San Antonio. It followed, generally, the route of the now defunct Butterfield Stage Coaches that carried mail on this warm weather road before the Civil War. He spoke of Indians, buffalo, sage-brush, great rock mountains with boulders rounded like pebbles, huge stands of Joshua Trees, Saguaro Cactus fifty feet tall on the high desert and side winders, the side slithering rattlesnakes of the brush country. Indian stories were obviously his favorite.

"Ridin' full gallop them Comanch' could fly twenty arrows in les'an a minut' shoot 'em stra'te too," he said. Roy spoke with respect for the savage Comanches who had once ruled the territory from the Arkansas River to the Rio Grande and from the mountains of New Mexico to the Texas Hill Country. "Sup'berb riders w'out saddles, them red feathers. They c'd drop to the side of them ponies at full gallop, present'in no target to the'r enemies. Them red skin's won tribal hon'rs, big gonads, by touching their enemies' bodies, with hand or weapon, while the enemy still lived. 'Magine that, right durin' battle,

29

you go up and touch the other guy–hen kill 'em–then cut off a part'ion of skin round the scalp–rip it off. By gobs, that takes big sweet breads," said Roy.

Roy rambled on, recalling the Warren Wagon Train slaughter that left seven dead. The bodies were mutilated, some tongues cut out, soft body parts burned and all heads scalped. "Don't be messin' with them Comanch'," he said, before being interrupted by Jake Busher, a cowboy who had quietly been drinking himself stiff at the end of the bar. Jake suddenly slumped to the floor, knocking over the spittoon. Roy bounced over to the slumped body, found Jake's money belt, relieved him of half his one hundred dollars and turned to Tex saying, "By gobs, he's damaged this places rep'itation. I fine him fifty dollars. That's my rulin'."

Tex decided it was time to saddle-up before Roy took a notion to make a "ruling" that would lighten his pockets. He said, "Roy I'm headin' to Bodie to see the elephant," as he stomped out with a cowboy's swagger.

Not ready to give out yet, Tex then bellied up to the bar at the Vaudeville. Thinking about Rosie, he ordered some suds and ogled the sporting ladies in pink tights dancing on stage. The Vaudeville was a booze emporium with a massive mahogany bar, cut-glass chandeliers, extensive rococo work, plate-glass mirrors, a gilt-framed painting of a well-proportioned nude and a grand piano. "Rosie still work here?" he asked the barman.

"Nah, went chasin' off with some travelin' drummer. Haven't seen her in over a year."

In the corner he noticed that some type of gambling was in progress. Beer in hand, he ambled over for a look-see. A dude in a silk shirt with gray pants tucked into his polished boots was playing with three half-walnut shells and a pea on the table. With a smooth easy tongue, he was working the crowd for bets. Placing the pea under one shell and moving the three around, he would get one of the cow hands to bet he could guess which shell the pea was under. He was winning most of the time and the ease of his victories seemed strange to Tex because he was sure he could tell where the pea rested.

The bartender called out, "Hey Soapy, you got some fresh meat just over there."

Soapy Smith looked right at Tex and said, "Want to try your skill?"

Tex recognized the challenge, a trap really, requiring him to step up to the line or crawl away branded a coward. "Sure," he said, " I'll risk a dollar."

Soapy placed the pea under the walnut in the middle and moved all three around for a time, "Which one," he said.

Tex pointed to the one in the center. He was right and a winner.

"Go again?" said Soapy.

"Pshaw, reckon not," was the answer. "Game's too easy, don't wann'a take advantage."

Soapy Smith, one of the best confidence men on the western plains knew when he had been had. He said nothing to the tall blond, continuing to work the crowd, seeking an easier mark. He had expected that the taste of winning would induce a higher stakes game, producing a killing, but it hadn't worked out. Smith knew from experience that some men could be neither challenged nor bullied into gambling away a lot of money, and he felt Tex was one of those, wiser than his age would have implied. He didn't want a ruckus, a fight that would end his game. There would be other cowboys, more careless, drunker. Soapy could wait.

Tex knew that rascals like this dandy were full of tricks and his many years with wranglers on the Chisholm had taught him about con men. The challenge had forced him to risk a dollar but having taken the gamble, he knew he could walk away with honor whether he won or lost. Escape, he thought, I have escaped the gamblers snare by doing and saying the right things. His plan had worked, but the result left him with an empty feeling stemming from his belief that he could beat Soapy at his game and he had not given himself a full chance. Next time he would be a little bolder! If he was to win, he must be willing to risk losing.

A stocky, well dressed, hard man, with the vacant eyes of a wild turkey stepped into Soapy's face, placing a twenty dollar gold piece and his Colt .45, taken from a shoulder holster, on the table. "One game, fop," he said.

Soapy smiled and ran the game. Ben Thompson, who had come down that day from Austin picked the half shell on the left, loosing.

"Keep your greedy fingers right where they are or I'll blow your dingus off," he said. Reaching out with one hand, he turned the other two shells over.

Ben found the pea under the center one. "I'd 'ave laid you out if it hadn't been there. You know that pilgrim," he said. Ben Thompson liked to kill and he was saddened that he had not caught Soapy out.

The fop was a cheat, a con man, without honor, the worst kind of low life. Soapy needed killing and Ben Thompson wanted to be his angle of death. Not tonight, but sometime, sometime soon, thought Thompson. "The game's over," he said. "Any objections?" There were none.

The next morning Tex bought a rasher of bacon, beef jerky and beans before setting himself back on the trail.

Three days out of San Antonio he was absent-mindedly allowing Moonshine to follow the trail. His brain was somewhere between the reality of the ride and the imagery of his past life. Like most young men, Tex had fallen in love several times, starting when he was sixteen with an Indian girl who had encouraged a rather sloppy tryst on the floor of an abandoned barn.

Betty Jane Allen, a more proper lady, was his most recent love. She lived with her parents on a modest ranch and had attended school with Tex, flirting and giggling like the other teenage girls. More recently she had enrolled at Mary Hardin-Baylor College in Belton, Texas.

One afternoon while wrangling stray cattle near the river, he came upon her clothes hanging from a low branch of a water oak. He dismounted and slithered on his belly, Indian fashion, up over the tree mound to where he could see the water. His loins prickled and his rod grew firm when he saw her bathing in the shallows. She moved her lithe, well-kept figure as she washed herself with sweet smelling soap. Her wet, smallish breasts and red nipples glistened in the reflected light from the river. She was reaching, turning and twisting while looking about with a twinkle in her eyes. Her sharp-featured face looked clean, fresh and pretty. A blond nymph, fully exposed, vulnerable, an angel or a devil twisting in the clear river waters watched over by a blond Texan, fingering his poker. He was hot, too hot to hold back and soon, his mouth, half-open, eyes glazed, he released his seed. Embarrassed and frustrated he squirmed back over the mound, spreading the gluey substance over his legs and abdomen as he made his retreat.

It was three days later when he saw her again at the regular Sunday

Baptist church service. She shot him a coquettish smile, her body language making it difficult for Tex to hide the hardness growing against his best gray pants. She was seated with her parents one row behind Tex and to his left. He couldn't help looking over his shoulder at her every chance he got, which was often, as the congregation sang the traditional hymns. About halfway through the chorus of Gathering at the River he saw her do something strange. She let him see, just for an instant, what she was holding in the small of her left hand, a bar of sweet smelling soap. Was it really a bar of soap, or was it a handkerchief rolled into a ball? He thought to himself. Why would she be sending me a signal? Why would she do something like that? Was she a tease? Was she flirting? What was it in her hand? Her hankie? It couldn't have been soap. It probably wasn't a signal—just something that happened by accident. Or was it? At the time of the incident, he was sure it was soap, but now after the passage of time he was less positive. Their eyes had met and he felt drawn to her, pulled by an invisible force more powerful than a giant horse.

"Repent ye sinners, lust not for the wickedness of the body, judge no man but thyself, but judge harshly if ye are following the path to damnation. Repent all ye for thy transgressions, misdeeds and wrongful thoughts," the old preacher had boomed, while looking directly at Tex who was praying also for deliverance, exodus actually, from church.

As Tex rode west images of Betty Jane and questions about her intentions kept invading his mind. Had she seen him and wanted him to see her? Had she liked the thought of exposure to his eyes? Did she know he was watching? Had she wanted to give him a proper show? Had she wanted to be with him? What had she had in mind, a flop on the riverbank or something else? It was shameless for Tex to harbor such ideas, but they were there, in his mind.

By the time of the following Sunday service, Tex was sporting a semi-permanent hard on. He couldn't stop thinking about the shiny soft gloss the soap made on her smooth white body. He was almost afraid to be seen in public, apprehensive that those lovely clean breasts would come to mind, causing a bulge in his pants. But Sunday service was not something one could easily avoid and he desperately wanted to see her again, so he found himself sitting in his usual place in his regular pew. He looked over his left shoulder and saw her sitting quietly with her parents. Tex realized that everyone always sat in the same places in church, much like cows that took the same positions in a trail herd. Why did people and animals act that way? What was the purpose? What made them go to their places? He thought.

His eyes and Betty Jane's did not meet that day and no sweet smelling soap appeared to perk his interest. She left quickly and was nowhere to be seen when Tex emerged from the holy place. Crestfallen, ready to depart, he noticed one of his regular sidekicks, Jim Lloyd, ambling in his direction on an apparent mission. He stopped, acknowledged Jim, and walked along with him for a piece, waiting politely for a fellow Texan to gather his thoughts before speaking. "She wants to know why you run 'way," he drawled. That's all he had to say but the words struck Tex mute. He had never been hit harder, not even by the kick of a horse. He couldn't answer, couldn't think, felt heat rising up his neck into his head, his breath became short, labored, and his pulse and heart were pounding.

Jim couldn't tell if Tex was mad or what, but like all young cowboys, he had been in plenty of fights. He knew that Tex was quick as a cyclone, strong as a bull and that he had a punch that hurt like the kick of a mule. Out of respect for those prior encounters, Jim pushed off out of harm's way, smiling to himself, wondering what it was all about.

Tex spoke not one word on the buckboard ride home with his family. Did she think him a peeper or worse? Why had she shown him the soap? And if she had known he was there why hadn't she bolted? Did she want him or did she want to humiliate him? If only he hadn't gone off in his Levis, it wouldn't have been so bad. It was all too mixed up for Tex; women were impossible to understand. He vowed, as he rode out to work the next morning, to forget her and not look down by the river any more.

▼▲▼

While Tex was deciding to forget her, Betty Jane Allen was deciding how to entice him. She had planted another seed in the courtship game that she planned to harvest. Should she let Tex catch her by the river this week or wait? A vexing thought. She wanted to feel his strong, hard body next to her in the cool river water and this week, just maybe, she would venture out to that special place by the water oak. Not to make love, mind you, just a little sport in the water, a few touches on those special places that create sensual, carnal vibrations that go tingling through the body. He could have a few kisses, but no more. But would he be there? Yes! For sure! Jim Lloyd had said he was spending every afternoon looking for strays near the river. Lost cattle or a found woman? She was sure she knew.

On Wednesday, she went out with her bar of sweet smelling soap, left her clothes on the oak and slipped into the water noticing that the nipples on her breasts were hard and her honey-pot tingling. She soaped and waited and soaped and waited, her fires gradually cooling, giving way to anger, hostility and cold water. Where was that slinky lizard? Was he really afraid? Or was it something else? Had she gone too far? Did he think her brazen? Was it the soap? It had been foolish, impulsive, using the soap that way. A bar of soap, in church, is that what raised his ire? Did he think her sacrilegious? It seemed like a devilishly good idea at the time, a little bit daring, youthful. But had it backfired! Was it a terrible mistake?

After an hour or more in the river, she climbed out, dressed, stalking off, leaving the courtship game incomplete. It was the following Sunday before she learned that Tex had gone to Bodie.

▼▲▼

Tex rode on through the hill country, heavily timbered with oak, pine and cedar, following the wandering course of the Guadalupe River which cut through the limestone sediments, transporting memories about an unconsummated love, reflections that raised unanswerable questions in his mind about himself and about women.

3

PETER QUINN AND JOHN RILEY WERE
decidedly Irish. They were big, strong armed men with round, red faces hardened
by the weather and "Irish milk." Peter had long, blond hair, a blond beard and
a large mouth given to constant use, eating and talking. John had a reddish
top and a freckled, clean-shaven face. John tended to himself.

Hailing from Cork, they came around the horn to San Francisco in
1849 and had worked in the gold fields since arriving. They had panned on
the American River and its tributaries near Sacramento, "rocked the cradle" in
the dry diggings near Placerville and had been at the funeral at Rough and
Ready when gold was found in the freshly turned earth of a grave-site. The
burial was halted while claims were filed. "Rough and Ready," said Peter. "Aye,
now that was a gold camp. Named for old Zac Taylor, they say. The settlement
was just a wide speck on the trail when prospectors found color. Rich diggings,
real rich, and folks 'round those parts knew how to salute. There was a red-
letter party when they made the find.

"Voted to secede from the Union in the spring of '50. Sure and by
golly they did. Can you 'magine—the tiny, little camp at Rough and Ready
getting out of the Union? Miners were mad, angry, they say. Went loony when
Nevada City was made the county seat. Ran off all the federal workers and
burned the post office. Torched the mail too, they did. Folks stayed drunk for
two days. That they did, and the Saints be praised. Then, don't you know,
fourth of July rolled 'round and they had no reason to celebrate. Weren't in the
Union no more. So what d'you think they did? They voted Rough and Ready
back in. Irish milk, that's what they wanted. Praise be to God for Irish milk and
the Union."

Peter and John had done most everything there was to do in the foothills of the mountains. They had found color, touched it, become obsessed by its allure. They had hope, a faith that fills a need in every man. "We be kno'in' what to do now John," said Peter. "But, we'd better be gettin' there first. Bein' first, that's the trick."

One night while drinking with and listening to a French Canadian trapper, Pierre Lovell at the Shamrock bar, it struck them that western Canada had all the things common to the Sierra's: mountains, great rivers, pine trees, grizzly bears. Why not gold? Peter said, "You Canad'a's are here for California gold. We ought to be goin' to your country to find yours?" And so, in the winter of 1857/58, the three of them set out for the far north, sailing to Fort Victoria, then striking overland with Pierre on lead.

They headed to the northeast. The plan was to go to Cedar Point on Quesnelle Lake, an old rendezvous for trappers. Pierre had seen rocks and other gold-like signs in that part of Canada. The signs meant nothing at the time but now, after working in the mother-lode, he could visualize gold. They reached Lillooet on their journey where they heard about the gold find along the Fraser River. No one seemed to know exactly where, just somewhere on the Fraser.

Pierre wanted to change plans, rush to the find, but Peter and John had heard mythical reports about bonanzas in the past and they were still seeking the advantage of being first. If the reports were true, there would already be hundreds working the Fraser and thousands more would soon follow. Before long this part of western Canada would be crawling with eager prospectors. If there was gold on or near the Quesnelle, it wouldn't be a secret for long. The parties could not agree so Peter and John headed toward Cedar Point, armed with a rough map provided by Pierre, while the French Canadian headed for the diggings on the Fraser.

One morning, in the early spring while prospecting along the eastern bank of the Quesnelle, Peter shouted, "Gold, the saints be praised, it's gold!"

"Where?" shouted John.

"Right here under me boots where the little people must have left it," was the answer. It was true, in a huge backwash, where the Quesnelle and

Caribou Rivers met, there was placer gold, piled up in thick pockets along the shore and on a large sand bar. They pitched camp and worked feverishly using rockers and pans. It was easy, almost too easy. Over a period of two weeks they filled thirty leather pouches with fine placer gold and had twenty more loaded with nuggets. Some of the nuggets were over two inches thick. They disbursed the bags, hiding them in groups of five bags each. John, the quiet one, kept a diary, noting the location of each cache, describing the find and chronicling their adventure.

Unknown to the Irish men, danger was near in the form of John de la Roach, a French Canadian trapper, a working member of the Hudson's Bay Company fur brigade, which held a fur trading monopoly in Canada. He and other members of the brigade would rendezvous at Cedar Point on Quesnelle Lake, far back in the northwestern mountains each fall to trail their furs to market. John was five feet eight inches tall, had dark curly hair, deep set hazel eyes, thin nose and jaw and the long fingers of an artist. Self educated and well read, he was a man possessed of great energy, a very hot temper and a killer's instincts. John was an avarice hunter, working the countryside for beaver, marten, squirrel, moose, deer, caribou and bear. He always arrived at the rendezvous with more quality skins, particularly the prized beaver and squirrel, than any of the others.

▼▲▼

"I am John de la Roche, the greatest hunter in these parts," he said outloud to the forest and its wildlife.

His mind drifted back, recalling a grizzly hunt one season in the high country. Them damned bears stink and they would as soon eat a French-Canadian like me as berries. Salmon, salmon and berries, that's what they go for. He enjoyed using those bits of information to kill seven of them during one season.

He was out trapping smaller prey near an unnamed river, roughly ten yards wide and ten to fifteen feet deep, for the early run of the powerful King Salmon that would return to the place of it's birth to spawn and die. As the waters cleared, the first of them could be seen struggling against the current and the odds. They came from the sea as sleek, shining trout-like fish weighing usually about twenty-five pounds. The male and female looked alike when caught from the ocean: whitish-silver sides and belly, dusky freckled top with a hint of yellow and many round black spots, both along the upper portions of the body and fins. In fact, all the species of salmon: King, Coho, Chum and Pink, had a similar look at sea which gave way when they turned in-shore for the spawn.

As the King struck fresh water the changes began—metamorphosis— that's what educated folks called it. The throat narrowed, the stomach shrank, appetite diminished progressively to none. The great fishes' color gradually changed to a reddish-orange and the meat, delicious when taken from the ocean or early in the spawning cycle, became less edible as the salmon, feeding primarily off itself, battled up river, leaping up water falls, bashing against rocks and fallen trees, avoiding predators.

The females exchanged their fast, smooth, polished bodies for the plump, round appearance of fish full of eggs.

The evolution of the male salmon was even more dramatic. He thinned, his head flattened, the upper jaw was reconfigured so that it curved like a hook over it's lower partner. Powerful, dog-like teeth were evident on both jaws; his eyes became sunken; he was gaunt, savage. I know that face, de la Roche thought. It's the face of the living dead.

The first arrivals could be seen in the clear water, moving against the current. They looked like soldiers, wriggling forward, then resting and then continuing their march. Their numbers increased in the days that followed, a seemingly endless line, an eternal transit of King Salmon moving hundreds of miles to fulfill their destiny, to provide life to their offspring. What drives these fish? Where do they get the strength and energy? What power propels them to continue the life cycle? He thought.

In the slow moving waters below falls or rapids, the salmon formed schools so thick that de la Roche felt like trying to walk across the river on their backs. It is almost unbelievable, a truly remarkable sight, a river thick with fish, crowded together. Wherever they bunched up, predators, like the seals, otters, grizzly bears and man, waited, fishing. Below the migrating salmon, Rainbow Trout and Dolly Varden were feeding off fresh salmon eggs; high above the eagle and hawk awaited a meal.

He located a place where the river fell from a small canyon over some huge boulders forming a large pool, an obvious holding spot for the salmon. His fishing hole was occupied by a fat, dish-faced, male grizzly bear. His grayish coat was covered with blood, and he was busy pawing King Salmon from the water and eating their flesh while they wiggled. The bear had a regal look of satisfaction when he dropped the fish heads and tails streamside for other predators. John de la Roche worked his way up, very quietly, to a position above the great beast, so that if he missed a clean kill with his first shot, the wounded animal would have to attack uphill. He is a great hunter and didn't expect to miss, but he is also a smart killer who knows that a giant bear can move around for a long time with a bullet deep in his body. This precaution, designed to provide time for escape, proved to be unnecessary. The grizzly went down soon after the first bullet exploded his heart. He skinned the huge animal, hung his coat out to dry and ate his meat for several days while continuing to work his trap lines.

Later the same year, he moved up river to a high lake where grizzly signs were almost everywhere, and the human-sounding, child-like cries of the bear cubs could be heard for miles. There was a small fordable stream on the inlet side of the lake with a sandbar at its mouth where salmon carcasses were piled thick enough to walk on. There were hundreds of trout feeding near the mouth of the stream, and a few had moved up into the relatively slow moving waterway. Beaver had built dam-houses along a timbered stretch of the stream about two miles from the lake, and half a dozen grizzly bears were pawing and eating salmon as they flopped about in the shallows.

At first, de la Roche saw two bear cubs walking on the animal trail he was following. They heard him, turned and one rose up on its hind legs before moving off into the brush as he came on. He left the trail, slipped into the trees, knowing that grizzly did not see well. He hoped he could move close and be undetected by the bear's sharp sense of smell. He crawled on his hands and knees over timbers, each four to six inches in diameter, small trees actually, that had been felled by beaver. He then eased around two large, thick pine tree trunks and found himself not more than thirty feet from a female bear who was fishing, and roughly sixty feet from a male grizzly who was feeding on berries. He shot and downed the female and watched the male disappear into the woods, wondering if he would attack or retreat. John remained, well hidden, for probably fifteen minutes, alert for any noise, any sound that would provide warning of an advancing bear. Hearing nothing, he finally moved to the site of the dead female where he commenced the skinning process.

As his work neared completion he sensed danger. He didn't know why—it was just a feeling—something the hunted seems to instinctively feel in the presence of an enemy. The earth shook, his space was filled with the low guttural sound of a charging male grizzly. He fired, then half ran through, half jumped over the stream, making it into a small grove of pine trees before the beast reached the female. Her scent or the effects of his lead slowed the charge and saved his life. He quietly drew his hog leg revolver, but did not fire, knowing that inaccurate shots from a light caliber weapon might be more dangerous than helpful. The male had stopped and was looking in his direction; he had lost the scent when de la Roche had crossed the stream. Using very careful, slow, disciplined motions, he reloaded his rifle, took aim and fired, dropping the already wounded animal almost in its tracks. Again, he waited, making sure the grizzly was dead before approaching the carnage, skinning knife in hand.

John de la Roche took four more giant bears that summer in the same general vicinity as they followed first the migration of the Kings and then, later, the Red and Dog Salmon into the higher reaches of the river. He used his knowledge, his understanding of the death cycle of the fish, to shoot grizzly and trap other predators who followed their migration. He felt like Azrael—angle of death—dwelling on the dark side, capable of the ultimate evil. While the salmon may view their transit as life producing, de la Roche saw it as an opportunity to enrich his fortune, fulfill his destiny.

▼▲▼

In the early spring of 1858, John de la Roche was hunting his way down the east side of the Quesnelle River, setting his traps in likely places along the shoreline, swollen by the waters from the spring thaw. He arrived at the junction of the Quesnelle and Caribou Rivers, two huge, dangerous, fast moving, turbulent, torrents heading west toward the Pacific Ocean.

John was surprised to see two men, miners, panning in the shallows of the Quesnelle. Panning, he thought, panning for gold. My god, those bastards have found gold! The prospectors were excited, totally absorbed in their work. They don't deserve the gold; this is my hunting ground! The dumb, greedy bastards haven't earned the right to pan my gold! Men, driven by greed; that's all they are. Foreigners too—must be foreigners—outsiders who don't belong in Canada, I can't let them take my treasure, thought de la Roche.

Unseen by the prospectors, he dismounted. With his carbine in hand, he approached with a hunter's stealth, demons possessing his spirit.

Up early at their work, unaware of danger, Peter was struck high in the back by the heavy bullet. He fell, face down, into the shallows of his dig, icy water filling his lungs, his body struggling to heal the fatal wound. Riley was also surprised, attacked without warning by the same wild man who had just killed his partner. De la Roche's knife cut into Riley's vitals before his fighting instincts were at the ready. He fell without throwing a single punch or putting up any defense. A cold, sad departure for two fighting Irishmen, delivered by an unexpected assailant. The prospectors' life cycles were ended, prematurely, at the height of their joy.

John scalped the two men, Indian style, dismantled their camp, carried them ten miles on mule-back up the Caribou, leaving them exposed on the ground. Their eyes were glazed, filled with outrage spawned by the attack and astonishment that their youth could be terminated. Did their eyes retain a picture of their last vision? John did not know, but all of their parts would shortly be eaten; nature's creatures would render them unrecognizable. When their bones were found he hoped their deaths would be blamed on Indians.

It would not matter to the dead how they died or what happened to their flesh. But it was important to de la Roche that the scavengers remove whatever vision their eyes held. He wondered if their spirits would come back in some other form to harass him. Would he meet them in another place, the hereafter, where they would extract retribution? Was there a heaven? A hell? Did the soul of man live on or was the end like a curtain falling on a stage play?

The curtain, that was the answer. It was the only thing that made some sense to him, besides it was, for him, a comfortable way to view the hereafter, given his mode of living. A vicious killer of both man and animal could not afford thoughts of hell. Wealth would fill his life, pervade his now, bloat his ego and satisfy his needs. The hereafter was born and fed by the foolish, those who placed immortality ahead of gold.

He scattered some of their camp implements and supplies near their bodies, built a small fire which he lighted using the pages from a notebook found in the freckle-faced man's coat pocket. He didn't take the time to read the diary, a costly error, but his mind was focused on not being found with a dead man's handwritten notebook. He extinguished the fire, returned to the Quesnelle and located the gold dust they had panned. It was all in five small leather sacks under a rock near their original campsite.

He never knew how much more there was to find. The locations of the secret hiding places described in the notebook had been consumed in the flames.

The miners had staked two obvious claims with rock monuments and John tried his luck with a pan, finding plenty of placer gold including several large nuggets. Over the next few weeks he filled twenty small sacks which he figured weighed a hundred pounds, a small fortune for John.

I will get more, the great hunter always seeks bigger, better and more, thought John. The demon in his heart, the demon greed would drive his future in directions he could not imagine.

4

JUAN OLIVERA WAS *MUCHO GRANDE Mejicano* in his own mind. Forty-six years old, four feet eight inches tall, thick boned with rounded shoulders that seemed to attach directly to his head without benefit of a neck, like a prizefighter. A round-faced man, brown eyes, brown up-turned mustache and a body browned by sun and genes. A pumpkin-like smile, accentuated by a missing front tooth, denied the sins hidden behind the eyes. His face was weathered by many journeys, and his soul filled with hatred for the *gringos*.

Juan's father had been killed in the fall of 1846 in the war between the United States and Mexico, a slaying he would never forgive or forget, sculpturing in his young mind an obligation to extract retribution. His pumpkin smile disarmed most of them; his strong arms, quick feet and agile wits could handle the others, when necessary. He was an instinctive entrepreneur; at age fifteen he was in business for himself taking strings of mules to the expanding gold camps along the western slopes of the Sierra Nevada Mountains.

His family farm was a few miles from Mission Santa Barbara, founded along with twenty-one other churches by Fray Junipero Serra and other Franciscans. The mission was located on a hill from which you could see both the Pacific Ocean and the Santa Ynez Mountains. The early adobe structure provided a place for schooling, religious instruction and services, first to the *Canoliño* Indians and later to other local residents and travelers. The Santa Barbara facility was part of a chain of structures built along California's *El Camino Real* in the mid-seventeen hundreds, each separated by a long day's march. Father Serra, a small, thin figure with a fox-like face, corded brown robe and large, long rosary, walked the trail selecting most of the sites.

Juan's family attended Mass at the mission and his mother went to the *Lavanderia* to wash clothes and exchange stories with local women. The *Lavanderia* was a man-made, trench-like ditch, roughly seventy feet long and six feet wide with firm adobe sides and bottom. Water poured into one end of the ditch out of the mouth of a masonry boars-head and left the trench on the far end. The women scrubbed their clothes on the sidewalls of the trench.

Juan learned English, arithmetic, history and the Franciscan version of Catholicism at the mission school. He absorbed a useful sense of economics, observed how the missionaries guarded their treasures, husbanded their gold, traded, planted and grew their possessions. They were religious men, praying often, and they were firm and definite in their opinions and views. Juan observed that such definite thinking was sometimes an asset and sometimes a liability, depending on the circumstances. Juan was also quick to observe that the Franciscans were suckers for a sob story, particularly if it was wrapped in the appropriate amount of contrition. He learned the value of saying *mea culpa*. "Through my fault, through my fault, through my most grievous fault," words used by the devout in many churches and by con men worldwide. Many people, it seemed, both good and bad, knew the value of apparent remorse. Spinning yarns to gain an advantage became a game Juan played with his Franciscan teachers and other associates.

Late one spring, he challenged his classmates to a contest to see who could catch the most wild horses in the hills the following Sunday. He offered the *el jinete* award, which was not well defined, to the winner. The kids rounded up five horses and two mules that were probably not all wild. Juan congratulated the two boys who shared first place, took charge of the livestock and left, promising to return with the *el jinete* prize.

Early the next morning he left for the gold fields that were located on the west side of the Sierra Nevada Mountains. He packed the mules with pots, pans, tools and other items he had mostly stolen, things he believed would have value in the mining community. He followed the mission trail north, soliciting sympathy and help from the priests. He was, after all, a poor, small child forced by circumstances to travel far with a string of wild animals. They gave him food, shelter, protection and hay for the livestock.

When Juan left Mission Santa Clara, he followed the trail that went around the east side of the bay through Corral Hollow, Somerville and on to Sacramento. He then turned east and walked up into the foothills until he reached the prosperous gold camp at Coloma where he sold the livestock for a price of twelve hundred dollars and the goods they carried for three hundred more. He was paid in gold dust. He earned the money in less than two hours, putting Juan into the trading business at a very early age.

Juan was carrying a lot of money, and he was a "greaser," surrounded by unfriendly miners. He sensed the potential for trouble. It was time to say "*adiós amigos.*" He slipped out of town after dark and hid one fifth of his poke in the hollow under a fallen California sycamore tree located roughly fifteen miles west of Coloma. It was his first cache, a trick used by Indians, Mexicans, miners and others to protect their plunder from those that would steal it from them. He covered the hollow with rocks and mud before he walked, mostly by night, to the coastal Spanish settlement of Yorba Buena, now called San Francisco. He planned to seek out his cousin, Jamie, who worked on the docks. Close family relationships were part of his Hispanic heritage and looking for a relative was a norm. He planned to learn the ways of the *gringos*, expand his knowledge of city life and take advantage of its opportunities.

San Francisco had grown from a small settlement of less than one thousand people to over fifty thousand after the gold find at Sutter's Mill. The harbor was packed with ships, goods were stacked along the docks, and people lived in tents or other hastily built structures. The city was alive with activity and new arrivals from England, Ireland, China, Mexico, Hawaii, Germany, France, Italy, Poland, Australia, Norway, Sweden and almost everywhere. They were mostly men with one common goal, to find wealth. There were also women, mostly sporting ladies and those seeking adventure.

Prospectors, who are instinctively aggressive, quickly availed themselves of the opportunities on the Barbary Coast which had developed into a sin-strip complete with saloons, dance halls, brothels and gambling houses. Prostitutes, often girls abducted from China, were easy to locate. Ships, abandoned by crews who were rushing to the gold camps, were often re-manned by potential prospectors. Men who had planned to seek gold found themselves aboard ship—shanghaied from one of the Barbary Coast's finer establishments. The seedy section of the new city was in strange conflict with the fashionable homes being built on Nob Hill and along the slopes of Stockton Street. The opulence was a product of the wealth already flowing from the Sierra Nevada Mountains and related ventures. San Francisco was continuously growing, burning down and rebuilding during the early years.

Juan lived on what he made working on the docks, never mentioning his gold. It was easy to find employment in 1851 because of the rapid expansion of the city and the flight of men seeking treasure. He helped with the off-loading of seedling fruit trees from a large clipper ship, helping himself to a goodly number. He found two lonesome barrels of flour and rolled them into a partly burned out section of an old warehouse, the same building where he stored the trees and other plunder picked up about town. His most prized bag was a double barreled, twelve gauge shotgun, pinched from a sealed crate which Juan opened carefully, then re-secured so that the theft would be difficult to detect. He stashed the gun in the rafters of the warehouse, concealing it well. He knew that pilfering a weapon would be viewed by the *gringos*, as a serious matter—much more serious than looting trees and other goods.

This particular June night was typical for San Francisco, cool, foggy and dank. The wind was swirling off the Pacific Ocean and then westward over Twin Peaks and out across the bay. The wind was wet and chilling because it was spawned by the cold, offshore water that had been driven by the forces of nature past the Aleutian Islands, Alaska and the Northwest Territory on its journey to the area west of San Francisco.

Juan's heart was as cold that night as the Pacific Ocean water. He filled his lungs as he walked west, uphill, away from the docks, with the adrenaline generated in his body by the thrill of the gun heist still firing through his veins. Firearms conjured up dark, evil, violent thoughts in Juan's mind. The whiskey he had purchased from Washoe Cete and sloshed down, helped match his mood to the conditions. It was a perfect night for a *gringo's* death, he thought.

A white girl, small, walking fast in his direction, materialized out of the fog, providing an opportunity to fulfill his need to take some revenge for his father. He blocked her path, brandishing his knife close to her breasts. She froze, blue eyes wide, mouth moving without sound, wet blond hair clinging to her head. "Be quiet or Juan Olivera will cut your tits off," he hissed to the sixteen year-old miss who cowered as he grabbed hold of her sweater and pulled her into the alley on the left. Strong, quick, determined, he brought her to the ground, sensing that she had given up, knowing death was at hand, much like a hunter feels the thoughts of his prey. Without passion or remorse he slit her throat and watched her body quiver as its life concluded. He stripped her naked, raped her motionless body, satisfying both his carnal and killing instincts. He then made a trip to the opium den owned by Sam Hing, a well-wisher he did not really like, but found useful. The police investigation turned up nothing. No one saw the knifing and Juan remained free like so many before and after who commit crimes that appear motiveless.

Months later, his stash grown threefold, he decided to head back home. Needing horse and wagon to haul the booty, he used his ingenuity and set fire to a downtown hotel. Knowing the blaze would draw a crowd, he hoped for an opportunity to make a snatch. It was a dark night, two days before Christmas, when the first volunteer fire fighters, Knickerbocker V, arrived sending one of their company scrambling up a long ladder to rescue a small girl from the burning hotel building. Juan stayed in the shadows waiting, watching, knowing that wherever tragedy strikes people gather, their baser instincts seeking drama.

His chance came when a teamster left his horses and empty wagon tied to a hitching rail as he rushed off to the fire and became lost in the crowd. Juan simply untied the animals and led them off to the hiding place in the warehouse where he loaded the wagon, slept for a few hours and departed before dawn. He was well south of the central city before he stopped to eat, buy additional ammunition for his shotgun and provisions for the journey, continuing to use money earned on the docks rather than placer gold. There was talk about a big hotel fire and a hero, a firefighter who saved a seven-year-old girl, Lois Hargrave.

The vigilantes, ad hoc law enforcers, were reportedly looking for an arsonist, a smallish man who had set the hotel blaze. Typically, the vigilantes had little patience, remorse or regard for the formalities of the law. They were angry men, fed up with criminal activity, often fired up with alcohol, who were all too willing to hang someone first and seek the truth later. Juan knew that they were active in San Francisco and the gold camps. He feared them, was glad to be getting out of the city, and hoped that they would be chasing some new villain when he returned.

Adiòs, he thought to himself. Goodbye, temporarily, to two men he had met through his cousin. Juan was planning to access their services in later business operations. Washoe Cete, dockside owner/operator of Cete's Liquor and Tobacco undertaking and Sam Hing a leader in San Francisco's *Yan Wo* tong and opium dealer. He planned to purchase whiskey from Cete and "powdered poppy" from Hing and transport them to the gold camps where they would bring a fine price.

Juan headed south, back along the mission trail telling the pastor of each mission about how his mother had taken ill and his sister's husband had run off, stories designed to gain their sympathy. He gave each mission pastor what he described as his "last few pennies." He ate their food, accepted their protection and stole whatever he could get his hands on without being observed.

Upon his return to Santa Barbara he and his sister, Maria, planted eighty sapling fruit trees, mostly oranges and peaches, carefully following the instructions for planting and watering provided by a friendly missionary. He hid most of his gold but gave the team, wagon, water-barrels, flour and other plunder to his family. Gifts for the family, an act proving his manhood—*macho*— a giving, consistent with the Hispanic way. His mother made old-fashioned tamales, the big fat type, filled with hot stuff and chicken, wrapped in cornhusks, tied at the ends and steamed until hot. There were advantages to being at home.

He presented his two winning classmates with their *el jinete* award, a "treasure map" showing the locations of the major gold fields in California. They were ecstatic and helped him gather twelve mules over the next few weeks. Then he loaded them with trade goods for the mining camps and started his next trip north. He was in business and would go back and forth many times in future years.

By the middle of 1852 Juan was able to convert his gold dust to bank deposits, coins or checks at the Wells, Fargo and Company Bank on Montgomery Street in San Francisco. Hispanic people were foreigners who were given little respect and who had few rights. Gold however, always had respect and Wells, Fargo and Company was happy to get it. A year later he could do the same things at numerous bank offices scattered around the gold fields. Henry Wells and William G. Fargo set up their business to transport people, mail, gold, coin, and to provide banking services to the California prospectors who came from all over the world and who numbered a quarter of a million by 1852. Juan trusted the *gringo* banks more than he trusted his ability to fight off the growing number of road agents working in Northern California, their ranks recently swollen by a shipload of hardened criminals delivered gratuitously by Australia.

Juan made numerous journeys to the early gold fields. One of the more memorable occurred in July 1853, when he was in the Tulare Lake Region of the San Joaquin Valley and ran into a group of Hispanic outlaws. He fell in with them, went on several robberies which netted him a wagon, four horses, a fine six-gun, a saddle, several blankets and other provisions. His fellow highwaymen did not fully appreciate the commercial value of the things Juan kept. They preferred to fight for money, gold or jewelry.

Late one afternoon, the one called Three-Fingered Jack caught two Chinese, tied them back to back by their pigtails and slit their throats. The slaughter generated no emotion in the cold heart of Juan Olivera who respected, but feared, the man with the missing digits. He would have enjoyed the slaughter more had the victims been *gringos*.

Early one evening while making camp, they were overrun by a bunch of deputies who came on without warning, firing from several directions. Juan fell to the ground, snaked his way into a gully and hid while the fight proceeded. Three Fingered Jack Garcia went down, dead, and the group's leader, Joaquin, fell to a deputy's bullet. Two of the others were captured.

Juan was very still, quiet. Throughout the battle, he didn't use either his shotgun or six-gun preferring to wait it out in the hope he could escape. It worked. The deputies didn't search the area, assuming that all those present were firing. They used Juan's wagon and horses to haul away the prisoners, the dead, and his loot from robberies, marking the end of his career as a road agent. He lost his plunder and learned a lesson. It's easier to cheat and rob the *gringos* when working alone. He was forced to recover the cache he had left years earlier near Coloma, under the tree, to finance his trip home. Later, Juan read that the head of Joaquin Murieta and the three-fingered hand of Jack Garcia had been preserved in some kind of solution in jars and were being paraded all over northern California. The deputies, "rangers," the newspaper called them, attacked the Hispanic group in response to the one thousand dollar reward posted for Joaquin. Juan learned a lesson. Work alone or with family and remain concealed whenever possible.

5

SEAN McCARTHY, A SHORT, STOCKY, round freckle-faced, redheaded, Irishman, came from Boston to California in 1850. He said farewell to his family and fiancee, Mary Hogan, boarded the narrow hulled, heavenly sailed clipper ship Andrew Jackson. He was suffering from over excitement and over indulgence. Sean had a passion, a fire in his soul for gold, a desire fueled by men like Sam Bannon, the Mormon store owner in San Francisco. Bannon was seeking self-enrichment, and he made it his business to hype the stories coming from the gold camps. The more people that came west, the more goods he sold, the more he made and the more he could donate to himself and his church.

The beauty of the departure was unforgettable as the sleek ship left its mooring from the wharf in Boston harbor and slipped silently out through the channel following the striped black and white buoys that marked its centerline. It left astern the rich history of the city called the "cradle of liberty," the site of the Boston Tea Party and the home of Paul Revere. They were sailing into a bright, rising sun that made the waters sparkle like diamonds on a jeweler's mantle. The ship moved easily, running before a modest wind that was on her port quarter. The tide was ebbing and they were slipping quickly past vessels of numerous sizes and shapes, some at berths and others riding at anchor. Her wake left a long, soft, straight trail on the calm harbor waters. The hills of Boston and the city's skyline faded into the distance as they passed out of Massachusetts Bay into the Atlantic Ocean. When the Andrew Jackson found deeper water the disposition of the sea changed from peaceful to choppy and then to a powerful swell. Strong, rolling waves followed the clipper causing her stern to yaw, swinging back and forth like the tail of a giant fish.

"Mind your helm. Mind your helm," he heard the captain order several times, but his commands seemed to have little effect on the yaw. To stop it, the ship's skipper "jibed" to a starboard tack, causing the boom and sails to swing across the deck.

When she reached the open sea, the ship took the wind first on the starboard quarter and later abeam as she swung southeast passing Cape Cod. Sean heard the command, "Hands aloft," and the crew brought the Andrew Jackson under full sail. The strong heavy waves leaning at regular intervals on the clipper's starboard side set her to rolling. "Reaching," sailing across the wind also added to her speed and that's when Sean began to feel sick, real sick, to his stomach.

Sean and others unaccustomed to shipboard life spent all the first day at sea between their bunks and the rail, giving to the ocean waters what had been eaten and drunk until they were dry. Sean felt terrible and his flu-like symptoms persisted for almost forty-eight hours before he began to get his "sea legs." After a time, his inner ear became accustomed to the new environment and his stomach problems eased. He learned how to stand and walk on the endlessly rolling, pitching and twisting deck of the clipper. He also began to appreciate the exhaustion felt by seafaring men after a long journey. Even when lying in his bunk, Sean's body was challenged to maintain equilibrium and balance. His body was constantly required to adjust to the instability created by the endless power of a mighty ocean.

He was fascinated by the men who climbed up into the rigging, eternally setting and trimming twenty-eight sails, each with its own name, attached in one way or another to the three masts, "fore," "main" and "mizzen." He learned the names of the sails, starting with the forward most, "flying jib," by sketching them with pen on paper and printing each name on its sail. He learned that the sails were trimmed to optimize their effectiveness under various conditions involving the wind, its force, direction, variability and the state of the sea. He heard about the skipper's goal, to sail from Boston to San Francisco in ninety days or less, which would require superb seamanship on his part and that of his crew. In fact, the training, skill and motivation of the sailors would be the key factor in achieving or failing their objective.

Sean was on deck one evening at twilight when he saw the first mate looking through a hand held, mechanical device that had the general shape of a chicken without much mass or feathers. He was curious and asked the mate what he was doing, never considering the possibility that he was creating an unwelcome distraction. "Wait one governor," was the response he got as the mate said, "Ready. Mark," and the quartermaster who was holding a watch, noted the time in a book. "Star bearing north by northwest, elevation sixty-one degrees, twenty-three minutes, eleven seconds," said the mate while the quartermaster copied. Turning in another direction, the mate adjusted the device and they repeated the procedure twice more.

"Aye mate," Charlie Winchester said as he turned toward Sean, "You no should'a trouble us when we shoot stars. Time's nipped. We hop to it. Shan't miss them first stars when th' light's just so. That's the 'ard part. Look sharp, hold your tongue. That's what you do. Put you square when last light's down, when we have a go at fixin' position."

The mate, Charlie Winchester, was a thin-faced, small-boned man of average height with brown hair and a neatly trimmed beard. He had the strong, weathered look of a man of the sea and the sharp eyes of a ship's pilot. He had learned his trade sailing out of Portsmith England with his father, as they fished and sometimes carried passengers or cargo to the ports on the northern coast of Europe. He spoke little and his dialect was hard for Sean to follow. He had some formal education and passed the pilots' examination, obtaining his papers when he was twenty. He found employment on several ocean going sailing ships, fell in love with a young lady in Boston, married and took up residence in the famous city, renting a small cottage near Boston Harbor. His aim was to become qualified as a ship's master, and he knew that navigating the Andrew Jackson to San Francisco in ninety days or less would accelerate his advancement.

Charlie's apprentice, the quartermaster, Rod Sherman, entered a crowded chart-house with Sean, and they began to teach him the language of navigation. All subjects have their own language, math, physics, chemistry, geology, economics, medicine, philosophy and navigation. Once a person understands the words, their meaning and their relationships, he can decipher the language, manage options and find solutions to problems or opportunities that present themselves within the framework of that discipline. Sean's first lesson in this science involved the use of the chicken-like device, a sextant. It's a mechanical contraption used to determine a ship's position at sea. Working the sextant requires knowledge of the language of celestial navigation, a blend of crisp science with practiced art, employed by sailors throughout history. He advanced his knowledge mostly by reading books loaned to him by Charlie and from the clear simple explanations communicated by his assistant, Rod. In the process of learning celestial navigation he developed great respect for the importance of clear, accurate, organized communications. Rod, a man with little education, was somehow better able to deliver such communications more clearly than his boss. None of his engineering teachers at college had exposed him adequately to one of society's basic fundamentals. Education is relatively useless unless its message can be communicated. Often those who know the most are unable to pass their wisdom on, he thought.

The brightest stars, called first magnitude, the moon and some of the planets can be seen by sharp eyed sailors at dusk and just before dawn when the horizon is also clear and sharp. The sextant, a mechanical device with a small telescope, fixed mirror and mirror on a moveable arm, allows one to measure the angle between the horizon and a celestial body. The process is often called "shooting the stars" The Nautical Almanac provides tables that describe the exact position of various celestial bodies relative to earth at various times of day. By measuring the angle between the horizon and a bright star at a known moment in time, one can calculate, using the Almanac, a circular line on the surface of the ocean along which the ship must lie. By shooting two stars, two lines can be drawn. The more stars you shoot the more lines you can draw. In theory, all the lines should meet at a point on the chart, fixing the ship's position. However, in practice, shooting the stars is an art requiring skill and practice. The science will always provide a perfect fix, but shooting celestial bodies on a moving ship in the half-light is a true art, like taking great pictures. Art is almost never error free and additional inaccuracies are introduced when some shortcuts are used to simplify calculating and plotting on nautical charts. In addition, the time on the ship's clock, called a chronometer, is never exactly right. Accordingly, a perfect fix is rarely achieved and the pilot or navigator must use some judgment in determining the ship's position.

Sean was fascinated; he was a young man craving for new knowledge on a long voyage that provided time to quench his thirst. He poured over the available books, learning about the constellations, the positions of the first magnitude stars, chart reading, tides, currents, clouds, weather and nautical terms. Sean located the Southern Cross and he took sightings on its southernmost star. He read about comets and hoped to one day be able to view a real big one. Later he gained agreement from Charlie and Rod to join the navigation team on their morning, noon and evening "shoots." It was a chance for Sean to expand his mind, moving its current limits outward, satisfying its never-ending hunger for new learning. For the mind, like the stomach, must be fed to grow the man. Lack of education, tradition, superstition, folklore, religion, hearsay and science all create barriers, rules and structures in people's minds which must be surmounted when new information sheds new light on the world around them. Such light was falling on Sean as he absorbed the language of navigation.

Rod said, "When we get close to land we no need sextant, can use dead reck'ning, 'nother way to find position. We take compass bearings on known landmarks—landmarks, you know—tall things that al' ready been marked on charts. We then find ship's position by what they call triang'lation. We still shoot stars to keep seaman's touch. We shoot sun too, at noon—the lower part—what they call lower limb. Sun gives one line on chart that marks our latitude."

Sean learned to take compass bearings on other ships they encountered in open water. If another ship was approaching the Andrew Jackson on a steady, constant bearing, the two vessels were on a collision course and maneuvering was required by one to avoid the other. There were very specific rules laid down by maritime law that set out maneuvering procedures and signals in dangerous situations. Sean memorized those rules and dreamed, dreamed often, about a huge ship closing on the Andrew Jackson and he would cry out, "Bearing steady, bearing steady. Bearing steady, bearing steady." But, in his sleep the words always went unheeded by a faceless, inert crew. He regularly awoke from the dream in a sweat, just as the two ships crashed together.

Sean took land sightings on Bermuda, taking note of the luminescent white waters near the island. Rod had told him it was bad water, unique to this area of the ocean.

Rod said, "Plenty ships gone down 'round Bermuda. Can't trust compass 'round these waters neither. Bad sea. Good place to go way from."

Superstitions of seamen, thought Sean, as they passed on to the south without incident, and he got a bearing on a small, unnamed island east of the easternmost tip of South America near C. de São Rogue. He became reasonably proficient in the use of the sextant and found the calculations required to complete the mathematics for a fix were simple in comparison to those related to calculus and other studies he had completed in pursuit of his engineering degree. Sean's father, a police detective, and his mother, a schoolteacher, had encouraged him from as far back as he could remember to pursue and cherish education. He learned to read at an early age and mathematics had come easily. He was one of the first Irish Catholics to graduate with honors in engineering from Harvard.

He would never forget the toast his father gave him after the graduation ceremony. "Books, yes books, you know. But what do you really know of life? Trust in God, start your journey to find your proper place. Work hard, reach high, never give up and build a loving family."

Sean thought often about those words. In a way they framed his character. His father had been happy living by those ideals and Sean was sure he would find success and happiness if he followed his father's example. Even here, on the voyage, he was adhering by advancing his education.

At eight degrees south latitude they altered their base course to south by southwest following the South American coastline past Rio de Janeiro, San Paulo, Motevideo, Buenos Aires to the Falkland Islands. They were making very good time, giving the captain a chance for his speed record, until they reached Cape Horn. The Cape was a dangerous and storm frequented passageway at the southern end of the Americas.

The sky was red that morning, reminding the voyagers of an ancient rhyme,

"Sky red at night, sailors delight, sky red in morning, sailors be warning."

"Batten down for heavy weather," was the day's order that Charlie Winchester put in simple perspective.

"Sticky business a-comin' me thinks," he said.

The steep sides on the southern tip of Horn Island, which rise up out of the sea to six hundred feet in the same places, were barely visible as they started the Cape passage, beating to windward in heavy weather. The clipper pounded into the huge ocean swells with overhanging crests which had grown to thirty and forty feet tall by Sean's estimation. Cold salt water poured over the bow railing each time her prow struck a new white capped wall of water. There was white foam and froth on the ocean surface, blown and fanned by a growling wind of around sixty knots coming almost directly out of the west, transporting thick, low, dark clouds that were passing swiftly overhead. Rain wasn't falling; it was shooting forward like pellets out of the nimbostratus clouds being pushed directly in Sean's face by the wind. The sky had been red that morning for good reason.

They had been warned, but what could they have done? Sean asked himself. And what would happen now? Would the clipper be broken apart by the pounding and shuttering? He had been on the water for over forty days and his sea sickness had given way to other feelings—feelings manifested today in a mixture of fear, exhilaration and helplessness. Fear for his life, exhilaration like that enjoyed when jumping a creek on a powerful horse at a full gallop, helplessness as man in his smallness attempts to grapple with the power of mother nature's demon sea. The clipper was slammed by a huge blast of wind that took some rigging and the top of the foremost came crashing down.

Sean heard someone shout, "Clear away the debris." And the hands turned out from what seemed like nowhere to carry out the command.

Lightning was all around. The Andrew Jackson was floundering and her seamen, while working, were holding tight to whatever they could grab each time the icy seas crashed over the deck. The noise from the sea, the bashing water and howling wind was sometimes so loud it drowned out the claps of thunder that followed the flashes of lightning.

He wanted to confess his sins but there was no priest and he was

forced to settle for a small sign of the cross and a couple of *mea culpas.*
"Through my fault, through my fault," he said before being interrupted by a
hard roll to starboard that almost pitched him overboard. Half frozen from the
effect of icy water and fear, Sean did not remember how long he held himself
fast to the binnacle housing but at some point his mind recognized a change.

There was an unexpected, sudden wind shift and a break in the gray
cover revealed a huge wide cloud with a towering anvil-shaped top directly in
their path. Lightening slashed down through its belly over and over as the
monster moved to swallow them up, flashing, flashing down repeatedly like a
serpent's tongue anticipating prey. The wind's force increased and the sky
turned greenish-gray as the ship floundered before her dragon. A waterspout,
tornado at sea, dropped from the giant cumulonimbus cloud just off the port
bow of the clipper, looking like a dragon's tail. The crew swung into action,
coming on a hard starboard tack and trimming what canvas was still aloft. The
lightening flashes persisted, framing the advancing waterspout that looked to
be from two to three hundred feet in diameter.

Sean, who had been holding tight to the binnacle housing which
contained the ship's compass affixed to a strong pedestal stand secured to the
deck, began taking bearings on the western side of the spout.

"Bearing steady, west-south-west," he said.

"Bearing steady, west-south-west," he said again a minute later.

"Bearing steady, west-southwest, collision course," he shouted as the
water tower closed to two thousand yards.

"Bearing steady, west-southwest, closing," and it was only one thousand
yards away.

Bearing steady," his dream sprung suddenly into a nightmare of life,
"and still closing."

Then, for no apparent reason, the waterspout vanished. It had been
bouncing along on the surface of the ocean waters like a spinning top and
when it took a jump it was sucked up into the belly of the giant cloud. The
gray-green hue faded in favor of simple gray. The wind slowed to its previous
speed and the rain returned to its forward leaping. The Andrew Jackson was
hurt and somewhat out of control but she had stayed afloat under the weight

of the devil's anvil. Where had the waterspout gone? Was it a miracle? Should I be thanking God or nature? Thought Sean.

The captain was issuing commands and the deck hands responded by cutting away the debris and setting a limited amount of sail. It took about fifteen minutes before Sean could stop shaking and give up his hold on the binnacle housing. He relaxed some when he heard the words, "Secure aloft." By then the ship was under control and the captain motioned him to his side. "Charlie was washed overboard. He's gone. From here to San Francisco you will be my pilot. I'll see you get proper pay and documentation for the work. I know you are well educated and I have followed your work with Charlie and Rod. You can do it."

"I'll do my best," said Sean, recovering his instinctive confidence.

"That's all I can ask; get started now. Cape Horn is over there somewhere, a fitting name considering the way we have been gored by that rum storm, don't you think? See if you can get some land bearings and a fix," said the captain.

They couldn't see the land because of the rain and low clouds so they headed west to make sure they would not go aground in the heavy weather. "Keep her into the wind," was the order given over and over to the helmsman during the night while Sean peered into the blackness as if he could see his way over the ocean. By dawn the next day the sky had cleared and Sean got a good celestial fix which allowed him to recommend a course to the northwest. He marked a course on the chart that would stand the ship out about fifty miles to seaward from the string of islands located near the western shore of South America. The captain double checked Sean's calculations, agreed that the suggested course was safe and thanked him for his good work.

The broken foremast could not be replaced at sea but the damaged rigging had been cleared away. Most other damage could be fixed while underway and the clipper was handling well as she swung to her new course. The captain considered making port in Valparaiso for repairs but decided he could reach San Francisco safely. They had lost two men and been through a terrifying experience that caused him to worry about the crew's morale. He did not want to put them on the beach in Chile where they might be tempted to jump ship.

There would be no speed record set on this voyage but they were still afloat and the clipper was sea worthy. They had been lucky and the captain did not want to stretch his good fortune too far.

The ocean currents, driven by the earth's rotation, moved counter-clockwise south of the equator pushing the Andrew Jackson on her way. The westerly wind remained brisk until they were well north of Valparaiso where gradually they began to shift into the warm gentle southeasterly trade pattern. It was hot when they crossed the equator where they sighted the Galapagos Islands and it did not begin to cool off much until the winds swung around to the northeast farther up the coast of North America. The ocean waters cooled considerably as they came abeam of San Diego; the current, now on their bow, was carrying water that had been cooled in its clockwise flow past Alaska. The wind grew brisk, coming across their port beam making for better speed. Near the Farallon Islands, they encountered light fog and trimmed sails, reduced speed, taking care not to go aground. They heard the foghorns and signal bells before sighting the entrance to Yerba Buena Harbor, now called San Francisco. The captain elected to sail in on a slack tide to reduce the effect of the water's strong currents on their movements.

The shoreline was rocky, steep in most places, spotted with trees and houses. Large white gulls flew overhead, leaving their droppings on the unlucky, and sea lions played in the water and snoozed on the rocks. Fishing vessels and boat docks lined the north beach to starboard and Mount Tamalpais towered over them to port. The fresh smell of a cold sea became mixed with that of docks, ships, fish, cooking and people, producing that unique odor only found in a commercial seaport environment.

Once well inside the harbor, they swung south, leaving Yerba Buena Island to port. They docked at a pier in the bay on the city's eastern coastline. The pilings groaned as the Andrew Jackson eased alongside with her crewmembers using fenders to prevent damage to the clipper's hull. They made her fast to the dock using lines and cleats in the ancient tradition of seafaring men who knew that the ship would rise and fall alongside the dock as the tide came in and out. A wooden plank, the gangway, was laid over the side between the clipper and the dock so that passengers and crew could go ashore.

An in-port watch was set and the captain sought out Sean to thank him for his efforts. He had been made an official member of the crew and was paid accordingly. The captain said, "The sea can use a man like you. If you want to apply for your papers I'll help you become a merchant marine officer. You can sail with me anytime."

But Sean had gold fever. That's why he had headed for San Francisco. He thought his engineering degree would give him an advantage over other prospectors. He knew something about gold, where to look for it, how it was formed. He had never been in a mining camp or down a shaft but he thought he knew what to expect. Like most Irishmen, his outlook was eternally positive, aggressive and reckless. Indestructible, like many youths, that's how he saw himself. The twinkle in his eye suggested he had kissed the blarney stone and believed in leprechauns; the swing in his stride revealed his self-assurance. He could find gold, build a tunnel and make a fortune! He knew he could! The voyage had been exciting and he enjoyed being the navigator, but he lusted for the color. He thanked the captain, who smiled when gold was mentioned. "There's more gold to be found in the sea than in the mountains," he said, leaving Sean to ponder his meaning.

He went ashore, carrying his possessions onto the Barbary Coast. It was crowded with fortune hunters of all types and descriptions, many coming from abroad: Englishmen, Irishmen, Germans, Italians, Frenchmen, Swedes, Spaniards, Chinese, Hawaiians, Russians, Poles and others, joined like an amalgam with a common purpose, their lust for gold. He had thought the word cosmopolitan fit Boston; now he saw that it fit this young city much better.

Crewmen, jumping ship for the gold camps, had become so common in San Francisco that sea captains could not find sailors and they consorted with bar owners to spike customers' drinks so that they could be pressed, unwilling, into sea duty. Sean liked the sea but he had no interest in being shanghaied and decided, in spite of his penchant for Irish whiskey and beer, to stay clear of the coastal watering holes. He located and boarded the first available riverboat to Sacramento.

He heard about a place called Wood's Dry Diggin's from noisy strangers on the riverboat. It was reportedly located on the north fork of the American River three miles upstream from the confluence of the north and middle forks. It was away from the area, crowded with prospectors, near Sutter's Mill and Mormon Island on the south fork of the American. A carpenter named James Marshall had found the first color in 1848 while employed by John Sutter to build a small mill on the south fork of the American. The first nuggets showed up when he was digging the millrace. He had used Mormons, recently discharged from the Mormon Battalion, as laborers and they made a second major strike on a sandbar down river.

From the W.M. Gwynn and H. M. House trading post, Sean purchased a horse and supplies to go along with the small tent, bedroll and tools he had brought from the east coast. The clerk at the store was angry, just like many other Sacramento residents. They were mad because they were still cleaning up the mess left by the great flood that occurred during the winter of 1849/50. Flooding in the Sacramento delta area was common but the rising waters of the prior winter were nearly cataclysmic. Great rivers including the Rubicon, American, Feather and Yuba all flow into the delta lands near Sacramento. When they crested their waters leapt over their banks and carried logs, green lumber, shacks, tents, wagons, supplies and people away. The torrential rains combined with waters from melting snow in the mountains had been too much for the riverbanks. The disaster had improved business for the trading post because folks needed to replace many things; however, the cleanup made everyone short-tempered.

Sean rode his horse upstream looking for gold in and around the river and on the dry ground away from its banks. He saw lots of miners working the sandbars between Sacramento and the small settlement called Auburn and there were others prospecting upriver to the east. He searched for several months before his scientific knowledge paid dividends. Early one afternoon about eight miles from the river in a hot, dry canyon he located what seemed to be an ancient stream-bed, one very difficult to spot because of surface erosion and undergrowth. He scratched in the dirt and rocks along its apparent course for several days keeping a watchful eye out for rattlesnakes that popped up almost everywhere along the western foothills of the Sierra Nevada Mountains. He had great respect for their fangs and the damage they could do to man or horse, but little taste for their meat; somehow eating the flesh of the poisonous serpent seemed unholy.

The temperature was high, over one hundred degrees, Sean guessed. The air was very dry as he dug down six feet into a brush covered, sandy layer of earth that may have been a pool or small lakebed along the course of the old dry streambed. Bingo! Gold! It was a thick layer of placer that had dropped to the bottom where the water had slowed. It could have been left there hundreds, thousands or possibly millions of years ago. Left there for him to find on this scorching summer afternoon. He concealed his digging and hid a pile of rocks under some brush to signify a miner's claim. His mind was racing! Hide, hide everything, then get to Sacramento as fast as you can and file an official claim. Be very careful, don't let anyone except the people at the filing office know about your find! There are men who will kill for gold and you are alone! Move fast, but with care and cover your tracks.

The following day Sean left his small mine, dragging a bundle of brush behind his horse to cover his trail. He thought, to himself, The venom in men's spirit is more dangerous than the venom in a rattler's fangs and man's venom is secreted for gold.

Sean scattered the bundle of brush as he approached civilization, stopped near the American River about twenty miles above the Auburn, and made camp with a few other miners who were just returning from their diggings. They shared their fire and some trout taken from the river. Sean was tired; it had been a hot, busy day. He was still excited about his find and concerned that someone else would be digging there before he could get back. He had no idea how much gold there might be in the old dry wash. It was quite a while before he could get to sleep but finally exhaustion overrode his excitement.

His eyes flew open when the quiet night exploded and he was shocked awake by noises, and the grip of fear. Thunk. Thunk. Crack. Crunch. There was the crackle of bark and a fresh arrow lodged in the tree near his tent. A second arrow cut through the side of the canvas pinning his unworn boot to the tent floor. He scrambled out on his belly, dragging a double-barreled shotgun and made himself as small as possible along side of the tree trunk where the first arrow lodged. He fired from the prone position at a shadowy figure in the dark about the same time that the other miners began to shout and shoot, mostly at monsters created by their psyche. They blazed away, not realizing that the battle had ended. The Miwok Indians had slipped off into the blackness. Two prospectors were dead, one was wounded and all remaining were both mad and scared. They agreed to track the Indians in the morning while Sean went for a doctor for their wounded comrade and for reinforcements. The Miwok, normally a peaceful bunch, were also angry. Their lands, which were whatever lands happened to suit them, were being invaded by others, mostly white men, who dirtied their water, ate their pine nuts and killed their game. This group of prospectors had gone well up river and had pushed the Indians too far.

Sean rallied the miners down river, encouraging them to join the hunt before they became the hunted, and almost all he talked to were willing to follow his lead. He sent word to Sacramento for a doctor and headed his army of twenty-four armed prospectors on a search for his attackers. The euphoria of impending battle, experienced by the invincible Irish spirit, grew in his chest as he joined the other miners who were hiding and waiting near the Miwok camp. The battle was brief, the miners routing the surprised Indians, leaving five dead and two captured.

Riding a ship through a great storm, finding gold and leading men in victorious battle produced feelings in man that could not easily be reproduced. Sean had experienced them all.

He filed his claim, obtained a wagon, water barrels and other equipment at various stores in Sacramento before riding out to his mine site under a blazing, white-hot, summer sun. It yielded eight thousand dollars in gold and silver over the next four months before playing out. It wasn't the mother-lode but the find set the hook deeper and deeper into his soul. He would be searching, forever seeking the exhilaration of another strike.

Prospecting is the engine that drives the entrepreneur and powers free enterprise. Greed is the fuel that powers the engine. Greed, in the form of a quest for gold, was now fully at work inside the person of Sean McCarthy.

He hadn't been to Mass since leaving Boston. The gospel of gold was his current reality, overwhelming his need to service his soul. The gospel of wealth is a reality resident in most men, including those who appear in church regularly, responding to social pressure more than spiritual desire. In the early gold camps, there was more social pressure to seek worldly treasure than to serve God. Had that gospel changed the soul of Sean McCarthy? Would he be driven to strange, foreboding lands on the other side of the mountain in search of new wealth?

6

LOIS HARGRAVE WAS SEVEN YEARS old and alone in her hotel room two evenings before Christmas. Her father, a doctor with an office near the Presidio, was independently wealthy. He had gone with her mother to one of the city's fashionable balls.

Lois, a bright, energetic youth, was reading by lamplight when she smelled smoke. Smoke, fire, escape, she thought. How did it start? Did someone set fire to the hotel? Lois had not seen the short, round-faced Mexican who torched the building so that he could pinch a team and wagon.

She opened her door to find the walls across the hall ablaze. She slammed it shut, ran to the window and started shouting, "Fire, fire, fire, help, help, help!" It was dark outside, but she heard the clanging of the fire bell, providing hope, as her room began to fill with smoke. She stayed at the open window, shouting and waving her white kerchief.

She felt the pressure of the rising heat at her back, heard the crash as one of the hotel's interior walls tumbled and felt her lungs gasping for fresh air. She was screaming, hysterical, tears in her eyes when a ladder smacked up against the outside wall next to her window and a man, wearing fire hat and jacket, came bounding up like a monkey climbing a tree. He reached out and his strong arm guided Lois to the rungs of the ladder.

They worked their way down together, Lois shaking and clutching as she went, shuddering uncontrollably when she reached the street. Her small arms went around the fireman's neck, holding him tight, crying from fear, joy, relief and admiration. Lois was in love with the strong, brave volunteer firefighter from Knickerbocker V. Placed on a gurney, covered with blankets, she was rushed, in shock, to a nearby hospital where she was treated and later released to her parents.

For years thereafter, this bright-eyed, quick-witted, resourceful, tough-minded, energetic, adventurous young lady followed the fire engines to their destinations, cheering her heroes particularly vigorously when they wore the symbol of the Knickerbocker V unit. She became a mascot first and, ultimately, the spirit of San Francisco's many fire fighting brigades, appearing on their wagons and posters and at their parades and fundraisers. She was seen all over town wearing her Knickerbocker Number Five hat with dark curly hair leaking out under its brim.

Lois was a fine student and in time she became an accomplished writer and communicator. She took voice and dancing lessons and learned the guitar. She was a hit on the San Francisco stage, performing often for the legendary buffoon, Emperor Norton, and other aficionados in this unique, colorful, young city destined to become one of the world's most revered. She was dubbed, "San Francisco's Brightest Decoration," by the Bulletin and she became a regular at fashionable events.

Adventurous sensually, she would often date several men on the same night. Once, she was engaged to two men at the same time, dating each every other night, changing rings to match her escort. She married a wealthy doctor, Harry Bolt, an arrangement that lasted ten years in spite of Harry's reported attention to other females. Lois took up various activities deemed inappropriate for a lady of her station, including playing poker, dealing faro and betting on horses. One night she dressed as a man so she could enjoy the adventure of attending a cockfight with Harry. The marriage dissolved in 1880 and Lois moved to her country place, vanishing from San Francisco's social swirl. Would she surface later, in Bodie? What fate awaited this adventurous young woman?

7

TEX WAS NOT SURE WHICH WAS THE best route west to Bodie from San Antonio. There were several options but the advice he had received from Roy Bean and others seemed to indicate that his travel plan was correct. Tex was heading northwest toward Fort Terrett.

He expected to follow the San Antonio-El Paso Road over the Pecos River to Comanche Springs, then follow the old Butterfield Stage route through El Paso, Yuma, Gila Bend and on to San Diego. During the early gold rush years, before Tex was born, the Houston press had suggested that route (according to his father) and many men had gone that way for years. Roy Bean had recently come from San Diego over that trail and he had described it clearly to Tex, even sketched him a rough map. During the early gold rush years, a trek by a lone rider across the territory called *Llano Estacado* by Hispanics and the "Staked Plains" by Texans, would have been a harrowing experience. By 1880, however, the trail was well worn. There were settlements scattered along its path and most of the Indians were either dead or penned up on reservations. It should be easy, thought Tex.

A lone rider making a long trip tends to loose track of things. His mind becomes bored and it reaches into the subconscious for entertainment. Tex was engrossed in his own thoughts and he lost track of the trail and what was going on around him. He almost came out of his saddle when Moonshine suddenly bolted, taking off, ears erect, at a full gallop, moving fast away from the puma he had spotted to his right. Tex lost a stirrup but managed to stay in his seat by grabbing the saddle horn with his left hand and a mitt full of mane with his right. He was glad his cowboy friends were not around to see him riding like a green horn. Heading off the trail at this speed provided little time for him to help Moonshine avoid the "devil" wire fence that suddenly appeared at their front. Together they made an incredibly sharp right turn but too late to avoid the terrible flesh ripping crash which nearly felled them both. Cut and battered, both rider and horse dropped into shock, but out of instinct, Moonshine stayed on her feet and Tex stayed glued to the saddle.

The puma, a natural hunter, smelled blood and knew her potential prey was in trouble, but she also recognized that the quarry, whatever it was, was much larger than things she typically hunted. The size of her target demanded caution.

Sensing the puma, Moonshine started walking, then trotting, picking up speed and falling into a natural, left-leading lope. The change of pace brought Tex around and he looked back to see the puma following at something less than her closing speed. A very big cat, over eight feet long, probably weighing at least two hundred pounds. She was very fast over short distances but lacked the stamina for a long race with a healthy Moonshine. The trouble was, both he and his mount were a bloody mess and they lacked the ability for a long course. Tex pulled his colt and fired two shots in the general direction of the hunter, a maneuver he suspected was useless. Hitting anything from a running horse with a pistol was almost impossible and striking the cougar on the move would be pure luck.

The mountain lion heard the shots and her mind registered danger. She broke off the chase, taking cover. She had heard that sound before; her mate had fallen, never rising again. She didn't know what it was or what the sound meant but the large animal she was following had some power she chose not to challenge.

Moonshine carried Tex several miles before slowing her pace, sensing that the puma was not in close pursuit. Tex pulled her up, dismounted in spite of the sharp stabbing pains in his leg and began checking both his and Moonshine's injuries. He found numerous gashes, cuts, bruises, slashes, a lot of blood and some swelling. The horse and Tex limped on their left sides. Moonshine's left shank, upper left foreleg and shoulder were bleeding badly and she tottered when walking. Tex was damaged above his boot and on the left hip, arm and hand. He took up one of his canteens and, using a fresh bandana, cleaned first Moonshine's and then his wounds as best he could while keeping a watchful eye out for the cat. He made some rough bandages from one of his clean shirts, doing his best to halt the bleeding. Tex knew they needed rest. It would allow the body to use its energy to heal rather than run. He was a cowhand, an adventurer, who had hunted big cats before. He didn't feel much like a hunter today but he was composed and determined to stand his ground. He built a fire, unsaddled Moonshine and gathered wood, keeping both his Winchester and Colt close to hand. He tied the horse to a tree and gathered grass and greens for her to eat. Moonshine drank water from his hat.

Tex sensed that the puma would attack. The fire would make her cautious but big cats had been known to come on, if hungry, in spite of campfires. Johnny Gray Wolf and Red Hand, the Indian scouts who rode often on the Chisholm, had told many stories about puma attacks and Johnny's life-cycle was almost ended one night when a huge cat came on while he slept in a bedroll. He was saved when the cougar went for his horse rather than his throat. Tex loved Moonshine and he wasn't going to let that happen here. He would stay awake all night, guarding himself and his friend. Tex loved animals, most of them, but not cougars or sheep and not the ones he shot for food; he couldn't love those. But in general, he had a strong affection for the creatures that shared the landscape with human beings.

As the lengthening shadows foretold the close approach of night, he gathered more firewood and moved with Moonshine into some rocks he thought afforded better protection. He didn't want to hobble the horse because of her injuries but he tied her up close by. Tex avoided cooking for fear the cat would become activated by the scent of fresh meat. He ate some beef jerky and settled down for the night.

He didn't plan to sleep, and he found himself thinking. I wonder if the cat's hunting us, following our tracks, considering, pondering, however cougars do such things? What does the animal think? Does it love us? Hate us, or just view us as a meal? Are there little ones to feed somewhere about? How hungry, how determined, how wise is the puma? Does she think or just act out of instinct? Does she relate in some way to the hunted, sensing its feelings—the fear—the will to survive? Will she spring at us from hiding out of the blackness or will we get a warning? Unsettling thoughts, the kind that helped Tex remain awake on this summer night.

Darkness produced coldness, a physical coldness and a coldness of spirit in a man. A chill stemming not from the temperature but from the absence of light and from the fear generated by evil creatures that lurk in the blackness. The demons that rise up at night are reinforced by those that reside in the reservoir of one's mind. Tex was scared but he was not going to give in to his fear.

The puma was nocturnal, preferring to hunt by night. Unlike men, her courage grew as darkness closed in. She moved up into a position where her prey was visible. There were now two animals, one large with four legs, a type she had hunted occasionally in the past, and a second creature with two legs that she had never stalked. She moved in, cat fashion, carefully, slowly, knowing that if seen, they would run. The night was long; she had plenty of time. Closer, closer, she advanced, unseen, easing around so that the wind would be in her face, carrying her scent away from the hunted. Her mother had taught her about the wind and shown her how to hunt. She learned when very young; ignoring mother's lessons produced careless attempts and resulted in extended hunger. She smelled blood, dried blood just before she got a nose full of smoke. Fire and smoke set off her danger responses. Halting, backing away, she bounded up into the rocks where she could still see the four legged animal but not be bothered by the smoke.

The stand off between the mountain lion and the smoke continued until about three in the morning when an exhausted Texan fell asleep and his fire died out.

The cougar had moved up several times during the night only to be chased by smoke. This time, she was more determined because of the hour and her growing hunger. Approaching, up wind, she smelled horseflesh, dried blood and sensed the kill. Coming on, yard by yard, slowly, quietly, she reached a rock twenty yards from the four-legged animal. No smoke, nothing to stop her now! She knew she could move very fast over short distances and the big cat sensed that her prey couldn't escape. She was gathering her strength, preparing to charge when the animal snorted, lifted its head, nickered and crow-hopped. Moonshine was making all sorts of noises. She was the hunted—sensing danger—just before being struck. "Crack, Crack, Crack." A flashing din pierced the blackness causing the big cat to leap sideways rather than toward her prey. She bounded up into the rocks, falling, rolling over. The puma lost her orientation as her hazard impulses overwhelmed her hunger.

Moonshine had saved herself, waking Tex in time for him to grab his pistol and fire three shots into the darkness blindly hoping the noise and gun flashes would frighten anything approaching. Fire, Tex thought to himself. Stoke the fire, get up a blaze, make smoke.

His breath was fast and his hands were trembling from the exhilaration of combat. He had no trouble staying awake until dawn. After first light Tex checked around camp, finding prints of the big cat less than twenty yards away. He was a tired cowboy, stiff and sore, with a horse that looked equally tender. He considered the situation. They needed to move on, making their next camp near water where they could tend their wounds, find better grazing for Moonshine and more opportunities to hunt fresh game. Tex thought if he killed a deer, he could skin it out, take part of the meat and leave enough to keep the mountain lion off his trail.

After breakfast, Tex was on foot, leading Moonshine, when they ran into a large flock of sheep near a medium-sized river, the Llano. The wool-covered animals were being shepherded by two small dogs and a shaggy looking company of Mexicans that included a wagon and some kids. The sheep smelled bad, like all sheep, an animal that Tex had been taught to hate. His parents had nothing good to say about sheep since the time he first learned to communicate, and all the cowhands detested the stinking animals that ate the grass down to the roots. Cattle were good, sheep evil, a truth he had been conditioned to believe by those who influenced him as a child, before he was experienced enough to judge for himself.

Teresa, one of the sheepherders, a bright Mexican woman, educated at the mission school, saw Tex and Moonshine approaching. A sorry looking pair, obviously injured. Worse, they had probably been taught to hate sheep and her kind. She had grown up a minority, learning about bigotry the hard way, experiencing it directed at her. She had seen it from early youth.

The curse of children everywhere, she thought, being taught to believe things that ain't true. Having their brains bent with no account ideas by bigots, rulers, teachers, slow witted parents and foolish friends. Oh, they don't mean no harm. They just don't know no better. It's no wonder that wolves, grizzly bears, pumas, mosquitoes and rattlesnakes are called bad. They have nasty tempers and they bite people. But sheep are gentle, tame animals that produce tasty meat and wool for fine coats and blankets. They give us much and ask for little in return. Are they called bad 'cause they don't smell sweet? Smell sweet, like cattle? Folks say sheep are rank 'cause they eat the grass down too short? Children have their brains twisted about more than animals. Savages, Breeds, Chinks, Spicks, Micks, Niggers, and Hebs are names used to chide different folks. Skin color, religion, manner, speech are things that rile folks and create hard times for those that are different. Who teaches kids that Indians are Savages, Micks dumb, Niggers lazy, Hebs cheats? The same folks that say what's right and what's wrong, what's good and what's evil, what's godliness and what's not. These are the same kinds of folks who called Joan of Arc a witch. They say, "I am right, you are wrong." That's the kind of thinking that put Christ on the cross, put the Christians to death at the hands of the Romans, put the Protestants to death at the hands of the Catholics. "I am right, you wrong!" That's what they say. And so the cattlemen kill the sheep men and their flocks. And so it goes, on and on throughout history, each person believing his view of truth and prodding others to obey—destroying life and evenhandedness along the way.

As Moonshine and Tex approached, Teresa came forward. "You look poorly," she said.

"Ran into the devil wire," he answered.

"Let's have a look," she said, setting about inspecting the wounds of both Tex and his horse. She was thin with dark hair, dark brown eyes, strong Hispanic features, a forceful look and confident manner. "Follow me," she said, as she moved off toward the old wagon where she found whiskey, liniment and bandages. She used them expertly to tend their wounds.

Tex thanked the woman, Teresa, and offered her two dollars that she accepted, graciously.

"Joining up with the sheep?" she remarked, with a sly grin.

"I reckon not," he responded. "Got a powerful hankerin' to see Bodie and the gold fields."

"Her expression changed as she spoke again. "Bodie! It'll be gone, time you get there!"

The memory of those words and her fish-eyed look would come back to Tex before his adventure ended.

Moving on, gradually working his way west, the landscape changed from rolling hills with thick vegetation to more arid, flat lands, broken by flat topped mesas that looked like huge cakes with slanted sides. He found himself frequently avoiding the sharp spines of several kinds of cactus. First, there were extensive groves of the kind with large pancake-shaped paddles, prickly pear cactus. Later he encountered many that looked like short people with stand-up hair. Yucca, they were called.

He settled himself one night at a watering place known as *Agua Escondido*, hinden springs, where a small fountainhead of cool sulfur smelling water bubbled to the surface forming a tiny rivulet which vanished into the ground nearby. His injuries and those of his horse were now healed. The puma had been left far behind, feasting on most of the small doe Tex had slaughtered near the Llano River.

He was just east of the Pecos River in the "Staked Plains," a semi-arid, mostly treeless region about two long days ride from Comanche Springs. The flat trail had once been totally under Indian control. He made a fire not far from what was left of the abandoned military camp known as Fort Lancaster. Tex boiled some of the venison he carried from the prior hunt. He added the wild onions and parsley he found growing near the spring. Moonshine grazed.

At dusk a rider approached from the east, a big man over six feet tall wearing a brace of .45's. He slowed as he entered camp raising his open right hand with the palm facing Tex, the traditional sign language of a greeting. Tex was alert, ready for trouble; highwaymen frequented the trail and strangers could not be taken at face value. Then he saw the star and relaxed and smiled. "I'm Dallas Staudenmire, Texas Ranger. May I step down?" he asked.

"Sure," said Tex, eyeing the well-mounted marshal with a granite jaw, sharp hazel eyes and auburn hair. He dismounted, unsaddled his horse, drank from the spring and then eased over to the fire. Tex offered food, coffee and companionship, and it wasn't long before Dallas was telling stories about his past adventures running down John Wesley Hardin, the infamous gunfighter, who shot Niggers and *tejanos* at random. Hardin's view of right was that all good Texans had an obligation to rid society of the hated Indians, Blacks and Mexicans. The second son of Reverend James G. Hardin, Wesley was one of the most sadistic killers in the history of the Old West and he had been chased by Staudenmire and many other lawmen for years until Captain Armstrong and Ranger Jack Duncan jailed him in 1877.

Dallas rambled on about other bad men, particularly a group from El Paso led by Jim, "Doc" and Frank Manning. He got his jug, pulled the cork, shared the red eye and talked into the night. Tex had a way of getting people to open up. Sometimes they would reveal their inner selves.

The more the ranger drank, the better the stories got. It became very late and Dallas said, "You heard of Pecos Bill, the small kid, the one who fell near the Pecos River from the old family wagon. They had so dern many little ones that Bill wasn't missed for days. When they figured out he was gone, no one knew where to look for him. Bill was raised by coyotes and he thought he was one of them 'til one day he saw he had no tail. He grew tall and strong and learned to sit a horse without a saddle. Mounted on Widow Maker, the meanest horse in the world, Bill became the most famous cowboy in Texas. Why, one day when angry with a gang of rustlers, he roped and saddled a puma, and got the old cat goin' by woppin' it with a rattler. Rode right into their camp, he did. "Them bad men was so scared they wet their drawers."

Pecos Bill, a legendary figure in western folklore, could be counted on to provide campfire whoppers covering all kinds of adventures. Tex had heard most of them on his trail rides but they always provided a chuckle. Funning was part of cow punching.

Dallas was out looking for Geronimo, the famous Apache Chief who had abandoned the San Carlos Indian reservation with about seventy-five Chiricahua Apache braves and slipped into Mexico. Dallas said, "There's rumors that he has crossed into Texas with Victorio, Chief of the eastern Chiricahua.

Victorio has been raiding into south Texas from various hideouts in Chihuahua, Mexico." Victorio was a charismatic leader, with long, flowing, dark hair, penetrating eyes, a square jaw, full cheeks and a high brow. He had escaped from the reservation in 1877. Dallas said, "Victorio's no one to trifle with." He explained the plan devised by a man he called General Benjamin Grierson, commander at Fort Davis, to deny the Indians and their ponies' water by controlling the area's water holes. The General, who was actually a colonel, had placed troopers at a number of the key locations and Dallas, along with a few other rangers, was patrolling those areas more remote to the Rio Grande. The Mexican *ruales* were supporting Grierson's strategy by sweeping northward, flushing the Apaches from their mountain camps.

"You're riding west, that right?" asked Dallas.

"Reckon to," was the reply.

"In six or seven days you'll reach the water in Quitman Canyon. You can't miss it 'cause of all the cottonwoods. Tell the soldiers there that I've seen no Indian signs out this way," said the ranger.

"Sure enough," was the reply.

"And be careful 'round the Pecos," remarked Dallas. "Remember, God sends 'em to hell on the Pecos."

Tex reached Fort Stockton, a settlement sited at the head of Comanche Springs. His first stop was at the military post where he met an old Captain named Bill Cullen who was a veteran of many years of campaigning. He showed a mild degree of interest in the meeting between Tex and Dallas Staudenmire and seemed pleased to find out that there was no Indian sign to the east.

Cullen liked to talk and show off and he spent some time telling Tex about Comanche Springs and the fort. "It's an oasis," he said. "One created by six fountains of clear water rising along an old fault line. Fault line. You know what that is? A big crack going down under the ground. Water comes from an underground river. Aquifer, they call it, hidden below the surface. Pressure down there causes the water to bubble up. The springs have been here for ages, attractin' both men and animals. The bones of real old horses, camels, dinosaurs, sloth—ancient beasts—the kind that no longer lives on earth, fossils they call them, can be dug from the dirt all 'round the springs. There's lots of arrowheads and Indian tools, pots, drawings, stuff like that, been dug up right over yonder.

"Old Spanish guy, name of *Cabeza De Vacā*, first found this place. Must have been three, four hundred years ago. The Jesuits built a settlement in '45. Called it Saint Gall. The first stage coach driven by Big Foot Wallace, you heard of him, the famous Texas Ranger and Indian fighter stopped here in the late '40s. Later, actually about nine years later, the Butterfield stage came this way," the Captain offered without being asked.

"Our fort has thirty-five buildings, mostly adobe, and we have a cavalry unit manned by both black and white troopers. The blacks, the Indians call them buffalo soldiers," he said. "Most of them are looking for protection, protection and security, the kind of things we have in the army. They're afraid that the folks down south won't let 'em stay free. After all, when you've been a slave, when your mother and father were slaves, well, you know, it's hard to believe you're goin' to stay free. Not everyone thinks the Civil War is over. It don't matter none to me why they came here. They fight real good and that's all I care 'bout."

Tex crossed Comanche Creek, reining Moonshine in at Young Store, a trading post with a wagon yard and corral. He provisioned for the ride west and enjoyed a cool afternoon in the shade of an oak near the clear waters of the spring fed creek. He was at an oasis, green, beautiful, like a flower, surrounded by the harsh reality of the high desert, an almost barren, dry, hot wasteland that would wilt the bloom of the flower of youth. The contrast was striking.

Tex by-passed another fort built to control Indians, Fort Davis, leaving it well to the south. He rode into the hard-rock mountains, spending one night at *Allamare* Hot Springs and way station. He reached a long valley full of yucca plants while making his way west on the north side of the Rio Grande River which, backed by the Chihuahua Mountains, created perfect terrain for hiding. It was late in July 1880 when he rode right up to the water hole in Quitman Canyon without seeing any signs of troopers. The cottonwood and willow trees provided cooling shade, a welcome relief from the hot, dry desert air. As Tex drank the water of the *Tinaja de las Palmas*, two soldiers appeared at his rear. Moonshine, also drinking, looked around warning Tex with a whiny. Tex also turned, finding the cavalry troopers observing him warily. He said, "Dallas Staudenmire, Texas Ranger, asked me to tell you there's no Indian signs out east."

"Good," responded Colonel Benjamin Grierson, who appeared with a sergeant from the rocks. "We're guardin' this water-hole with part of my troop. One of my scouts spotted Victorio and his band headed this way. He's not comin' with a raidin' party with a dozen braves; he's got a full war party in his followin'. Should show up tonight or early tomorrow. I've sent for reinforcements. Hope you won't mind stayin' on 'til they get here."

Tex looked at the colonel thinking over what he had said. Grierson had a strong face, full head of hair, long nose, commanding eyes, a heavy beard and the bearing of a military leader. "You want me to stay and fight Indians?" he asked.

"Right," said Grierson, "We need your' gun. If you ride on and run into a passel of them alone, you won't have a chance. Stay here and we pay you like a scout, five dollars per day plus keep. You do yourself and your country a favor."

Tex gave the matter a few more moments thought before extending a hand to the colonel and saying, "Guess if I got to fight Indians, might as well get paid for it."

"Good", the colonel said, "Sergeant Riley will find you a place."

Pat Riley led Tex and Moonshine to a nearby shallow gulch where other horses were hobbled. He recorded the name, "Tex Garland," in his pay book along with the time and date. Together they located a suitable hiding place in the rocks, brush and trees where Tex could observe the waterhole without being easily seen. There were a few others scattered about in similar locations, creating a field of fire over the target area. If the Indians advanced directly on the waterhole, as expected, they would come under heavy fire. On the other hand, if they sent scouts in early or came stealthily on foot, using the terrain to cover their advance, a bloody battle could result.

The colonel had his own "eyes" out watching the possible approaches. His "eyes" were his scouts who would signal the advance if they were able. The plan was to let the main body of the savages come right up to the water hole before opening up. Riley told Tex, "Keep your head down, keep quiet, no campfire. Don't shoot. Don't do anything until you hear me order "fire." Then throw as much lead as you can at the red men fast. Can you shoot straight?"

"Reckon so," he answered. "Never shot at people before, though."

He settled down among the rocks with his Winchester, Colt, a pile of ammunition, beef jerky, his canteen and corn provided by the army. There were about half a dozen soldiers, best Tex could tell.

They waited as the sun set. Some parts of the soldiers' minds hoped the hostiles would come while other portions of the same wills prayed they would not. The thrill of adventure and sensation of battle caused part of the mind to look forward to the engagement. Reason and judgement caused another portion of the id to decry combat. The colonel made his rounds about 9 P.M., stopping to visit with Tex and each of the troopers in turn. He called Tex by name, telling him to get some rest while his men traded off keeping watch. Tex offered to help out, to take his turn on watch, but the colonel was firm.

He tried to sleep, but each time he dozed off, he was jolted awake by a vision of an Indian's hand touching him from out of the darkness; the hand of a warrior, touching his enemy before the kill. Red Hand said that touching the enemy during battle was a symbol of Apache bravery. They called it "counting coup." The Indian's fingers were always holding the top of his head in a position to cut off his scalp. Red Hand told him, "*bitsa-ha-digihz*, his head top cut off, that's what we do to white-eyes."

Apaches did not like to fight at night. Tex had been hearing that since he was very young and Red Hand had confirmed that his people feared that their spirits would become lost if they were killed in battle after dark. Now he was alone, and did not completely trust the conventions of the past. Men were always somewhat unpredictable and Indians were men, capable warriors and dangerous. Apache, the *Zuñi* word for enemy, was fitting. He truly wanted to sleep, slumber close to the others, die, if he must, with friends, now comrades bonded together by the stress of impending battle. He wanted the others near, breathing in harmony with his own breath, thinking, acting in concord with his being, providing peace, the same peace sought by many Indians. However, military logic suggested it was wiser to fight from individual positions, lone solitary stations. No child is born for mortal combat! No soldier should die alone! No youth should face danger without his mother. Tex was in need of closeness and comfort; he could not rest. The Indian's fingers, fingers attached to a ghost like hand, fingers that would rip his scalp from his head, were always on his mind.

He could visualize his enemy. His face was painted. His eyes were blazing and his breath was strong and fast. He had a lean body, well conditioned to battle, with a bag of pollen hung from an *Izze-kloth*. The *Izze* is a loosely braided string sash with four strands of hide. It would be draped across the warrior's body from right shoulder to left side. *Izze-kloth,* the medicine cord, "killer of enemies," bandoleer, made by an Indian "war" *di-yin*. Its pollen, provided power from the "Supernaturals" in war, according to the red men.

About four in the morning, fifteen additional troopers, Buffalo Soldiers, lead by a black officer, arrived and took up positions with Tex and the others. Dawn came slowly. He was stiff, groggy, heavy-headed when the first golden red rays of the morning sun began to splash long shadows over the landscape, driving the demons of the dark from his consciousness. He wanted to get up to stretch but knew better. He drank from his canteen, ate corn and jerky and settled down for what he hoped would be a lucky day.

At around eleven o'clock, Tex saw a flash, a glitter of light from the sun striking a bright metal or glass object. The light fluttered on and off several times. A signal! Could it be a sign from one of the colonel's scouts? Or, could it be red men talking to each other? Or might it be just a product of nature? He got his answer a few minutes later when Pat Riley moved up stealthily, talking to each trooper and saying to Tex, "They are on the way, more than sixty, about one hour out."

"Saw the signal," said Tex. "Your scout sent you a message using light same as they do on ships."

Pat nodded saying, "Wait for the order to fire."

Sometime after the sun had passed overhead, Tex saw a whiff of dust and a few moments later some movement in the brush about a quarter mile from the waterhole. An Indian came into view, moving slowly, cautiously, using rocks and trees for cover. He was obviously a scout, checking out the landscape. Tex made himself as small as possible embracing his rocky crib. He thought about the game he had played called "The Fort" and wondered if the impending battle would be his Alamo. The red man came on, reached the water, drank and moved past it looking carefully into the surrounding terrain, satisfying himself that he was alone. He turned, cupping his hands in front of his mouth making the sound of a wild turkey, producing, in short order, a band of about sixty of his kind. They rode right up, watered their horses and began dismounting when he heard the Irish sergeant shout, "Fire." The order brought the landscape alive with violent explosions! A fusillade! Tex took aim at a mounted savage near the waterhole but, before he could pull the trigger, the Indian's horse fell, hit, and his rider scrambled into the undergrowth and disappeared. Tex fired, aimed and shot again as fast he could at other rapidly vanishing targets. He could see eight ponies down and four bodies near the waterhole. The others had dissolved into the countryside like ants. Here. There. Then suddenly gone.

Pat Riley made rounds again and found no one in his group injured. He had Tex and the others shift, undetected, to new positions on higher ground. Smart, thought Tex, Very smart for an Irishman.

Riley said, "Keep down, don't give your new positions away, wait for my command, stay alert!"

A half- hour passed before Tex saw movement followed by the crash of spasmodic gunfire from hidden locations scattered about the landscape. The red men were trying to draw their fire, get them to reveal their positions. He heard the clatter of arrows striking the rocks near his position. Gradually the gunfire moved closer, savages stalking their prey, seeking the enemy position, fighting for control of the water. He saw one crawl behind a rock near where Riley was hidden. He had come in from the rear, out of the trooper's line of vision. Tex raised his Winchester waiting for him to show his head. Suddenly he was on top of the boulder behind the sergeant, tomahawk raised in hand. Tex fired, hitting the red man square in the chest, knocking him sideways to the ground.

He heard Pat shout, "Thanks! Fire at will," and the battle was begun again, this time with an unseen enemy. The black lieutenant, Leighton Finley, attacked with his detachment of black men, carrying the fight to the Indians for a time before being driven back. Troops C and G of the Tenth Cavalry arrived, improving the situation, but the Indians still had the numbers. The fighting was scattered and spasmodic. There were occasional pops of fire from both sides as the Indians gradually closed in. Hours passed. The sun dipped lower and lower in the west, its light casting lengthening shadows, making it harder to see. To make matters worse for the soldiers, a stiff breeze came up, creating movement among the brush and trees, further impairing vision, adding to the dappled scene. The gods seemed to be turning their elements in support of the Apache.

Had Tex been alone, he might have tried to escape but that wasn't possible because he was part of a group, a fighting team, where each member draws some of his strength from fellow members, multiplying fighting ability many times. Tex was sure of one thing; the Apaches would never take him alive. He had no interest in being tied up, buried up to his neck and plastered with mesquite juice. Mesquite juice, something to attract the ants and to encourage them to eat out his eyes and into his brains while he still lived.

Tex saw the flashing light in the hills again, coming from a new location. A signal, but what for? Heliograph, that's what they call it, using a mirror to signal. Army scouts and quartermasters were trained in its use. But what was the report? What did the signal mean? Thought Tex.

War whoops, gunfire, a cavalcade of arrows filled the air all about the position occupied by Tex. The red men were attacking from three sides and Tex realized that he might not see the sun dip below the horizon this night. He looked for targets but the Apache were lost in a jungle of shadows and movement. An arrowhead crashed into the large rock near his head and his eyes felt the sting of the chips it broke loose. He fired once in the general direction that the arrow had come from, without result. A bullet whistled into the dirt a few feet from his boot and a painted Indian appeared about twenty feet from his hide, moving directly on his position. He fired as the Apache dove behind the rocks.

Then, Tex, who had the instincts of a warrior, moved. He half-crawled, half scrambled to a new location. Changing positions was something all experienced Indian fighters did when in close combat. They knew that a moving target was hard to locate and hard to hit. Tex hunkered down behind his new set of rocks just as the Indian leaped, hatchet in hand, on what he thought would be his foe. Tex fired his Colt four times, dropping the red man, leaving the dead Indian on the ground, hand outstretched, trying to touch the body of Tex, an enemy, an enemy who was gone. His instinct said move, move again, but before he could he saw two large bodies of mounted troopers riding down on the rear of the Apaches from both ridges. Captain Nicholas Nolan, Troop A, tenth Cavalry, was leading the column to the right. He heard the war whoops and saw the red men moving out in full retreat as the cavalry came on. Tex dropped into the firing position and opened up on the retreating enemy, continuing to shoot until after it was over.

The battle, which started so slowly, had come to an abrupt end, leaving Tex shaking uncontrollably, suffering from shock and dehydration. The anxiety, apprehension, terror, exhilaration and excitement of combat had sapped his energy and fluids, staggering his mind and body, producing the uncontrolled trembling. He didn't understand what was happening. He was embarrassed and he wanted to move, hide, escape so that the others would not find him shaking, but all his body would let him do was lean against his boulder and wait. Tex was exhausted from the passion of battle. He didn't know how long it had been since the cavalry rode past, charging the Apache, but when he felt Riley's hand on his shoulder, he came out of shock.

"Good work, Tex, you saved my ass, hair too, with that first shot. Got one or two more I think. Smart. You were smart to change positions. You fight like a professional. Comes natural, I guess. We could use you in the cavalry," said the sergeant. He produced a bottle of red eye, giving Tex a long pull before adding, "Really, we could use a man like you. How 'bout joinin' up? You could help us wipe out the Apache Tribe, erase their sign from the west." The sergeant said those last words while using his right arm to portray the Indian's vertical zigzag symbol.

Tex wasn't thinking about becoming a soldier but he was happy to be accepted as one of them, ecstatic to have won, pleased to be rid of the shakes.

But Tex was tired, exhausted actually, emotionally drained form the fury of combat. He had traveled through the cycle of battle, survived in both body and spirit, escaped the gods who favored his enemy and avoided the hand reaching out for his hair. "If it's all the same to you I'd rather not," said Tex, "Fancy findin' some Bodie gold."

He stayed the night, supped and celebrated with the troopers. Pat Riley gave him a paper signed by the colonel, authorizing him to draw two days pay, ammunition and provisions at Fort Bliss in El Paso.

" Talk to you later," said Tex as he waved good-by and rode northwest toward *El Paso del Norte*, the pass to the north. El Paso was a settlement split in half by the treaty of Guadalupe Hidalgo in 1848 when the governments of the United States and Mexico agreed that the Rio Grande formed the dividing line between the two countries. It was a major event in the history of Texas and Tex had heard all about it for years. In school they taught him about the importance of the treaty because it stabilized and clarified the border situation between the two countries. He remembered the old drover, Tim Nelson, saying, "Them Mexican whores don't charge much. Don't wear much neither. I go 'cross the river over to the Mexican side, Juàrez they call it, when I get 'round El Paso."

There wasn't much to the American portion of the settlement when Tex arrived. It was nothing like the wild cow towns of Texas and Kansas. A sleepy village, an infant town of mostly mud huts which would wake up soon when the rails moved in. Soddies and dugouts were sprinkled about among real wood and adobe homes, stores, shops and other commercial buildings. It was easy to understand why Tim Nelson went across the river.

Tex rode into the town's center. It was framed by strong ridgelines to the west and northeast and big mountains to the southwest. He stopped at the Coliseum Saloon for a beer and supper.

A man named Frank hailed him asking, "Where you from and where you bound for?"

"From Houston, headin' for Bodie," he responded.

"A hard place, Bodie," said Frank. "The bad man from Bodie is real. My brothers Doc and Jim passed through that country few years back; man

85

died every day 'cord'in to Doc. Shot down, mostly. Best keep your powder dry out that way."

Tex nodded, thinking. Frank looked like trouble; he had the eyes of a reptile. And the names, Frank, Jim and Doc. I heard them before. Where? Was I being warned? Why? Who told me to take care? He couldn't remember.

"Play a little draw?" asked Frank

"Been ridin' all day," said Tex, "Maybe tomorrow night."

Tex headed to Fort Bliss where the night duty lieutenant was impressed with the paper he presented that was signed by the Colonel. He got a bed for the night, the first time he had slept in one of those in a month. He ate a big breakfast in the morning, then received his pay, ammunition and provisions. Moonshine had her fill of oats, new shoes and a rub down. The horse looked fully recovered from her injuries, rested and ready to go. Down at the stable, Tex made the mental connection between Frank, Doc, Jim and the Texas Ranger he met on the trail. His instincts had been right. They were trouble! He rode on without taking up the challenge of poker. His charge, after all, was to his aces in Bodie.

He crossed the Rio Grande at Mesilla and wound through a thick, extensive stand of yucca before reaching Las Cruces. He stopped at a bar and restaurant for refreshments and filled up on beer and lamb chops. Tex wanted beef, but none was served. Imagine, he thought. Me eating stinking sheep right here near the Texas border, right here where cattle is king. The meat was strong tasting and not what Tex preferred, but it cost only two bits and was filling.

The bar owner told him that Las Cruces was named for the three Spanish crosses on the hill that overlooked the city. "The crosses mark the massacre. Long time ago, early days," he said.

"The Mesilla Valley, that's what they call this land. It's rich. Good for farmin' and good grazin' for sheep and cattle. We be sittin' right on what some folks say is the oldest road in North America. *El Camiño Real we calls it.* My great grandfather came this way headin' from Chihuahua to Santa Fe 'round 1600. It was rough in them days. Not much here, not much anywhere out this far west," he added.

"We got herds, big herds a sheep in these parts. Spanish settlers brought the first ones out here years ago. Most folks cotton to lamb over beef 'round here. Sheeps' always been better'an cattle. Wool's good for makin' all kinds of fine things. Them Navaho Indians that still lives 'round here makes the warmest blankets you ever seed. Best looking too, best I ever seed. Startin' back in the '50s, we trailed sheep to them hungry California gold camps. You be usin' the same trail we be a followin' back then. Those gold miners paid big, real big for sheep. Lamb or bear meat, that's what them prospectors was thinkin'. Lamb tastes lots better than bear. We made a bundle. No more. Long trail rides are 'bout over for us. Cattle and sheep be movin' all over the place by rail. We use trains for some sheep, but the money ain't big no more. There're more cattle and sheep out west than people can eat. 'Sides, the gold mines on the west side of them Sierra mountains is pretty much played out. The big mines be still workin' but there ain't much good ground left for prospectin'. Those folks left up there can get beef or lamb from close-by ranches. It's cheaper'an ours," the bar owner said.

"Sheep," snorted Tex. "Down Texas way we don't cotton much to sheep. They stink and kill the grass."

"Bull," was the response. "Out this way we put sheep and cattle on the same range. They get along. And since when did cows start smellin' so good."

Tex was surprised to hear the bartender speak up for lambs. No one mixing drinks in a Texas bar would dare to take up for sheep. Were his views wrong? He reflected. Or was the bartender full if it? He wasn't sure and felt it unwise to carry on the discussion.

"Talk to you later," said Tex as he finished his meal and left.

Moonshine moved along the westbound trail at his fast walking pace, undisturbed by the rustle created by the swift road-running bird that jumped out in front of him. A funny looking bird, unlike anything Tex had seen before. A fast bird, very quick, that seemed to want to run rather than fly. Roadrunner, he realized, recalling the story Red Hand had told about the, "moccasin game."

At Fort Grant Tex heard stories about the Red Rock Stronghold in the nearby mountains which had been the camp for the famous fighting Indian chief, Cochise. Tex recalled Red Hand saying, "Cochise, what eyes he had.

Could see right into the heart of his enemy. Eyes with steel, wisdom too. And his voice. You could hear it anywhere, anytime. It was carried on the wind. Cochise was a chief, one you white-eyes won't forget. He led raidin' parties all 'round Arizona. They burned, took captives and destroyed white settlements for more than a hundred moons. He was protectin' his lands, Indian Territory, ground that his father knew. For a time he raided so hard the Butterfield Stage stopped goin' for almost sixty moons. No passengers, no mail. They say Cochise killed twenty-two stagecoach drivers 'fore the Butterfield was shut down."

"Never thought I'd see it happed. Lone rider, like you, makin' this passage." said Jim Gable, a ragged, old Lieutenant at the fort. "He took hostages, tortured captives, scalped, burned and raped. Respondin', that's what he was doin', respondin' 'in kind' to the bounty offered on Apache scalps. This was Chiricahua territory, country they'd hunted for years, their home ground where they sprang from nowhere, striking down white settlers and soldiers. After a battle they would vanish, you know, be gobbled up by their mountains. Actually they would retreat to their stronghold. It's a wooded area lying in a rampart of granite domes. Those sheer cliffs in the Dragoon Mountains sheltered them from prying eyes and advancing soldiers. The Dragoon Mountains were named for the Third U. S. Cavalry. The soldiers were stationed in the area when Cochise was 'round. You can go and see their stronghold if you like. It's some thirty miles southwest of Willcox. Might be a few red men 'round up there to give you a welcome." The Lieutenant gave Tex a "fish eyed " look when he said "welcome."

"The Indians fought pretty smart and they were brave. They died protectin' their honor and families while Indian mothers cried for their fallen children," said the Lieutenant after a pause. "They're folks just like us and they fought in spite us havin' so many against 'em. Some of 'em are still up there somewhere, fighting and dyin'."

Tex thought it strange that an officer, an Indian fighter, would have such high regard for his enemy. He was too old to be a Lieutenant and Tex wondered if his career in the army had been retarded because of his beliefs. He also wondered if the army folks knew that the demise of each Indian marked the beginning of his nameless spiritual passage into the future. It's a nameless trip because it was improper for Apaches to speak about the dead. Red Hand had told him that the name of a dead warrior was never mentioned after the burial ritual. "Nameless, but not forgotten," were the words his Indian friend had used.

The Lieutenant spoke up again. "Realizin' they were outnumbered, Cochise made friends with a white man and used him to make peace in '71. That's when he signed a paper with General Howard and moved his followers to a reservation. Not all of the Apaches accepted the treaty; many fought on and small bands of Chiricahua are still loose in the mountains. Sometimes, those raiders are led by Geronimo. Now, he's my idea of a rough man. Just the mention of his name brings fear. Geronimo, he's a devil, he's killed thousands."

Tex had met the red men at Quitman Canyon and he wanted no part of another battle with Indians. After he left the fort and got back on the trail, he rose early and moved fast, alert for trouble. He stayed well clear of the "Stronghold."

As he made his way west his thoughts wondered. Where is an Indian's home? Is it wherever the buffalo roam? Where the deer and the antelope play? The different tribes fought each other all the time before the whites came. They fought over water holes, hunting grounds and the like. The Sioux pushed west, taking whatever lands they hankered for. They run the Comanches off the northern plains. In turn, the Comanches pushed the Apaches south, toward Mexico, and both tribes raided wherever it suited them. The so-called Comanche trail was over a thousand miles long. The Indians grabbed what they wanted from the land, other red men, Mexicans, whites, whomever,

Where is the white man's home? Where the buffalo roam? Where the deer and the antelope play? Where gold shows itself? White men grab what they want from Indians, Mexicans, Chinese, fellow whites, whomever.

How are the reds and whites different? Who is right? Wrong? Truth be known, on the barren southwestern desert where there is no law and different folks don't give a frig about each other. "Right" drifts to the fittest. The Indians are being prodded out, planted on reservations, destroyed, not because of right or wrong, but because they are outnumbered, outgunned and sometimes outsmarted.

Gray purplish hues gave way to streaks of red, yellow and orange as the early light from the sun cast its beams over the piles of rocks and boulders that formed a pass through a narrow canyon. It had huge smooth rocks, many six to fifteen feet across sitting around on top of each other in a random fashion. Some were tipped on edge; some were hanging over the edges of others. It looked as though an enormous wheel barrel full of gigantic domino-like boulders had been dropped from the sky. Dropped by a rascal. Beautiful and strange, thought Tex, like nothing I could have fancied. Even more striking than had been described by Roy Bean. Tex thought of it as, "Ambush Canyon."

They passed on into the dry countryside with sharp, rough-looking mountain peaks scattered about, very different from the flat-topped mesas he had left behind. Late one afternoon, Tex tracked and shot a small mule deer, carting it to a hastily selected campsite. The light was failing while he was gutting the animal and as he looked up into the lengthening shadows, he saw a man, a huge fellow, standing motionless with two thick arms held outstretched. Tex had been too busy to notice much when he brought his kill into camp and he had no idea how long the newcomer had been standing there, frozen, faceless, watching. The light was fading fast now and Tex could not make out the man's features clearly. He couldn't locate the eyes. They would reveal much of his qualities.

He set his hunting knife down, handed his Colt without drawing, before moving forward to confront the observer. Closer and closer he edged, no eyes, Scarecrow, he thought. He looked like one of the big stick people folks dressed up to scare birds away from gardens. Frozen, without sound, unresponsive to his greeting, Tex closed in to within a few feet before his eyes could clearly define a Giant Saguaro cactus, the first he had ever seen, something that he would encounter frequently in the Arizona territory. It was ten feet tall and had two thick arms. The cactus had observed much since its birth over one hundred years earlier but unlike man, the Saguaro had no eyes, no soul, no heart and no way to communicate its counsel.

In this country, Tex carried two extra canteens and he learned how to cut the top off a barrel cactus, dig out the melon-like center and suck on it for it's moisture. Red Hand had told him a great deal about living off the desert lands, taking advantage of the lifegiving things nature provided. Almost all types of cactus contained some fluid in their centers and could be used to keep one alive when water was in short supply.

During mid summer, the season called "Large Leaves" by the Apaches, there were many opportunities to harvest the fruits of nature and he kept his eyes open for wild onions, potatoes, grapes, mulberries, juniper berries, strawberries and raspberries. The area near the trail was picked over but when he chose to wander off the well traveled course, his search was often rewarded. Wild onions and potatoes were wonderful in trail stew, a mixture of whatever meat, greens and other edibles one might have.

Tex also tried a fruit from a prickly pear cactus after rubbing the spines clear with sand. He had learned how to handle the prickly pear from Red Hand but after trying one, decided to leave the rest of that fruit for the Apaches.

Indians ate all kinds of things that grew in the desert and surrounding mountains. In the early fall, the season called "Thick With Fruit," they harvested nuts from the *piñon*, live oak, walnut and other trees. Some were eaten fresh but most were roasted and stored or ground into a powder similar to flower that could be used in a wide variety of cooking applications. Seeds from the spurge, tumbleweed and sunflower were dried and eaten. Mesquite beans and fruit from the giant Saguaro cactus were also staples.

The Apache product that focused his thoughts best in this hot desert environment was a tall cool glass of *Tula-pajh*, a corn beer that, according to Red Hand, stimulated memorable festivities because it spoiled quickly after brewing and thus required rapid consumption.

The long desert ride had become stimulating for Tex, in great part because a Chiricahua scout had shown him what to look for, how to harvest the landscape's treasures that others would ride over. Would he be equally able to harvest gold? he asked himself.

With prickly pear cactus all about the trail, Tex rode into the high desert valley town of Tucson. He twisted about on his saddle looking at the dry mountains that surrounded the settlement. The old pueblo along the eastern bank of the Santa Cruz River, originally surrounded by a twelve-foot tall adobe wall to protect its citizens from the Apache, had expanded to nearly seven thousand people living and working well outside the enclosure. Sentinel Peak, a small, tall mountain just west of the center of town was no longer manned continuously by lookouts. Most of Tucson's buildings were brownish-orange colored adobe with the traditional Spanish architecture. The adobe kept them cool in the desert heat and warm on cold nights. The streets were windblown, dusty and dirty, like most of those Tex encountered in all settlements west of San Antonio. The air was very dry and Tex presumed that the temperature over one hundred degrees.

Tex tied Moonshine up at a hitching rail in front of the Congress Hall Saloon on Camp Street and went in for a beer and something to eat. Inside he felt conspicuous and uncomfortable. This wasn't a place frequented by cowpunchers. It was full of what appeared to Tex to be lawyers, bankers, businessmen, mostly dressed like dudes. They talked about the arrival of the new Southern Pacific Railroad with track connecting all the way to California. One of them had a plan to put live sheep in a rail car and ship them west while others were discussing alternative business opportunities connected with steam locomotion.

Tex, beer in hand, moved away from the conversations about the railroad and found himself eaves dropping on a discussion between the owner of the saloon, Charles Brown, and a well dressed Spaniard, Jaime Cortina, writer on the *El Fronterizo* newspaper. He heard Jamie say, "Satan, there's a Satan in all who believe my point of view is right and yours, if different, is wrong. That Satan is reinforced by prejudicial training, provided by parents, teachers, ministers of the gospel, associates, club members; he is reinforced further by society itself, tradition and culture. He comes wrapped in righteousness, passing his rules on from generation to generation, creating all sorts of problems because there is nothing so dangerous as a brain convinced that something is so, when it is not so. War, conducted in the name of crusades, slaughter in the name of racial supremacy, denial of truth in favor of false gods, rape of the landscape in the name of progress, all those things and many other horrors grew their roots from that Satan who resides in all of us. He is overcome, not by prayer, but through education which provides one with the mental agility and confidence to break ranks with the slavery of biased thinking. Education needs to be a core value for all societies. The Chinese know these things but many other cultures don't, mine, for example.

"What do the Hispanics value? I'll tell you. Family, that's important to all Mexicans and we think a lot about how we appear in the eyes of others. The need to look good shows-up in the way we build our homes and dress. We love to fiesta. In fact, any reason is a good one for a party. Religion too, that plays a major role for us; the poor go to Mass and pray for forgiveness and help; the rich honor God by having a party. Yes, the poor pray a lot, but God doesn't teach people to read. Most of my kind, Spanish speaking folks, particularly the ones that are poor, can't read. What we need here in Tucson is better schools and better teachers from the first grade on up through college. Yes, a university right here in Tucson would be a great addition but most of all, we need parents willing to encourage their kids to attend school and study. Every Spanish and Indian speaking person in this community must be able to speak, read and write in both English and their native tongue. They need to know the numbers too, and be able to work them. When I was out west, I met Chinese children who were fluent in three languages and they worked the numbers very fast, with accuracy, using beads on a rack called an abacus. The Chinese know the value of education. My people?

"You and the other community leaders should put education first on both the legislature and social agendas. The churches must also support proper schooling. Some already do but too often others teach only their narrow view of God and morality, claiming that their fallible, man-made rules come straight from the all-mighty. Small-minded men, seeking power, forgetting that God will sell himself. After all, almost everyone seeks immortality and all Gods promise life after death in some form. The churches and schools need to teach people to read, write and think so they can determine the shape and nature of their own gods. There is a Satan in all of us. If we want him struck down, educate society so that each member can deal with his own prince of the kingdom of evil."

It sounded to Tex like Jaime was preaching a sermon. A very special sermon delivered in the finest English. But as he thought about it, that's what newspaper people did, they preached with pen. Teresa the sheepherder knew about Satan. As Tex and Moonshine approached her near the Llano River she was thinking that he had probably been taught to hate sheep and her kind. Tex didn't know that. He hadn't been able to read her mind. He knew education was important but he hadn't thought about it in the context of his own beliefs. Was his education insufficient? Was he brainwashed? Was he sure that certain things were true, when in fact they were not true? He would have time on the trail to consider such thoughts.

Tex finished his beer, had lamb chops, potatoes and green beans. He left, full of food and provocative thoughts and set out taking the road to the northwest that followed the Santa Cruz River. Approaching Picacho Peak, he fantasized about it being a giant clipper ship, riding on an ocean of Saguaro Cactus, ready to sail him westward to Bodie. The bighorn sheep he spotted on a cliff could well have been her master and crew. How easy and peaceful it would be to ride on a sailing ship instead of a horse, he thought. He had never been on a real seagoing vessel but it must be fun, he said to himself, just as the words spoken by Jaime Cortina came thundering back into his mind. Convinced that what is so, is not so. Maybe it's not so easy to manage a ship at sea, he thought. And what do seafaring men think about education, family, religion, hard work? How do they raise their children? Given the ruckus they made in the Port of Houston, its plain to see sailors love to party. Out at sea for months, doing whatever they did, then coming into port for a time much like cowpunchers who had been on the trail. Maybe they weren't so different, maybe it wasn't easy, maybe they needed to let off steam like cowhands when they reached town. Tex didn't know it, but he was learning as he had always learned.

Tex made camp on the Gila River, south of the small settlement of Phoenix. Another man with a horse and two burrows was making camp across the water. Tex hailed him and invited him to cross over for a few pulls on his jug and some trail stew. The man seemed aloof, cautious, but the down-home manner Tex presented and the offer of red eye lured him to the south-side camp.

"Make yourself to home," said Tex as the new arrival tied up his horse.

They sat sipping from the bottle while Tex tried to draw the stranger into conversation. When that didn't work, Tex told him about his trip from Texas. The longer he talked the more the newcomer seemed to relax, finally saying, after an hour or more, "They call me Dutchman."

Tex nodded, waiting for quite a spell, hoping for more, but nothing additional came out of the Dutchman's mouth. After a very long pause Tex said, "I'm headed for Bodie to find gold."

He saw the other man's eye's twinkle at the mention of gold, his face softened, his body slacked. He smiled and said, "Know anything about gold?"

"No, not really," was the reply.

"It's not like finding strays. It's hard to locate and even harder to work."

And so it was that Tex got his first lesson on prospecting that night while pulling on a jug with a newfound friend.

The Dutchman's real name was Jacob Walzer. Born in Germany and a graduate engineer from Heidelberg University, he had worked in the gold fields of California in the late 1850s and early 1860s. He told Tex about how gold was born underground where the rocks are subjected to huge temperature and pressures. "They get so hot they turn into thick molasses-like liquids and gas—gas similar to steam from a hot pot. I think of it as a bunch of stuff that squeezes its way up toward the earth's surface from time to time along faults. In some cases the rising hot stuff contains, gold and silver, usually in combination with other minerals like quartz. As the stuff cools and hardens, it forms rocks with the gold, quartz and other minerals mixed together. Sometimes the veins reach the surface, sometimes they don't. When the waters from rain, snow and ice wash over the hills and mountains, they wear away the earth's surface exposing the veins. The water breaks up the rocks and carries the gold into streams headed for inland lakes or the oceans. Gold is very heavy and it tends to fall to the bottom of the creeks and rivers wherever the waters slow down. Sometimes it goes to the sides where the current pushes the heavy material to the outside. Prospectors dig into creek bottoms, in backwashes, on the lee side of boulders, in the upstream end of the gravel bars in eddies and at bends. They also search the roots of streamside plants to see if they have captured color. They call gold found in streams, placer deposits. When a find is made, miners often divert the creeks, dig up the dirt containing the placer gold and wash it with pan, sluice box, Long Tom or cradle to separate the valuable mineral from the dirt and sand.

"Smart prospectors know that placer deposits foretell a vein somewhere upstream. They seek it out and then work it by mining. They dig a hole into the rock containing the lode and continue the hole until the vein runs out. Mines can become very long, deep and complex. Many need lumber to shore-up the top and sides and heavy equipment to lift and crush the material. The rocks taken from the mines must be broken up and washed to separate the good stuff from the trash. Gold, silver, diamonds, opal and other riches often come from the same source rock," he continued.

"The minerals may have been formed hundreds of thousands or even millions of years in the past and the courses of creeks and rivers are often altered in only a few years or days. Experienced prospectors look for placer deposits in old streambeds, dry washes anywhere that might have held an old lake or stream. Most of them are probably never found, like most of the lodes that never surface, lost in the womb of mother-nature. Her mysteries enticing prospectors who are always looking and always dreaming. They are determined like no other breed, occasionally finding but rarely having the wisdom to keep what they locate. The first ones into a new area always have the best chance to strike it rich but those that do usually give it up to 'canaries,' con men or road agents. The best way to find gold is to marry an Indian girl who knows where it is. The best way to keep it, is to stay out of gold camps."

The flood of conversation and information that had just bubbled out of the Dutchman's mouth almost overwhelmed Tex. It was like the mention of gold had unlatched the spring; the device that held the old man's talking box shut. And, what a way of talking, thought Tex. The Dutchman didn't sound much like the cowpunchers he was used to hearing.

"How do you pan, or what's the word, sluice the stuff?" asked Tex.

"It's easy," was part of the answer. "Just keep in mind that gold is very heavy and, if agitated in water with other material, it will tend always to work its way to the bottom. Get yourself a fourteen-inch pie pan with gently sloping sides and fill it with stream bottoms. Find a spot where the water isn't moving very fast, submerge the pan just below the surface, tipping it slightly away from you. Move it in a horizontal circle with a slight jerk each time around, swirling the water on the top to remove the light sand and course gravel gently over the lip of the pan. Repeat the process several times, tapping the pan periodically in a horizontal position to keep the gold on the bottom. Bring the pan out of the water, tip it away and alternately dip and rotate, letting the water carry away the lighter material. Brush out the larger pebbles with your hand and continue to dip and rotate until only gold and the finest particles of sand remain. Save the concentrated material for either finer panning or treatment with mercury. You need to practice a bit to get it right and you must take your time. It's a slow process. An experienced miner can do only about three pans per hour. The sluice box, cradle and Long Tom all operate using the same principle as the pan, agitating the stream bottoms and inducing the heavy material to go down."

"What's all this about gettin' together with a squaw, an Indian squaw?" asked Tex.

"That's my secret formula for finding gold. It's the best way. Actually, it's the only way, the only way I ever found anything significant. Married a young Apache in Phoenix and she lead me to the hiding place of the Indian Thunder God's gold in the Superstition Mountains. I've been taking from the Gods ever since.

"Indians have Gods, lots of them, and plenty of myths and fairy tales to explain natures wonders.

"In the Chiricahua Apache tribe the creator, Yusn, the life giver, built the universe. He used four spirits to fabricate the world. Each worked on the basic structure and when his part was completed he added his individual touches. The spirit, Black Water, gave earth its blood by making the rivers run. Black Metal added hills and mountains. Black Wind provided the breath of life and Black Thunder added trees and grass.

"Yusn created White-Painted Woman sending her to earth to live with a son, Killer of Enemies. White-Painted Woman gave birth to Child of Water, a youth fathered by lightning.

"The earth had four monsters, bad folks, the kind that ate people, limiting Indian population. Child of Water, slew each of them in turn; Owl-Man Giant, Buffalo Monster, Eagle Monster Family and Antelope Monster were all done in by Child of Water.

"Ultimately, Child of Water, became the spiritual leader of the Indians while Killer of Enemies became Chief of the white-eyes.

"The Apaches explain the mysteries of man and earth using animals as spokes-people and in games," he continued. "Coyote and Badger are key animals and the myth of the 'First Moccasin Game' is told over and over. The contest pitted the birds and other good creatures against the monsters and bad beasts. The stakes were continuous daylight against everlasting darkness. The birds were winning, thanks to the special assistance of their power songs and the unique skills of roadrunner, thus the bad creatures fled. Many of the bad animals were killed but some escaped, including bear, snake and owl. The game was never fully completed and, as a result, the earth has both day and night, good and evil. Various Gods are held responsible for the good and nasty things that nature produces. The Sun God, Lightning God and Thunder God are examples."

Tex nodded, he had heard all those stories before from Red Hand. The Indian scout had made them more elaborate but the content was essentially the same. They were important stories to the Indians, but how did they relate to gold? thought Tex.

" I know all this sounds crazy to a white man educated in Christianity, but think about this. How would you like to try to explain things like the Immaculate Conception, the Resurrection or Noah's Ark to an Apache? Our religious stories, rituals and beliefs would sound strange to him, I think. People believe what they are taught as children, at least most do, particularly those without very much education. Apaches have their *Yusn*; Christians have their Christ.

"Apaches killed my squaw because she had betrayed their Thunder God by telling me how to find his gold. They cut out her tongue before she died. Then they tried to cut me down. She was a good person. I'm sure she lives in a better land where maybe, just maybe, white and red people live together in harmony. She was raised in a Chiricahua tribal family but later married a Tonto, an unusual match, because Chiricahua view Tontos as inferior. *Bini-ê-dinê*, people without mind they called them. Her brave was killed by a force lead by a Major Brown at a cave in the Superstition Mountains in '72. I took her as my squaw a year later.

"The Apaches fear the owl, *Búú*, most of all, and their fear extends to the other bad creatures that escaped from death in the Moccasin Game. *Búú* comes out at night when his body is inhabited by ghosts. Ghosts, you know, the spirits of dead people. His hooting–the voices of those departed, threatens the living with darkness sickness–an incurable disease. It will kill a person unless he is treated by a *Shaman*. A spirit man, one who gets powers from the owl. The Indians believe that most ailments are caused by the spirits. To get help a person needs someone who gets his power from the spirits. There are many Apache myths that are passed on from generation to generation, molding the minds of their young to the rites of their elders. Superstitions are used by some to benefit the tribe and used by others to benefit themselves.

"I had a wooden owl made in Phoenix; it's with me always. I put it up close to my camp at night to keep the redmen away. Learned how to hoot too. Should have gotten another owl constructed for my squaw. It might have saved her life.

"Everyone in Phoenix knows my story and that generates my biggest problem, keeping prospectors, outlaws and Indians off my trail when I head out and return. I go by different trails every time. Twenty-six men have come after me. None have ever returned! Dispatched by Indians, cougars, rattlesnakes–or something, I guess," he said with a wry smile.

"Lord a'mighty," said Tex, thinking about the torrent of words he had unleashed. "How much gold have you taken out?"

"Enough," was the only answer he got, not surprisingly. "Time to turn in," said Jacob Walzer, "Don't get lost and stay off my trail tomorrow lest you become number twenty-seven."

"My gold's in Bodie, not the Superstitions. I'll be leavin' first light. Won't get lost. Will you, Dutchman?" The last words from Tex were spoken with a smile. He rode west the next morning, thinking about how both he and the Dutchman had used the owl to gain something from the Apaches.

Jacob Walzer told Tex nothing about the location of his find or the amount of treasure he had taken out or left behind. He didn't confide in Tex or anyone else and he took the secret of the location of the "Lost Dutchman Mine" with him to his grave in 1891.

8

JUAN OLIVERA WAS NOW FORTY-SIX years old, slightly stooped, weathered from hundreds of trips to the north. His face, neck and hands looked like the trunk of a mature pepper tree, full of furrows, lines and cracks. He was on his way again, this time with his thirteen-year old son, Pedro and a dog, a dog of average size and mixed lineage named Trigo. The dog's coat resembled, in color and texture, the wheat fields in the valley. Trigo was an important member of Juan's close knit family unit that included his wife Teresa, oldest son Oscar, younger son Pedro and two daughters Felicia and Maria. Juan's aging mother also lived with the family because each member of the unit recognized the need to take care of their own. They all looked after the farm. Having over five hundred fruit trees, eight water wells, irrigation ditches, a small herd of white-faced cattle and several dozen horses of mixed breed, it should now, more properly, be called a ranch. The horses had been purchased, stolen or gathered from wild stock run down during Juan's travels.

Most Mexicans had lost their California properties. Their lands had been "stolen" by whites both "legally" and illegally. Juan Oliver had been more forceful than many of his race. He stood his ground and, when necessary, cleverly eliminated antagonists. He never challenged *gringos* openly but somehow people knew that Juan should not be taken lightly. His reputation made it easy for people to leave him alone. Juan hated the *gringos* and he would injure or even kill one with little provocation. When threatened he worked alone, at night, and took care of his business. There was no gold on Juan's property and there was an abundance of vacant land available in California. There was no need for most folks to risk life for the Olivera ranch and white folks generally left him alone.

Juan had learned the secret of back hauling early in his entrepreneurial career. Back hauling is a procedure used by freight carriers who haul something to one place and return or go elsewhere with something else. They try to never go anywhere with an empty wagon. Juan had twelve mules, each packing Mexican pottery, leather-goods, costume jewelry, fruit and other items that would sell in San Francisco. His two wagons, pulled by six horses each, were loaded with fresh oranges. He drove one wagon, his son the other. The mules were strung-out behind the wagons in two lines of six each. They stopped at each of the missions along the trail, trading goods for meals, lodging and a place for the livestock. When they arrived in San Francisco, they peddled the goods, purchased whiskey and tobacco from Washoe Clete's Wholesale Warehouse and opium from Sam Hing's brother, plus canned food, tools, warm clothes and other items that would bring a high price in the remote mountain camps. Washoe was an opportunist who, in the early 1850s, had sold the city of San Francisco a shipload of cats which were turned loose on the docks to kill rats. Can you imagine, thought Juan, knowing a man who could con a city into buying cats?

They learned that Washoe and Sam were in Bodie, a very tough settlement far from San Francisco, located high up on the backside of the Sierras. Juan had never been there. He wanted to go. The things he had accumulated in his wagons and his livestock would bring a very high price if he could get them all to Bodie.

In San Francisco Juan and Pedro heard about the Comet, a sun grazer they called it, a big one, that could hit something in our solar system. The sun and the earth were possible targets according to some reports. It was due in September, about the same time they would arrive in Bodie.

Using maps and information gleaned from people he knew in the City, Juan planned their trip. They would go from San Francisco to Stockton, Copperopolis, Angel's Camp, Carson Hill and Melones. Then they would cross the Stanislaus River at Knight's Ferry and push on to Jamestown, Sonora, Twain Harte and Barry's Station. From there the road would take them up Deadman's Creek and over the Sonora Pass. From the top it would be downhill over a steep course to the meadow and the Walker River. They would push on southeast through Devil's Gate, south to Bridgeport where they would find the Bodie road. Juan was familiar with the path as far as Twain Harte from previous visits but he had never been over the Sonora Pass which topped out at nine thousand six hundred feet above sea level. Reports from various people indicated that it was a very narrow, rough and dangerous trail.

Pedro had never been to San Francisco before and Juan encouraged his son to explore. Juan had been there, working on the docks, when he was only fifteen. The community was much rougher then, he thought. Pedro should be able to find his own way around while I enjoy an opium den and a *señorita*. He'll be fine, just fine. He should learn something too.

▼▲▼

Pedro felt his brown eyes grow wider and wider as he made his way around what the white folks call "The City," "The City by the Golden Gate." Homes and other buildings, thousands of them, all packed together along streets with cable cars that climbed up and down steep hills. Restaurants, hotels and saloons were clustered and scattered throughout the city, some catering to the wants of specific segments of a very diverse population. There were German beer halls, English pubs, French *cafés*, Mexican *cantiñas*, Italian spaghetti houses and Chinese *chop suey* joints.

It was a beautiful harbor packed with ships and boats of all descriptions, some with tall masts; others with steam power. There were junks manned by Chinese, *feluccas* with Italian sailors, stern wheelers taking cargo and travelers around the bay and up the Carqinez Straits to Sacramento, whalers used to search for the hump back's, and other fishing boats of all types and colors. Most fishermen had given up the gold fields and returned to the sea. They had given their boats exotic names hoping that such titles would help them harvest the wealth grown in the Pacific Ocean.

The warm fertile ground in the nearby San Joaquin Valley was producing all types of edibles, particularly grain. The produce was being eaten locally and it was also being shipped from San Francisco to the east coast and to Europe.

Juan rode the cable cars all over the city on tracks that must have been near a hundred miles long. He went up and down Telegraph, Nob and Russian Hills many times just for the thrill of doing such a trip. He went to the Presidio, to the Golden Gate Park and to the Cliff House at Land's End.

A cable car conductor said, "What's your name, son?"

"Pedro, Pedro Olivera," he responded. "What's yours?"

"Roger Grant," he answered. "Been drivin' these cars ever since a Scot name of Andrew Hallidie, wire rope maker, invented this cable car system. Smart man, must have been. So far none of these cars has run 'way and crashed."

The conductors were all willing to talk about the city. They described the elegant homes owned by the rich and powerful. The best one was a villa that belonged to the former governor, Leland Stanford. There was the huge brick fort protecting the entrance to the bay called the Presidio. There was the Cliff House, a place where the power of the ocean was pitted against the majesty of the rocky cliffs of California's shoreline.

But the place that held Pedro's interest the most was the great new hotel called The Palace. He was determined to get inside and he made his way into the circular marble-paved courtyard. It was big enough for carriages to enter and circle around. Pedro looked up at the magnificent seven story structure, each floor having it's own gallery and promenade. People above looked down on him as he stood, bathed in the soft natural light let in by the amber-colored, transparent ceiling of the courtyard.

Finely dressed guests were coming and going assisted by coachmen, doormen and bellboys. Coaches were circling, horses hoofs were clattering on the hard surface of the yard. The horseshoes produced a rhythmic beat, one that caused his heart to pound out the words, "I must get in. I must get in."

He watched, waiting for an opportunity to pop inside, unnoticed. His chance came when a team of horses reared, reacting to a small barking dog that had escaped from the arms of a fancy, feathered lady guest.

Pedro slipped inside and up the stairs to the second floor where the first person he encountered was a young lady of his race who was cleaning rooms. They talked quietly as she moved about one of the suites on its thick carpets. There were heavy drapes and highly polished furniture made of hard woods, mahogany and oak. Pedro could sense the former presence of General Grant sleeping here in the huge four-posted bed.

There was a tube near a roll-top desk. Pedro guessed that it was a pneumatic tube, one that used air to transmit cylinders carrying messages. His class had studied pneumatic tubes in his last year at school. They were the latest advancement. he couldn't resist the pen and paper on the desk and wrote, "Pedro is here." Next, he put the note in the tubular message cylinder and sent it rocketing down through the pipe to the hotel desk.

"*Malo muchacho, muy malo,*" said his lady friend, in a tone no longer friendly.

Pedro left quickly, scampering down the stairs and out onto the courtyard before anyone had time to react. He ran, full tilt, out onto the street, jumped aboard an open sided cable car traveling fast down hill and mingled with the other passengers.

Pedro had escaped from the Palace Hotel and would soon depart for "the ground" that was responsible for the building of all the major structures in this great city. The ground was a small piece of foothill territory, sixty miles long and twenty miles wide. The ground was only dirt but it had delivered the power and wealth that had produced the beauty of the Palace Hotel, the majesty of the Cliff House and the genius of the Cable Car. That same ground produced another kind of power, the might that had given this part of the world many evils, killing, deceiving, conning, suppressing the people of his race, Chinese, Indians and other minorities. Strange, he thought. How five hundred gold camps on a small patch of ground could change the face of a city and the spirit of its men.

▼▲▼

It was a cool windy morning when Juan and Pedro left San Francisco in their fresh smelling cloths washed by Wan Lee. Wan was one of the early Chinese businessmen in San Francisco. He had become the key leader of the people of his race and he helped build China Town. He was a man of influence,

105

the kind of man Juan liked to know. After all, he might be useful later. That's why Juan had gone there and spent money to have his clothes cleaned up.

They took the steamboat and soon found themselves deposited on the opposite shore of the bay. It warmed considerably as they moved east through the hills and small mountains that had been turned brown by the summer sun. It became clear and very hot when they reached the great central-valley. The early part of the trip was made on a roadbed well defined from years of travel by man, horse and coach to the heart of the mother-lode country. Their trip through Stockton and the agricultural center of the huge valley was uneventful, boring to Pedro, until they reached the gently sloping foothills of the Sierra Nevada Mountains. His father had told him that the low rolling country gave up *mucho oro,* and Pedro imagined himself with pockets full of nuggets. Dreams of treasure, the timeless fantasy of child and the fancy of child in man. Youthful fancy, tending to be more optimistic than that divined by someone more mature.

As they moved up into the foothills the countryside gradually changed. The northern Sierra Nevada Mountains were structured like a tilted rectangle, rising gradually as someone approaches them from the west, falling off abruptly as the traveler passes over the top. Juan and Pedro did not know about the forces that made mountains; they saw them only as they appeared on the surface, the way people usually see most things including their fellow men. The hills were brown. The bright spring colors of blue lupine, orange poppy and yellow monkey flower had given way to the summer sun and a shortage of water. There was plenty of food for the stock and shade from oak, sycamore, buckeye and some scruffy looking pine trees. Juan admonished his son to look out for rattlesnakes that could be encountered everywhere on the western slopes below the heavy snow line but Pedro was unconcerned. He had heard such warnings before, about the Santa Barbara hills near home, and he had never seen a rattler. Deer, rabbit, fox, pheasant, quail and wild turkey showed up trail-side, usually early in the morning, but they did not stop to hunt. Their wagons were full and they had plenty of food. Pedro was glad; he knew it was sometimes necessary to hunt to eat but he did not like to see animals killed. In fact he preferred not to think at all about death.

Pedro knew he was in gold country when he reached Angels Camp, a vibrant mining town with hotels, saloons, a big jail house, plenty of mines and heavy equipment. It was a settlement made famous by Mark Twain when he wrote about its annual jumping frog contest. Pedro thought it would be fun to enter the contest and he also wanted to try his luck in the gold fields but they had work to do elsewhere.

They pushed on, moving higher into the pine forest reaching Carson Hill. It was another gold camp, part of the ground that delivered so much wealth and power. Juan told Pedro about Carson Hill's unique beginning. It owed its birth to a gun. A man named Raspberry was first to find color in Carson Hill when he jammed his muzzle-loading riffle with its ramrod and shot the rod into the ground to clear the barrel, striking and breaking open a rock laced with gold. Raspberry mined ten thousand dollars the first three days he worked the claim and he eventually dug himself a fortune. The hill was now honey combed with shafts and Juan told his son that a single nugget found here once brought forty-four thousand dollars to its owner. The trees that used to live on Carson's steep hillside had been clear-cut to provide access to the mines and timber for their shafts.

The next settlement, called Melones, was named after the Spanish word *melofis*, their seeds resembling in size and shape the gold found in this part of the Sierra Nevada Mountains. They crossed the Stanislaus River at Knight's Ferry. While pointing at the bridge, Juan said, "Second one built here. First one washed 'way. Water comes way, way up one spring–picks up logs waitin' at sawmills for cuttin'. Then they come crashin' and bashin' down river. Masahed everythin' standin'. Remember this, Son, when floodin' time comes 'round stay clear of this country." They stopped at the sawmill downstream so Pedro could take a look at how tree trunks were turned into lumber. Juan said, "Fresh cut boards are as val'able as gold; they're used for the mine shafts and for buildin' 'most everythin' that goes to makin' a town. Hear me now, lumber's gold!"

In the old settlement of Jamestown, Pedro learned about the fire of 1866 which downed most of the early wood framed buildings. "Most mountain gold camps burn every few years. Some folks call it a cycle; someone finds gold, prospectors rush in and throw up wood shacks, business people follow with stores, saloons and pleasure houses. Then one day, it burns down. If the load is still payin' out they build again. If not, you have a ghost town, endin' the cycle," said Juan.

Outside of Jamestown where they had seen a funny looking, soft, dark green rock, they camped near a party of six men and a woman led by a lean, bright looking *gringo* with long auburn hair, a high brow, flashing blue eyes and a great beard. At five foot nine inches tall, he was not a physical giant but his trim, fit presence commanded respect; he was clearly the leader of the group. While sitting on a rock near their campfire he held court for all those who chose to join him, including Pedro. He described the wonders of the Sierra Nevada Mountains including the Yosemite Valley, Vernal Falls, Nevada Falls, Tenaya Lake, Mirror Lake, Yosemite Falls, Inspiration Point and Half Dome. He talked about glaciation, erosion, volcanic activity and some of the traditions of the Miwok Indians. He went on at length about the beauty of the countryside. There was a giant Sequoia tree with a trunk so large loggers cut a tunnel through its center while the tree still stood and lived. "Man, wagon and horse can drive through the hole in the tree like a train goes through a tunnel," he said.

"To the south there's Mount Whitney, her granite cliffs rising to almost fourteen thousand five hundred feet above sea level with sheer snowcapped faces overlooking the world in all directions," he said while pointing in the general direction of the highest mountain in the United States.

"Remember the huge lava mountain we saw from Jamestown? The lava flowed like thick hot soup out of the earth, covering whatever stood in its path until it cooled, forming the forty mile long black rock mass called the Table Mountain. "Prospectors," he said, "found gold nuggets the size of hens eggs on the eastern slope of that old mountain."

Acting like a teacher, he pulled from his pocket a piece of green rock that he passed around in the group. Pedro thought it felt like a piece of soap with a waxy texture that broke in slivers.

The leader asked, "Did any of you see the outcrop of this rock today?" No one in his party answered. Their eyes were down, each acting with the mind-set of an ostrich, wishing to be invisible.

Only Pedro raised his hand saying, "I did, outside of Jamestown."

"Good," said the captain. "At least one had his eyes open. Who knows what it is and its significance?"

A young man responded, "Serpentine, a rock often found near gold and other precious minerals."

"Right," said the teacher. "It was located less than twenty feet from the trail. You know what it is and what it implies but before you can use your knowledge you must use your eyes. Tomorrow let's try to keep them open.

"Serpentine is a strange rock, but it's not the only unusual thing found in these mountains," he continued. "The east side of the Sierras around Mono Lake not far from the gold camp at Bodie. Now that's a foreboding landscape. Much of it is barren like what some scientists expect to find on the moon. The lake has too much salt, a problem that limits habitat. Brine shrimp and a few other salt-loving things grow in its waters. Volcanic cones, explosion-pits, craters and domes are everywhere and there are clear signs of earth movement along fault lines particularly around Lee Vining. A stark countryside ripped in the past by great glaciers and earthquakes.

"It was March 26, 1872, and I was in Yosemite Valley when the sounds of night faded, animals came on the alert, rigid and frightened. The air became thick just before the first jolt hit. More followed that night and for weeks thereafter. It was a monster earthquake, centered in Owens Valley. Twenty-five people died, most in Lone Pine where the town was demolished. Lateral slippage along the fault line exceeded twenty feet in places and vertical uplifts were as great as thirteen feet. The quake hit hard all along the eastern slopes, particularly in communities like Bishop, Lee Vining, Bodie, Mono Diggings, Bridgeport and Aurora. It really shook things up for me in Yosemite," the leader said.

"Many strange things happen along the eastern slopes of the mountains," he added. "A huge, unexplained, night time explosion in Bodie on July 8, 1879 killed ten people, injured a bunch more, pitched giant boulders into the settlement's street and felled large buildings. The cause is still unknown but many of the destructive forces we experience are man, rather than nature made. That's why all of us need to enlist the aid of the government in protecting the high country. The nation's scenic treasures belong to all of mankind. Join with me," he said. "Go down the right trail. Follow the path of a true human being, true to one's self, true to friends, mankind and rightness. Crusade to save the wilderness, follow my vision before it's too late!"

As the fire cooled, the six University of California geology students drifted off to rest but Pedro, captivated by the magnetism of their teacher, remained behind. A giant, persuasive figure, thought Pedro, small, in stature but huge of mind, a leader ahead of his time who had sprung full blown out of a people-less wilderness. What had given him *the* wisdom to speak as he *did*? Was he from some other time or place, set down in the mountains to show mankind a better way? Pedro felt his power, sensed his greatness, and wondered. What would it be like if he could pass his own views on to others? And what would happen to his family, to Trigo, if he were transported to another world? Was it a flight of fancy or inspiration residing in the mind of a child/man who had just encountered someone extraordinary?

The man came forward saying, "What's your name, son?"

"Pedro. Pedro Olivera from Santa Barbara. We are going to Bodie."

"I am John Muir," he said. "And you need to take care in that part of the country. It's a very dangerous place. Seems like someone gets killed there almost every day. There are natural disasters, shootings and strange unexplained happenings around Bodie all the time. And don't listen to those crazy *Veda Madre* stories folks are peddling. That's just a bunch of bunk drummers use to sell mine stock. *Veda Madre* indeed! There's no such thing!" With that he turned, took the hand of his lady friend, Louie Wanda Strentzel, and left.

9

SEAN McCARTHY WAS STILL ON A mission. He had taken the first steps on his journey of life but he had not yet satisfied his quest for wealth. But, he also needed companionship, a wife and a family. He used part of his gold dust to built a small, sturdy cabin in the foothills just east of Sacramento and sent word to his fiancée, Mary Hogan, to meet him on the east side of *Istmo de Panama* at a rooming house he had heard about in Colōn.

Ship's crews were still in very short supply in San Francisco and Sean had little difficulty convincing the skipper of the Molly Jane that he was an experienced pilot who had lost his papers in a fire. He navigated the ship to Panama, received his pay and walked the fifty miles across the Isthmus to Colōn, picked up Mary, put her on a mule and lead her back to Panama. They followed the path pioneered by John Butterfield and other early trailblazers. It was a hot, painful journey. The air was moist and thick, the country was infested with mosquitoes, cockroaches, snakes, flies and other assorted tropical amphibians and insects. Conditions in the equatorial latitudes sap a man's strength, eating up his energy, shrinking his courage. Everything is hot, the air, water, earth, the human body, everything boils as the sun's rays pour down on those foolish enough to march in its glare. Sweat, never ending sweat, with almost no relief, even from the night. Tropical conditions, ideal for germinating the microbes of disease and cultivating the squalid segment of man's nature. The smell of death hung in the air, stalking their progress. Mary, a Northeasterner, could not believe that people lived in such a place and by the time they reached Panama she was sorry to have come but afraid to retrace her march back across what she preferred to think of as the *Istmo de muerto.*

Sean found employment as a mate on another ship using his pay vouchers as evidence of his seafaring experiencing and rank. Perception was more important than truth in the old west and people often made themselves out to be something that they were not. Mary's outlook improved when they sailed into San Francisco Bay where she was reminded of the beauty and the cool breeze of Boston Harbor. They were soon married and Sean took her to his cabin outside Sacramento.

Sean spent the next ten years in the gold fields on the west side of the Sierra Nevada Mountains, prospecting whenever he could and finding employment building bridges, sawmills, roads and mine shafts to maintain his growing family when his gold seeking luck was poor. Mary gave birth to two boys and a girl and Sean added two rooms to the cabin. By the time he carried his poke over the mountains through Carson Pass and headed for Bodie, he possessed some of the most productive assets known to man: education, experience, work ethic, loving family and greed. His lust for gold was unabated and Bodie offered a new challenge.

He stomped about in the Bodie Mountains for six months and found some color, but concluded that harvesting the lode would require heavy investments in men, machinery and deep mine shafts. He had watched others profit in the camps by taking the gold from the miners rather than the mountain and he devised a plan for a second hand treasure hunt. For twenty-five dollars per acre he acquired a homestead in the flat, sage-filled valley a few miles outside of Bridgeport. Using the names of his wife, children and various eastern relatives, he filed homesteads on additional acreage and obtained water and timber rights. He surveyed the property and laid out an engineering plan to clear the sage, channel the water and irrigate the rich, dry, valley floor. He hired Chinese Coolies to do the work and build a ranch house, barn and corral. Sean managed the foreign workers by using clear, crisp communications, like those he received on the subject of navigation from Rod. They cleared the sage, put it into huge piles and built magnificent bonfires to warm them at night. He obtained a bank loan, built a sawmill near a large creek, clear-cut the trees, turning them into lumber for use in construction around Bridgeport and Bodie. He had Coolies build a small shack on each of his homesteads to make it difficult for the government to reclaim the land. The very cold winter and huge snowfall of 1861 impeded his early progress but Sean was determined, the engine of greed driving him to harvest his fortune from gold without pan or rocker.

It was so cold in 1861 that the famous Norwegian immigrant, Jon Torsteinson Rui, had difficulties in the snow-covered mountain passes. Jan, known in the Sierras as "Snowshoe" Thompson, carried the mail on his back during winter, ninety miles between Placerville, California and Carson City, Nevada. He traveled the route for twenty years, starting in 1856 when he responded to an advertisement for a mail carrier in the Sacramento Transcript. Mounted on homemade skis with a twelve foot balancing pole and carrying a sixty pound pack, the big, blond, powerful man usually made the trip in three days. In 1861, he was often late. It was the only year anyone could remember his not being on time.

Bridgeport became a center of commerce, communications and travel for the Bodie camp and others at Lee Vining, Dogtown Creek, Mono Diggings, Aurora and Taylor. Sean bought interests in a shipping company, hotel and saloon in Bridgeport and a livery in Bodie. The irrigated valley land supported cattle, horses, sheep and pigs in the summer and provided a short growing season for grass, potatoes and hardy vegetables. He made plans to expand the ranch house that was now surrounded by a fine stand of young trees.

Mary and the children were happy in their new home in the summer but nearly froze during their first, very long, cold winter. Each winter thereafter, Sean arranged to move Mary and the kids to warmer quarters in Smith Valley where their livestock also spent the cold months.

Over the next eleven years, business flourished. The grass grew thick and strong, fed by the fresh, cool mountain waters in the irrigation ditches. Gradually, the tiny waterways became populated with small trout. The towns of Bridgeport and Bodie grew and thrived. The original sawmill ran on two shifts, weather permitting, and the shipping business was brisk.

In June 1878, Congress passed an Act permitting any U.S. Citizen to acquire one hundred sixty acres of timberland for two dollars and fifty cents per acre. Federal legislation usually results in unanticipated actions by people and commerce. Some people call it, "The law of unintended results." Sean gobbled up timberlands along with other entrepreneurs in the area who used both ethical and unethical means to grab as much cheap land as possible. The less scrupulous filed false documents and made purchases in the names of small children, relatives and sometimes the dead. Paper corporations were created, mills were built and treed lands were clear-cut. In some instances trees were slashed to the ground leaving the surface of the earth exposed to unnatural amounts of erosion. Sean did his share of land grabbing and he opened a second lumber operation on the another creek and increased his logging activity.

Other less predictable things occurred as a result of the new law. For example, "Rocket," a thirty-six foot by ten foot steamboat was transported in sections on wagons from Carson City to Mono Lake where it was first used to pull barges loaded with lumber across the lake to the shore nearest to Bodie. After a time, Rocket became a sort of party boat, taking sightseers around the lake and to Paoha Island. Later still, the little steamboat contributed to its own demise by moving almost three thousand railroad ties per day in support of the construction by the Bodie Railroad. In late 1881 a narrow-gauge line of track ran from "The Company" sawmill through Bodie to the northern most mines. The mill was sited in a ravine, roughly five miles south of Mono Lake. "Tybo," the first of the railroad company's puffer bellies, made the first trip over the new track. It had been hauled into the area on wagons pulled by sixteen mule teams. Other engines, little engines that could do almost anything, named, "Mono," "Inyo" and " Bodie," followed and they were soon running along the three-foot wide track, delivering lumber and supplies to the mines and the town. The townsfolk and mill operators cheered when the trains pulled in. Some folks fall in love with trains, treating them like they are almost human. They give meaningful names to the engines, coal cars and caboose. They think of them as friends, look forward to the rumble of their wheels and the sound of the whistle, thought Sean.

The lifecycles of the new machines were begun as a result of a federal law, the same Act that resulted in the early demise of many forests. The useful life of the steamboat was ended by the railroad, a rail line that would later be abandoned because it went no place important.

The Act changed the western environment. It helped some people and hindered others. Sean was one of those who was assisted but his growing holdings faced a challenge, finding experienced, skilled, cowhands to handle his livestock. All men who came to this part of the world went to the gold camps. He was excited when he saw the tall, blond, well-seated cowboy ride up on a Sunday to his hitching rail. He hoped he would become a friend, a companion and possibly even his foremen. He needed a good cowhand, someone he could trust and befriend. He needed people around him who would listen to his stories. He had spent months in the mountains seeking gold and he hated the loneliness. He enjoyed going to Bodie from time to time to attend the fights, common distractions in gold camps, and he wanted someone to share his adventures.

10

JOHN DE LA ROCHE WAS TENSE, ALERT, exhilarated—all at the same time. His hands were on a fortune. But how could it be taken out without sharing with the others in the brigade and the Hudson Bay Company itself? And what if the dead men were found and connected to his gold? After all, he thought, death makes one important and gold makes the mystery of death worth solving. Would the murders bring him down? No, no. He could not let that happen—not now. Not when he had his hands on the key to a glorious future. There must be a way, he must find it, achieve a victory; he knew that success meant grandeur, renown and promise, while defeat spelled the opposite. Failure is the only true crime, he thought.

His mind was racing, struggling, pondering; he was anxious to devise a scheme that would provide his solution. Slowly a plan took shape. He would dismantle the rock piles identifying the claims, abandon the old campsite, wipe out all evidence of its existence, hide his gold and set about trapping. He would fix a camp upriver, three miles from his gold, work out of that location, snaring, hunting and skinning for two weeks, then panning for two weeks, alternating these cycles throughout the summer. He would return to Cedar Point with fewer furs than usual, feign ill health, resign from the Hudson's Bay Company and wait until he got back to civilization. When free from the company and the other trappers, he would purchase a string of mules, return to the back country before the coldest part of the winter set in, recover his cash, which would be hidden in places unlikely to be covered by deep snow or ice. If winter came in too fast he would wait until spring.

The brigade members took pleasure in kidding John about his lean haul when they met at Cedar Point. It was always fun to see the "king of the hill" knocked down. Under normal circumstances, John would have reacted with a hot temper and fast moving fists, but the soft color hidden in his sacks and the two big nuggets in his pocket soothed his person. Triumph was near at hand. He would enjoy the last laugh.

The hushed majesty of winter snow lay thick on the ground and hung heavy from the pines as John made his way back to the confluence of the Quesnelle and Caribou Rivers. He located his stash, packed the mules and hid the gold under some furs he had withheld from the company. He rode out southwest trailing a string of eight—eight mules that owed their existence to the mating of the jackass and mare. The snow was light, temperature cold but not severe as he passed out of the timber country. He reached the great valley with its sparkling lakes and small creek with hundreds of beaver ponds where he had trapped in the past. He felt the warm sense of familiarity that comes with a return to a place where a person achieved success.

He climbed out of the valley, traveled down into the rolling hills and came upon the small trading post just east of Williams Lake. Following the well-marked trail, he turned south and stopped at small settlements including Lae la Hache, Boyd's House and Cut-Off Valley before reaching the larger town of Lytton. At Williams Lake he first heard about the gold find on the Fraser River and the stories about the placer deposits and big nuggets grew as he moved south. They included tales of outlaws killing miners for their dust and he decided to hide his cash outside of Lytton, a town alive and bustling with activity even though it was caught deep in winter's grip.

Litton was busy because it lay astride the main trail to the Fraser River and not far from the gold strike. He sold six of his mules for ten times their worth and holed-up in a small summer cabin owned by a trapper friend. It was cold and the unfinished house was ill suited for winter lodgers. But John was used to rugged living and it served his needs perfectly. A small barn was suitable for his horse and two mules. He made several trips to Lytton obtaining supplies, tools, grain and hay for the livestock and established himself in the community. He made an appointment with Louis DiSimone, one of the leading bankers in town, and asked him to keep an eye out for a good business that was for sale.

His coat needed mending and someone told him about a young widow lady, Roxanne Bordeaux. Her former husband, a logger, had been killed in a forest accident, causing her to take in sewing. She was a friendly lady, not beautiful but attractive, with long brown hair, a shapely figure and a happy laugh. John, the Frenchman, saw himself as an amorist, a lady's man, and he set his mind on Roxanne. He also saw her sunny personality as an asset he could use in a plan forming in his head. A coat and hat making business scheme where he would provide the furs at their market value and she would turn them into fine, warm, coats and hats which would be sold from her home. They could split the profits above the value of the raw furs. John had heard stories about gold rush territory. People came from everywhere wanting everything. Simple things like shovels and buckets reportedly fetched as much as a hundred dollars each. Prospectors apparently came and went but mostly went broke, leaving their gold with businessmen, sporting ladies and gamblers. Lytton was the gateway settlement located at the convergence point of the Fraser and Thompson Rivers. It was also on the natural route from Fort Victoria to the Quesnelle country where he knew that the gold strike he had made would soon be found. Warm coats and hats would be a start; other goods, services and recreation would follow under the control of John de la Roche.

During the winter months he purchased a small store. John made it larger by converting the upstairs living quarters into storage space. He contacted several trappers he knew to be trustworthy, letting them know that he was prepared to pay a good price for illegal furs that were traded outside the Hudson's Bay Company monopoly. Using those black market furs with others he would obtain by trapping himself and still others purchased from the Company, he could keep Roxanne busy and stock the new store. He would buy just enough furs legally to make it difficult for the Hudson's Bay Company people to close him down.

He made trips to Fort Victoria and Vancouver with some of his gold, established banking relationships in both cities and arranged to purchase large quantities of tools, supplies and other merchandise for his store. He also bought two wagonloads of whiskey which he took, along with former store clerk Peter Hayse, back to Lytton in late February. John spent gold in Victoria and Vancouver, simply telling people he had spent a few days on the Fraser. He made prospecting sound so easy that Hayse quit his job to ride north, winter not withstanding. John knew that his stories and the gold he flashed would accelerate the stampede of seekers, helping his business in Lytton. He was following the example of others in San Francisco, men like Sam Bannon who had spread exciting rumors and accelerated the rush west in the early 1850s. De la Roche went out of his way to show color in some saloons near the docks, a dangerous practice but worth the risk. He knew that the sailors and stevedores would spread the word, causing the Canadian gold strike message to be carried quickly to Seattle, San Francisco, Los Angeles and other ports. He also expected that Peter would find prospecting too difficult and he had the perfect position for a clerk in his store.

History is pock marked with deceit and other evil deeds that have been energized by the forces of greed. This time it was John de la Roche, a man willing to destroy others for his own sake who was being spurred by his craving for power and riches. Injustice, contempt for the rights of fellow men was the norm for the French Canadian who viewed concepts like fair dealing as a ritual dance designed for suckers. His way was better because it was conceived to reward the most clever person. His true nature, if exposed, would lead others to believe that people are no damn good.

In March, he bought the vacant property next to the store and arranged for the building of an adjoining downstairs restaurant and saloon with a brothel upstairs.

As spring spread light and freshness over the territory, he yearned to return to his "golden" river but he was afraid that his mining presence on the Quesnelle would be discovered, causing the Royal Canadian Mounties to question him when the bodies of his victims were found. If they made the connection between his sudden wealth and the two Irishmen it could mean, at worst, a hanging, at best, a major problem with the Hudson's Bay Company over the ownership of gold he mined while in their employ. Either way, the risk was too great.

Early one morning he heard a horse and rider approaching the cabin. Carbine in hand, he went out to find his trapper friend and the property owner, Barry Larkin, riding up. There was surprise, hostility and anger in Larkin's eyes when he found John living in his lodge but his mood changed when he learned that John had been stuck there during a heavy storm and decided simply to ride out the winter. John offered to pay Barry for use of the cabin and barn but the offer, as anticipated, was refused. Larkin was satisfied that nothing had been harmed. In fact, the property had been improved by John, not out of generosity, but because of his need to shield out the icy winter winds.

Barry told John that the Hudson's Bay Company no longer had the exclusive right to trap in western Canada and that he was headed upriver to work for himself this spring. John exchanged his two mules and some traps for a twenty-percent interest in the furs Barry brought back. Two days, several jugs and many stories later, Barry was on his way.

Later that spring John moved into a rooming house in town where he had a fifty-percent interest and he moved his horse into the livery he had recently acquired. He needed to be closer to his expanding enterprises and Roxanne.

He had gotten closer to Roxanne, so close in fact that one cold winter night they found themselves fingering each other's hot parts on top of a pile of furs in her cabin. As their foreplay continued and their passion grew, their clothing found its way to the floor. Soon they were making love on the body covers of dead animals. When their first desire cooled, they rolled off the pile of furs and fell into Roxanne's bed where they spent the long, dark winter night enjoying each other's bodies.

For John the act was simply rutting. It was an exhilarating experience, similar, he supposed, to that felt by the animals. For Roxanne, the same act was an expression of first love. At one point near dawn Roxanne found herself kneeling over John's body holding his limp member in one hand, his sack in the other trying to arouse his spirit one more time. It worked; soon they were coupled together, Roxanne on top, rocking back and forth, alternately squeezing and relaxing the muscles of her vagina on his long firm rod which had proved to be better suited to this sport than her former husband's.

Since that first winter encounter they had grown close and Roxanne was showing the signs of love, signs that did not go unnoticed in the settlement.

John's business associates teased him about marriage, something he considered. It would allow him to enjoy the profits from her business and she could work for him, cooking and keeping his place without pay. She was an exciting partner in bed and marriage would not prevent him from enjoying the favors of other women.

Many of John's trapper associates came to him starting in late spring, with prime furs for sale, growing the hat and coat business and causing Roxanne to hire two ladies to help with the sewing. A flood of prospectors also arrived, dumping money into the de la Roche enterprises. They purchased mules and supplies before making the steep hike up "Jackass Hill." By late fall Peter returned from the gold fields, broke and despondent, ready to take over the day-to-day store operations. The saloon, restaurant, brothel, livery and other businesses flourished. As John's wealth and statue in society grew, his feeling of invincibility intensified. John's self-appointed divinity thrived. He did not appreciate that the spider who wove the largest web was the one most likely to have it broken by the bear.

John and Roxanne, happy and prosperous, were married and decided to honeymoon in Seattle and Portland. Roxanne had never been outside of Canada and she wanted, desperately, to see another part of the world. John sought contacts south of the border and new business opportunities. The trip was financed by money derived from double murder. Vice, de la Roche' vice, was about to be exported to a new part of the northwest.

They arrived in Vancouver British Columbia in the late fall, boarded an in-straight steamer for the trip, "Magnificent Passage," of less than one hundred and fifty miles. The daylong saltwater voyage was spectacular and in the early evening as they made their way down Puget Sound they could see the mighty mountain ranges on both sides, the Olympics to the west and the Cascades to the east. "My God," said Roxanne. "Look, look there! It's, it's a giant snow-castle in the sky! What a mountain! Must be the most spectacular peak in the whole world." It was Mount Rainier, ablaze in the fast setting, slanting sunlight. Truly a behemoth that seemed to rise right out of the waters and up to the far reaches of heaven. The gigantic volcanic mountain that stood over fourteen thousand feet tall was usually obscured by rain this time of year but on those few days that it appeared, it presented a sight to behold, even for the natives.

The docking near Seattle after dark was also spectacular. The lights, sometimes scattered, sometimes bunched along Puget Sound, illuminated sawmills, canneries, docks, other businesses and residences and twinkled like stars pulled from the sky. They lighted the way after dark and when they reflected off the rippling waters they looked like silver shivers on a dark *sombrero*.

It was the first of many trips John would make to Seattle and other port cities in the Northwest Territory in search of knowledge, contacts and opportunities. Each of the new settlements springing up in the west had it's own unique beginnings. John studied such things and listened to the natives because he knew that knowledge was power and he believed that his ventures would be better served if he understood what he was experiencing. I will take advantage of every opportunity to outdo others and expand my fortune, he thought.

John was interested in the Salish Indians, the early inhabitants of Puget Sound. It was their country, their territory, and who would know it better? Big Mike, the huge-boned, Irish bartender at "Billy the Mugs," said, "Them Salish. Now them's a peaceful lot. They build wooden shacks, live off the things that come from the sea and land. They fish, dig clams, lots of clams in these parts. Them red men hunt small animals and gather nuts and berries. Chief Sealth, he's their leader. He's always carryin' his hand carved, painted, cedar talking stick. Damned thing must be six foot long. It's a small totem pole. Could be used to bludgeon a man but not Sealth. He makes it his business to find bloodless ways to communicate with us eastern arrivals. Came from Maine myself. The Indians 'round here use talkingsticks to bind a bargain. You know, sort of like us white folks use a handshake. First, there was the explorer, Charles Wilkens in '41. Then came the Denny party of settlers in '51 and the Yesler Mill in 1852. Those early explorers and settlers were soon followed by new arrivals to share the land with the Salish Indians.

"Denny and his people rowed ashore from a schooner. Exact. That was its name. They landed at Smaquamox, point of land, just west of the

Duwamish River. They built log cabins and started this city. Seattle, they named it, after the friendly Indian Chief. Here, on the eastern shore of Elliott Bay the fishing, hunting and logging is fine, fine as Irish Milk. And them Indians don't bother us none."

John would make numerous subsequent trips to Seattle. He would leave Roxanne behind so that he could have some fun. Each time he came, he painted the town red, intoxicated by it's beauty, excitement and charm. He liked the soft rain that seemed to fall most of the time and he loved the green countryside that was spotted with multiple lakes, streams and great rivers. He visited the best restaurants, theaters and gaming houses. Exciting places, he thought. Places that were much better than anything available in his part of Canada.

He particularly liked the red light district, called the "Lava Bed" that was located south of Mill Street. It was complete with saloons having exotic names, including "Billy the Mugs" and "The Graves of Daphne," and there was plenty of opportunity to work the sporting ladies or gamble on pool, billiards, pigeonhole, cards, whatever. Big Mike knew his way around the Lava Bed. He knew the best whores by their first names and he could always find a friendly game of chance. John befriended him and got Mike to show him around whenever he came to town. Big Mike was a gladiator, a man from the lonely, cold state of Maine. He knew how to cut the wolf loose when in town. It didn't matter that he lived in the city now. His spirit was still daring someone or something to stop him. The Lava Bed was the perfect place for two men who reveled in self-pleasure.

On their very first trip to Seattle, John and Roxanne went exploring. They sloshed along the mud street in front of the general store, livery, blacksmith-shop and barbershop. It was wet and dirty most of the time. The roadway was wet from the frequent rain and dirty with trash, garbage and human waste. However, the street's conditions didn't discourage commerce. One could buy all types of goods including staples like "Dill's Best Cut Plugs," "House of Lords Whiskey," "Coronet Dry Gin," mining supplies, spices and coffee. A haircut was twenty-five cents, a shave fifteen cents.

John liked the city and he was fascinated by the green hills and mountains, tall trees and breathtaking waterways. But on this first trip nothing, not Roxanne, the night life or the scenery, perked his interest as much as the sawmills. They represented another way to make big money. The California gold rush and growth in Hawaii produced a huge demand for timber, a need that was being satisfied, in part, by lumber from the Puget Sound Mills. The hard wood could reach San Francisco by steamship in a few days. The wharf-side saw mills were located in front of stores, hotels and saloons. Set away from the commercial buildings were cottages, small houses that resembled those found in early England. They had Victorian designs and slap-board sides that were painted white. There were white picket fences and the owners had carved signs displaying their names and hung them over their doors.

The lumber vessels were tied-up stern-to the docks and they were loaded, hold first, by friendly Salish Indian stevedores. When full below, the wet lumber was piled on the decks and lashed down. The ships were invariably overloaded and top heavy and some sunk before they reached port. Big Mike said, "We lost a lot of them, ships and seamen. The ships go over, just roll over when the swell first hits the hull. Water's cold, too cold for swimmin'. The men got no chance."

The ships came and left the wharf in a steady stream and the sawmills operated with virtually no inventory and little space for storing or drying the fresh cut wood. John went into the hills to see how the timber was cut and moved to the mills visualizing what it would take to exploit the logging and sawing opportunity that was surely headed his way. There were plenty of trees, available lands and waters in Canada, no need to import lumber. De la Roche had a new dream, spawned in Seattle, framed by the alchemy of converting trees to gold; a dream he could afford to pursue because of the fruits grown out of his slayings. He contacted several bankers, deposited some gold, repeated the Frazer River gold story and determined the requirements for his new venture in Canada. He met with prominent people, Yesler, Horton, Phillips and Denny and, on this, his very first trip to Seattle, John ordered the equipment he needed for a sawmill.

After completing his business in Seattle, John took Roxanne to the newest state in the union, Oregon.

John wanted to look smarter, wiser and better informed than other folks. Before leaving Litton he read about Lewis and Clark. He knew there would be a time when he could show off his wisdom. On the trip south John told Roxanne. "Just after the Louisiana Purchase, President Thomas Jefferson hired a survey crew—one plannin' to find a northern route to the Pacific Ocean. He hired a couple of men—former military guys. Meriwether Lewis and William Clark, to lead the party. Hired twenty-five other men and headed for the northwest out of Saint Louis, startin' in the spring of '04. Followed the course of the Missouri River through Nebraska and the Dakotas and into western Montana. Crossed the continental divide and picked up the headwater of the Columbia River. Added a Shoshoni Indian squaw named Sacagawea, 'bird woman,' to the group. Some newspaper halfwit said the Indian girl showed them the way. The story sounded good—made good copy—the public ate it up. No one who knows anythin' believes that fable. Women aren't trailblazers. No squaw could follow the track. I bet they took her along for the 'ride' she gave the men. Now her husband, Touissant Charbonneau had French blood. A man with a name like that could be a scout—a trailblazer even. He could have taken the lead. Don't you think?"

Roxanne bristled. It was one of the few times John had seen his wife angry. She didn't say anything for a time. She just looked him in the eye while raging inside. Finally, she said, "You men do lots more dumb things than women. Lots and lots more. I don't know nothin' 'bout the Indian girl but a woman could find her way. A smart lady could lead. You men think you know everythin' but you don't. You'd be surprised what women can do without no help from you."

"Oh, you think so? You ever been on a hunt? Ever found your way over a mountain pass? Fought a grizzly? No, you ain't! You don't know what you're talkin' 'bout. Trail finding is man's business," said John. "The guy with the French name, he's the one probably helped Lewis and Clark travel over the mountains. Maybe he got them the canoes to paddle down the Columbia River."

John rambled on, failing to notice that Roxanne was no longer listening. "I hear that river's course cuts 'tween two huge, snow-topped, mountains.

Volcanoes they say they were, Saint Helens risin' to the north and Hood to the south. They say that sailin' down inside the huge river gorge sittin' 'tween them two monsters was somethin'—really somethin' to see. And dangerous, too dangerous for some girl to lead. The Columbia's bigger, faster even than the Frazer."

Western Oregon and Washington looked very green with fertile, timbered lands that got more rain than the natives liked to admit. Rich soil, long summer days and rugged landscape produce magnificent sights. A landscape worthy of the artist's brush, thought Roxanne, ignoring her thick-headed husband.

"It took that troop eighteen months to get down here. Long time, don't you think, for Lewis and Clark to wait to dip their tired hands and feet into them very cold waters 'round here," said John.

"Guess so," mumbled Roxanne, still fuming.

They encountered the local inhabitants, the flat-headed Salish and Chinook Indians who carried huge, colorful, hand-made totem poles. Each pole displayed the clan or family crest. Roxanne had heard that the Salish Indians were the southern segment of a group of tribes that lived along a narrow strip of the northwest coast that lay between the coastal ranges and the offshore islands. At the top of Alaska the Indians that were related to the Salish were called Tlingit. Farther south lived the Haida, Tsimshian, Bella Bella, Bella Coola, Kwakiutl and Nootka. Someone had told her that the cultures were similar and they were over ten centuries old. She knew that all of the tribes were very artistic and that they produced magnificent ornaments. She had seen pictures of the artwork done by the early Greeks and Egyptians and she liked what the Indians did better. Roxanne had some of their work: a colorful hand carved canoe, two bent-cover boxes, a drum, a mask and some jewelry. I'll figure how to get John to buy me some more, she thought. It's the least a man can do, especially such a big man. One who knows everything.

John and Roxanne watched the Indians fish using dip nets and harpoons. They were frequently after sea lion, otter, porpoise, salmon and various fish in the bays, harbors and rivers. Roxanne was surprised to learn that the local Indians accepted slavery, taking mostly women and children when they raided neighboring tribes. Slavery was a practice that appeared to be inconsistent with their religious beliefs that stressed purity of heart and goodness of conduct. It also seemed unusual because they were generally so peaceful. However, she had heard stories about Indians all her life. She knew that some tribes raided, killed whites and took hostages. As a child she dreamed that a red man had come for her, dragged her away, raped her and made her his slave.

Roxanne was surprised to learn that the Salish Indians searched incessantly for their guardian spirits. Supernatural beings that they believed could help with their hunting, fishing, war-making, trading and health. In fact, she found that the Indian guardian spirits could help with almost anything. The Indians have a faith, a faith that is not unlike the one enjoyed by Christians. They believe that some spirit, something they can't see or touch, controls what happens in their lives and takes care of them in the hereafter, thought Roxanne.

John de la Roche stopped on the Lower Columbia River to watch the trading of people, furs, food and artifacts. A Haida Indian Chief purchased a graceful, fawn-like, girl for his concubine. The transaction suggested a thought to John. Could he buy, or better yet, steal slave girls for employment as sporting ladies in Canada? On one of his future trips he purchased two young girls for his purpose. One ran away and the other died at the hands of a drunken miner. His plot was spoiled. He never tried again. Failure was something he could not tolerate. There were others who used slave girls for prostitution successfully. There were also others who invested in a variety of ventures that John had not tried. He was prepared for the risks of trying something new but he was not able to accept failure. If cheated he would kill the cheat but once beaten in a business venture, John would quit trying to make a go of that activity.

John knew that the early fur trappers and traders employed by Pacific Fur and the Hudson Bay companies followed the route taken by the Lewis and Clark exploratory party into the area in the early 1800s. While in Dalles, a small town at the terminus of the Oregon Trail, John was eavesdropping while having lunch with Roxanne. He heard someone seated at a nearby table say, "The first settlers led by Nathaniel Wyeth came down the Columbia River

Gorge in '32. Larger groups followed in the '40s creating what some have called the Great Migration. Folks come from all over the country. They came with hope! Hope's what propelled them. They came in response to stories about rich, bountiful lands and gold. I believe that most folks came for the gold. Gold gets under a man's skin, makes it itch."

John knew some gold had been found in this part of Oregon but that was not the engine that was driving the communities of Fort Vancouver and Portland. These two settlements were booming vibrant communities supported by salmon canning facilities, sawmills and docks for fishing and shipping. Furs, grain, lumber, apples, canned fish and other produce went south, out of the docks on all types of ships. The land, the rich, wet soil and the long summer days, those were the things that made this part of the northwest successful, thought John, who saw many opportunities being exploited in the Columbia River terrain, business systems that could be transported to his empire in Canada. He would consider them and use what he had learned to gain an advantage in his part of the world.

Upon their return from the honeymoon John studied the sketch he had made of the de la Roche saw mill including a bunkhouse, cook house, dining room, office, file shack, meat house, stables and blacksmith shop. Some day soon he would build it at a key site in the Canadian gold fields. He needed to select the best possible location and buy the land. The equipment he had ordered in Seattle would soon be on the way.

John and Roxanne now found almost everyone in Lytton was talking about the big gold strike on the Quesnelle and the skeletons of two persons found in a nearby location. The Mounties said that the dead men were probably Peter Quinn and John Riley, prospectors, who had gone to Cedar Point in the spring of 1858. They were found near the Caribou River some ten miles from the place where other prospectors were now panning. A bullet from a carbine was lodged in the bones of one of the skeletons, a matter of concern for the Mounties. A man named Pierre had indicated that Quinn and Riley were very experienced, skilled miners, men unlikely to miss an obvious gold play along the shoreline of the Quesnelle, a river that they had planned to explore.

Shaken by the story, John de la Roche began to dream. The spirits of those he had killed, returning spirits, filled his nightmares. In part of the dream blue eyes seemed to fill a round face. It was a face that was partially covered by long, blond hair and a blond beard. And in another part of the repose, the gray eyes gleamed from inside the freckled face of the second Irishman. The eyes! They were the central elements in his dreams! Eyes that were staring directly at him! Eyes that had seen him kill, seen him plunder, held his secrets. Were they capable of revealing his sins? His conscious mind sealed out the thoughts of exposure, captivity on earth and hell in the hereafter, but his subconscious would not. The dead men's glossy eyes were always there, watching him in his dreams. The eyes were full of outrage and astonishment and they regularly reminded him that man's reason knew death was inevitable while his animalistic instincts anticipated immortality.

The godless animal that occupied the conscious part of John de la Roche's mind could not deal with the hereafter or tolerate worldly failure. While fear grew in his soul and his intellect screamed, "Sell out, run," his animality shouted, "Keep your gold, wealth and power." His internal struggle between fear and greed, being decided, by the degree to which the animal in him felt invincible. John elected to stay; he had known fear before. He had seen men try to run from the grizzly only to be brought down by the bigger, quicker predator. Running makes one the hunted. His intellect suggested that the recent gold strikes would draw thousands of prospectors who would be accompanied by many scoundrels, con men, claim jumpers, bandits and swindlers. The Mounties will have their hands full with current crimes, and they are spread very thin.

No one saw me kill the prospectors and no one knows where my gold came from, he thought. Leaving the bullet behind in the body was a mistake, but almost everyone has a Carbine. I am a legitimate businessman, important to the community, married, settled down. Why should they bother me? His conscious decision did not end the nightmares which often included a Mounty on the doorstep, outrage in his eyes. His nightly mental struggle drained his strength, deep-set his eyes and darkened his life but the Mounty did not come. His conscious mind accepted the risk of disclosure but it rejected thoughts about the hereafter. His subconscious had questions and was struggling with both risk and God. His id asked, "Would the risk prove too great; would he be captured, or did God have another fate in mind for de la Roche?"

His enterprises grew and prospered until the nearby gold began to play out. By that time John was well propertied. He had sawmills, timber, other lands, interests in diversified enterprises, stocks in growing companies and bonds offered by strong firms and stable governments. He had come a long way since the spring of 1858. Invincible, he thought, really invincible. That's how John still felt when he first heard about a remote settlement in California. A place called Bodie, and something else, something new, a huge vein of pure gold that folks called, *Veda Madre.*

11

APACHES ARE A STRANGE LOT, thought Tex, as he rode west following the general course of the Gila River. Tribe members are expected to follow certain rules, rules and traditions. They are told, no actually called upon to share, to be unselfish, to work for the good of their tribe. Red-skins aren't supposed to hanker for the things most folks want like treasure, fancy places to live, things like that. They wallow in tribal tradition, fear the spirits and respect those in their roundup. It's important for them to be accepted, liked and respected by their fellow Indians. They have pride in their deeds but don't cotton to change and they don't give a frig about what outsiders say. In fact, they chide those who are different. Indians believe it's fittin' to take what's needed from the land or others by raiding outside their tribe. They burn, plunder and take slaves. They must be brave in battle, and raise their children to be like their elders.

Red Hand had told him these things about Chiricahua ways, teachings that gave birth to new questions in his young mind. Issues and questions that Tex had heard discussed by politicians when they were seeking votes. Did the Indian ways make for strong family units, closeness, cooperation, harmony and strength? Or was the Senator he heard speak in Houston right when he said, "Their social structure hosts the seeds for academic, economic and cultural constipation." Was their education too narrow, too backward aimed? Jaime Cortina didn't think much of their ways? He said they couldn't read. Many Indians had fought long and hard. Some tribes had disappeared while others carried on even though they were giving ground. Most Indians were like cattle on a long drive. They tended to take the same place in the herd of life every day. They were unable to change the course that was taking them to the slaughterhouse. Was it their breeding, their limited education, their red skins or just their lack of numbers, that was causing them to be split wide open."

His father and the politicians knew the answers to all these questions. Most folks from his father's generation also knew the right answers, or thought they did. They believed the Indians were a problem and that most everything they did was wrong. Many felt that the right solution was extermination, the same solution they favored for grizzly bears, rattlesnakes and wolves. Most other white folks wanted the Indians kept on reservations, far away, where there was no gold and the land was poor. Five years ago, Tex would have agreed but now he wasn't so sure. He knew enough about the Apache Culture to recognize that these were vexing questions—questions with no clear answers.

The mind of a young Texas cowboy was at work trying to sort out the issues of right and wrong. He had been engaged in battle with the Apaches and been victorious in a contest that could impact the Indian lifestyle for many future years. He had been asked to stay on and to help wipe out the Indians and was glad that he had declined.

Tex and Moonshine made their way west along the trail, leaving the Apaches behind. Using the same trail as the now defunct Butterfield Stage, they entered the land of the Yuma Indians, a place called Yuma Valley made prosperous by the waters from the Colorado River.

On the far side of Yuma he ran into sand, real sand, like that he had slept on at the beach on the Gulf of Mexico, South of Houston. The old stage trail cut to the south, going into Mexico to avoid the sand. There were several miles of rolling sand hills followed by what appeared to be an old dry lakebed devoid of most vegetation.

The intensity of the desert inferno was impossible to appreciate without firsthand experience. The rippled strata of the heat waves could be seen shimmering in the distance, beckoning a traveler to the scorched landscaped below. Searing, lip-parching winds came up almost every afternoon, sucking the moisture from Tex and Moonshine. No soft cowboy songs came from cracked lips that were caked with, dry, white, salt-like deposits. Little twisters, baby tornadoes, hopped across the landscape producing sandy, cone-shaped swirls that bent the chaparral and punched the loose tumbleweeds. And the signs of death, broken wagons, animal skeletons, an occasional cross, were scattered along the road.

Each morning the sun was up early, it's blazing energy pressing down on Tex and Moonshine. It seemed to Tex that the days were unusually long. Red Hand, the Apache Scout, had told him that the sun's moccasin strings are made rotten by the winter rains causing him to slow as he stoops to mend them during summer. Late in the year, the sun got new strings, made of Yucca fiber, permitting him to move faster, shortening the days of winter. Tex didn't believe the Indian myth but somehow he hoped the hot white ball would move faster, even get new moccasin strings if that was necessary. Tex wished for an Apache *di-yin*, a medicine man, an Indian who comprehended the form of things that create changes in the weather. The *di-yin* might have the power to bring rain but Tex had been at war with the Apaches so they would be unlikely helpers. Besides, he was too far west for Apaches. If he wanted to use Indian myths to bring water he could kill a rattlesnake, turn it belly up and hope for a storm. However, south of the salt sea, in this desert, making rain in mid-summer takes more than the underside of a reptile. And anyway, he thought, he was too far west for Apache medicine to be working.

Tex found water at Cook's Wells and Alamo Mocho. He climbed out of the valley and continued west by north, stopping at various way stations including Indian Wells near El Centro, old Carrizo and Vallecito before he took the Wells Fargo Express trail fork at Warner's Ranch and Trading Post. The road led over the mountains via In-ko-pah, Tecate Divide and Cameron Station to San Diego. The trip up the east face of the rock strewn, barren mountainside was steep. Tex had to stop frequently to rest Moonshine and reposition her saddle because, as they went up, it tended to slip too far back on the horse's hindquarter.

The wind was strong, gusty and sometimes full of choking dirt and sand. Water was dear and the heat oppressive. The course was marked by many broken-down wagons, animal skeletons and gravesites, attesting to the difficulties others had experienced. Up and up they went. Over four thousand feet, thought Tex. As they approached the crest, the air became cooler but the wind did not abate. Green vegetation, grass and timber gradually replaced the barren landscape. By the time they reached the summit it was actually cool. Probably thirty degrees cooler, thought Tex. There was fresh, chilled water at the higher elevation which was savored by both Tex and Moonshine.

They continued, down slope, westward onto the dry, brown hills east of San Diego. The grass on the lower level hills was dry from the summer sun and lack of water, normal conditions for the area at this time of year. The sky was clear, blue, reaching out over the edge of the world to meet the equally blue vastness of the Pacific Ocean. Tex first saw it from the top of a rise. He was struck, awed, by the beauty of the great expanse of water, the bay and the settlement of San Diego. The town, with its colorful Spanish architecture framed by the grandeur of the sea, produced a magnificent picture, one that would remain in his mind for years. He felt the cool breath of the breeze created by the cold Pacific waters, a cold ocean giving birth to a chilly wind, so unlike the humid blows that grew out of the hot waters of the Gulf of Mexico or the dry, torrid, blistering gusts spawned by the desert sands to his rear.

He had supper in "Old Town" where he listened to the local residents talk to some other strangers about their city. He learned that the big, fort-like building he had seen from the hills when he rode in was called the Presidio. It was built in 1769 by Spanish soldiers and it housed California's first mission, *San Diego de Alcalá* that was founded by Father Junipero Serra. There was also a portion of the city called "New Town," which was laid out over one hundred years later near the wharf. New Town existed to support commerce moving over the sea. Tex felt more comfortable in Old Town, where the classic Hispanic character of the community and the Mexican food reminded him of his roots in South Texas where the Spanish influence was strong.

He slept on a white sandy beach, the waves pounding and receding with a rhythm that produced feelings of tranquillity, joy, security and harmony with the environment. Man, an animal that had, in the beginning, evolved from the sea—man returning to the place of his origin, to sleep, in concord with its majesty.

He then followed the old mission trail north, stopping at each ministry, San Luis Rey, San Juan Capistrano, San Gabriel, before reaching Los Angeles. The fertile river basin area was bustling with activity from agriculture and commerce; oranges were being grown and shipped via the Southern Pacific Railroad to San Francisco and then to the east coast. Water, mostly from the Los Angeles River, was being used to support the activities of over ten thousand people scattered about the large bowl-shaped area bounded by mountains on three sides and the Pacific Ocean on the fourth.

The fertile ground, warm sun and long summers were ideal for crops. They grew in abundance wherever sufficient fresh water was available. But a smoke-like haze hung over the city. The brownish-gray cloud, caused mostly by man-made fires, was pushed by the prevailing westerly winds against the curvature of the mountains where it became trapped. As Tex passed through the haze his eyes became itchy, his lungs heavy, his nose stuffed, and he developed a rough cough. I wonder what they call this kind of air, he thought. Can't be too good for folks.

He continued north to the Mission San Fernando before turning northeast in Placerita Canyon, site of one of California's first gold finds. The canyon would lead him over the mountains and down to the western edge of the Mojave Desert. He rode over the top with a powerful wind beating on his back, thinking to himself, what a place for a windmill. He could see the shimmering ripples of the heat waves rising from the valley floor, a wasteland with character but little life. His vision told him it was hot down below and his body began to experience the torrid reality of one of the world's worst summer climates. He rode into Willow Springs, then past the Queen silver mine and on to the settlement of Mojave, a place where the temperature in the shade was often over 110 degrees F; a desert area that had been known to reach up to 130 degrees.

Vegetation was mostly mesquite, sage, cactus, desert holly and pickle-weed, and animal life was measured in terms of small creatures, coyote, fox, kangaroo rat, lizard and rattlesnake. The leaves on the desert plants were all small, designed by nature to minimize evaporation of what little moisture they held. I'm back, thought Tex. Back in the desert. Back in country like that west of Yuma. Back with the searing winds and little tornadoes.

He pressed on to the northeast through Red Rock Canyon where he got his first closelook at the old lava flows which had formed pillars, dark six-sided, post pole-like columns, standing together. Each pillar was much taller than a man; some were broken, most were assembled massively together. The lava itself was nearly all black but the iron and other minerals it had given up to erosion helped create the reddish ground color. Red Rock Canyon, that's what they called it and for good reason. He followed the small creek that ran along the canyon floor, moved up through Walker Pass and continued north past cinder cones and other volcanic debris. He was in a landscape that had been molded by the powerful hands of nature, hands that had worked overtime for hundreds of millions of years. Tex didn't recognize the lava or know what a cinder cone was but he could sense the power and see the products of nature's work.

He camped near a large salt lake with no outlet before following the Ownes River up the valley to Lone Pine. It was a high desert valley over five thousand feet above sea level flanked by the fourteen thousand foot Sierra Nevada Mountains on the west and the twelve thousand foot Inyo's on the east. The mountains gathered water running off the slopes, funneling it into a winding river that terminated in a saline lake named for the early explorer, Richard Owens.

The granite cliffs of Mount Whitney, the highest peak in North America outside of Alaska, looked down on the small community of Lone Pine where Tex found lonely people who were more than willing to talk about their community.

"The countryside 'round here's a mess," said the town's mayor and saloon owner. "The geologists say it's a hodge-podge of faults—you know—cracks in the earth that were made by earthquakes. And hills made from jumbled rocks left behind when the glaciers melted are called moraines. And strange looking rocks, hard black pillars that grew from the hot molten lava that came out from underground. There's lots of quartz rock and some strange looking glass-like stuff called obsidian. And, there're some light stones that are full of holes. They look sort of like moldy Swiss cheese. None of the stuff the geologists talk about means much to us regular folks except for the gold and the earthquakes. Some of the quartz rock is laced with gold. Many years ago it squeezed its way up along fault lines as a thick liquid and then hardened when it reached our cool mountain air. We dig it out, crush it up and get the gold. It makes my blood boil just to think about that grand yellow metal. Earthquakes are a problem if you are near where one is centered. We got hit, struck eight years ago by a monster earthquake that moved the west side of the ground upward at least thirteen feet and northward roughly twenty feet."

Folks elected to office and preachers, boy how they like to talk, tell tall tales, and use big words, Tex thought.

The mayor went on talking endlessly about the huge earthquake and the gold finds in the area but it was not until Tex ran into Ray Keats that he developed real respect for the quake.

The part-time blacksmith and full-time minister, Ray Keats, told Tex all about the huge shock which killed ten percent of the local population and brought down all the buildings in the community except for a few wooden shacks. The quake was felt for hundreds of miles in all directions. Working very late Keats, a large, strong man, had been thrown to the ground. His left arm was still scared, burned by coals from his forge. He spoke with the bravado of a minister, saying, "A dead calm came over the countryside just before the shaking started. It was as though the animals, birds, trees and plants were holding their breaths, collectively, afraid to be found by the impending onslaught, like a human might hunker-down in quiet trepidation, lungs frozen when threatened. God must have provided her creatures with a sense of approaching danger. It started with a low moaning rumble and a shaking of the earth, followed by a huge, deep, powerful, guttural roar, accompanied by a sharp, violent movement so strong that one could not stand. And the sounds, coming from the bowels of the earth were like tones from the low notes on a piano. The noise could have been mistaken for the cries of the angry dead, calling from their wooden, buried caskets. The ground continued to wrench, jerk and growl for a long time, the big jolt being followed by others throughout the night and into the next day. In fact, the local world continued to shutter, creak and grumble, moving periodically for over a month, as its parts below adjusted themselves to their new, temporarily less stressful, condition."

There was a mixture of drama and fear in his voice as he continued. "According to the geologists it could happen again—anytime, around these parts. Before you leave you can stop and see the common grave, and if you're not afraid you can follow along the fault scarp for a piece. Fault scarp, you know what I mean, the area where the earth ripped apart–split–was sheared. The ground slid up and to the north, twenty, maybe thirty feet. You can see it clear as day. Ride along its course for a piece, if you like."

"Reckon you knowed how to give a man a powerful hankerin', said Tex." I'd sooner wet my whistle for now but when I drift north at first light I'll be havin' a look." And that's–that's the God's truth."

"Good," said the minister. "Ride with God on your saddle horn."

It was easy to find the places where the ground had moved. There was a sharp rise with jumbled rocks and the land had a fractured, broken appearance. My god, the power of it, thought Tex. What monster forces were at work under the ground 'round here? He didn't know it but many of the scrapes and slashes on the earth's surface that were obvious immediately after the earthquake had been covered up or obliterated by new growth and erosion. Nevertheless, Tex was able to follow the scarp for a distance before he decided to rejoin the trail north.

He was excited, nearing his goal. Bodie was not far now. He pushed Moonshine along the track through the small settlements of Camp Carlos, Camp Independence and Bishop. The trail was very rough, often steep, and the countryside was spotted with cottonwood, *Piñon* pine, live and black oak, Jeffery pine and white fur trees. It was nothing like the land in his native Texas.

Shortly after leaving Bishop, the trail went upwards into a set of tall, rugged, tree covered mountains that still had patches of snow left over from the prior winter. He reached the top and started down, down into the Mono Valley. It was a foreboding sight, complete with saline lake, mostly barren, jagged landscape and harsh, cratered countryside. The valley was alive with signs that nature had given much of herself to this place but scattered hot springs, recent fault and volcanic activity suggested she wasn't finished. Placer gold had been found in Lee Vining Creek and a small town had grown up there. Mines were operating around nearby settlements in Monoville and Lundy. He turned northeast, following the trail on the north side of Mono Lake through Cottonwood Canyon to Bodie, a trip of roughly fifteen miles from Lee Vining.

His ride revealed nothing of the mysteries that lay in store for him on the Cottonwood Canyon Trail in the future.

Tex was staggered by the size of the Bodie community, the number of people already there, and the diversity of structures, buildings and businesses. Set in a barren, desolate looking, treeless, high-mountain valley, the town was laid out in the lower, flatter terrain, in all directions. The surrounding hills and mountains were spotted with mines, slag piles, mills, flumes, equipment and other buildings Tex could not identify. He could see some tree stumps and he assumed that the timber had been cut to build up the town. The downtown streets of the settlement reminded him of the cattle towns along the Chisholm Trail: saloons, dance halls, hotels, rooming houses, markets, stables, even a brewery, all packed together. Main Street looked like Abilene, Kansas, Tex thought to himself as he rode about to get a feel for his new hometown. He could hear the noise—bang, bang, bang, bang, bang—coming from the mountains but he did not recognize its origin.

King Street was obviously different. My God, he thought. What kind of settlement is this?

A Chinese colony with dried fish, ducks, chickens and dressed hogs hung up in shop windows. Short, squat, dark haired, pig-tailed people were bustling about with their wooden soled shoes clattering on Bodie's board-walks. Some of their shoulders were bent by the weight of goods carried on the ends of long poles. Many wore straw hats some covered their heads with silk bonnets. There were large lodging houses, wash houses, opium-dens, gambling halls and outdoor peddlers hawking vegetables and other goods from stands and racks. It smells, thought Tex. It was a strange, different odor, unique to China Towns worldwide.

On the ride he located a post office, a telegraph, barber shops, bakeries, churches, banks, a land office, blacksmiths, an assayers office, union hall, fire stations, a stage office, newspapers including the Bodie Standard, Free Press and News, an Odd Fellows hall and businesses of all kinds. He counted over fifty saloons attesting to the value of alcohol in the souls of the adventurous.

He reined up at the Tuolumne Stable on North Main Street asking, "Where does a man go 'round here to hunt gold?"

The old codger at the stable groused, "Anybody knows that—likely be there—not likely be tellin'."

"Come all the way from Houston—big town in Texas—to find the stuff. Won't likely leave 'til I do," said Tex.

"Most come from way off. I come all the way from hell myself—still there too. Found first color here in 'fifty-nine. Folks been pannin', rockin', chippin', and diggin', ever since. Miners—crazy bastards—do all kind-a stupid things. Why just last winter Robinson and Anderson blew themselves to hell while tryin' to thaw their frozen blastin' powder in their wood heated oven. Blastin' powder—in the hot stove. Can you 'magine? Ain't much left of them or the cabin. Some ten thousand of them dumb bastards is here now, lots of rabble, greasers, chinks and scum. Prospectors, the real seekers, mostly moved on to fresh diggins. That's the way it always is. The prospectors come first. If they spot color, others follow—miners, whores, gamblers, outlaws, bobtails—all kinds of raff. The followers, smart business folks like me, end up with mosta' the gold. Prospectin' 'round here's 'bout over. Deep mines, that's where the work is now. Won't last much longer. Mine stocks be fallin', fallin' soon, you see," the old fellow said.

"You want a job down under, go up to Standard. I heared their hirin'. Ever done work down under?" he asked.

"Reckon not," said Tex.

"You got a lot to learn son. Hope you come with plenty time and money. It ain't easy findin' or minin' gold. Don't rightly know how you're gonna make it 'round here."

Tex thanked the codger, who's name was Nick Boule, proprietor of the stable, and took directions to the Standard Mill located just at the base of Bodie Bluff. He was craving to see, touch and hold gold. He yearned to feel the soft yellow metal in hands. It was, after all, the thing that had drawn him to this place.

Riding up to the mill he got his first close look at the tramway, a cable hung about twenty feet above the ground. It ran from the mill up the mountain about a half-mile to the mine. The cable was held up by towers, tall structures, each separated from the other by about fifty yards. There were rectangular buckets hung to the underside of the cable that carried rocks down from the mine dumping them out at the mill. The cable was a continuous loop, like a rubber band, which circled the empty boxes back to the mine. At the mill, Tex learned that the continuous conveyor was able to deliver forty-five tons of ore in eight hours. The tramway had been designed and engineered by A.S. Hallidie. He was the same gent that designed the San Francisco cable car system.

Steam engines provided the power to move the cable on its drive wheels. The steam was generated from water, heated in two huge boilers about three times taller than Tex with diameters about equal to his height. There was an engine with the power of one hundred and twenty-five horses. It had a huge flywheel that looked as if it weighed more than one hundred men and was taller than the boilers. The stone and cement foundation for the engine and flywheel was six foot in depth, attesting to their great weight. BANG! BANG! BANG! BANG! BANG! The noise was louder up here and the earth seemed to shutter with each blow.

A lady named Janet Arlett who worked in the Mill administration office gave Tex a paper to fill out. It was sort of an employment application. He wrote down his name and prior work experience and answered questions about his honesty, jail record, parents, sex, color, race, age and religion. She suggested that Tex go to the Bodie Tunnel the next morning and she made arrangements for him to go into the mine with an engineer who would be inspecting the tunnel. Tex hadn't actually asked for a job. Janet just assumed he was there to apply and her sweet smile, soft green eyes, golden hair and round, ample bosom made it easy for Tex to cooperate. He didn't think he wanted to work for someone else. His own mine was locked in his dreams but he knew there was much to learn so he figured that a few days mining would be a wise investment.

Tex took a bed in town at the Stewart House on North Main Street where board was eight dollars per week and meals were served at all hours. He drank at the bar and listened to miners talk before turning in. It was late but he had difficulty sleeping, suffering from apprehension, a crawly feeling, in anticipation of his journey deep underground. He had heard stories about cave-ins, fires, explosions, poison gas and accidents in mines and his Bodie goals did not include termination of his young lifecycle in a dark black hole.

He dreamed of Vulva Woman, a beautiful Chiricahua. Red Hand had told Tex the story about Vulva Woman, the mythical lady that had a vagina that was full of teeth. Stories about her were useful in helping to control promiscuous youthful sex. In his slumber, he visualized Coyote feeding a stick into her orifice and having it chopped up. He could sense a cave-in. Timber cracking and breaking up under the weight of the earth. A confused reverie about holes, dark dangerous passages, underground and elsewhere.

Tex was up early, riding to the mouth of the Bodie Tunnel below the bluff north of town where he met John Von Ludwig, the engineer from Standard who had been invited to check out the deep vein material now being encountered in the Bodie mine. John and the other people at Standard had experience with the quartz rock that was very hard near the surface but could be dug out with a shovel at depth and the Bodie Tunnel staff wanted advice.

They entered the huge hole in the ground, heavily timbered on the sides and top, wearing miners hard hats. Von Ludwig was doing the "Miners Walk," and Tex copied his movements. The walk is a stooped shuffle used by men working below ground as they attempt to avoid bashed heads. Out of habit it tends to be used even in places where people can stand erect.

There were two parallel sets of narrow gauge railroad-like tracks on the floor of the tunnel over which trolley carts, carrying ore, muck and supplies, were pulled by men and mules. At the bar last night he heard the story of a runaway mule. His thoughts drifted back to that tale. The mule had been frightened in the Standard/Bulwer Tunnel. It had broken into a gallop, pulling the heavy cart behind, crashing against the sides of the Tunnel and crushing a miner along the way. The mule slipped and fell and the cart ran over the body. Two dead, one a man and the other an animal. Tex wished he hadn't heard that story, particularly now that he was making his first trip into a mine.

The tunnel, some three thousand feet long, sloped slightly upward so heavy loads could be moved downhill and the underground water would drain naturally. Tex thought he could feel the weight of the huge mountain overhead pressing down on him, gaining power over his spirit as the outside light faded, giving way to the glow from lanterns. Von Ludwig explained, "There's the first drift, a crosscut shaft following the first vein cut by the tunnel, one of twenty-one loads we will hit ranging from a few inches to twelve feet thick before we reach the end of tunnel."

"Are you sayin' this tunnel's just dug up into the mountain in a straight line and it happens to bump into twenty-one underground gold-filled bunches of rock?" asked Tex.

"Yes, that's the idea. We call the rock arrangements formations. Geological work on the surface located some of them and scientists know roughly how they wind their way down. The miners cut the tunnel into the mountain and feel fairly certain about hitting the gold-bearing formations as they dig up," answered John.

Unfamiliar sounds accompanied them on their walk through the flickering light of the gallery-like shaft. Next they encountered a vertical pipe and Tex twisted his head around so he could look up. "What's that?" he asked.

"It's an air-shaft to the surface. We call it a winze," John answered. They found more drifts and winzes as they trudged deeper into the earth. Miners were seen taking ore from the open sides of the crosscuts, loading the trolley cars, and picking, digging. Wooden beams and planks were being set in place to shore the top and sides of the drifts; muck and slush filled the floor. John handed Tex a whitish, speckled rock about the size of his fist. "Quartz rock," he said, "Contains some gold and silver; it goes to the mill for crushing, washing and processing to recover the minerals."

Tex looked at the rock, thinking. Have any of the miners tried to take some of these rocks out in a pocket or boot? He didn't ask Von Ludwig because he was afraid that the question would mark him as a potential thief. In fact he was, for deep in his soul he yearned to take a little quartz rock home.

They stayed in the mine all day breathing the thick, sometimes choking air. The foul atmosphere did not seem to bother anyone but Tex. It made him think about another story from the bar. The housing works at the Goodshaw Shaft caught fire. The hot flames sucked up all the available air. Four miners died.

A big miner, with arms like the blacksmith's in Lone Pine, reminded him of the earthquake. What happens if the earth takes a notion to jump about while we are down? thought Tex. When he thought about such things, fear grew in his heart and he realized that a man who permitted himself to dwell incessantly on the dark-side of things could be caught in their net, paralyzed into inactivity, giving up his strength, his will. That wasn't going to happen to Tex Garland, not today, not ever. He would show the miners, Von Ludwig, Janet, all of them, that a hole in the ground could not sap his energy. You are what you think about, thought Tex. I will think about finding gold, keep my mind on exciting ideas, block out the dark-side. No one would ever know that he had been just a little bit scared.

The miners were pleasant to him. One, with the wire-like body of a cowboy and a pick that looked like it was too large for him to swing, introduced himself as Ben Ablard. He said, "Have a sandwich, kid. Marilyn always makes too much fer me."

"Thanks. Thanks a lot. But I'm not hungry," said Tex, who was too embarrassed to accept a handout.

"Ah come on kid. You can eat this. Don't like to throw food out and Marilyn will kill me if I brings it back. She's always bitchin' that I am too skinny. You'll be helpin' me out."

Ben's words put a new spin on the offer and Tex was glad to be able to accept. He had not thought to bring something to eat. Two of the other miners offered to share parts of their lunches but Tex refused. He had never taken charity and he couldn't bring himself to do it now, particularly because the miners would not let him help with the digging. Tex couldn't understand why they wouldn't let him use their tools until Ben said, "It's ain't you, kid. It's the union. Miners got union rules. No one digs lessen their in the club. You can figure that can't you, kid? Cowboys got unions too, don't they?"

"Nah," said Tex. "Cowpokes ride alone."

He heard an unseen voice shout, "Fire in the hole." Tex watched those around him duck down, then heard the noise, felt the shock wave, and then the dust came billowing out from ahead. They were using dynamite to lengthen the tunnel. The thick cloud reminded him of riding drag on the Chisholm and he wished he had a bandana.

John Von Ludwig looked at the soft, quartz vein located in the deepest drafts and conferred with the Bodie Tunnel engineers. Miners were using picks and shovels to get the ore out but there was more than the usual amount of water to deal with and shoring was difficult because the soft rock tended to cave in, making the miners cautious. Time was being lost because miners didn't want to work out from beyond the timbered shelter. John was showing the engineers and miners how to shore and timber as they advanced, affording themselves maximum protection. He was speaking forcefully, his German heritage demanding obedience. They were nodding, responding to John's leadership; some were regaining the will to continue.

Tex heard the whistle, the signal that it was time for this shift to depart. He watched the miners secure their equipment and start to trudge and slosh out over the muddy floor. They were tired, dirty and ready to leave. Although Tex had done no real work, he felt exhausted. Anxiety, concern about the weight and power of the mountain, had sapped some of his energy. As they progressed he began to see the light at the tunnel's mouth. It was faint at first, but growing steadily, a glow of hope. A sign that he would soon be bathed in the friendly colors of the sunlight.

Glad to be out, happy to see the sunset, Tex rode back to town with Von Ludwig who rambled on about mines and experiences. "The Bodie Tunnel slopes up but there are other vertical shafts going straight down. The Lent mine is one of those. At Lent they use heavy equipment to bring ore, muck and debris out and lower pumps, pipes and timber. They also pass people in and out in cages."

In cages, thought Tex. I don't think I would cotton to being hauled up and down in a basket.

Von Ludwig rambled on. "In July of '79 Mr. Shay, the hoisting engineer at the vertical Summit shaft had four men down two hundred feet in a cage when a blast of air hit him. He pushed the foot brake, stopping the cage just before the hoisting engine and its housing disappeared, blown up by a huge explosion at Standard. The brake saved the men from a hundred-foot fall. Scared the hell out of all the miners working everywhere around Bodie Mountain. They all crawled out of their holes like ants. They say that ten people died because of the blast. Most of them went right away but at least two lasted a time before they died of their injuries. The biggest problem is that no one knows what caused the blast. Folks talk about it all the time around campfires and in saloons. Some people think it was witchcraft. Was the explosion man made, a work of nature, something else? No one has ever found out."

Strange, thought Tex. Had the mountain been violated, and was it taking revenge? An Indian might think so, or was something else going on around these parts.

Von Ludwig continued. "There're some inclined shafts cut at a downward angle into the mountains following the dip of the vein. In these shafts the miners stay with the ore all the way down. You know, they just follow the formation that contains the gold. It's very efficient because all the rocks coming out can be sent to the mill for processing. It's also very complex because the dip of the load changes as you go down making extraction hard. Engineers drive verticals down to intercept inclined shafts. The vertical tunnels provide air and permit the lowering and raising of hoisting cages and pumps.

Simple inclined and vertical mine shafts are also used by individual miners at their shallow diggings. They build a frame over the shaft to hold a windless, windless you know, its a roller with a crank handle and ratchet wheel. The ore bucket and tools are hand cranked up and down in the same way one uses a water bucket at a well. The miner uses a ladder. Often two miners work together in these shallow diggings."

"Do things ever fall down the holes?" asked Tex.

"Oh, hell yes!" answered John. "Lots of miners working at the bottom of vertical shafts have been smacked by boards, buckets, lunch pails, rocks and tools. Killed a few of them but miners are determined. They keep climbing down into their holes looking for the big strike. Hope. That's what drives 'em. Guess everyone needs something to hope for.

"Deeper mines, down as much as three hundred feet, often use a whim which is a rotating drum that winds up a hoisting rope to raise and lower the bucket. One, sometimes two horses, walking in a circle, are employed to rotate the whim. Operating this equipment requires someone on the surface to handle the animals and control the clutch and brake."

Tex couldn't imagine Moonshine walking in a circle day after day.

What a terrible way to treat a horse, he thought.

"The deepest inclined and vertical mines require more sophisticated power systems such as steam driven engines to lift the heavy iron buckets known as Cornish Kibbles. Big frames called gallows are constructed over the holes permitting the Cornish Kibbles, full of ore, to be lifted well clear of the mine mouth without having to be manhandled. This kind of mining is very expensive and requires large investments," said Von Ludwig.

"What's it like, ridin' in and out of a mine in an iron bucket?" asked Tex.

"Riding is easy enough but it can be dangerous. A number of miners have fallen out of the buckets and been killed. They probably encountered a pocket of poisonous gas on the trip and panicked, falling or jumping out. A few buckets have also broken free and tumbled to the bottom.

"In some of the deep holes there's so much water Cornish pumps are used to suck the fluid out. A sump lift pump is put at the bottom with a series of several force pumps placed above. Such a system is capable of bringing fifty, maybe sixty thousand gallons of water to the surface every hour," said John.

"One more thing, Tex. The mine owners must take care of their ore and even better care of their finished gold. Gold does something to the spirit of man. It creates a privation—a starving for the color—a kind of madness, really. Honest folks become thieves, high grading they call it because high grading sounds better than stealing. Most everyone will take a little ore or a nugget if they get the chance. I pinched a few samples when I was younger.

"That's enough about mines for today. Tomorrow we can talk about how we process the ore," Von Ludwig concluded as they reached town.

Tex rode out to the Standard Mill the next morning to continue his education. John Von Ludwig was there to help.

"We've been talking about getting the ore out but that's just the beginning of the process of capturing the gold. The rocks must be moved in some fashion to the mill where first the big one's are broken up, often manually, with a heavy hammer. The guys who bash the rock usually aren't too smart, mostly Niggers, Swedes, Irishmen, folks like them. The medium sized rocks are then reduced in size by rock crushers of various types. The crushers are usually run by steam power. After being crushed, the crumbled material is then moved, by conveyor, to a battery box. Think of it as a big sandbox roughly ten feet square having three foot tall sides made of heavy iron. Each battery box has it's own set of stamps. A stamp is an eight hundred-pound cast iron hammerhead. The stamps are hung over the battery box on stems, long iron bars hung vertically. The stems attach to a rotating shaft. When it turns, the shaft raises and lowers the stems causing the hammerheads to mash down on the rock and then lift back up. The stamps, you know, the hammerheads only get about a foot above the battery box floor but because of their weight they make a huge amount of noise as they drop down, one at a time, in sequence. BANG! BANG! BANG! BANG! BANG!

The noise is earsplitting, the force ground shaking, death blows for the ore and birth-blows for the color of profit. Clean water is let in one end of the battery box. It pushes the crushed rock and slime out the other end. The Standard Mill has four battery boxes, twenty stamps, and four conveyors," said John Von Ludwig.

Tex had heard and felt the thumping since arriving in Bodie but he hadn't experienced the thunder up-close until now. He couldn't make out much of what John was saying over the din but John was so animated Tex could literally see what he was trying to communicate. It would be more fun, thought Tex, to watch folks make wine. Sloshing around in a tub full of grapes and squishing them with bare feet wouldn't be so noisy and dirty. They wouldn't get gold but wine could make one forget his passion for the yellow stuff.

The slime discharged from the battery boxes was carried in water troughs to one of two rows of ten settling tanks where the gold and other heavy material was permitted to settle to the bottom. The heavy stuff was then drawn off and put into tubs with gear driven central grinders where it was pulverized. Mercury, the heavy metal called quicksilver, was then introduced into the tub where it reacted chemically with the gold and silver forming an amalgam. "Amalgam, that means the gold and silver were joined chemically with the mercury," explained John. "It's heavy. When we wash it into settling pans, it falls quickly to the bottom. Next we take it to a furnace so that the three minerals, gold, silver and mercury, can be separated. The gold is then taken to a refractory where it is poured into bricks. It takes, on average, three million pounds of ore to get one thirty-five pound gold brick," said John.

My god, thought Tex, I'm glad I didn't ask if any of the miners ever tried to take a piece of quartz rock out in a boot. Wouldn't be hardly any gold in, just one piece.

"Where does the mercury come from?" asked Tex.

"Cinnabar, a type of rock called cinnabar," responded John. "It's mined in Almaden and New Iberiá."

There were numerous other processes going on to handle pulp and slime, recover clean water, manage the tailings, bring new water from the spring and handle the silver. In its totality, the milling operation was the most impressive undertaking Tex had ever seen. Mentally he weighed the value of his fourteen-inch pan against the enormous mine and mill activity he had witnessed realizing that fulfilling his dream would require more than he had reckoned for. Was Teresa right, he thought. Was his vision of Bodie gone?

The mine superintendent was with Janet when they returned to the administrative office. He offered Tex a job as a miner in the Standard Mine, an inclined underground tunnel system having great depth and complexity. It seemed obvious to Tex that Von Ludwig had recommended him so he thanked both John and the superintendent for the opportunity. He asked if it would be okay to take a day or two to think it over. They agreed that if he wanted to go to work, he should report the following Monday morning.

That night Tex stopped at Wagner's bit-house, at the intersection of Main and King Streets and asked the barkeep to point out people who might give him a look at a small mine. It was a big, busy place, with two hinged glass doors at the front, a large long bar on the left wall, a chop stand offering steak and chops on the right and gambling to the rear. People were playing faro and twenty-one, games of chance favored by miners as compared to the cowboy standard, poker. Someone was banging on a rinky-tink piano near a small stage.

He met two Irishmen, Jack Kennedy and Joe Gleeson, who had a small inclined shaft of their own. They downed a lot of sour mash they believed was "fine as silk" and chased it with pints of dark, heavy local beer. Each drink cost a bit, twelve and one half cents. "Bit-houses, that's what folks call these western taverns," said Jack.

Joe and Jack got red-faced but they kept going until after midnight. When Tex tried to get up and walk, the walls of the saloon began to spin and he learned why a mixture of beer and whiskey is known as tangle foot. He stumbled and might have fallen if Joe had not reached out and grabbed hold of his arm. Both Irishmen were laughing as they helped Tex back up onto his barstool. Still chuckling, Joe said, "Sure now, me thinks you've had a mite too much. We be sweatin' it out at the diggins on the morrow. Indeed we'd be happy to have you a joinin' us."

Tex had a tongue that was thick and fat, and his words came as slow as a tortoise in July. He drawled, "Been . . . itchin'. . . to . . . see . . . a . . . small . . . mine. I'll . . . be comin'."

The next morning, suffering from thirst and big heads, they met at the diggings on the side of a hill south of town. The hill was called Sugarloaf. Joe and Jack had opened an inclined shaft. They were digging down, following the dip of a skimpy quartz vein that was only about twenty inches thick and had mined down eighty feet. They took their ore to the Miners' Mill on Aurora Road four miles from Bodie. The Miners' Mill had been built to process material not controlled by the major mines. The "Big Guys" had their own mills. The Miners' Mill got its equipment from an old Silver City milling operation that had been shut down.

"The timber and other supplies we're usin' cost more than the ore brings," said Jack, "but the thick part's comin', comin' soon. The little people are showin' us the way."

The words of a prospector, thought Tex, searchers, driven by hope. Believing in themselves and luck. Convincing themselves that the next few shovels full of dirt will expose the mother-lode. Von Ludwig's words came back into his mind. Hope, that's what drives them. Everyone needs hope and every prospector has it.

Optimism and greed were the picks and shovels that drove the Irishmen deeper and deeper into the mountain. As they went down, their problems grew; ore and muck were hard to get out, water disposal was laborious without pumps and lines, the vein meandered requiring turns in the tunnel. The Irishmen were energetic diggers and Tex joined them at their work for the day. He sensed the futility of the effort but enjoyed their company and his first real chance to get his hands on gold.

They drank gallons of water, cooling the fires produced by alcohol, a hot summer sun and very dry air. Water was dear around Bodie; the mills used huge quantities and more was needed for people, livestock and commerce. There were few creeks in the area and they had limited flows during the summer. Springs were not plentiful. Fresh water cost a dollar a barrel and the Irishmen brought theirs to the diggings by wagon.

At the end of the long day, Tex went back to the Stewart House to ponder his situation. He had followed the dictates of a dream, traveled roughly two thousand miles on horseback, battled cougar and Indian and suffered many hardships to search for gold. It was here, but finding and mining it looked impossible, he thought, as the words of Robert Louis Stevenson came to mind, "It is better to travel in hope than arrive."

"Well, I have arrived probably twenty years late. What should I do?" he said, half out loud to himself. Give up, go home? No. No I can't do that. What would I tell my friends? What would Betty Jane Allen think of a man who rode all the way to California for gold and came back with nothin'. I will stay and figure things out. Make a future in one way or another. Nick Boule told me I had a lot to learn. Nick was right. Well, I can learn, I will! I must! It's ability that counts in the gold camps, ability and hard work. I can get experience and I can stand the work, he thought. It was his Texas pride that was reinforcing his spirit. Pride, a powerful force, when harnessed—particularly when hitched up in a yoke of greed.

It was Friday morning when Tex rode up to the Sandard Mill to tell Janet that he wanted to see the Standard Mine. The truth was he wanted to see her. They talked awhile and she gave him the name of the mine foreman. Tex wanted to ask her to supper Saturday night but couldn't get up the nerve. He left for the mouth of the Standard Mine feeling empty. When he arrived, the foreman was nowhere to be found; he was probably below, somewhere in one of the shafts. Tex waited around for a time and then went back down to the mill, and told Janet he had been unable to locate the foreman. She laughed and said. "If you want to find a miner, put on a hard hat and go down. If you want to find gold, get a shovel and start digging or get a pan and find a stream. If you want someone to smile, start with a grin of your own. Whatever you want, reach out for it, go get it."

Reach out. Go get! Don't be pussy-footin' 'round. If you want a date, ask, thought Tex.

"How 'bout supper Saturday?" he asked.

"Why, why thanks, Tex, sure that would be nice," Janet responded. "Come over to my house, meet my parents and have dinner there. We usually eat about six."

Tex had his best clothes scrubbed at the Chinese wash house, got a shave, haircut and bath at the barber shop, had the kid who hung around the stable polish his boots, saddle and silver bright work.

Janet's father, Paul Arlett, was a stern, bearded, old man with the rigid bearing of the military. He talked about his life in the early gold fields of the western Sierra Nevada. He made a strike on Carson Hill and found a nugget weighing over sixty pounds that brought sixteen thousand dollars. He grew his stake in Virginia City, later in Aurora, and now he owned two saloons, a hotel, part of the Standard Mill, and interests in other mines and businesses, all concentrated in Bodie. Tex had wondered how Janet, a woman, had got a job at the mill.

After all, ladies didn't make good workin' hands, he thought to himself. Important jobs were better done by men. Women get too flustered, they titter too much to figure things right. That's why they don't have the right to vote or own property in most places. Women have few rights, 'cause they don't deserve 'em. They wouldn't fight. Nice women don't go to saloons, or gamble or smoke. They're fun in bed on cold nights, good for tending children, and for washing, cooking and doing choirs, but the hard things, the real jobs, are done by men.

Now he understood how she got the mill assignment; her father owned the place. He also realized that she, rather than Von Ludwig, was responsible for his employment opportunity in the mine.

Janet's mother seemed pleasant enough, said little, nodded her blond hair and flashed her green eyes. Green eyes that her genes had passed on to Janet.

They had a fine supper, chicken, biscuits, green beans and apple pie for dessert. After eating Tex and Janet sat on the porch looking at the stars. Tex couldn't remember ever seeing them appear so clear and bright. We must be closer up here in the mountains, near enough to almost touch 'em. Are we close enough to be connected, united somehow, linked for communication with the spirits of space? he thought.

She broke his spell by asking, "How did you come to be in Bodie?"

"Came to find gold," Tex responded.

Janet smiled. "Everyone comes for gold; very few leave with much. Prospecting is a form of gambling; you place your bets and mostly lose."

"Your father won," said Tex.

"True, but Father is a rare bird, smarter than most, very frugal. So far he has done well but he could lose it all if Bodie goes down," said Janet.

"What do you mean by that?" he asked.

"Bodie's booming, so were all the other gold camps he's been to. They've all gone down. Some are ghost towns. The gold runs out and everyone leaves. It'll happen here, someday. Father says the Bodie formation is different. The veins on the west side of the ridge slope down at an angle, dip he calls it, the veins dip down underground toward the east while those out-cropping on the east side dip down to the west. Dad thinks the veins join together at depth forming what the Spanish folks call a *Veda Madre*, great mother vein.

"I have heard the so-called experts talk. Geologists, they call themselves. Some believe in *Veda Madre*, others don't. I think the underground is too jumbled in these parts for men to figure out. The ground around here has faults and lots of folds and twists, and there's been melting, exploding, quaking, eroding. It's chaotic under the earth, too much to figure or explain. No one knows what's down below in this country. Dad has all his assets invested here believing in *Veda Madre*, immortality for this community. The other camps had life cycles but not Bodie. At least, not in Father's view. He is sure, just like all the other prospectors and gamblers who are always positive they're going to strike it rich. That's the problem, when you are convinced that something is assured and you are wrong, that's when there's big trouble. Remember the song:

> Cold blue morning
> Game is done,
> Everybody's lost,
> Nobody's won.
> Light's dim out,
> Prospectors too.
> Town's dead,
> So are you."

Tex was thinking hard and he took a long look at Janet while she was talking. He knew women prattled more than men but he had no idea their words could be so weighty. She could be workin' with that newspaperman in Tucson. What was his name? Oh yes, Jaime Cortina. She speaks of things reserved to men. How could that be? Could my notion of the woman's place in society be wrong? Is it a product of my upbringin'? "Maybe," the Apaches often said "maybe" 'cause nothin' was certain, thought Tex. Another Omen? Teresa had said, "Bodie 'ill be gone time you get there." Well, it isn't gone yet, but two women he had recently met were predictin' its end. Females, people who aren't supposed to hold such deep thoughts.

Janet then asked Tex about his travels to Bodie and she listened with interest as he recanted the adventures with many of the people he had met: Roy Bean, Soapy Smith, Ben Thompson, Dallas Staudenmire, Benjamin Grierson, Jaime Cortina, Jacob Walzer and others. Tex described the Battle of Quitman Canyon, the attack by the puma, the fault scarp in Lone Pine and the crash of the ocean waves along the coast. Tex said, "There is a Satan in all men, one that gets us to believein' things that ain't true. He can be driven out by education. The Mexican newspaperman, Jaime, first said that to me and you just said the same things. Is your father listenin' to Satan."

"Could be," she responded.

"You ever thought 'bout workin' on a newspaper?"

Janet smiled. "Yes, I have, always wanted to write something important, something that would change things for the better. But it's a man's world today. You men don't pay much attention to what the ladies write, or for that matter, say; not yet you don't. But that will change. There'll be a lady President, a female Prime Minister some day. You'll see." With that she leaned over, gave Tex a quick kiss and said, "Next Saturday?" Then she went in.

On Monday Tex found himself four hundred and fifty feet down in the Standard Mine working a drift following a huge forty-foot vein that struck in a north/south direction and dipped to the west. It was a quartz-vein surrounded by clay and it was being worked by Tex along with other miners with picks and shovels. Different miners timbered or filled carts with ore for transport to the skip that would be hauled to the surface. Drills were employed to make holes in the rock that could be packed with explosives. The dynamite was used every few hours to break up the load. The pay was four dollars a day. The work was hard and dangerous.

Tex continued to stay at the Stewart House and saw Janet every Saturday night. On Sundays, weather permitting, he rode Moonshine into the hills and mountains looking for promising outcrops, placer deposits or other signs that might allow him to stake a claim. He was happy when with his girl or his horse, gloomy when underground, but content to be out of the freezing conditions which came with winter. Bleak, frozen, harsh conditions, possibly among the worst anywhere in the world, described winter around Bodie. The temperature fell, minus ten, minus twenty, even minus thirty degrees. And this was a mild winter in comparison to the prior year when woodpile thefts had been common.

For a person from Houston with thin blood, conditioned to the high temperatures and stifling humidity of the Gulf Coast, it was a long, very long nightmare. A Bodie zephyr struck in December, slapping snow and ice hard into the faces of anyone that ventured outside. The wind was so powerful it lifted the three-quarters finished Goodshaw Hoisting Works, a building ninety-five feet long, twenty-five feet wide and twenty feet tall, built with eight inch timbers, off its foundation without breaking a stick of wood.

One cold December night before Christmas, Tex felt lonesome and decided to ride out and pay a visit to Janet. He knew he would be welcome. He was right, when he arrived her long, golden hair was flowing down over her shoulders. Her smile was radiant, and her body seemed to be open and inviting. "Mom and Dad are in Bridgeport overnight," she said. "They went to a wake."

"Oh!" Tex responded. "Want to go to a saloon and wet your whistle?"

"If it's all the same to you, I'd rather not," she said. "Dad has too many friends about who might tell him I was out, acting improperly. You know how some people are, the ones that get pleasure from being tattle-tales. It's a pity that so many folks enjoy creating misery for others."

"Yeah, I know," he answered. "I'll fetch some wine and cheese if you like."

"Oh good. I'm starving," said Janet.

When he returned they sat on the couch, the only place in the room for two, and drank sweet red wine and ate cheese and crackers talking and enjoying each other's company. They were together a long time before Tex got up enough courage to lean over and give Janet a kiss, a soft gentle kiss, one that she returned. They held each other close, their hearts beating faster.

Tex experiencing the rapture of amour, not a new experience but somehow different. She was soft, sweet-smelling, tender. They extended the kiss, he stroked her long hair, rubbed her back, whispered softly in her ear. His left hand slid around in front lightly caressing her breast that was firm and willing. Slowly he opened her bodice and they leaned back on the sofa, legs dangling over its side. Still kissing, Tex fondled both breasts while they squirmed and twisted against each other before Janet said, "Stop, we can't do this; its going too far."

Tex had a hardness that was pressed against his Levis and he didn't want to end the trip they had started. He didn't want to force Janet but he didn't want to stop either. She eased him off, got her breasts back under the cover of her bodice, saying "Tex, I can't. I never have. It's not right for people who aren't married." She gave him that soft smile. It eased the tension without lowering his carnal craving.

"It's all right, I understand," said Tex, as he rolled himself over to the wine bottle for a long pull.

Stretching as she rose from the couch she said, "Thanks Tex, some day I hope we can finish the dance. It probably would be best if you went home now, please."

"Talk to you later," said Tex, as he sidestepped out the front door while trying to hide his hardness.

12

WHEN JUAN AND PEDRO OLIVERA reached Sonora, Juan said, "Bad city, this. No need slowdown 'round here. Once Sonora was our town, started by folks like us. The gold should'a been all ours. Gringos, *gringos*, drove us out! They called our kind for'ners and greasers. Charged us twenty dollars, twenty dollars every month. Called it tax, tax on us folks that talk Spanish. Chinese too, made everyone who wasn't English pay up. They tried to tax my farm in Santa Barbara but I took care'a that. The tax made big trouble 'round Sonora but mostly it was just us 'gainst them. They drove two thousand'a our kind out—usin' guns and threats. They done it for gold. Bad blood," Juan grumbled, "very bad blood boiled over one night when a bunch'a whites found three Indians and a Mexican burnin' two *gringo* bodies. Sheriff showed up, stepped in, saved the four from a necktiein'. Sheriff stopped the vigilantes that night, locked the Indians and our kind up in jail. After that the lawmen picked up every Spanish-speaking folk they found 'round these parts. Herded them, over one hundred of 'em, into a corral and set out guards. They held a trial and what d'you know? Them two *gringos* was dead when Indians found 'em. They stopped their prospectin' to build pyres. Can you 'magine? Pyres to burn white bodies so their sprits would go to the Happy Huntin' Ground. The Indians and Mexican was let go. But the *gringos* didn't get no more 'umble. The hunger for gold, the hunger in the hearts of them whites, that's what drove them. They would'a done the same to us in Santa Barbara if the prize had been gold 'stead of farm land."

On the way to Twain Harte, they stopped to drink from a small stream. The water was cool, refreshing, and after filling himself and his canteen Pedro rested against the side of a digger pine tree when Trigo started to bark. It was the frantic bark of a dog in combat. Jumping up, Pedro found him bobbing in battle with a large diamond-back rattlesnake coiled in a fallen tree stump. The snake's head was jerking in and out on its swivel neck with beady eyes and deadly fangs. Trigo had never seen a rattler but his sense of danger, natural instincts and quickness had thus far kept him out of harm's way.

Pedro froze, not knowing how to help but Juan arrived pitching stones at the snake as he came. Following his father's example, Pedro picked up a large boulder with both hands, heaving it much as one would launch a medicine ball. The big rock rose in the air and then fell almost straight down. Crunch-thump, a direct hit, lucky and effective. "Get clear," shouted Juan.

Pedro took his dog back to the tree looking around very carefully before taking a seat. Juan followed in a few minutes with the headless body of the snake in one hand and the rattles, twelve in all, in the other. "Make a fire. We'll have this fellow for lunch," Juan said, as Pedro's eyes became as large as miners pans and his stomach ill.

Eat rattlesnake, not me, he thought as the fire came up, but it wasn't long before the fragrant scent of the rich meat eased his fears and following his father's lead, he filled his belly. He had learned two things from the encounter: to pay attention when his elders warned him of danger, and that nature provided strange things that could be eaten.

When they reached Twain Harte, they sought out Emanuel, a distant cousin. Looking up relatives was an act consistent with the family traditions of Hispanics. Emanuel was working the tailings at The Old Thunderbolt Mine located north of town. Pedro had his first close look at a flume. It was a man-made, V-shaped creek with wooden sides that took water from the Tuolumne River to the mines and mills. The water had multiple uses, most importantly, the separation of gold from the other rocks it lived with in the natural state. The flow in the flume was fast; its construction was complex and intricate, impressing Pedro, causing him to ask many questions. Emanuel, who had been working in the gold fields for thirty years, recognized Pedro's interest and he related a true story about a flume at supper.

"It was in the camp they call Columbia where old John Huron Smith, drunk as a hoot he was, when he roughed up Martha Barclay in her bar one night. I was there–right there havin' a beer–when her man, John Barclay, shot Smith dead. John Smith had friends in the vigilant's. They got liquored-up, held kangaroo court–found Barclay guilty and decided on a hangin'. The crowd carried him down Gold Springs Road to a flume, a big one, towerin' some forty feet 'bove ground. The sheriff rode up sayin', "break it up and go home." Now he wasn't much of a lawman, no power in his talk, no shotgun. They grabbed him–tied him to a tree, for sure they did. A little *gringo* got a rope over the flume, 'round John Barclay's neck, and then–oh Lord they hauled him up. But, what do you know, them dumb white folks had forgot' to tie his hands. Some sight! Barclay holding the rope with both hands high over his head–his body swingin' back and forth under the flume. The vigilant's tried jerkin' the rope up and down but John Barclay wouldn't let go. The little *gringo* climbed out on the flume and started bashing John's hands with his pistol. Can you 'magin' a man hangin' from a flume just bashing away on your hands. John started screamin' but didn't let go. He was thrashin' and kickin' like crazy. He was holding his own too. Least 'till the pistol must'a broke some of his fingers. Oh Lord, how his head snapped back when he let go the rope. John's body jumped, face turned real blue and his eye–oh Lord, how they bulged 'fore he died."

"Was it was fun, watchin' *gringos* kill one of their own, 'stead of our kind?" asked Juan.

"Fun, oh Lord no. No, no, not fun at all! Didn't want to watch but couldn't stop. No one should die like that," said Emanuel.

Pedro shuttered; the story was too gruesome, hideous in fact. Death was bad enough but to be killed in such a manner was inhuman. He had always thought his father wrong about *gringos*; those he grew up with had treated him well. Maybe Juan was wiser about some things, but not this, he thought. The vigilantes had killed a white man, they were wrong, they would probably kill a Mexican with less remorse. He would treat white men, particularly white vigilantes, more carefully; his travel and adventures were serving to make him more aware of the dangers in the adult world.

Emanuel introduced Juan to the mine foreman who bought their mules, most of the tools, some clothes and tobacco at a price about four times their

San Francisco value. Their load lightened; they were now ready to go over the top.

From Twain Harte they traveled northeast, following the ridgeline trail between the south fork of the Stanislaus and the north fork of the Tuolumne Rivers. In the gray light of morning they could see the Great September Comet streaking toward earth. As the crow flies, it was only about forty miles to the summit but on the twisted road that gained six thousand feet in elevation, it was long, slow and tedious.

Just outside of Twain Harte, they encountered the westbound Wells Fargo Stage. The driver pulled the coach over to the side of the narrow road and stopped to let Juan and Pedro pass. He looked tense and picked up his shotgun as soon as the team was settled. He eyed Juan and Pedro carefully before deciding they were probably harmless. When he finally spoke his voice cracked. "We've just been held up! Robbed on this very road, in broad daylight too. A rough highwayman he was. Dressed in a long, white duster and wearin' a flower sack, a sack with eyeholes that was pulled over his head. The black hearted devil was heftin' a double-barreled shotgun and a heavy ax. Looked like he knew how to use 'em too. He didn't hurt nobody," said the "six-in-hand" teamster from his seat behind a half dozen fine brown coach horses. The passengers are all fit, but he got the strongbox that was full'a gold from the Red Cloud Mine. And, he left a poem! Can you 'magine? A road agent leavin' a poem!

"Can I see it?" blurted out Pedro.

"Don't see why not," the teamster answered. "Didn't think none of your kind could read."

Pedro took the paper and Juan jumped down to look over his shoulder while they read:

> *"I've labored long and hard for bread,*
> *For honor and for riches,*
> *But on my toes too long you've tred,*
> *You fine-haired sons-of-bitches."*
> Black Bart The PO8

Pedro was laughing as he passed the poem back to the teamster. "Thanks, he said."

"You see him, stay clear," said the driver.

"Sure you're all right?" asked Pedro.

"Thanks kid. Yeah. No one hurt, just riled and a little jumpy," the stage driver responded.

Pedro and Juan rolled their wagons past the stagecoach. Must be a smart man, thought Juan. It's an able fellow who can rob a stage, get away and leave a poem,

Pedro was shocked. How could one person stop a Wells Fargo Stagecoach with a driver, who had a shotgun and four armed passengers, and get away? he asked himself.

They moved on through a stand of sugar pines and past the Miwok Indian village. They were taking their time moving up trail as the wind grew stronger and a mountain chill set in. They could see patches of snow and the remnants of glaciers on the high mountains.

At Barry's Station, a muleskinner suggested they go a bit out of the way to see a magnificent glacial lake surrounded by an incredible stand of pine trees called Pinecrest. Pedro wanted to go; he also longed to try his luck with the fishing pole and small hooks they were packing and Juan had promised they would find time to catch some trout. They left their teams and wagons at the way station, traded a bottle of firewater for two saddle horses and rode to Pinecrest where Pedro got his first look at one of the most beautiful places in the world. The clear, blue-green waters were cold and deep and the shoreline was well defined by granite and pine. The lake was tucked away in a high glacial valley that had been carved out by ice millions of years earlier.

They dug some grubs from a small outlet creek and Pedro hooked one up and began to fish in a deep hole while standing on a partially submerged rock. His line and pole tip jerked as the first native fish took the grub and Pedro's excitement grew as he dragged his prize to shore. His hands were shaking, his heart pounding, when he took hold of the very slippery catch that was flopping and wiggling about trying to escape. He felt sorry for the beautifully colored fish, struggling to breathe, as he held it.

He did not like to see things die but he had taken many fish out of the ocean and they were good to eat. His parents had told him that fish, unlike warm-blooded animals, had no feelings and he believed that to the degree necessary to keep his catch. He collected a half dozen trout ranging from ten to sixteen inches in length, strung them on a line and tied to it a small tree. The fish were in shallow water and still flopping around, meaning they would be very fresh and tasty when fried.

He was now down to the last grub and he wanted to get another big one. He cast as far out as possible. The fish hit almost at once; the rod bent double. Pedro held on tight knowing he had a lunker on the end of his line. At the same time a huge brown bear ambled out of the pine forest not more than thirty yards from Pedro's position. The grizzly stopped and used her keen sense of smell to locate the fish. Her eyes were inherently weak but the great beast recognized motion. She rose up to her full height, standing on rear paws, and let out a horrible sound. Help, thought Pedro, still holding his fishing pole.

In panic he turned to run and suddenly found himself over his head in the chilling water. He surfaced, gasping for air, partly from fright, partly from the cold, to see the bear advancing toward him at a lope. He realized he was still holding the pole and that his fish was pulling him gradually out farther into the lake. He let go and began a hard swim toward the shore away from the grizzly. He looked back, seeing the huge, smelly beast standing on his rock gorging herself on his string of flopping fish.

Pedro angled toward shore, climbed out of the water and ran as fast as he could toward where they had tied up the horses. Juan had built a small fire and he was taking a *siesta*, his head resting on the seat of his California style saddle. He and the horses were startled by Pedro's high-speed advance. The boy was shaking from fear and cold, talking, half yelling, in Spanish staccato, about the huge brown bear who had eaten his fish and was still hungry."*Oso, muy malo oso*", he screamed. The horses were banging their hoofs, ears up, heads bobbing up and down, whinnying.

"*Leña, mucho leña,*" shouted Juan as Pedro dutifully began tossing firewood on the small blaze. Juan went for his shotgun, loaded it and turned toward the lake. He saw her, rise up, front paws making heavy markings on the trunk of a tall thick pine tree, advertising that this was her territory. The fire came up slowly as wet hands placed damp wood and sticks in a pile on the hot embers, but fortunately for Juan and Pedro, it generated a great deal of smoke. The grizzly made up for her lack of good vision with a keen sense of smell and the smoke triggered her response system, alerting her to get away. She went back to the forest, following her own trail, feeling safe in the knowledge that there had been no smoke on that path.

Pedro took off his wet clothes and boots, placing them on the sticks near the fire to dry. He covered his shivering body with a saddle blanket and stayed close to the blaze that now had a bright red/orange color and spoke with a crackle. It took almost an hour for Pedro to thaw out and get his things dry before they could start back to the way station. It was getting dark and Juan worried about finding the way back to Barry's as well as encountering the grizzly along the trail. He considered remaining by the fire for the night but chose to make the short trip.

As they rode into the thickening blackness there was a sharp crack on the left side of the trail, a noise that sounded like the snapping of a large tree branch. The horses, already shaken by the bearsighting and smoke, shied and Juan had trouble keeping his seat as they bolted down trail at the full gallop. "*Cabeza bajo,*" shouted Pedro, the better rider, as he instinctively gathered his small frame into the fetal-like position of a jockey, head and body low, driving for the barn. Juan had both hands on the saddle horn, his teeth full of mane, his heart thumping with fear. The horses knew the way back to Barry's but their frantic flight caused the riders to feel slaps, scratches, bumps and bruises from low hanging, trailside tree limbs and brush. Juan relaxed as he saw the way station lanterns come into view and failed to recognize the danger as the horses maintained their uncontrolled gallop.

"*Salto*" shouted Pedro as he left his mount for the hard ground, but Juan held tight until his horse crashed headlong into the barn's lower half door, catapulting the senior Olivera into a huge pile of manure on the far side of the barn. The soft landing saved his neck but did nothing for his *macho* image or his dignity. Around campfires all over the Sierra slopes, *gringos* would laugh about the old greaser being pitched into a pile of manure as The Great Comet approached. Was he goosed? Goosed by its tail? They would joke and speculate.

Up early to avoid the laughing eyes of the *gringos* the father and son team moved out. Going higher and higher, the air thinning, becoming colder, still colder, and very dry. They began to feel short of breath and the horses labored. Pedro's lips were dry and cracking, his ears plugged and his throat became sore. He yawned to clear his ears, greased his lips and at Juan's suggestion, sucked on a piece of hard candy to ease his throat. Patches of cold, dirty snow started showing up in shaded places as they approached the permanent snow line. The tall pines gradually gave way to thick, scruff brush, a few scattered hemlock trees and some foxtail pine with thick trunks and few branches. The higher they went the more barren the mountains looked and felt. There was snow all around as they made camp just below the summit on Deadman Creek. Pedro pulled his coat tight around his body and kept it there even after the radiation from their campfire eased some of the cold out of the air.

Juan and Pedro rose before first light, determined to view sunrise from the top of the trail. They reached the summit before the sun's rays turned the blackness of the countryside below into a breathtaking, panoramic, montage-like spectacular. The early light gradually revealed, first the steep eastern mountainside, and then it slowly exposed a huge cavity containing mountains of its own, valleys, rivers, lakes, old volcanoes, cinder cones, moraines and trees. There were thousands and thousands of beautiful, tall, majestic green trees forming monster forests wherever there was water. A blend of high mountain/high desert terrain was being exposed by the rising sun, producing the kind of picture that could be taken in only a few places in the world.

The sun had broken over the horizon and the scene gradually came into clear view a frame at a time; reality revealed piecemeal as dark gave way to light. Pedro, intoxicated by the vision that had unfolded below, was speechless. He was looking almost straight down, thousands of feet, into a huge valley surrounded irregularly by hills and mountains. He had no idea how they would get down or what they would encounter along the way but he knew it would be a challenge worth enjoying.

The road down was steep and hard and there were signs that many folks who had tried to come west on this trail had lost their lives. Old wagons, animal skeletons and gravesites marked the path and Juan decided that they would return from Bodie on an easier course. Some people think it's easier to go down than up but it's not; the animals are hard to control, the wagons difficult to brake and the turns difficult to navigate.

Pedro, an inexperienced driver, was struggling. Juan was making them go very slowly, stopping frequently to scout ahead. The fall to the outside of the trail was vertical, dropping thousands of feet. Looking down made Pedro shiver. There were tingles in his arms and hands, his stomach fluttered, his mouth became dry and there was sweat on his hands in spite of the cold. Each time an animal bumped toward the outside or a wagon wheel struck a rut, the level of Pedro's tension rose. He planned how he would jump out, away from the cliff if the team or wagon began to topple over. He had heard that some people feared falling more than others and he was sure that his discomfort was greater than that experienced by others. He stayed lightly on his seat, ready to spring out, but not wanting to abandon his team and wagon or anger his father. He was holding his breath most of the time, scared of falling but more frightened of quitting.

Juan was scared too but he could not let his son know it. The road was narrow and the canyon sheer, capable of taking man, horse and wagon to an unmarked grave thousands of feet below. The trail was also very steep causing the wagons' weight to push the horses hard, encouraging them to rush down, run away ahead of the trailing load, killing them all. He pulled hard on the wagon brake forcing the team to virtually drag the burden, holding them back but still moving, sometimes too fast. Juan stopped often and acted as if he was searching ahead when, in fact, he had lost his nerve and couldn't go on without gathering himself. He was moving again, making a sharp left turn with the cliff on his right when the rear outside wheel bumped up sideways on a slanted rock and slid off the right side of the road hanging itself by the axle over the precipice.

The team, stirred up by the noise and the change in condition of the wagon, dragged Juan and the load along, the axle scraping over the cliffs edge, the wheel squawking. "Eeeeeek . . . clunk . . . bunk . . . lunk . . . eeeeeek . . . clink . . . bunk . . . lunk". Juan pulled on the brake and reins as hard as he could but the team couldn't stop. He felt everything slipping farther to the right, toward the edge. He jumped out to his left scrambling on all fours up the high side of the road to safety, presuming the loss of horses and wagon. But for no apparent reason, the wagon and team seemed to shift into a slow motion, then stop.

Juan, shaking, took some time before he climbed down from his safe perch to find the right wheel firmly caught up with a small, tough, white bark pine, its tap root sunk deep into the rocky cliff side. The pine with its six-inch trunk had been stronger and more effective stopping the run-away than Juan. He and Pedro settled the horses, unhitched and hobbled them before unloading the wagon. When empty, they used Pedro's horses to ease the wagon back away from the pine tree before they levered the wheel back up onto the roadbed. They changed the wheel, greased the axle, and checked the wagon thoroughly before reloading and starting down the mountainside again.

The trip from the summit to Leavitt Meadows, about six miles by air, had a fall of roughly two thousand five hundred feet and both drivers remained tense and uneasy until reaching the West Walker River near the way station. They stopped, refreshed themselves and decided that their horses had gone long enough that day. They made camp near the station and after being assured that there were no bears around, Pedro tried his luck in the river. He had lost his fishing pole at Pinecrest but Juan's was still in the wagon. Pedro made a fine catch, producing a scrumptious dinner. While Pedro fished, Juan took a late *siesta*, dreaming about the *mucho hombre*, Snowshoe Johnson, the famous Scandinavian mail carrier. His real name was Torsteinson but folks called him Johnson. He was a man, a giant, who had toted dispatches over the Sierra Mountain passes on foot during winter. Impassable mountains in winter, impossible journey. *Montañas en ventisqueros*, he thought, when he woke, *el grande hombre*.

Juan hoped to make Bridgeport the next day but the trip from Leavitt down through Pickel Meadow, then back up through Devil's Gate was too hard. They camped on the east side of a ridge in a meadow with a small creek, a few miles past Fales Hot Springs. The hot springs were a new experience for

Pedro and they had taken time to immerse themselves in the warm sulfur waters. They panned for about an hour in the creek near their camp, mostly to show Pedro how it was done. Pedro found a little color that they packed away. The canyon was beautiful, many pines, abundant grass and wildlife was everywhere. They saw signs of logging along the road foretelling the nearness to mines, towns, and people.

They watched the comet in the night sky, closing in on earth, its tail twisted out to the side like fire coming from a dragon's mouth. The comet was a stranger, an alien object in these parts, in a way, much like the camels that had been brought west. The comet came on its own, for its own reasons. Camels, strange desert animals, had been imported to carry man and burden across the Mojave through Devil's Gate to Virginia City. The camels were useful because they could go on and on across the desert in the scorching heat, seemingly forever without water.

The unknown produces fear and both the comet and the camel fell outside the norm for these parts. From the earliest time man has feared comets and in the west just about everything living gave ground to the camels. They spooked horses, stampeded cattle, and sent the grizzly into panicked flight. Pedro had never seen camels and part of him hoped for an encounter along the trail while another segment of his being wanted no part of such an engagement. The camel, thought Pedro, was here to do a job. What about the comet? Did it have a mission?

It was almost all down hill into the Bridgeport valley which gathered water from a multitude of creeks, streams, springs, and rivers which join the East Walker River on its northeastward course. Originally a high semi-desert valley with sagebrush, tumble weeds and chaparral on its floor and pine with other hardwood trees near the creeks and on the ridges, the Bridgeport area had been transformed by man and commercialized to fill some of society's needs. The valley floor had been cleared; cattle and horses were grazing on the rich grass supported by irrigation ditches; ranch houses were scattered about in the fields, mostly fenced by wood and devil wire. Approaching town from the northwest it was hard to take the eyes off the massive gray mountain range, its peaks resembling the teeth of a huge irregular saw rising up to the southwest. Smoke curled up into the wind from kilns located below the saw-tooth range and it was obvious that the trees had been clear-cut to the ground around the sawmills and from nearby slopes. The deep canyons gouged out by ancient glaciers and worn down by the waters from Buckeye and Robinson Creeks could be seen as they worked their way down onto the valley floor.

Bridgeport was not the largest community in the area but it was the most important commercial center and travel hub. It lay astride the main north/south route running between Virginia and Carson Cities to the north and Los Angeles to the south. Gold moving from the major mines in Bodie, Aurora, Lee Vining, Lundy and Dunderberg passed through Bridgeport on its way to the mint at Carson City while lumber, supplies and people moved from the north and west through Bridgeport to the mining settlements. The valley was high, roughly six thousand feet above sea level, pleasant during the short summer season, very cold in the winter, suitable for growing grass for livestock, less conducive to raising crops. Grain, potatoes and a few vegetables survived in spite of snow flurries in late June, July and sometimes, even August. The town, sighted on the west side of the Walker River, was typical of the early settlements containing saloons, pleasure palaces, liveries, places to eat, drink, sleep, supply and play. They stopped at the Simmons Building where Juan had a beer and Pedro, sarsaparilla.

They crossed the bridge over the river, continued south to Virginia Creek and then southeast to the Bodie cut-off. They were being followed by a train of wagons, pulled by fourteen mules, loaded with bales of hay, lumber and other supplies. The road turned east, followed Clearwater Creek to Mormon Meadows where they made camp for the night. It was clear and cold at seven thousand feet above sea level and by morning the grass had a silver sheen that crackled when trod upon.

Two miles up the road at Murphy Station they were assessed a toll for traveling over this private trail, fifty cents for each wagon and fifty cents for each pulling animal. Juan bristled at having to pay *gringos*. The charge renewed his hatred and generated the same kind of get even feeling he felt when he killed the girl in San Francisco. I could kill and burn again, he thought. I could kill a *gringo* any time, anywhere, for any reason.

169

13

THE SPRING OF 1881 CAME, MELTING
snow and ice making Main Street, Bodie, a muddy cesspool filled with human
waste, garbage and thick murky water. Rats and other varmints fed on street
garbage, creating an environment for disease. Bodie was just like all the early
gold camps, dirty, unkempt and unhealthy. People remained there because of
the opportunity, the gold, the commerce and the adventure.

As the declination of the sun gradually shifted to the north, it rose
higher in the sky each day, getting closer to Bodie little by little. Its rays
penetrated the cold ground and energized the smiling face of spring. The
wonders of life began to unfold slowly, graciously.

Tex Garland saw tall Indian rice grass jump from slumber; the trees
and brush returned to life; fresh parsley appeared along the spring fed creeks.
Snowberry and gooseberry offered their tender, sweet taste to both man and
bear as they all emerged from hibernation. The creamy, yellow, spatula-shaped
flowers of the antelope bottlebrush opened in red, yellow, purple, and blue
wildflowers appeared. The sugary aroma of sagebrush soon filled the air that
was populated by bluebirds, blackbirds, sparrows, hawks and other sometimes
less friendly flying bugs and insects.

Mosquitoes swarmed out of the ground around the melting snowfields
attacking man and horse, whichever ventured near. The *Piñon* pine restarted
its growth cycle producing pine nuts that were harvested green and roasted
whole over an open fire. The heat vaporized their pitch and provided a delicious
food that had filled the bellies of many Washoe and Paiute Indians long before
the miners came. Signs of black and brown bear, bighorn sheep, deer, coyote,
badger, beaver and other smaller animals marked the landscapes where one

walked with a watchful eye for rattlesnakes. The native cutthroat trout with its sweet, tender, reddish meat became active in the fresh water rivers, streams and lakes as food washed down with the spring run-off and insect hatches spread natural tidbits on the water's surface.

Tex took pleasure from the fact that he had learned much about nature from his travels and from Red Hand. Spring brought all the signs of new life, new opportunity and new love. For the animals it was the rutting season; for humans, a time for weddings, church bells, flowers and white dresses. For Tex, it was also a time for change. Weary of the choking, black, wet under-earth caves and inspired by the bloom of the new season, his spirit sought its heritage, a heritage rooted in sunshine. The cowboy, the cowboy residing in the soul of Tex was determined to surface.

The Apaches had a saying, "Man's heart must lead him, may yours be wise." He had heard that ranchers were hiring cowhands in Bridgeport as they trailed their herds up from Smith Valley. He didn't want to give up his quest for gold but he wasn't prospecting for himself while down in the mines. He told himself that he could seek color while moving cattle about on the surface. He was better prepared now, knew what to look for, thus improving his chances over others who were searching above ground.

On Sunday, his day off, he headed for Bridgeport locating the ranch owned by Sean McCarthy. Tex rode up to the large two-story main house framed to the west by the magnificent Saw-tooth Mountains, silvered by a heavy snow-pack. A stand of young ash, popular and pine trees grew near the house and cattle grazed in the high grass in all directions. There was also a large barn and corral; pigs were swilling in the mud and chickens were clucking and scratching loose in the yard.

Three barking ranch dogs greeted him as he approached, dismounted and tied Moonshine to the hitching rail in front of the barn. Sean McCarthy, alerted by the commotion, met Tex as he walked up to the front door. They exchanged introductions and Sean invited Tex to join him for coffee. They spent almost two hours together, Sean asking questions, Tex responding, in what seemed to be an eternity of talk for a quiet Texan. Finally Sean said, "Let's see what kind of wrangler you are."

He took Tex to the barn, saddled his bay and led him into the pasture. He mounted and gently prodded his horse into an easy walk, chatting as they rode. "That's an awful big mount for a cow pony," he said.

"She is that," Tex responded.

Sean gave the orders and watched Tex handle the cattle with the fluid ease of a well-practiced professional. He worked the horse without using a quirt and when asked to rope a cow he only needed to swing his *lariat* once. For over an hour McCarthy issued instructions and Tex showed his stuff. They gradually made their way north until they reached a small river where, without warning, McCarthy pitched a large pinecone into the fast moving water shouting, "Shoot it, now!"

Tex drew, fired four times, hitting near the pinecone twice before Sean raised his hand to stop. Tex was embarrassed. He had fired four times and missed every shot. It was tough to shoot a handgun from a horse and even tougher to hit a cone bouncing around on a fast moving river. He knew that, but the ranch owner apparently didn't. Did he need to shoot his way into a job as a cowpuncher? Had he lost his chance with Sean? Would he need to go back underground? His thoughts were spilling out. He was suffering–hurting because he felt inadequate but also sensing that he had been taken advantage of by being asked to do more than was reasonable. He said, "Give me another chance. Reckon I can do better."

"Another try," said a smiling Sean, "Nobody I know can hit a pinecone movin' down this river, not even a shootist. You did great, kid. Good shootin', but most important, you are the best cowpuncher I've ever seen. There's no one in this valley that can handle cattle as well as you. I like your know how, your skill and your easy way with me. You've a sense for leadin', I can feel it. You'ill be able to handle cowhands. The ranch needs a foreman. The pay's one hundred and fifty a month plus keep. Sundays off. The chow's good, the bunkhouse warm. When can you start?"

Tex was stunned, and he hadn't reckoned to get a job offer, at least not right off, and he never had considered foreman. Foreman, foreman on a big ranch, a job for a man who couldn't shoot straight. What a day, he thought. Tex made four dollars a day as a miner and had to pay for a room at the

Stewart House and buy his meals. One hundred and fifty a month with a free bed and good ranch beef would be much better for him much better for sure, and he could carry a pan in his saddlebag. "Reckon I could ride over to Bodie and get my kit. I want to let the people at the Standard Mine know I have a new job. They've been dern good to me at Standard. Seems like it's fittin' I tell 'em face to face. Also, there's a lady; she needs to know. Think I could be back by sundown tomorrow, if that suits you," said Tex.

The Irishman nodded. They shook hands, sealing their agreement, commencing a new work cycle for Tex. By becoming a cowhand again, he was going to his place, much like people find their special seat in church and much like each cow takes its spot in the heard. He was finding his place and himself and it was the beginning a fresh friendship that would last much longer than either he or Sean could ever imagine.

Tex liked being on the McCarthy Ranch and Moonshine was acting like a young yearling. Working cattle in the clear, cool air was a reward, a prize. It captivated their spirits.

Sean was an educated man and he kept up with the news. He was active in local politics, a pillar of society and a person of vision, respected in the community. He planned, someday, to run for the state senate. Sean was still following the logic that had been fixed in his mind by his parents. Logic that declared that one should seek high levels of achievement through hard work, education and family strength. The ranch was friendly, managed in a humane manner, a style atypical of the times.

Sean often invited Tex to join the family for supper. After the meal he would sit and tell stories about his own adventures, discuss his philosophies and report the news. Like Tex, he had been personally involved in an Indian fight, an event that had triggered a powerful interest in the red men. He had spent many hours reading books, stories, articles, listening to others, and generally advancing his knowledge of the Native Americans.

One evening after supper he said, "I figure there were some three hundred tribes of Indians, each with its own way of talkin', thinkin' and actin'. Near a million of 'em were located west of the Missouri River. When the California gold strike was made, prospectors pushed across the frontier in huge numbers, bringin' guns, cavalry, stage coaches, forts, buffalo hunters and later the telegraph and the railroads. The trappings of a white man's civilization intruded into the wilderness, a place that had been inhabited almost entirely by red men.

"There was no stoppin' the seekers, their resolve incessantly drawing them to color like a child is drawn to his mother's bosom. The cattlemen, settlers, most of the others who followed were almost as determined. The model early American lifestyle that had embraced God, duty and country as the standards gave way quickly. In the expanding west, gave way all too quickly, to greed. Never underestimate the power of greed. It makes men single-minded, determined, foolhardy, brash, thoughtless and dangerous! But when men focus their energy on a single objective, their accomplishments can sometimes seem super human.

"Unlike the whites," Sean contended, "the Indians were an unfocused, disorganized lot without unified goals or singular leadership. They possessed long traditions of individualism and war among themselves. Oh yes, they knew how to fight. In fact their customs, superstitions, and mythology drove their young men into battle, tribe against tribe. Honor in battle was special for Indian braves.

"Back in the early '50s, the Indians had a claim on most land west of the Missouri but they had no organization or unity. Up north, the Sioux with brave Chiefs like Sitting Bull and Crazy Horse, were busy makin' war on Crows, Kiowas, Omahas, Pawns and others. Farther south, Apache, Comanche, Kyowa and Crow raided each other. Had these diverse groups been able to unify against one common enemy—white men—the intruders from the east, the outcome in the west might have been very different.

"You've read about Custer, the Last Stand they call it. The Indians got together and ganged up on him and look what happened. Long Hair, the Indians called him because his red-gold locks reached down almost to the collar of the buckskin coat he wore in the field. General A. Custer and his Seventh Cavalry from Fort Abraham Lincoln moved into the Indian camp on the Little Big Horn River in June, '76. His head scout, a Ree Indian named Bloody Knife, was unfamiliar with the terrain. He had a half dozen Crows who were native to the territory but they still underestimated the size of the Indian encampment. In fact, Sitting Bull, Crazy Horse, White Bull and other tribal leaders had gathered a big force of mostly Cheyenne and Sioux with other warriors from the Arapaho, Blackfoot, Miniconjou, Sans Are, Brule and Oglala. The Indians outnumbered the cavalry three to one. The soldiers attacked and fought a confused uncoordinated battle that cost Custer his life. The red men took prizes. White Bull took the general's saddle, leggings and pants; Noisy Walker, a Dakota, took his sorrel."

Sean took a deep breath.

"The Indians fixed the guy they called Teat. Isaiah Dorman was his real name. He was a black soldier and a good friend of Custer's. Oh yes, they fixed him good. Teat was found after the battle with all his body parts slashed. He was riddled with arrows and nailed to the ground with an iron picket pin that was driven through his balls. His penis was plugged into his mouth. The Indians made sure—damned sure—that Teat would not look too good in the world of spirits.

"Roughly, three-hundred cavalry soldiers were killed and many others were wounded. Many also escaped. The red men lost about forty."

"I bet them red men cut loose that night," said Tex.

"You're probably right about that, Sean," agreed.

"Those Indians have lots of dances. They dance for their gods, for rain, for death, for birth, for courage and they must have a dance for victory. Let's hope there were no white captives there for the red-sticks' celebration," Sean continued.

"You know somethin', Tex, the Indians won at the Little Big Horn because they outnumbered their enemy; they were united, confident, determined, cornered and angry. They were fighting for their land, their women and children. They had leadership, single-mindedness, focus and determination, the same kind of drives that motivated the early prospectors.

"The Indians fought united in one great battle and won, but for the most part they lost. As a result, their culture is fast fadin' from the western landscape."

Tex had heard about Custer's Last Stand but never had it been described the way Sean had framed it. "Reckon you're right 'bout them red-sticks," he said. "They're fadin' fast like the grizzly bears in Texas. Lots of 'em once, not many left. Pity, in a way, but them bears and some of them Indians was real salty."

One afternoon Tex was checking on a small herd in a meadow where there were few trees but a great deal of ground cover and vegetation. He stopped for a cool drink from the waterway that was only about two feet wide and shallow. He always carried his prospector's pan as he rode about over ground that could contain riches almost anywhere. He brought up some creek bottoms from a spot on the eastern edge of the meadow where the waters made a sharp turn and found, to his surprise, signs of both gold and silver. He worked his way up stream toward the saddle-shaped ridge from which he could look down on a lake. The signs of color vanished as he went west. On his way back to the ranch he dug in the creek down in the canyon east of his find and located fresh shows of placer deposits.

It's there, he thought. A vein of gold and silver bearing rock is up on the side of that mountain right over there, he said to himself.

He didn't understand how he had developed the skill to isolate the probable location of the lode but he felt proud that he had the ability. Many of the facts tossed at him by friendly miners must have been absorbed into the deep recesses of his mind, returning now as insight, even inspiration. Almost by instinct he knew how and where to prospect, much like a trained minstrel knows what notes to play, seemingly without thinking.

He knew the find was on McCarthy property and decided to discuss it with Sean after supper. All he had found was a few scattered thin placer deposits in a small creek that thus far would be difficult to pan economically. However, the signs implied that a vein of ore-bearing rocks existed somewhere above the creek along the watershed that flowed into creek east of the saddle.

Sean was very excited to hear of the discovery and he promised Tex a fifty percent share of a mine if it could be worked. Sean saddled his horse immediately and insisted on riding directly to the place Tex had described. The fire in a prospector's heart had been rekindled.

"Great work," said Sean. "Tex, you're right. There must be a vein up on the side of the mountain somewhere. Could take some time to find it. Might never. Could be too small to work. Then again? You need to get to runnin' the ranch. I'll look 'round for a time. Let's keep it under our hats, you know, keep it quiet. No need to have a bunch of prospectors getting in the way."

And so it was that Tex became an owner in what would later be called the Longhorn Mine, located on the steep slope above the meadow at over seven thousand feet in the air. It produced mostly gold along with some silver and it was profitable.

Tex had learned some prospecting and mining skills and now he had become a mine owner. But more importantly, he had developed his skills as a ranch foreman, a manager of men, using the knowledge that he had gained from the examples set by others he had observed. The lead cow Old Blue, the Indian Red Hand, Charles Goodnight, the point rider John Dursh, his boss Sean McCarthy and other leaders had shown him different ways to manage. He handled the men smoothly, encouraging the eager with positive comments and driving the lazy, batting one alongside the head when necessary. He learned the meaning of loneliness—the solitude that resided with leadership. He was alone when managing the men but in a partnership of good company when with Janet.

Tex and his crew worked the cattle into the late fall, then headed up a November drive to Smith Valley where they would winter.

During the cold dark winter months he worked on ranch gear and spent most of one day writing to his parents in Houston. He described many of his adventures and bragged a little about his good fortune.

As foreman, he remained on the ranch payroll year round, finding by spring that he had a few dollars in his jeans, an interest in a mine, a future that looked as bright as the color of the early mountain flowers. He spent another exciting spring and summer leading men, working livestock, managing the farm, handling the duties required of a ranch foreman. He used some of his free time on Sundays to work his mine.

He rode to Bodie almost every Saturday night to visit with Janet Arlett and he was particularly looking forward to the journey next Saturday that would permit him a good view of the comet on its close approach to earth.

The Bridgeport Chronicle called it the Great Comet of 1882. He planned to go to the fights first, then take Janet out to view the heavens. Some people said the comet would end the earth's cycle of existence but Tex didn't believe unfounded predictions of doom.

Comets had come and gone before, and the earth was still rotating normally. He would go out with his girl, watch it, defy it. Sean had studied the heavens and he had no fear of the comet. He would ride out with Tex, visit Bodie, go to the fights, "cut the wolf loose."

14

TWO MILES AND THOUSAND FEET
further up the trail Juan, Pedro and Trigo had already pushed into Bodie. They struck out first to find Washoe Cete, the scoundrel Juan befriended in his youth in San Francisco. Cete, an old man now, was found at his wholesale liquor warehouse, knurled and scarred by both the ordinary struggles of western life and his self created battles.

He was taller than most men of his time, near to six feet. He was thick boned, had the short, fat neck and powerful arms and of a heavyweight, and the killing instincts of an assassin. Washoe had mean, crazy eyes like those of the owl. He had been burned badly along the left eyebrow that had grown no hair since being struck by a hot branding iron. Cete was also scared deeply on his right cheek that had been opened by a broken whiskey bottle during one of his many bar room brawls. He greeted Juan, ran his left hand across his thin, dark, unkempt hair, exposing the hand without an index finger, bitten off by an angry miner who lost his life for the insult. That incident started people calling him "Bad Man From Bodie."

After the introductions, it wasn't long before Washoe was bragging, using the worst kind of saloon language about his fistic victories, female conquests and business tricks. He spoke in a high-pitched nasal tone originating in the twisted tubes of his oft broken nose.

Juan then traded his whiskey for gold at roughly four times its San Francisco cost being careful to strike an agreement with Washoe to have a free room at his Bodie Lodging House for three nights. Cete talked about the big fights set for the next night. A cock battle at Joe Rouse's saloon would be followed by a badger against the dogs at a nearby embankment used for such activity. His eyes gleamed, full of crazy, as he described the killing that would take place. Juan listened carefully while thinking how he might profit from the conflicts. Pedro, appalled at he idea of the men inducing animals to destroy each other for sport, sat in silence. Pedro thought his father saw Pete as *el hombre grande* while Pedro considered him *el hombre enfermo*. In truth, Juan hated all *gringos,* including Cete, but he found him useful. Anyone who didn't know the value of his own whiskey in San Francisco and the cost of freight could be exploited and Juan Olivera had just taken him; he was *el hombre estúpido,* in Juan's mind.

Cete didn't like greasers; he had shot several and helped hang another. However, he found Juan useful. He bought spirits in San Francisco from his own warehouse, a profitable business for Washoe. He carried the booze all the way to Bodie where he sold it back for only four times the cost. Pete would water it and sell the stuff for six times what Juan charged. Greasers, he thought, are all stupid. "Will you put Trigo in the badger fight?" he asked Juan, while Pedro stood by, his eyes growing large—so large that each orb seemed to be as full as the moon.

"Don't think so," he answered. "He's family."

They left for China Town to find Sam Hing, a short, stocky, dark haired man with a flat nose, alligator eyes and a pigtail. Pedro thought most all China men looked alike; he didn't understand why they bothered to have different names. Sam Hing was just another one of them. Washoe Cete had told them how to find Sam's house. It fronted on King Street and adjoined his opium den.

Pedro slipped unnoticed up to the door of Sam's opium pleasure house and had a look. There was a big, stuffy room and users lay back on bunk beds placed along the room's walls. They were smoking, sniffing or eating opium, Pedro supposed, for the feeling of extreme calm and wellbeing it was reputed to provide. Good feelings that some people said lasted forever. Temporary feelings lasting until the user became addicted, suffering ugly nightmares, mental breakdown and ultimately death, according to others.

Pedro knew quite a bit about opium. One of the older boys in his school, Tim Stone, told him all about the drug. Stone was a fat kid who liked to tell outrageous stories and he claimed to have used opium many times. The drug, made from the juice of the opium poppy, could be turned into heroin, morphine or other powerful opiates. Dens were not illegal; in fact, opium derivatives were available from drummers, as laudanum and other medicines or tonics.

Juan traded the opium he had brought from San Francisco with Sam for gold, earning another substantial profit and ending a very good day for the Mexicans. He deposited the gold in town with Wells Fargo, stabled the twelve horses and two wagons, before devouring a fine supper at Brown's Hotel with Pedro and then bedded down. Juan kept his shotgun close to hand. He didn't trust any of the *gringos* and certainly not the rough uncouth, Washoe Celt, owner of the place where he was trying to sleep.

The night passed without incident and the next day Juan traded his twelve pulling horses and two wagons for gold plus two good riding mounts, saddles, one mule and other gear that he knew he needed to make the trip back to Santa Barbara. The ride home would not require wagons. Bodie had nothing worth hauling back except gold and silver and it was much too dangerous to move that type of cargo. They would go home the long way, down the Nadeau Road. It went south out of Bodie to Lee Vining, Camp Independence, Red Rock Canyon and then into the desert. He would turn westward when they reached Placerita Canyon that would provide them a windblown route over the mountains.

In past years Juan had brought livestock and supplies to the Queen, Yellow Aster and Tropico mines located along the southern portion of the old Nadeau road and he knew the southern part of the way home. Without wagons they could move fast, a good thing to do along the eastside of the Sierra Nevada Mountains where hard people congregated.

Sam Hing was married and had two sons. One named Lee Sing was about the same age as Pedro. While Juan and Sam talked, smoked and drank Chinese Rice Spirits, Pedro was sent to visit with Lee who was in a small room in the back of the house working on numbers with beads hung on a wooden frame. Pedro had never seen such a thing and he was curious.

Lee said, "It's a Chinese abacus used to add subtract, multiply and divide. You can even do square roots." Lee showed Pedro the thirteen columns of beads with three above the center and five below in each column. "The first column is for ones, the second for tens, the third for hundreds and so on," he said. "Each bead below the bar has a value of one, each above has a value of five. You add and subtract the same way you do with columns of numbers." Lee Sing showed Pedro how to do a few simple calculations and then let him do some himself. It wasn't hard and Pedro caught on quickly, realizing the value of an abacus. He decided to get one for himself.

Lee Sing told Pedro that his father beat him with a stick if he failed to get perfect marks with all his schoolwork. "The abacus helps lots with math," he said. "Father says that being smart is most important. You need to be smart to have success. He claims he learned that from Confucius, a preacher from long ago. Confucius wanted folks to be responsible. You know, to do the right thing. Father says that means folks need to be smart and work hard. That's why he's so hard 'bout my grades. I read a little Confucius. He had a lot of good things to say, like, 'What you do not wish for yourself, do not do to others.'

"I'm not so sure Father feels as strong about doing nice things for folks. He's not unusual, I guess. I see lots of grown-ups who only hear what they want to hear and abide by what pleases them. They don't pay much mind to what preachers say. My father thinks that only the rich get into a good place in heaven. You buy your way in. Success in business—that's the way to get a fine spot in up there. He really believes in richness, but Confucius didn't have much to say 'bout that."

While Lee Sing was talking Pedro's mind was working on his father's view of what was important. Family, certainly family was first, but what about other things? He was never beaten for not getting good grades; in fact, schooling was hardly ever discussed at home. They left that to the Jesuits at the mission who taught him to read, work the numbers and to know the Divine Trinity. It seemed to Pedro that the ideas expressed by Confucius were not unlike those taught by Jesuits. Juan didn't talk about education or hard work but it was obvious to Pedro that his father was a driven man, motivated by a need to support his family and whipped by his hatred for the *gringos*. His parents seemed concerned about how relatives, friends and neighbors viewed them.

They yearned for praise and acceptance in their society. The appearance of prosperity dominated a major part of their thinking and directed much of their activity. Vain, they were vain.

Mexicans also lived for the *fiesta*, attending a party at least each week. *Fiesta* is a requirement for most Hispanic families. *Fiesta* is a happening, complete with music, food and tequila. *Fiesta*—an event where everyone eats and drinks too much, is an obligation for the people of his race. When a new *casa* is put up, a fuss is always made about building large, decorative rooms where guests can be received. The big ornate rooms attest to the owner's prosperity and provide a facility for the *fiesta*. The other rooms in the house are downsized to serve the frugal part of the Hispanic nature. Pedro's thoughts solidified. Were Juan's values family, outward appearance and fiesta? How would such standards compete with family, education, hard work and belief in the hereafter? And what about the hereafter? Did people buy their way into a heavenly place of importance? The Jesuits certainly didn't teach that. But were they right?

Pedro liked Lee Sing. They appeared to have a common antagonist. Pedro was no longer comfortable with white men. When he started the trip his feelings were that his father was wrong to hate them but now he was not so sure. The *gringos* treated Mexicans, with contempt calling them greasers, stealing from them without remorse. They also mistreated the pig-tailed Chinese, ran them off and killed them when it suited their purpose. But, worst of all, they pit their animals against each other in fights to the death. Papá may be right, he thought. *Gringos* may be mostly evil. A common enemy breeds a bond, a sense of closeness and mutual support between the children of the oppressed. The *gringos* had unknowingly forged a bond between two young minorities in the wilderness settlement of Bodie. A bond similar to others fused elsewhere, wherever oppression exists. The closeness between Pedro and Lee Sing had developed quickly and Pedro wondered if a similar tie extended to the relationship between Sam and his father.

While their young were forming a new relationship, Sam Hing was busy telling Juan about his bold leadership of the local Yan Wo Tong, a secret fraternity, one of several that pervaded the Chinese society. Most of what he said was exaggerated and in almost every conversation he overstated his importance. Hing bragged about how he headed nine hundred men, from a previous Tong into battle in 1856, against twelve hundred of the Sam Yap Tong at Chinese camp on the Western Sierra slopes. The issue was face. He said, "We went after each other with whatever we could find, spears, daggers, battleaxes and pikes. I killed one of 'em with my bare hands. Got wounded too and tossed in jail. There was no winner or looser. Face was saved on both sides. When I 'scaped jail I joined other Tong big shots and we planted a locust tree. You know, the tree of heaven. The kind that Chinese folks are growin' wherever they make camp."

Sam recounted some of his more recent adventures including the charge of arson brought against him for burning one of his insured properties, the shooting of two Chinese and the lifting of various treasures from whites who had too much opium. He was careful to omit one story of murder. He didn't want to let a greaser know that he had killed a poor Mexican—a kid actually—who had allowed his mule to graze in Sam Hing's vegetable garden.

Sam Hing was a shrewd businessman, using his power as a tong leader to extract favors from fellow Chinese and using the power of his opiates to take mostly form whites. He felt justified in both actions because Chinese tradition allowed rewards for those in power. The whites, while acting superior, were actually part of an inferior race deserving disdain and victimization. Sam recalled with pain how his inferiors had beaten him at times. Once, he had tried to organize his countrymen so that they could earn higher wages and pay tribute to his tong. They were living in a camp two miles north of Mono Lake, working to grade the Bodie Railroad. Company employees with guns and numbers routed the Chinese, forcing them to retreat. They ran to the small steamboat named Rocket. It took them to the relative safety of Pacha Island where they waited until things cooled off.

There were many lessons Sam could have learned from that defeat. He took the message that suited his nature; his mind became steeled against all those from different cultures with different colored skins. He would steal from them, cheat them and kill them when it suited him.

Greasers, Red Sticks and Niggers were also inferior, almost as bad as

Japs, according to Sam who viewed himself as a fine judge of people. He didn't care for Juan, a dumb greaser, but he was sometimes useful and the opium he had bought relieved a supply shortage in Bodie. He had paid only four times the value in San Francisco, a steal in this country. Accordingly, he was obliged to be hospitable. He took Juan across the street to the upstairs pleasure house that featured a trio of ladies, one Chinese, one Hispanic and one white. If you could have a go with all three and not leave your load behind, the tricks were free. Juan tried but lost his money.

Left to themselves, Pedro and Lee worked for a time on numbers and other school tasks and speculated about the approach of the Great Comet which might hit the sun and end the world. Eventually they got bored and their thoughts and conversation turned to a subject common to youth. "Woman, have you ever had one?" asked Lee. Pedro shook his head. "You should tonight," said Lee. "If the stories about the Comet are true, this may be your last chance."

Pedro didn't know what to say. He wanted to, had dreamed about it, but was afraid. Take all his clothes off? In front of a woman?

"Come on," said Lee Sing leading Pedro to the back of a building on Main Street. He knocked on the door four times. A big breasted, heavy, white brunet in a silk gown came to the door, recognized Lee Sing and let them in. "Is Daly here?" he asked.

"Sure, Lee" said the woman with big tits. "Did you bring some poppy for me?"

Lee Sing handed her a small bag and asked her to take Pedro, his friend, to Daly. She took Pedro up the stairs to a room where Daly Storm both lived and worked. Pedro stood back as she knocked.

"Who's there," said a soft, pleasant voice from inside.

"It's me, Marynette," was the response from the buxom madam. "Got a young one for you."

"Fine, show him in," said Daly.

Pedro felt flushed as the door swung open. Part of his nature wanted him to run while another element of his senses required him to stay. He was frozen in front of the door and Marynette had to give him a little push of encouragement to get him to move forward. He walked ahead, shyly, while trying not to look directly at Daly. His eyes flittered about the room that was decorated mostly by things that had red and black colors. Pedro jumped when he heard the door close behind his back. He was scared, trapped now in the bedroom of a beautiful woman.

She had brown hair, light blue eyes, white skin, red lips and a modest build. "Take off you clothes," she said, leading Pedro by his hand to her bed. She slid out of her robe to reveal a naked body except for black stockings and red garters. She leaned back on the bed revealing herself to Pedro while he fumbled with his buttons. "Ever done it before," she asked, watching him carefully as he shook his head. "Good," she said, "You'll be clean."

Daly wasn't overly bright but she was nice, appreciated the freshness of youth and still got some sexual pleasure from her work. She had become a heroin addict and prostitute when she was fourteen while living in Auburn, a foothills mining community on the western slopes of the Sierras. Her mother had died of diphtheria when she was twelve and she had never known a father. Lady Ball, a local madam, saw her potential, introduced her to the opiates and started her working. Daly didn't mind. She functioned in harmony with her surroundings by staying high on drugs. She left Auburn when Lady Ball's place burned down along with much of the town in a huge fire.

Reaching out, she helped Pedro off with his shirt and pants, taking his member in her hand as he had done for himself many times. He released himself in her hand almost immediately, unable to hold back, ashamed, embarrassed. "It's all right," Pedro," she said, "It only takes a minute for a young one like you to get ready again."

She would take her time with Pedro. Lee Sing had brought enough opium to pay for an all night trick and she would enjoy watching Pedro get it up again. In fact, it took him less than ten minutes and she took his hardness into her soft pleasure hole with ease, rocking him in her arms like his mother had done when he was very little. But this wasn't his mother; it was Daly Storm and the feeling was very different.

She showed him how to move up and down and soon he had lost it again. This time it took longer for Pedro to feel the blood but it came back again when she leaned over putting her soft lips around his shaft. This time she sat on top of him and did the bumps and grinds herself. It was erotic, a fantasy come true, *macho* in every way. He had made it three times with Daly; he was in love.

He told Lee Sing all about his experience and they vowed not to tell the fathers. It was a pact made between the young, the oppressed—an agreement that strengthened their bond.

When Juan returned, he took Pedro back to Washoe Clete's place, leaving him with Trigo, saying that he was going to the fights with Sam Hing. He left some money with Pedro to pay for his supper.

"Don't be goin' out tonight," Juan said. "The comet's too close. Things in the sky don't scare me much but no one knows what other folks might do. No one really knows what will happen!"

15

THE LETTER FROM TEX CREATED AN event for the Garland family. They shared it with their friends and neighbors, including Betty Jane Allen, a young student at Mary Hardin-Baylor College in Belton, Texas. She stopped at the Garland home from time to time to find out if there was any word from Tex. Her eyes sparkled when she was encouraged to read his letter. It described his good fortune; foreman on a big ranch, part owner of a gold and silver mine, named Longhorn, adventurer who had fought the Apache, forded the Rio Grande, picked gold from the deep Bodie Mines and horse-backed over snowcapped mountains.

The fire in her breast grew as she thought about Tex and the excitement he was enjoying. It was risky to chase about the country scratching in the ground for gold, the soft yellow metal that drove men and women crazy, but what Tex was doing was successful, even admirable. She wanted to be a part of his destiny. Since that day by the river, her dreams had been filled with his eyes. Betty Jane longed for his strong arms. She would go to Bodie, find Tex, corner his love. She was smitten and sometimes overcome by fearful thoughts. Did he have a girlfriend? His letter made reference to the nice people he had met, but he made no mention of a woman. Would he be spoken for by the time she got there? Would she be too late? Had she gone too far by using the soap? Did he think of her as a hussy? The soap in church. Was it something she should not have done? Has she lost him because of the soap?

According to Tex, Bodie was a grown up city with a school and a newspaper called The Free Press. Betty Jane wrote to the editor, stating that she was an experienced schoolteacher in search of a position out west. It was a small lie. Betty Jane was a good student and capable of teaching. She knew that the men and women of the west were always telling folks that they were qualified to do things that, in fact, they could not do.

She had heard stories about a bar owner named Roy Bean who was prosecuting justice on the Pecos River. He called himself judge but he had never read a law book. Some of the Texas Rangers delivered their prisoners to him, knowing he had no official authority. It was easier than trailing the bad men back to civilization.

She had read the story of Charlie Parkhurst, one of the Wells Fargo teamsters. Charlie had driven stages all over the Sierra Nevada Mountains for almost twenty years. When he passed away in 1879, it was discovered that he was a she!

There was also a man named Stokes in San Jose, California who flipped a coin to determine if he should be a doctor or a carpenter. The coin came up favoring doctor.

If Bean could pass himself off as a judge, Parkhurst as a man and Stokes as a doctor, certainly she could claim to be a teacher. In the west, it was the perception that others had that made the truth. Did such thinking apply outside the west? Was perception greater than truth? Elsewhere? Everywhere? Betty Jane Allen was a smart lady, capable of harboring deep thoughts and instructing children.

It was September before Betty Jane completed her studies at Mary Hardin-Baylor College and was able to travel. She knew that the fastest route to Bodie would be to take the Texas-Pacific Railroad west through San Antonio and Del Rio to Sierra Blanca. There it met the Southern Pacific tracks that ran roughly along the old Butterfield Stage route through El Paso, Demming, Lordsburg, Bowie, Tucson, Yuma and Los Angeles. From southern California's, "home of the angles," she could take the valley line to Sacramento and Reno. However, as a prospective teacher, she was interested in the major historic events of her time; she wanted to ride the route taken by the first transcontinental railroad.

The line was built in two sections; the Union Pacific portion ran from Omaha, Nebraska through Fort Kearney, North Platt, Julesburg, Cheyenne, Laramie, over the Wasatch Mountains and down into the Great Salt Lake

Basin. At Promontory, Utah, it met the tracks built from west to east and originally laid by the Central Pacific Railroad. When she was a young girl in the spring of 1869, she had read everything available about the building of the road and the meeting of the tracks at Promontory where the dignitaries drove a golden spike. She wanted to experience, first hand, some of the exhilaration the railroad engineers must have felt when they first traveled across their own bridges and trestles and passed through their own tunnels. She wanted to see the Black Hills and the Rocky Mountains, and she wanted to view the rivers that had supported the early trappers and wagon train travelers. She wanted to see the namesake of Paiute Indian Chief, Winnemucca, a small settlement that was located in the high desert country of Central Nevada. The experience would help her describe more accurately the things many of the parents of her pupils would know first hand.

The anticipation Betty Jane felt as she prepared for her adventure was almost overwhelming. She got out the old family trunk and packed, then repacked it several times. She had plenty of cloths for hot summer weather but her wardrobe was very narrow and she had almost nothing that would be effective during the long, deep, cold winter months common to Bodie. She considered buying a heavy coat, hat and boots from a Houston store or possibly ordering them through the mail. However, she decided instead to obtain what she needed when she reached Saint Louis or Omaha. Certainly, she thought, the stores in the northern cities would have a good selection of warm clothing.

Betty Jane withdrew from the bank the money her grandmother had left when she died and purchased a coach ticket to New Orleans. She also arranged passage via riverboat from New Orleans to Saint Louis, and then on to Omaha.

It's exciting, she thought. I can't wait to get going, to be on my way. And Tex is at the end of the trail. Tex is in Bodie with a pot of gold. Is he digging at his mine, riding over the high mountains, fighting Indians, herding cattle and leading men? Is he alone or has he found another woman? I must find out, even if I go to hell trying.

Betty Jane felt time was her enemy. The longer she waited in Houston the greater the chance that Tex would find someone else. It seemed like an eternity before the departure day arrived.

Finally she was on her way, armed with her graduation certificate and the letter she had received from the town's mayor, advising her that her teaching services would be welcome. The letter indicated that the Bodie schoolhouse had been completed in 1879 and that it could be found on Green Street. The school usually had forty or fifty students and there was plenty of work for a second teacher. He also communicated that the battery of attorneys working in the Molinelli Building also had openings for employees with sufficient education to work as legal assistants.

She headed by stagecoach from Houston to New Orleans where she planned to catch a riverboat. It would transport her north, on the Mississippi River, to Saint Louis. There she would switch to a smaller boat going up the Missouri River to Omaha. She would be sailing on the same waters that had carried most of the railroad supplies and construction materials that were used to build the eastern portion of the transcontinental railroad. Rails, spikes, switches, signals and other essentials were fabricated in east-coast factories, shipped to New Orleans and then moved on barges to the beginning of the track in Omaha.

The coach clattered onto the cobbled streets of the French Quarter, announcing her arrival in New Orleans, the Paris of America. New Orleans was a fascinating city packed with music, glamour, theater opera combined with gambling, fancy brothels and opium dens. Ornate restaurants that served Cajun delicacies like crawfish *étouffé* were scattered about the French Quarter.

The city, sitting at the base of the Mississippi River delta, is mostly below sea level. It floods easily and sometimes the bodies of the dead that were buried underground rose to the surface. For that reason, most modern graves were built on the surface.

It was a miserable, hot day, swamp-like, unhealthy, much like Houston and typical of Gulf Coast cities, when Betty Jane arrived. Walk slow on the shady side of the street. That's what the natives say, she thought. The streets were dirty and the city looked unkempt. She worried about getting yellow fever, one of the many known diseases that germinated in New Orleans. She also thought about hurricanes, the huge storms that frequently smashed into the community. When they came, they were led by a string of swirling tornadoes that could rip up trees, batter down the strongest buildings leaving injured and dead people scattered among the ruins. Rain fell in seemingly never-ending sheets and the wind was heavy with it's power. The sea surge that ran before the storm swelled up like a huge, moving mountain as it found the shallows near the shoreline. It's waters crashed into the city flooding destroying and killing. New Orleans is certainly an imperfect place, she thought. Yet, it was an exciting place where residents with mostly French, Spanish and African lineage could invent reasons for parties regularly.

Exciting, yes this place is certainly that, thought Betty Jane as she recalled some of the history of New Orleans. Such an old city, claimed for France around 1680 by the explorer, Sieur de La Salle. It became United States territory in 1803 when the Louisiana Purchase was signed. And later, there was the big battle when the city was defended against the British in 1815. New Orleans was saved by an unlikely combination of forces. Andrew Jackson and the pirate, Jean Laffite, fought side by side to win the day. Imagine the chagrin of the wealthy city folks who needed the help of a buccaneer to protect their homes.

In the early years, cotton and slave trade supported commerce in New Orleans. Cotton and sugar cane came by boat and barge down river from ports like Memphis. By 1880 the railroads had displaced much of the river traffic and the Port of New Orleans was open to seagoing steam ships that hauled products to worldwide markets.

She boarded the Lyon, a paddle wheeler with two very tall, well-decorated, smoke stacks. The flat-bottomed steamboat was soon on its way north up the Mississippi River. It moved against the current, dodging sandbars and sometimes touching bottom. Their departure was punctuated by the ship's horn, the creaking of the pilings at dockside, the churning of the stern paddle wheel and music from the boat's minstrels. The canopy over the afterdeck provided some relief from the steamy air and blazing sun, and the movement of the vessel produced a breeze that provided relief from both the muggy conditions and mosquitoes.

The passenger areas aboard the Lyon were generous, like the trappings of a fine hotel. Thick carpets, gold framed paintings, thick, rich drapes, marble topped tables and mahogany furniture adorned the small cabins, dining areas and gambling casino. The boat provided a perfect setting for romance, but Betty Jane Allen had her heart fixed on her blond Texas cowboy. She worried throughout the trip about what he might be doing, what adventures he might be enjoying without her. She also worried some about the comet. Some people said it would destroy the world. Her educated self knew better but her emotional self worried. She asked herself, What does Tex think about the Comet? But, more importantly, what does Tex think about me and why did he leave without saying good-by? Her fear of the solar visitor was much less powerful than her concerns about Tex, her love. Strange, how something as unique as a comet can give way in ones mind, give way to earthly emotion. Love is like wine, to sip it is fun, to drink the whole bottle can be a headache, she thought.

Many of the ante-bellum river plantation homes could be seen from the deck of the Lyon as she glided up river.

An old, tall, pillared, white house lurked behind the *allée*, an aligned grove of live oak trees between the river and the main house. The *gavconniéres*, guest quarters, stood on either side of the entrance. In the back she imagined the *pigeonniers*, carriage house, cotton gin and slave quarters. There were beautiful dark green magnolia trees surrounded by slightly unkempt camellias, roses, palmettos and Spanish Dagger. Spanish moss hung thickly from the trees in the *alleé*. She spotted a young woman sitting on a swing in the gallery that ran around the plantation house. Everything showed signs of decline and decay, common to many plantations after the Civil War.

They tied up at various ports along the Mississippi River, the largest being Memphis that was a cotton and hardwood center and Saint Louis, a trade and manufacturing hub. In Saint Louis she changed to a small paddle wheeler that took the smaller Missouri River past Kansas City to Omaha.

Lewis and Clark, Brigham Young and most of the early trailblazers and mountain men had followed this same Missouri River route. "Brigham Young," she said out loud to herself. Another religious leader driven far away from his chosen land by those who objected to his religious beliefs. It's always the same in every culture. The unalterable spirit of man, in its ceaseless quest for immortality, finds ways to be destructive.

Omaha became a railroad center when construction started on the transcontinental railroad and it now included upwards of seventy five thousand people. It was a good place for Betty Jane to shop for winter garb. I like shopping, she thought, it's fun to pick out something new. She found the things she thought she needed for the Bodie winter, but Betty Jane had no real idea of just how cold it would get.

She boarded the train in Omaha and headed west, imagining what the troop that had built this part of the line looked and felt like. Spread out over three hundred miles ahead of the end of the track were some ten thousand men; former soldiers both Union and Confederate, freed slaves, Irishmen, Englishmen, Germans, and others. They were split into working groups, lead by the survey party, which included the chief engineer, rod men, flagmen, chain men, ax men, teamsters, hunters and a small military escort. The survey party laid out the course the track would follow. Next, came the location team. They staked out the exact grade and curves getting them ready for the graders. The grading crews blasted, cut and filled the grade, following the instructions left by those who proceeded them. A continuous train of wagons brought supplies, materials, tools, food and water to the thousands of graders who worked feverishly. The bridge and trestle men came next. They were pressured to remain ten to twenty five miles ahead of the track crews. The last section in the long parade actually laid the track, ties, rails, fish plates, switch stands and the like, using their hands, hammers and spikes. There are five ties to every twenty feet of rail, she recalled. They worked, five on each side of a rail, lifting in unison. Each long slab of metal, weighing seven hundred pounds, rose into the air and was dropped, on signal, close to its proper position. The rail was then "lined" to grade, tapped into proper position, with hammer. A mile a day had been the standard until General Grenville Dodge, head of the Union Pacific's Railroad "Army," got his crews into full swing. Two miles a day—then three miles a day became the new target.

"Hell on wheels," construction camps, sprang up along the line of march. Camp followers, sporting women, gamblers, whiskey dealers and thugs showed up in numbers at the construction camps. They were leaches, sucking on the wages of the work crews. General Dodge cleaned them out, military style, from time to time but they always came back or were replaced by others. They seemed to be indestructible, like cockroaches. Supply trains ran from the Hell on Wheels camps to the end of the track daily, fulfilling all the needs of the workers. What an adventure, the birth of a railroad, thought Betty Jane.

Her train rumbled on out of the deep valley formed by the Platt River and up into the Black Hills, passing over the gradual grade of General Sherman Pass. It was an easy way through the mountains, a route found years earlier by Grenville Dodge when he rode in uniform under the command of General Sherman.

While the Union Pacific was striking to the west from Omaha, the Central Pacific Railroad Company was building eastward from Sacramento, California. The work on both ends of the line was triggered by the Pacific Railroad Bill, passed by the United States Congress and signed into law by President Lincoln in July, 1862. The Bill also triggered a one hundred gun salute that was followed by an all day and night drunk in San Francisco.

The eastward construction was motivated and partially financed by four San Francisco merchants: Charles Crocker, Mark Hopkins, Collis Huntington and Leland Stanford. It began in 1863. Government money and land financed most of the drive across the treacherous slopes of the Sierra Nevada Mountains, sixteen thousand dollars per mile for level land construction, forty eight thousand per mile for mountain construction, and twelve thousand acres of land per mile of track.

One of the first big problems faced by those Central Pacific builders was finding crews. Most men who lived in California and who were capable of physical labor were either prospecting for their own gold or working in the mines for four dollars a day. They solved the dilemma by dispatching agents to oriental ports and authorizing the agents to hire Chinese by the batch, a thousand at a time. Central Pacific was required to guarantee the return of Chinese bodies to their homeland if one of their number was killed on the job. The people of China were hungry in the early 1860s, and they were willing to take work almost anywhere as long as their remains could lie in rest with their ancestors. They came to America without benefit of citizenship, as minorities who were discriminated against by almost all the whites. Like other minorities, they had almost no legal rights because they were not permitted to testify against whites. They worked for very small wages, but still managed to say, "May Buddha bless you," to their oppressors. At the time of peak construction, over seven thousand Chinese worked alongside a few thousand whites on the western portion of the railroad.

Betty Jane Allen thought back on stories she had read. Getting over the Sierra Nevada Mountains, called "The Hill," by railroad people, was an incredible miracle of engineering. They crossed the great river canyons eaten away for millions of years by runoff water and glaciation. They scaled the sharp granite cliffs that, only a few years earlier, had been impassable for horse and wagon. They braved the powerful winter winds, the snow and ice. Trains usually stopped for ten minutes on the canyon rim called "The Horn" by railroad folks, so passengers could have a good look at the yawning abyss. In the foothills at the lower elevations, the mountains were spotted with sycamore trees and stands of oak including white, blue and live. Higher up were pine trees of all types, fir and mountain hemlock, a place where bear, deer, mountain lion, beaver, coyote and squirrel could live in harmony with nature.

Close to the top near Donner Summit was an underground town. It provided winter quarters for crews and contained a restaurant, communications center, office, shop and turntable. As the train went eastward over the top, the passengers could look down the sheer side of the mountains and have a perfect view of Donner Lake. The lakesite is marked by many graves and headstones reminding one of the unfortunate people who had followed George Donner and been unable to climb over the summit in the winter of 1846 and 1847. Eighty-six people had started out together from Independence, Missouri, Thirty-six perished.

The passengers' view from the train in the high country was often blocked by snow sheds. They were sturdy wooden tunnel-like structures, built over much of the track to protect the road from twenty to thirty foot drifts of the white stuff that would frequently build up along the track. Some of the snow sheds had movable sides that could be pulled open during the summer, permitting passengers a better view. The engineers did everything they could to make the track safe and usable year around but sometimes their efforts were still not enough. In 1872, a Central Pacific passenger train was snowbound near Donner Summit for two weeks.

Betty Jane's head was full of images. It was almost as if she was a part of the pictures she had formed in her mind: people building tunnels, trestles, cutting trees and laying track. When she dreamed like this, Betty Jane's soul became part of the early west–the soul of a traveler making its way over the countryside. Her spirit, in fact all of herself, was also with Andrew J. Russell, photographer, who had mounted his studio and darkroom on a springboard wagon and headed west. Then she was a pioneer, an explorer, riding with Kit Carson, John Fremont and the others. She was at Sutter's Mill when gold was found; she was panning in the American River when the color was so thick you could feel its weight in your hands. Gold! That's what built the eighteen hundred miles of track she was now moving on while dreaming about the past and anticipating the future.

When darkness fell, Betty Jane stared out the window at the Great September Comet flashing through the sky. It seemed as if it were traveling with her, taking her toward some unknown destiny. Leading her, she thought, out of her dream world and back to Tex.

The track ran to the north of the Great Salt Lake, that huge inland body of water that has no outlet to the sea. The train by-passed Salt Lake City, founded in 1847 by Brigham Young after leading his Mormon followers west. Betty Jane recalled from her reading that the first group of Mormons had left Illinois in the dead of winter in 1847; driven out because they were different, had views that didn't square with the locals. They believed, for example, in polygamy and saw themselves as "chosen people."

The Mormons stayed on the north side of the Platt River to avoid contact with other folks as they made an orderly march west. Organization was one of their strong points. They tied a rag to one of the wagon wheels and counted its revolutions each day. Knowing the circumference of the wheel and its daily revolutions, they could compute the distance they had traveled. They built bridges and put up signs to help future travelers.

Betty Jane had not read *The Book of Mormon* but she had heard the story about how the seagulls had saved the settlement. The Mormon camp was taken under attack in 1848 by locust, short-horned grasshoppers, the kind that bunch up into massive, migrating, airborne swarms. When the locust descend to feed, they eat everything that is green along with leather goods, cloths and softwood. A large cloud of the beasts could clear hundreds of square miles of territory in a very short period of time. The swarm that had attacked the Salt Lake area was met by a gigantic flock of gulls, lake gulls actually, the kind that live near saline inland lakes, feeding normally on brine shrimp and insects. The gulls were hungry and the locust retreated, leaving the Mormon settlement alone.

Betty Jane's train rolled on without regard to history. It swung around the lake, passing through Promontory and then moving westward through many small, desolate, whistle stop settlements in western Utah and Nevada. The melody of the train as it clattered over the iron rails and the rock and roll created by the movement of the train had captured the spirit and imagination of Betty Jane. She experienced a bonding with the engine and its cars. They were friends on an adventure, rolling across the bleak, hot, high desert, western landscape.

At Reno's depot, a modern, ornate stopping point, she saw him, Chief Winnemucca in full battle dress, complete with feathered headgear, standing on the platform. He was telling chilling stories to travelers about the Indian wars, making a living by "haunting" the Nevada depot as an employee of the Central Pacific Railroad. He provided excitement, something for the passengers to remember when traveling over the boring terrain in Nevada. Most of his "Digger Indian" followers had left Nevada to build their crude wickiups on reservation land in eastern Oregon. In fact, the Paiute, Cheyenne, Sioux, Shoshoni, Kiowa, Osage, Pawnee, Kansa, Arapaho, Blackfoot, Oglala, Miniconjou, Brule, Ute, Wichita and other Indian tribes had mostly disappeared from the lands she had just traversed.

Betty Jane was soon on her way south to Carson City and prepared herself for the final leg of the journey by coach.

The Wells Fargo stagecoach ride from Carson City, south to Bodie followed the east fork of the Carson River, named for the famous explorer. The coach moved quickly through the hilly country just east of the high peaks that formed part of the Sierra Nevada Mountains. Betty Jane could see small patches of snow left over from the prior winter on the higher eastern slopes. Lake Tahoe lay on the other side of those rugged granite cliffs, but the clear, deep waters were not visible from the stagecoach. The high desert countryside that stretched out to the east of the river was brown and dry from the warm summer sun.

They bumped and rattled over the irregular trailway through Genoa before turning southeast, away from the river and made several stops to refresh themselves and change horses. They had supper in Wellington and then continued traveling in the dark; a thick, heavy, cold darkness that caused the passengers to huddle under their blankets. They looked into the night sky for the comet but it seemed to be hidden in the blackness, a thick black shroud, foreboding, blocking out the light from the moon and stars. The horses were working hard, pulling up the Sweetwater grade.

They were at the summit when something happened. The team became unsettled, almost impossible to handle, and the teamster halted the coach. There were lights—ights that had pierced the dark shroud—lights in an unusually still, black sky. The horses became unnaturally quiet and a hush came over the forest. Betty Jane stared out the window and saw a string of three, possibly four lights, moving about in the air, far to the south. The night air, though cold and dry, felt thick and seemed to be filled with something heavy. The passengers and horses had became frozen in place, watching the lights as they played in the night sky, moving—turning, changing directions and then unexpectedly shooting up into the blackness. There were definitely four of them—four fiery lights—like roman candles rising up into the blackness.

Had Tex seen whatever it was? She wondered, thinking that he must have.

No one slept the rest of the night as they resumed their journey and rattled downward to Fletcher's Station where the breakfast table buzzed with conversation about the sighting. What was it, something from beyond this planet? Had it landed? Where? Would it return? Was it dangerous? Were they moving into harm's way? There were no answers.

They continued south, heading directly toward the place where the strange lights had disappeared. They were in Aurora at ten in the morning. Don Southerland, the coach driver, had babbled on about the town during breakfast. In fact he had made a pest of himself talking so much about the huge gold finds in Aurora when everyone else wanted to talk about the strange sighting.

Betty Jane remembered one of his interruptions. "Aurora's one of the biggest gold camps in these parts. Rich. Fine placer gold and deep mines. Folks made so much dough they built most houses with brick! 'magine! Brick! Fetched by clipper 'round the Horn to Frisco. Then hauled by riverboat, rail and wagon to the diggin's. The miners figur'd this to be one settlement that wouldn't burn down. Gett'en color was awful good 'round these parts for years. I shoud'a been digg'in, not driv'in."

Aurora, she thought. Goddess of dawn. A gold camp on the east side of the great mountains, facing the rising sun and built with brick to keep it from burning up.

They changed coaches in Aurora and arrived in Bodie early that afternoon. A tired, Betty Jane Allen had reached her destination thirteen days after leaving Houston.

Bodie was there but her man was gone. She would locate people who knew him and visit the ranch where he had been foreman but no one would be able to tell her what had happened to Tex Garland.

16

JOHN DE LA ROCHE WAS MUCH OLDER now but he still craved excitement. He missed the mountains, trapping, killing, having his hands on raw gold, building an empire. His life was too settled. He wanted action and Louis DiSimone suggested a high stakes game, one John could enter without going into the backcountry. The game was stocks, ownership rights in the Bodie mines.

"You can buy them," said Louis, "and take advantage of the chance to hit the *Veda Madre*. You know what they are saying about the big mines around Bodie! All the gold-bearing veins will meet deep below the mountain forming a huge mother lode. All the rock at that depth will be gold—pure gold. Imagine a golden lode that looks like a great, long loaf of bread. A loaf that is maybe forty, fifty, sixty feet thick that runs for miles. The price of the mine stocks will go up and up. If you owned enough of the stock you could become the richest man in the world. You could buy shares on margin, actually sort of borrow the money. That way you could own more shares without having to raise much cash. I think you could get hold of a million dollars in Bodie mine stocks for as little as a hundred thousand."

Louis didn't talk about what would happen if the stock prices fell. He also failed to mention that he would get a little richer too, thanks to the sales commissions he would receive if John purchased stocks.

Easy money, thought John. If I were Louis I would keep my mouth shut and buy all the Bodie stocks for myself. In the summer of 1879, John de la Roche plunged into buying Bodie mine stocks including Red Cloud, Blackhawk, Noonday and Paris. He bought as much stock as he could on margin and paid for the rest with money borrowed from the DiSimone Bank and other financial institutions in Vancouver, Seattle and San Francisco where he had established lines of credit. The Bodie mines had been popular speculations on the San Francisco Stock Exchange Board for some time, and the price John paid was near their record highs. He didn't realize he might be paying too much and his sense of invincibility prevented him from checking. The quest for *Veda Madre*, that was the thing—prospecting, hunting, seeking—provided the orgy he required to fill his reservoir with vitality.

But in the early 1880s the Bodie mine stock prices began to fall. They dropped slowly at first, and then faster and faster as the Exchange called margins and people began to panic. John's paper was called as well and now the banks wanted their money—millions of dollars. He would be forced to sell his properties, his sawmills, canneries and possibly even the hat and coat business. His wealth would disappear and his status would evaporate.

John knew he was not responsible for the falling stock prices, it was the doing of the bankers. They took advantage of him, did not advise him properly, failed to disclose the risks and took his money. They would not give it back. He would fix Louis, fix him forever! A hunter, a trapper against a banker would be no contest. He left a note under DiSimone's door after dark that read, "Come to my office at midnight tonight. Come the back way. Don't let anyone know. Try not to be seen." It was signed William Prescott, Royal Canadian Mounted Police. John knew DiSimone would find the note when he came to work in the morning and that he would comply. He knew the route, could stalk his prey and make a kill in the dead of night.

At around midnight, Louis DiSimone stealthily made his way toward Prescott's office. He was making sure no one saw him, as instructed. Suddenly, out of the dark, a man approached from the rear wielding a heavy sledgehammer. Louis went down without seeing his adversary. He died instantly. His money belt was taken along with a gold ring, watch and pocket change, making robbery the apparent motive. The note was removed from DiSimone's wallet, eliminating the connection between the untimely death of a prominent banker and John's carefully planned trap. He burned it and buried the money belt, ring and watch. The connection between the rendezvous and the death had been broken, relieving John of the fear of an exhaustive investigation that might turn up other motives.

A week later he left for Bodie bent on finding out what was happening, who else was responsible, which others needed to die. No one could cheat the invincible de la Roche and live. He contacted his banking associates in Vancouver, Seattle and San Francisco and found a common thread; the key to the Bodie collapse resided with a man named Paul Arlett, a prominent person who had convinced the bankers that the *Veda Madre* would be found. The bankers, Arlett and others were stupid. They deserved to die for their incompetence but he would deal with the cheat next Paul Arlett, the swindler with a story about a huge mass of pure gold, very deep underground. "Buy shares in the Bodie mines," Arlett had told them. "Buy into the deep mines with tunnels headed toward the bonanza."

De la Roche got more bad news: all the major mine values were still falling. Virtually all the mines had been unprofitable or marginally profitable; all were unable to pay dividends, all required huge capital investments in machinery and all were labor intensive. And the worst message was that most knowledgeable geologists did not believe in the *Veda Madre* concept. The bankers told John that Wells Fargo Bank had levied attachments on the Red Cloud and Noonday Mines and that they would be shut down; in fact, all the Bodie Company stocks John held were near bankruptcy and close to ruin. He was deep in debt. If he sold now he could not cover the losses; his empire would collapse, be sold off piecemeal. He would be insolvent, broke, a friendless looser; his dreams turned to dust. The financial web he had woven had been broken by the bear. Ripped by the bear market for Bodie mine stocks. Paul Arlett and the bankers had bought him to death's financial door and they would be made to pay.

John de la Roche took the stage to Bodie, got a room at the Stewart House and began investigating his prey. It took less than a full day to learn everything he needed to know about Paul Arlett, where he lived, worked, whored. His two ladies of the night were Daly Storm and Nellie Moore. John purchased five gallons of kerosene and waited for night to fall.

A visit with Nellie Moore was first on his agenda. It cost only a few dollars to get into her room and arrange for a trick. Before they got started he asked, "Your friend is Paul Arlett, yes?"

"Paul comes 'round," was the response.

"Often, very often, yes?" he asked.

"Sometimes," Nellie answered, in a tone indicating she was tiring of the questions. "You are his friend, his lover, and I, John de la Roche will kill him, his family, his friends. You are the first."

He reached for his gun too late. Nellie produced a double-barreled tit gun and shot him in the right forearm. She hustled out the door, shouting for help.

He slipped out the open window and made his way back to the Stewart House where he tended his wound and his pride from the same jug, one filled with "panther piss," a mixture of many different alcohols. The bullet had cut clean, missing the bone and passing through. There was a lot of blood but no serious damage except to his ego. Ripped and frustrated, he snarled to himself:

Panther Piss
Panther Piss,
spit it out
and hear it hiss.

Panther Piss
Panther Piss,
watch the comet
see it miss.

Panther Piss
Panther Piss,
Nellie Moore
will pay for this.

With this injury, John sensed the winter of life closing in. He'd progressed from young hunter to murdering prospector to business tycoon to the gates of ruin. And now, John de la Roche, the self-proclaimed great hunter had been shot—shot by a small woman. Anger and humiliation obsessed him. He must get even with the people who cheated him out of his greatness. He would kill Paul and his family tonight. Then he would backtrack, taking out Nellie and the bankers before retreating into the Canadian Mountains where he could start a new lifecycle. He was still, after all, a great hunter, able to care for himself in the backcountry—indestructible.

He drank until two in the morning, took his kerosene to Arlett's house, splashed it carefully all around, adding sticks in places where he thought they would help create a fast, hot fire. He lighted fires on three sides and slipped into the shadows created by a combination of the fire, the comet and moonlight. In his drunken stupor he did not realize that he had set fire to the wrong house.

The next night he headed for the cock fights at Joe Rouse's Saloon where he watched Nellie Moore and another woman, both dressed as men, bet on the old sick looking bird, the one with a missing toe. How stupid, he thought, while placing his money on the young rooster. When the fight started, the sick bird miraculously seemed to come alive, suddenly attacking, pecking, clawing and killing. The shrieking chicken had pecked and clawed away both the life of the other bird and de la Roche's money. A trick, another con, a trap laid by others for him! He was sure. They beat him again, taking his money, his honor, and his pride. He wanted to fight, to kill the barker, Washoe Cete, the man who took the bets, but a tall blond kid beat him to the punch. Cete wasn't dead but he was badly hurt and off somewhere with a doctor. De la Roche followed Nellie and her friend to the fight between the dogs and the badger but this time did not wager with the replacement barker, a Chinese. They had trapped him before and he would not be ensnared again. He made a side bet with an old, dumb Mexican. He could beat the greaser, beat or cheat him, he thought.

17

SOME PEOPLE BELIEVE LOIS HARGAVE headed for the Sierra gold camps after her divorce, in response to the demand from many community leaders for talented stage performers. They speculate that she was seeking escape and adventure. But some say she didn't ever leave her comfortable San Francisco area retreat. In any event, her talent suited the gold camp an environment perfectly.

There were other gold country entertainers who seemed to emulate her style. One such musician named Nellie Moore looked and acted a lot like Lois. Traveling over the Sierra Nevada Mountains by coach and dressed as a dance hall singer, Nellie reached Virginia City, Nevada, one of the more civilized gold rush towns in the west, in 1880. Her hair was long and it was dyed red.

Was Nellie really Lois, disguised so she could sing, dance and deal twenty-one at the Virginia House Saloon and not be recognized by casual acquaintances? No one knew where Nellie hailed from and in the gold camps no one cared much about what had gone on in folks prior lives. That was particularly true of beautiful, adventurous women.

The Virginia City silver bonanza was winding down but there were still over twenty thousand people in the town, mostly men, who she entertained, sometimes two or more at a time.

Later that same year she moved south after hearing about a man worth meeting. He was called The Bad Man From Bodie. She set herself up dealing and entertaining at the Opera House Concert Hall, built to produce legitimate theater but later turned into a saloon and dance hall. Nellie soon found there were many men who carried the handle, Bad Man From Bodie. Over the next two years she took up with most of the bad men including Washoe Cete, Red Rowe, Rattlesnake Dick, John Wheeler and Mike McGowan.

She had known Mike in Virginia City where he had a reputation for biting off noses and ears.

Nellie had plenty of adventures and some close calls. That's why she always carried a tit gun, a small two-shot derringer, in her bodice. She shot a crazy man just last night when he threatened to kill her for pleasuring Paul Arlett. She thought, He was crazy. Was it the approaching comet that turned him mad?

That night Nellie went to the cockfight dressed as a man with her friend Dally Storm. She saw and desperately wanted to meet the person she believed was the real Bad Man From Bodie, a tall, square-jawed, blond, cowboy who beat the hell out of Washoe Cete. He was fast, strong, handsome, with a tail, she imagined, like that of the comet approaching earth. A tail she wanted to feel in her hands, mouth, between her breasts and legs. If the earth was going to end, she hoped it would end with him, plunged deep inside her well.

18

JUAN TOLD PEDRO HE WOULD BE BACK
late. Pedro was glad he was not expected to go to the animal fights. He did not
want to see animals hurt and he had the sweet memories of Daly to occupy
his mind.

The cockfight was held in a smoke filled place called the Joe Rouse
Saloon. Such fights were common in Hispanic communities and Juan had a
keen eye for the aggressive spirit of eventual winners. Washoe Cete was there,
barking at people, taking bets. Juan bet ten dollars on the cock that had an
obvious scar on his neck and was missing one claw. He attacked immediately,
wings thrashing the air and pecked an eye from his dispirited foe. He followed-
up clawing, pecking, screeching, killing in whirlwind style.

Juan waited in line behind a tall, blond, square-jawed, young man
dressed like a cowboy, to get his money from Washoe.

"You owe me a dollar," said the kid, as Washoe looked up from his
book.

"Don't pay off less'an a five 'til everyone else gets theirs. Get to the
back of the line," he said, pushing the cowboy backward into Juan.

"You owe me a dollar," the kid repeated.

Pete laughed with a sneer, responding, "You need a dollar now, pass
the hat, don't come 'round askin' men for that kind'a money, not when real
hombres, real gamblers are waitin'."

Juan edged back, sensing that the blond young man was not going to
be put off, and he was right. Without saying another word, the cowboy hit
Washoe Cete. Hit him hard, straight on the jaw with a quick left hand. The kid
then moved in, throwing a stout right to the mid-section. Cete bent over forward

just as the cowboy delivered a downward falling right to his cheek. There was a crunching sound and Washoe screamed while twisting around and going down. He fell hard, on his back. The cowpuncher dropped on top of Cete pounding both knees into his ribs and both fists into his face. He continued to batter Washoe's body until several in the crowd pulled him off.

"Keep the dollar to remember me by," he said, in a low but clear voice. One "Bad Man From Bodie" was down, a legend destroyed. Washoe Cete would no longer carry that handle and in the eyes of some people, specifically Nellie, Tex would take his place.

Sam Hing, Washoe's gambling sponsor, took over the money. By default he became the barker. Sam was quiet and not well suited for the job of drumming up excitement in the crowd of mostly white folks. However, he was a leader in his community and the custodian of the money being wagered. He seemed to have no choice but to take charge. He paid Juan and the others their due and then led the group to the embankment where the dogs would fight the badger. Prospectors were instinctive gamblers willing to bet on almost anything. They worked hard, digging and scratching in the earth all day, playing by night. Very few had wives to go home to and they were adventurers. Bodie, like all gold camp environments, provided just what the miners wanted; golden poppy, a woman's favors, saloons and gambling. These things had a nighttime value that exceeded the daytime worth of the color sweated from the mountain. Miners seemed driven to find gold and equally driven to give it up. Sam was not very good at barking but the money flowed in because of the spirit of those he was leading.

The badger set his back against the bank. Five dogs were turned loose against him, one at a time. Sam Hing set the betting odds, favoring the badger in the early encounters, collecting and paying out money after each engagement. Four dogs were dragged away dead before the odds turned even. The badger was cut, tired and bleeding. The fifth combatant, a bulldog, went on the attack to the shouting and jeering of a drunken, bloodthirsty crowd. The fight went on a long time before a badly slashed bulldog rolled over on the bloodstained ground, his heart given out. The badger was panting by the bank, alone, red with his own blood and that of five dogs. He had won, but the drunks who had lost their bets were incensed. They attacked the lonely badger with a vengeance. The tall blond from Texas saved him by firing a shot in the air and commanding everyone to leave the badger alone. The miners had already seen Tex in action and no one challenged him.

Juan had been to badger fights all over the Sierra Nevada Mountain in the early gold camps and in the cities of San Francisco and Sacramento. He was familiar with badger courage, fighting skill and will to survive. He bet each time on the badger and increased his poke by over one hundred dollars, paid grudgingly by Sam Hing. He also made an even money side bet of fifty dollars with a French Canadian named John de la Roche but he vanished in the crowd after loosing, giving Juan one more reason to hate *gringos*.

The Mexican couldn't find the French Canadian hunter but de la Roche, well hidden in the trees and shadows, had a good view of Juan. He kept him in sight, a target he planned to strike. No toothless greaser was going to better him. He kept Juan in view for a long time, watched him meet a boy of about thirteen years, saw him depart for town with the Hispanic youngster and the two women who were dressed as men. He followed, keeping out of sight, waiting for an opportunity. He presumed that the boy was Juan's son. If he could snatch the kid and kill him, that would be revenge; even a dumb Mexican would probably be hurt by the loss of a child.

19

JOAN AND FRANCES DEQUILL WERE vindicated the morning of June 10, 1995, when the Bridgeport Newspaper printed an Extra covering the strange sighting reported to both the local and state police by numerous residents and tourists.

Linda McCarthy had the paper at breakfast and she read most of the article to all those present. When she completed the story she looked straight at me and said, "Frances, you and your mother were right, you saw this thing, whatever it was, and none of us believed you. Tell us more about it. Did you hear any noise?"

"No. No noise," I said. "But you could feel it, sense its presence. The air was thick—the animals all sensed it—they froze and watched. It came down as one ball of light with a tail, moving fast, then stopping, then moving again. It came right at us. Got real close, then went overhead traveling with great speed. It came down as one object but split into four parts as it headed south. The four lights circled to the southeast, somewhere near Bodie, I think. One may have gone down for a time. Then it came back up and the four objects went up—almost straight up into the blackness. I could count them, one, two, three and four—shooting up into the sky—following each other. It was something, something I will never forget. It seemed to have an essence, a presence that was not human. Don't laugh. You asked me to tell you what I saw and felt."

"We won't laugh, not today Frances," Linda responded.

It was good to be elevated from the post of a fool to that of the exalted; a position shift experienced by many as life delivers its joys and punches.

Too late, I called Reuters News Service finding that they already had the story from numerous eyewitnesses. Why hadn't I acted sooner? Why had I failed to have "faith and belief" like the old Kingston Trio Song, Desert Pete, suggested? I could have had an exclusive! Feeling the fool, I left breakfast, mad at myself and madder at those who had shunned our story. My spirit fell back into one of life's valleys. I called the local paper and gave Sandra, a reporter, my story. It turned out to be consistent with others she had received.

The following day, there was an article in the paper about a strange group of five people dressed in old fashioned western garb with a yellow dog. They were first seen walking south on the western bank of Mono Lake by a local policeman. Some time later, in Lee Vining, they were picked up by the state police. The strangers seemed confused, disoriented, out of place.

I didn't usually read the local paper when at the ranch but the sighting perked my interest, and secretly I hoped to find my name in a follow-up report. Old news, however, gets little space in a newspaper and although there was another story about the strange object seen on June 9th, the local subscribers' versions of the story were used rather than mine, the outsider.

The horses at the ranch run loose in the pasture at night. They are rounded up at first light and brought to the barn, first for oats and later to be saddled by the wranglers.

After breakfast, around eight-thirty, the dudes mount up and mill around in the yard adjusting their gear, shortening or lengthening stirrups, taking pictures and settling into the saddle. It's always the same, a time when dudes yawn and stretch; farting by the horses is socially acceptable.

There are three rides almost every morning. The "fast" group goes out first anticipating a long ride and a good deal of loping, creek jumping, river fording and other activities suitable for experienced horse people. The "medium" bunch goes next, planning on shorter lopes and less rigorous sport. The "slow" group walks out last with older folks, inexperienced riders and little kids.

Still angry, I went on the morning ride with the fast group. On the first lope I kicked my mare on the lead, bringing her to a full and somewhat reckless gallop, knowing that my superior equestrian skills would permit easy jumping of the small creeks and ditches in the meadow. I did it hoping some of the dudes following, those who had been smart asses when first told of the sighting, would get thrown or at least bounced around dangerously. As expected, the wrangler in charge of the group chastised me for taking the lead and told me to refrain from passing him again. He expected me to be embarrassed, knowing that I had been out of line. Instead he got a sunny smile, one that said, "I got even." The gallop had delivered my spirit from an emotional trough to a mirthful peak.

When the horses are heading back towards the barn, it's prudent for all riders to go slow. The big, strong animals sometimes get excited at the prospect of returning to their home and if they are permitted to run they may take the bit in their mouths and go like hell. Many good riders have been forced to jump off galloping mounts racing headlong into the darkness behind an open barn door.

The people in the fast group were walking their horses back to the barn, facing southeast toward Mono Lake when I suddenly made the mental connection between the sighting and the strangers reported by the newspaper. The fast moving objects had dipped down behind the mountain between this valley and Lee Vining. Four balls of fire going down, three coming back up and circling before going down again, four coming back up and moving out. What happened to the fourth object? Had it landed? Was it connected with the strange people picked-up by the police in Lee Vining? Questions a real reporter would ask but I'm not a newspaperwoman, just a stringer who pens an occasional story.

Should I forget it or follow-up? Was someone else already tracking down the answers? Was it worth the trouble? All of these questions were invading my mind as I stepped down at the hitching rail in front of the stable. I made a decision. "I'll not ride this afternoon; I'm going to chase the story. If there's a connection, it's mine. It might be good for a Pulitzer Prize," I said, half aloud, not really believing I could actually win but enjoying the fantasy.

I went to the newspaper office, talked to Sandra, the reporter who wrote the first sighting story. I was careful not to mention the article about the strange group of folks who were picked up while walking towards Lee Vining. I didn't want Sandra to make the connection. I was afraid she would go charging after my story and she would have the advantage of local contacts and friends in this area.

I stopped at the local police station and got their account of the sighting. Next I drove down Highway 395 to Lee Vining and started canvassing local businesses to find out what people knew about the strangers. I introduced myself as Tip, the reporter, and no one questioned my credentials.

Todd Williams, an employee at the Chevron gas station, said he had seen them, a funny looking bunch who appeared confused. "Drugs, or maybe too much to drink," he said. There was a young, blond man, about six feet tall. And there were two women dressed like the kind of dance hall girls you see in the old John Wayne movies. One had red hair. There was a short, stocky, round faced Irishman wearing an old fashioned bowler. And there was also a young Mexican boy with a yellow dog.

I then talked to the cook at a local restaurant where they made the greasiest fried chicken in North America. He had seen the state police pick them up. I found a Hispanic clerk in the C-Store, a customer in the drug store, the owner of the Texaco Station and a dozen others who claimed to have seen the strangers. The Hispanic woman, Angel Commondoza, had gone outside to get a close look. "The kid's name is Pedro and he calls the yellow dog Trigo, Trigo, that's Spanish for wheat," she said. All of them provided similar descriptions of the group: two men, two women, one Hispanic boy and a yellow dog. Carefully, I recorded the names and addresses of all those interviewed.

Clearly the group was unusual, obviously strangers in the small town of Lee Vining. During the discussions, I determined that the State Police from Bridgeport had made the pick up. One young woman, Laurie Frazier with a flash in her eye, mentioned a cute trooper named Patrick Clayborn attached to that office.

I drove back to Bridgeport and stopped at the state police office to ask about the strangers but no one could give me any information. There seemed to be no record of an arrest or pick up, and the desk clerk suggested I contact the office at Mammoth. I asked about trooper Patrick Clayborn and was told he was off duty. Looking the clerk straight in the eye I said, "Have you ever heard of the Freedom of Information Act?"

The young clerk looked straight back with clear blue eyes and said, "No!"

Perplexed, I drove north over the Walker River Bridge and parked downtown, across the street from an old hotel. I crossed over the highway for a drink in the old bar which had a dinner napkin hanging on the wall signed, Louis L'amour. The only problem was that Louis was deceased by the time the napkin was signed by an impostor who convinced the hotel owners that he was the famous author, writing a story set in Bridgeport, and that the old hotel would act as a centerpiece in his new novel. They gave him their best room, wined and fed him, receiving for their trouble only a signature on a napkin. He left one morning without announcing his departure, his con having exhausting itself, and it was several months before the hotel owners found out that Louis had been dead for over a year.

I called the state police at Mammoth from the pay phone, getting no more information than I had obtained from the cops in Bridgeport. I then looked up the number for Patrick Clayborn in the local directory and dialed. When he answered, I asked him about the Lee Vining pick up and was shocked when he denied any knowledge of the strangers. Baffled and frustrated, I had a second glass of wine in the bar before going methodically over my notes. "Strangers show up in Lee Vining. Half the townspeople either see them or hear about them. There's an article in the paper about their arrival. The state cops pick them up and then can't remember that they did it."

Why? Over and over I write why? Why? Why? I was feeling power, the power of a reporter closing in on a story. I wasn't Frances the housewife, I was Tip the reporter. I had another glass of Chablis and began to write how? How? How? How can I get the answer? Should I go to the chief of police, threaten him, bring in an attorney? They can't silence all those witnesses. But what if the police won't talk? How much pressure can I bring to bear? Who will care about the strangers? Smoking and drinking too much, I forgot about dinner at the ranch and mother. I stumbled out of the hotel bar at nine in the evening, much too drunk to drive, and took my car out onto the road and headed for McCarthy's ranch. I got as far as the hospital before two police cars, one state and one local, pulled me over. A breath test and a quick trip to the Bridgeport tank followed, consistent with California law requiring the immediate dispatch of drunk drivers to jail.

On the way to the jailhouse, I asked the local cop about the strangers and confided the reason for my drunkenness. A frantic call to my husband produced, after a time, an attorney who was unable to spring me. I wondered how long I would be held.

At about five in the morning, a man in a dark gray, pin-stripped suit stopped by and asked the duty clerk to let him see Frances privately. He met me in a small office, did not give his name, and told me that if I forgot about the Lee Vining strangers, the drunk driving charge would be dropped. Humiliated, hung over, thirsty and in need of a bath I agreed, finding freedom within thirty minutes.

Back at the ranch, apologies completed, I pondered my plight knowing that I had hit on something big, really big, a *Veda Madre* for a reporter. Mother, the wise old gal, had always been good at solving problems so I told her the story, asking the questions why and how. I considered calling my husband, Brodrick, but figured he would be mad about having to pay a lawyer to get his drunken wife out of the clink. He'd give no help, only a lecture.

Mother and I talked all morning. I was getting frustrated while going over my notes out loud for the third time when mother said, "The girl, Laurie Frazier in Lee Vining, use her, she knows the policeman. What's his name? Patrick. Get her to tell you what he knows. Make a game out of it; she'll be able to make him talk. If you get her interested, involved, she'll want to know. You know how people are, everyone wants to know secrets and very few can keep form telling. They tell because they want to show people how smart they are. He won't be any different, he'll want to talk to her about the strangers. It'll make him feel important. And she'll want to tell someone else."

We got Laurie's phone number from information and she agreed to meet me after work. She asked if her name would be in the story. I assured her that it would, if she wished, reemphasizing her importance and the vital nature of her information. We had a couple glasses of wine at a local gin mill while I listened patiently to Laurie's story about the strangers; the same tale I had heard before. Laurie then got very relaxed and added a few embellishments before I finally said, "I talked to Patrick Clayborn about those people. For some reason he didn't want to admit he was here." I caught a flash in Laurie's laughing eyes.

"That's Pat for you. He adores police secrets. Makes him feel important."

"Oh," said I. "Well, he sure wouldn't open up for me." Being cautious, I changed the subject ordering another round before casually remarking, "I wonder where they took them, don't you? Do you suppose Patrick knows?"

"Don't know," said Laurie. "But I can find out Saturday night."

We chatted on and I bought our dinner. As we were leaving I said, "Okay if I call you Sunday?"

"Sure," said Laurie, "but not before noon."

I couldn't wait for Sunday to roll around. Not wanting to appear anxious, I waited until quarter to one before calling Laurie who answered on the first ring. We talked while about her date with Pat before getting to the point.

Laurie said, "Pat didn't want to talk about the strangers but I made him. Promised not to tell anyone else, though."

I held my breath. Was this another dead end? I waited, my instincts screaming to ask, knowing I should not press, suspecting that Laurie wanted, like Mother said, to share secrets. Hell, I know that most people need to share secrets, desperately. How could I help it happen? Finally, I said, "How did the dog act. Was he friendly, or a biter?" It broke the spell and got Laurie to laugh and start talking again.

"He didn't talk about the dog but I didn't see any teeth marks on any part of his body, nowhere," she said with a titter. "The kid's name was Pedro Olivera, the big blond was Tex Garland. There was an Irishman; I don't recall his name, Sean Mack something I think, and the ladies were called Daly Storm and Nellie Moore. Ladies of the night, probably. A man from the F.B.I. was there and a colonel from Edwards Air Force Base after they made the pick up. The F.B.I. wants it kept quiet. That's why Pat wouldn't talk."

I said, "Wow, F.B.I. and Air Force. Wonder if they come up this way often to visit with strangers?"

Laurie laughed. "I haven't seen them, that's for sure. The F.B.I. guy came all the way from Pasadena. Flew up on a small plane. They took the strangers somewhere. Pat doesn't know where. Back south he thinks. They took the dog too."

We chatted for a long time. I probed for additional information but got none. Laurie had told all she knew and I suspected that she soon would be telling the secrets to other special friends, providing an increasing number of Lee Vining locals fodder for speculations. Surely other reporter's would get wind of this unusual situation and start following the story. Speed was important if I was going to get recognition for breaking this news.

I went over my notes again, asking the same kinds of questions as before, "What happened? Why? Where are the strangers? How can I find them?" I spent another few days at the ranch, researching the history of Bridgeport, Bodie, Mono Lake and Lee Vining. I thought it was important to go back to the days of panning, digging and rocking because of the physical appearance of the strangers. I read about the early trapping in the area by Jedadiah Smith in 1827, the trail blazing of Christopher "Kit" Carson in 1829 and Lieutenant Joseph Reddeford Walker in 1833, the men responsible for opening the mountain passes to the coast. I learned how some of the prospectors who came west in 1849 and thereafter to seek their fortunes on the western slopes of the Sierra Nevada Mountains ended up on the east side. They ran short of the fertile ground and easy color and gradually worked their way over the passes down the eastern slopes of the same mountains. Strikes at Virginia City, Aurora, Candelaria, Bulleville, Washoe City, Como, Pine Grove, Rockland, Mono, Dogtown, Bodie and other places all followed.

Since the strangers had been seen coming from the direction of the Bodie Mountains when approaching Mono Lake, I was particularly interested in Bodie, a camp that had gone full circle from the first finding of gold and silver in 1859 on Silver Hill by W.S. Bodey. It reached its peak with nearly ten thousand people in 1880. There were many deep mines and their owners were hiring anyone they could find to dig frantically. Each mine owner wanted to be he first to find the gigantic, pure gold deposit called *Veda Madre*. Mine stock prices rose dramatically. The prices went up and up on the San Francisco exchange. But then, the news began to change. "Was there really a *Veda Madre*? someone asked. "Were Bodie mine stock prices too high?" The stock prices began to fall, faster and faster. There was no *Veda Madre*, and in the 1990s Bodie became a ghost town.

I drove out to the old settlement that was now managed by the State park authority. Large mining companies had reopened some of the diggings but what was left of the old town was still lifeless. I was struck by the smallness of things, chairs, tables, doorways and the like which were much smaller than what people use today; a reflection of how much mankind has grown in size, if not wisdom, over the past one hundred plus years. It had been a very rough place where a killing a week was not unusual. Parents told their children to be good or the Bad Man From Bodie, might get them.

The Bad Man story reminded me of the university course I had taken. We studied Indian Culture. The Apaches had a *Godeh*, a character who was used to frighten, control and discipline small children. The *Godeh*, the bad troll of the Chiricahua and the Bad Man From Bodie, characters with similar roles in very different societies. Strange, I thought, how two such diverse cultures found common ways to control their young.

According to Mark Twain, Bodie had only two seasons. The breakup of one winter and beginning of the next. Monster winter winds called zephyrs and hot dry santan blows ripped across the high valley either freezing or searing the landscape. The trees that once struggled to survive in the unfriendly environment were hacked down for commercial use and the few streams and ponds around Bodie were mostly polluted by mining operations. Human waste ran in the streets of Bodie washing up against drunks lying fallow in the mud. A nasty place, I thought.

The structure of the gold producing earth in the area was also discordant, disorderly and unsettled as my work revealed. I had been riding horses around Bridgeport since I was old enough to get my boot into a stirrup and I knew that the Sierras had a sharp steep eastern slope much different from the gradual grade of the western side. I had ridden to the top of Eagle Creek, over nine thousand feet above sea level, and looked down to the east from the high ridge above its headwaters where you could view Bodie Mountain and the eastern countryside for hundreds of miles, with its valleys, mountains, lakes and rivers. My blood always ran cold when I sat in the saddle looking down the sheer eastern slope where a few false steps could end one's days on earth. But I rode back up to the top many times because of the thrill the beauty of the scene provided.

I knew the mountains but not the forces that built them and the environment for gold and silver to appear on the surface. My research provided new insight. The upper part of the earth is divided into several rigid segments called plates, each plate consisting of a continent. These plates, which make up the earth's surface, slide about on top of the material below, a sticky viscous substance like Shoe Goo before it dries. The North American plate was once attached to the western edge of Europe and Africa and the South American plate was connected to central and southern Africa before they slid apart. As the North American plate moved westward it ran into the eastbound Pacific plate that was forced to dive beneath it. This slow motion collision of heavy weights created an enormous amount of heat and pressure, causing the brewing of a thick, underground, stew. Geologists had names for parts of the stew: igneous and metamorphic rocks, molten granitic magma, gold, silver, copper, serpentine, iron and other minerals. Some of the stew squeezed its way up to the surface where it cooled and became hard. The underground pushing and shoving caused the surface of the earth to fracture, twist and tilt. Mountains rose up where none had been before. Molten lava spewed out onto the surface covering whatever stood in its path. Volcanoes formed and then erupted, blowing hot ash and debris thousands of miles. Ocean waters were driven back. New rivers and lakes formed. The northern portion of the Sierra Nevada Mountains were tilted upward along a line of sheer faults on its eastern side, creating the gradual western rise and steep eastern slopes. All this activity took hundreds of millions of years and is still going on but none of it matters to most people unless they find themselves near a fault that moves, a volcano that erupts or an outcrop full of rich minerals. The area around Bodie had a long history of subsurface throttling and surface extrusion, accompanied by deep veins of gold and silver.

As the winds blew from west to east carrying moisture from the Pacific Ocean, the clouds they brought delivered heavy snows and rains, particularly on the mountains' western slopes. During the ice ages, huge glaciers formed and carved out magnificent valleys like Yosemite and defined future river courses. As the earth warmed, the ice melted leaving mixed piles of rocks called moraines, like those near Mono Lake. Rivers with waters that sought the sea or inland lakes developed and gold and silver, copper, iron and other precious stones and minerals were eroded away by the fluid traveling downstream. The migrating waters deposited part of their load along their course and part at their destination. Most of the early gold finds were made in rivers and streams where the waters slowed, leaving the heavy minerals on the bottom. Lee Vining Creek and other creeks and dry washes around Bodie were good examples.

Earthquakes jolted the area near Bodie. Such tremors being caused, according to the devout–those who decry scienc–by the spirits of the damned rocking the core of the earth in their useless efforts to escape. The instability of the land around Bodie was well chronicled, highlighted by the monster earthquake in the Owens Valley in the 1870s, another, near Fallon, Nevada, in the 1950s and very recent movements along Highway 395 south of Lee Vining. Was the surface activity in the area related to the extraterrestrial or the spirits of the dead I wondered? Or was it just associated with the continuing struggle of the plates below the earth's surface, as the current version of science suggested? Whatever the reason, the earth in the area around Bodie was discordant, disorderly and unsettled, and its condition caused the curious to ask questions.

I continued checking around town, at the courthouse and library, using low profile approaches, not wanting to alert the police to my continuing investigation. I recognized that the story had newsworthy value but nothing like it would have if I could locate the strangers. If I release what I have, a stampede of reporters with better support and contacts will find my people, tell my story and win my prize. If I keep quiet, the missing might never be located. Hope resides in Pasadena, Edwards Air Force Base, the Freedom of Information Act and my head start. Pasadena and Edwards are close to home. I decided to continue to dig.

I drove south on Highway 395, rolling over the repaired roadbed near Lee Vining that had been recently ripped apart by an earthquake. I flew past the small airport near Mammoth and on through the old mining towns of Bishop, Big Pine, Independence, Lone Pine and Mojave before reaching the windmill spotted hillside that marked the pass between the desert and the

Los Angeles area. Very high winds pour over the pass almost continuously during the summer months, blowing from west to east. They are so strong and consistent that the government tested an electrical power generating system on the hillsides using windmills. It must have been a hell of a pass to ride a horse over in the old days, I thought.

From my Pasadena home I continued the research, aware that people had reported unidentified flying objects for many years. I am skeptical, a norm for reporters and consistent with mankind's tendency to reject new ideas. I also know about coverups and have no doubt that those high up in government had both the propensity and ability to carry them out. The story I am working on gives rise to the possibility that my skepticism about extraterrestrial encounters has been misplaced but it also reinforces what I believe about government. I spent my first two days back home studying UFOs, and found, to my amazement, that there had been literally hundreds of sightings reported, many of them preceding man's adventures into the sky. I was particularly impressed with early reports west of the Mississippi, which I summarized in my notes:

1873 Fort Riley, Kansas. Cavalry horses bolted when a shining object roared over parade ground.

1873 Bonham, Texas, northeast of Dallas. Shining object zooms and counter-zooms over a party of field workers. One man killed in the panic.

1882 Bridgeport, Bodie, Lee Vining, California. Strange lighted elliptical object seen descending from the sky and later going back up. Thought to be a comet or related to the Great September Comet. Some said it had several parts.

1897 Benton, Texas. Search light reported shining form a saucer.

1897 Kansas City, Kansas and Missouri. Disk shaped object bearing colored lights

1899 El Paso, Texas. An illuminated disk sighted at terrific height.

1899 Prescott, Arizona. Same as El Paso.

It struck me that Sean McCarthy had vanished from Bodie in 1882.

Laurie had said an Irishman named Sean. Sean something was with the strangers. A connection? A connection after one hundred and thirteen years? Ridiculous, I said to myself.

I read the theories of various UFO aficionados who had a passion for proving that visitors from outer space were real and they made arguments suggesting that some very early art, sculpture, biblical passages, Egyptian gods and other antiquity described extra terrestrials and their space craft. I found that there was a national UFO society with branches in most major cities.

Space vehicles were described in various ways: cylindrical, aspirin-shaped, domed, disk-like, egg-shaped, circular, saucer-shaped, elliptical, frying pan-like, Japanese-box-kite-appearing. Some reportedly have pulsing lights; others are luminescent, balls of light, balls of fire, multi-colored. They appear both alone and in bunches. Most are fast and move in all directions, stopping and starting at will. Some are silent and some noisy.

Oscar Linke and his daughter Gabriella described their experience along these lines, "I noticed a large object whose diameter I estimated to be between thirteen and fifteen meters. It looked like a large covered frying pan sitting on the ground. It seemed to me as if it were supported by a cylindrical plant which had gone down from the top of the object through the center, rising into the air. The cylinder on which it was supported had disappeared within its center and had reappeared on the top. The object rose to a horizontal position, gaining altitude. Then it disappeared in the direction of Stockholm."

I was stunned by a news report from the Soviet Union's official government controlled newspaper. The notoriously staid Tass was quoted by Reuter News Service, in part, as follows:

Voronezh, Soviet Union:

An ENTIRE city in central Russia is spellbound by reports of giant aliens making a downtown visit.

They came from outer space, three-eyed monsters, landing from a shining ball-like craft—that's what everyone says.

Feverish excitement about UFOs is sweeping Voronezh, an industrial city of 900,000 people about 300 miles southeast of the Soviet capital.

"It happened on September 27th, 1989, recently, very recently," I thought out loud. A Soviet scientist was quoted as saying "We measured the landing site and recorded unbelievably high levels of magnetism," said Genrikh Silanov, head of the Voronezh Geophysical Laboratory. Two boys and a girl, ages 11 to 14, made the initial sighting which ultimately drew a crowd. Ten foot tall, three eyed, aliens, wearing silvery overalls, bronze boots, chest disks and two foot long side arms, came out of a ball about ten yards in diameter. A sixteen year old boy from the crowd was shot, vanished, then reappeared when the space vehicle departed.

A hoax by Russians, involving Tass, including the geophysical laboratory? Unlikely, I thought. Very unlikely!

Abductions were also recorded in the literature. Betty and Barney Hill claimed to have gotten out of their Bel Air automobile to observe a landed UFO in 1961. Becky Anderson and her family in 1957, Antonio Villas-Boas and his brother in Brazil in 1957, Jim and Jack Weiner, identical twins, and a lady named Clair, a horse farm owner, all claimed to have had encounters with aliens. Most of them experienced a form of suspended animation. They felt that they were floating through time while in their custody. All were returned or escaped, absent a piece of their lives and altered to reflect their experience. Some were able to describe their captors, space ships and provide other details.

Not every encounter with these visitors ended well for earth people. In an area of the Atlantic Ocean known as the Bermuda Triangle, numerous UFO sightings have been reported over a very long period of time. Ships, aircraft and people have been lost. Compass malfunctions, equipment failures and time discontinuities are the norm. The sighting involving Navy Flight 19 cost the U.S. Military six aircraft and seventeen men. In another incident near the Triangle a flight leader named Thomas Mantel reported that he was following a huge metallic cylinder. Did its weapons shoot him down? Early mariners avoided the strange looking sea in the area near Bermuda and they told stories about fish-like monsters that come from that part of the ocean. More recently an American and a Soviet nuclear submarine reportedly collided underwater some three hundred miles from Bermuda, creating an incident that almost triggered nuclear war. In fact, the Triangle seemed to have produced so many stories from such a diverse universe of people that it was almost impossible to disregard all of them.

Then there was Roswell—Roswell, New Mexico. The story started with a sighting at three in the afternoon on June 28, 1947, a sighting of nine saucer-like aircraft flying in a line at ten thousand feet. Kenneth Arnold, a businessman, saw them just to the east of the Cascade Mountains. Was it the same nine objects or something else that caused the powerful radar stations in Albuquerque and Roswell to track numerous unidentified flying objects that flittered around southern New Mexico starting on July 2nd? Did the United Airlines pilot, flying over Idaho, falsify his report involving nine flying disks, bigger than aircraft on July 4th? What happened? What really happened late at night on July 4th when a brilliant lighted object fell to earth near Roswell?

Why did the Air Force keep the Roswell incident under raps for more than forty-five years? What did their belated 1994 report about secret experimental equipment operating in the area really mean?

From my research, it became clear that recent movies involving close encounters with UFOs drew some of their material from the same kind of data I was surfacing.

Some of the sightings were thought to be comets. That caused me to expand my reading to include those strange solar bodies that have vexed people since the earliest times. Their origin unknown to early civilization, their make-up still sometimes debated, comets have brought fear and morbid speculation to people of science and religion for centuries. Flying about the sun in their egg-shaped orbits with star-like heads, some the size of earth, tails up to a million miles long that always point away from the sun, each comes and goes like the passing of a fast train on a black night. "Save us from the devil, the Turk and the comet," was the prayer of the early Christians and more than one scientist had predicted the end of the earth when a comet approached.

As The Great September Comet rocketed toward earth in 1882 such predictions were rife in the gold camps of the Sierras, and nowhere were they more strongly sounded than at Bodie where the outlandish and grotesque were the norm. Approaching like a giant silver horse with its long tail pointing away from the sun, it appeared as a single nucleus, very bright compared to a star, bright as a quarter moon on a dark night. You could still see it after the sun rose over the horizon. That comet came out of that small space in the sky from which all comets that will get very close to the sun approach. Scientists call them "sun-grazers." They all reach perihelion very close to our sun. Comets that get that close are worrisome. If one hits the sun, earth or one of the other planets all hell could break loose. Some astronomers thought that The Great September Comet would hit the sun, unleashing fires that would end life on earth. Such thoughts fueled the fear fires of the comet occultists and mystics of that time, rekindling the stories about how comets carried disease, like the plague, in their tails and were responsible for the demise of the dinosaurs. In the early years, comets were part of the unknown and like most things people don't understand, they created fear, fear that generated myth and fantasy.

David Gill, her majesty's astronomer, working for England at the Cape of Good Hope in 1882, photographed the Great September Comet. In Ireland, at the Duw Echt Observatory, Ralph Copeland and J.G. Lohse used a spectrograph on it in one of the first attempts to determine the mineral content of a comet. They found iron. Other astronomers all over Europe and North America followed the advance of The Great September Comet, hoping its silvery radiance would shed new scientific light on extraterrestrial matters. Observers were puzzled by this comet because it approached as a single entity but departed split in four parts, looking like a string of pearls, all traveling at slightly different speeds.

Known comets return to the earth's area at mathematically predictable cycles. This one would be difficult to predict because of the varied speeds of its parts. Most scientists explain unusual things in terms of existing accepted logic and language. Few are able to extend their thinking out into the unknown. Gill and other astronomers theorized that the Great September Comet's break-up was caused by solar tides, something that could not be proved or disproved.

Were they right? I thought. "In 1882 the September Comet came down towards earth as a single entity but it went back up as four separate things. That's a scientific fact! Whatever I saw in the field near Bridgeport with mother came down as one and went back as four. Could there be a connection, a relationship, a bond?"

Scientists today would have us believe that they know all about comets. But do they? Not long ago, scientists decried chiropractic, acupuncture and herbal remedies and they praised a good hot breakfast of bacon and eggs. What would they say today? And how would they explain the Apache's use of a herbal blood thinning tonic made from a weed they called *zagosti*. Doctors prescribe it today for cardiac patients under the name Coumadin.

Sightings and abductions, are some real and some imagined? Are they related or unrelated to comets? Do scientists really understand them? And there are similarities between the comets of September 1882 and June 1995. Are they related or is the similarity a coincidence? Sean McCarthy disappears in September 1882 and Sean-someone shows up in Lee Vining in June, 1995. In both instances, the earth was being approached by a sun-grazing comet. What's going on?

My mind flashed. Brodrick has a friend, Hiam Yehuda, at Edwards Air Force Base, a fact I almost overlooked. They had gone to medical school together and I had talked with him at several conventions and parties. A ladies man, one whose ego required constant female adulation. They fawned over him and he loved it. A psychologist with fine medical credentials and a colonel or general or something in the Air Force. I picked up the phone, got the number for the base, called, and to my surprise he was on the line in short order. I invited him to lunch the next day and he accepted without question—a man who enjoyed a rendezvous. I asked him not to tell Brodrick and I suspected that the request heightened his interest.

I arrived at Edwards just after eleven in the morning, having planned my approach with Hiam the previous evening and practiced on the drive up.

The base was well guarded and the staff security conscious. Edwards housed many secrets, experimental equipment, stealth technology, newly designed aircraft and weapons. Many UFO sightings had been attributed to things put in the air by men and women at Edwards Air Force Base. I recalled from my research another UFO sighting on the eastside of the Sierra Nevada Mountains, one seen by thousands of people including folks not far from Bodie.

On April 17, 1962, the thing was over New York, headed west. It was later reported over Kansas City and parts of Colorado. It was bright enough to light up the streets of Reno, Nevada before it turned southeast passing near Bodie and then it moved on toward Las Vegas. The North American Air Defense Command (N.O.R.A.D.) tracked it on radar before it vanished from the screen being monitored by Nellis Air Force base personnel. Major newspapers including the *Los Angles Times, Nevada State Journal, Las Vegas Sun* and others reported its passage and the papers had stories of the sighting from a pilot and controllers in towers at Reno, Elko and Las Vegas airfields. Most people speculated that whatever it was crashed in the desolate region somewhere east of Las Vegas. The Air force investigated. The public heard nothing. Was the thing related to a secret project at Edwards, I mused?

Traditionally the Air Force had the lead in dealing with matters related to UFOs, so one of their people showing up in Lee Vining was consistent with that role.

The Air Force and the F.B.I. had acted quickly in response to reports about the strange people who had arrived in Lee Vining. A Continental Airline pilot, driving a delayed flight from San Francisco to Houston, had called in an emergency while traveling over the area. Powerful military radar installations at or near Edwards Air Force Base, China Lake Naval Weapons Center and Nellis Air Force Range, all reported unusual activity over the Bridgeport Valley on June 9th. The sightings were confirmed from satellites, commercial radar installations in Carson City and Reno and individuals. It was communicated on ham radio as well as commercial radio, TV and newspaper.

Trouble, possibly danger, almost certainly speculation by those who believed in UFOs' was lurking about. In fact, government computers were programmed to compile UFO sighting information and identify those instances when extra terrestrial activity was potentially real. It had happened before and officials knew that they must act quickly to contain publicity and maintain cover. Hiam Yehuda and an F.B.I. operative were immediately ordered to take charge.

Hiam met me in the administrative office and we went to a small quiet restaurant in Mojave where Hiam sat patiently sipping his wine, waiting for me to break the ice. After some small talk I looked him in the eye. "A kid named Pedro, a dog called Trigo, a tall blond called Tex, Sean, Nellie and Daly, all picked up in Lee Vining on June 10th by State Troopers. An officer from your base is involved along with the F.B.I. The cops are trying to hush it up but that's impossible. Do you want to tell me what you know or do you want a bunch of big time reporters from the *Times*, *Post* and other influential newspapers and wire services here waving the Freedom of Information Act? Tell me, off the record, what you know and I promise to keep you out of it if that's your wish."

I had Hiam on the defensive. He looked a little pink around the ears and it was obvious that he didn't like his position. I waited.

Hiam cleared his throat to gain time. He wanted to respond but he knew he shouldn't until he had gathered his thoughts. He didn't want to tell me that he was the leading psychologist on the base and that he went to Lee Vining, met the F.B.I. investigator and picked up the strangers at the Bridgeport jail. He had spent a week debriefing them. He knew they had an incredible, almost believable story that was being checked out thoroughly by Air Force and F.B.I. staff. Everything they said seemed to ring true but it wasn't logical; it couldn't have happened. He hoped their game would be found out. He'd faced this sort of thing before. There's almost always a hoax or a freak of nature involved.

One thing Hiam knew for sure. The emotional press and the gullible public could not be told. It would be too much for the world to take. What would the government say? What could the Air Force do? We have no star ships. Panic would follow, he thought.

Hiam knew it probably would get out one way or another. Too many people knew. Being cast as a bad guy, the man who had stonewalled, lied, concealed the truth was unappealing to psychologists, at least one like him, who craved adulation. Trapped, he needed a way out, time to think and instinctively he fell back on a basic technique used by members of his profession when in doubt. He started asking questions. "What do you think is going on?" he said.

I sensed his dilemma, recognized the question as a diversion and realized that Hiam probably wished he had not answered his phone yesterday. In fact, I anticipated the problem he would have, thanks to mother's teaching.

I was prepared. "I think I know what's happening," I said, raising my hand in a friendly gesture. "But I don't mean to sound like a prosecutor. Let's try to think this through together. You don't need to say anything, just nod if I am on track and shake your head if not. How does that sound?"

Well we can try it," Hiam haltingly responded, relieved to have avoided a confrontation.

I touched his hand saying, "Thanks," before starting a well-rehearsed series of questions.

"Are some of those picked up, strangers let's call them, Americans? (Nod)

"Are they all Americans?" (Shrug)

"Were there two men, two women, a boy and a dog? (Nod)

"Do you know the person from Edwards who picked them up? (Nod)

"Well?" (Nod)

"Is the person a he? (Nod)

"Does the person work with you?" (Nod)

"Are the strangers still at Edwards? (Head Shake)

"Did they have a unique story?" (Nod)

"Did you hear it?" (Nod)

"Did you believe it?" (No Response)

"Were they abducted?" (No Response)

"In 1882?" (No Response, Expression Change, Discomfort)

"Did they come from some type of flying vehicle?" (No Response)

"If they had come from a flying vehicle, could it have come from Edwards?" (Head Shake)

"Some other Air Force base?" (Head Shake)

"Are the strangers still in California?" (Nod)

"Is the Air Force holding them?" (Head Shake)

"Is the F.B.I. holding them?" (No Response)

"In Pasadena?" (Partial Nod)

Hiam put up his hand. "I can't give you any more. I've revealed too much already. I was the officer who picked them up and did the initial debriefings. Don't use my name! I could get into a hell of a lot of trouble for just talking to you. Their story is unbelievable. We'll probably find out it's all a hoax. It wouldn't be the first time. It's also a dangerous area for you to play in. Give it up! When certain people feel that National Security is involved almost anything can happen!

"By the way where did you get 1882?" he asked with a concerned look.

"The Great September Comet. String of Pearls, they called it. Came out of the sky as one. Went back up as four bodies. I read about it in the astronomy books. I saw the same thing on June 9th in the fields near Bridgeport. This thing started out as one silvery structure, broke into four parts, went behind the mountain, returned as three, went down again and then came back and left as four. Clearly four separate objects rising out. Seemed like quite a coincidence. Then there was Sean McCarthy. I stay at his ranch in the valley. He disappeared from Bodie in September, 1882."

Hiam blanched. Sean McCarthy's name had struck a chord and I had provided him with something new, something he didn't realize could be found out. It was true, Sean had been abducted; I could see it in his eyes, feel it in the air. He was tense, knowing I knew, realizing the jig was up.

20

TEX SHOUTED FOR THE BLOOD-
thirsty men to halt but no one paid any attention until he fired a shot in the
air. He stepped between the badger and the men, saying in a firm, quiet voice,
"Reckon the ruckus is over, this fellow won. He don't deserve to die. Leave him
alone." One of the drunks started forward with his club but Tex lowered his
gun in the man's direction and he stopped, remembering what happened to
Washoe Cete. "Go home, go wherever you want, like I told you, the fight's
over," said Tex.

He watched the crowd break up and head back toward town where
they would be swallowed up by saloons, gambling halls and pleasure houses.
Sean McCarthy and two small men lingered behind. One offered to help in a
voice that sounded unusual to Tex but he accepted.

They managed to get the badger into it's cage and started to carry
him back toward the Tuolumne Stable when a Mexican boy with a wheat-
colored dog appeared out of the darkness followed shortly by a short stocky
old Mexican *hombre* with a missing front tooth. The noise and excitement
had lured the adventurous spirit of youth out into the street, then to the
embankment. Pedro didn't want to see the fight but he couldn't stand not
being a part of such a happening. He had seen the final engagement, felt sorry
for both animals and like Tex, he wanted to save the badger. The tall blond
cowboy, a hero by his measure, needed help and Pedro wanted to be part of
the badger's salvation. Tex suggested that they would have an easier time if
someone went into town and rented a buckboard and Pedro jumped at the
opportunity. Tex handed the young Hispanic some money to pay for the rig
and Pedro started off immediately with Juan and the two smallish men who

wanted to go along, leaving Tex and Sean with the badger and the approaching comet. Juan had planned to take the money and not return but he realized that his son wanted genuinely to help the animal and the other two were equally determined. He was forced to go along.

Pedro had been distracted by the badger's plight and had not looked carefully at their companions. One of them whispered softly, "I'm willin' any time you are, Pedro?" My God, he thought, recognizing Daly Storm dressed in men's clothes, realizing suddenly that both his new companions were female. When they reached town the ladies broke off, telling them to wait at the stable for them to return.

The women quickly changed into alluring, traditional attire designed to get the attention of the handsome cowboy. Tex couldn't believe their transformation. Two small men left; two shapely ladies bedecked like dance hall girls returned.

They then loaded the badger on the buckboard and headed for Cottonwood Canyon where Tex planned to release the wounded animal near the creek. The water would help him and it seemed fitting to leave the animal near the trail Tex had taken on his way to a new life in Bodie. Would this place provide a road to a future life for the little fellow, or would the harsh world of animals be too much? thought Tex.

They moved easily along the well-marked trail by the light of the moon, stars and approaching comet. No one noticed the French Canadian man following, evil thoughts filling his black heart. De la Roche moved with the stealth of a hunter, the Winchester he had retrieved from his hotel room in town in hand, his colt strapped tight to his leg. His instincts sharp, crisp, on point; his body, tense, in pursuit of his quarry. There were seven of them, three men, two women, a boy and a dog. It was a large group and it would be hard to cut them all down.

The cowboy was armed, tough, and the two other men and at least one of the women carried guns. He made a plan. He could tell that the boy was favored, like most kids, favored by everyone. If he shot the boy some of them would rush to his aid making themselves easy targets. He would shoot the youngster and one or two more before slipping away into the blackness, using the trees and brush to cover his withdrawal. He would ease back toward Bodie, find a hiding place near the trail and wait for their return. From ambush he could chop down one or two more. Then he would move again, this time all the way back to town. The survivors would not be able to identify him but they would be easy to find in Bodie the next day where they would be relating their horror story. If any of the four he really wanted was still alive, he would eliminate him or her in his own time.

The group stopped and John de la Roche slipped down behind a recently cut tree stump sighting the boy's back with his Winchester. It was light enough to see his target, easily. The comet was helping him. It was quiet, actually very still, an unusual condition for the forest. He took a deep breath, preparing himself to fire. His hands were steady, the blood in his veins running cold. He enjoyed killing, relished the idea of downing his prey. He started to squeeze the trigger, slowly, when suddenly—without warning—the semidarkness gave way to total blackness.

Tex and his procession had stopped and found an unusually quiet place to release the badger. They were about to start back when the soft light of the night suddenly went out. The night air had become thick and heavy and Tex felt the cold hand of fear gripping his heart. It's like being down in a mine, with all the lights out, he thought.

It seemed an eternity but it was actually only a few seconds before a strange white light appeared, coming from the north. An elliptical object moving fast, splitting suddenly into four parts, one descending, three swooping, circling. Tex was transfixed, Juan awestruck, de la Roche unable to squeeze the trigger. All were frozen, caught in the spell of the eerie light, a light that seemed to carry with it a strange thickness.

Then the descending cylinder of light stopped moving and hovered near the earth.

The thing looked like a giant luminescent mushroom. Its glow gripped the travelers. Their clear understanding faded, ebbed away, the way strength slowly departs the dying.

21

HIAM YEHUDA ROSE FROM THE LUNCH
table, nodding politely, and paid the bill. We seated ourselves in his car and
moved out into traffic in silence. It was some time before I said, "I know I have
no right to ask or expect anything more but I am driven to find them. Can you
give me a clue, anything that would help me?" I got no response until we
reached my car in the administrative office parking lot.

Before he parted he said, "I can't tell you where they are. I can't even
tell you where Trigo is. But if you continue the search be careful, Frances.
Remember, Bodie is a ghost town."

I left with his warning ringing in my ears.

My mind thrashed about, speculating as I drove home. Why did Hiam
mention Trigo. Trigo means wheat. Food. Does food have something to do with
all this? Could I find the dog? Would he lead me to the strangers? Crazy. All
this UFO stuff must be messing up my mind, I thought.

What is the F.B.I. doing to the strangers? And why am I in danger?
Someone with power got me out of jail; he freed me from a drunk driving
charge, a serious matter in California. I promised to let go, give up the
investigation, but hadn't. Could they take me, break me, make me a prisoner?"

I was willing to take personal risk because the story had me caught in
its power.

Imagine the reaction! People whisked away. The same people returning
more than a hundred years later. What things would they bring back with
them: wisdom, knowledge, disease, changed attitudes, new abilities,
inadequacies? Abductions by some unknown power. How bizarre! I thought.

Paula, my bright daughter, provided one of the answers. "Our dog goes to the kennel when we go away," she said.

Twenty phone calls later, I found a woman who said they had a yellow dog named Trigo at their kennel and animal hospital on North Fair Oaks Boulevard in Pasadena. This seemed too easy. Had Hiam known that I would find the kennel? Was he suggesting that the strangers were nearby?

I left immediately for the kennel. When I arrived, Trigo was bouncing about, yipping and barking softly. I asked the attendant if anyone named Pedro ever came to see him and was told that no one came to visit. They had been given a thousand dollars to cover his keep and a phone number to call when that ran out. For twenty dollars, I secured the number and then drove randomly around, hoping for some kind of break. I was familiar with this part of Pasadena and knew there were a lot of hospitals and rest homes in the area.

I decided to spend a few days asking questions. At one point I used a pay phone to call the number I'd gotten at the kennel. It turned out to be a Wells Fargo Bank in the area but that was all I got.

On the morning of the third day of searching, I spotted a gardening truck manned by a polite Japanese.

"Good morning. Maybe you can help me," I said.

"Glad help, glad help," he answered, bowing each time he spoke.

"This may sound strange but I'm looking for some people who were brought here, to one of these rest homes or hospitals, within the last couple of weeks. A boy, Mexican, about fifteen, a blond man who looks like a young cowboy, an older Irishman and two ladies, one with red hair, dressed like, well, fancy ladies"

"*Hi*, I see them. They come in Air Force cars, three of them. They stay at the Vista Oaks on Fair Oaks. Fourth floor, I see boy at courtyard window on fourth floor when I do yard."

"Thank you, thank you," I said, my heart pounding.

We parted and I got the exact address from a phone book at the Albertson's Market nearby, drove to Vista Oaks Rest Home and Hospital and feeling like a detective, "cased the joint." It was fenced. There was an entrance in front with a guard desk. Getting in would take some planning; I needed time to think, to catch my breath. They are there, right there in the Vista Oaks and I am very close to getting their story—my story. I will get in.

22

TEX KNEW IT WAS MORNING, different from others somehow, in a way he did not understand. He could vaguely remember sleeping on the hard ground during the night. It was a sleep unlike others, a deep slumber, as if he had been very drunk. But he wasn't hung over. He was a few miles northeast of Black Point on the shore of Mono Lake not far from Cottonwood Canyon.

Things looked changed, not like Tex remembered. The lake's water level was way down, there was wire strung from tall poles and the trail was covered with a hard black substance. He could see carriages moving along a roadway far in the distance. His companions, Sean, Pedro, Nellie and Daly were still asleep. They had all been on a journey, one he could not recall or grasp, but Tex knew they had been somewhere together and now they were back where it started. He felt like he had been riding on a peaceful river, a waterway that went on and on—no start, no finish. Had he been in heaven or in Hell?

Tex recalled the sermons he had heard about the grandeur of God's celestial home and the inferno in the adobe of the damned. Neither description squared with whatever he had experienced. Have I been to a land, a world where things just went on and on, without nature's cycles? he thought. No birth, no aging, no death, no color in the leaves of fall, no chill of winter, no blush of spring, the rutting season without the urge to mate. Somehow he believed he had spent time with those who lived in such a place, suspended in a fluid environment. He could only remember vague images, shadows covered by a blanket of thick, dark stillness. Had they found peace, harmony, equilibrium with the cosmos, a state sought by the Hopi and other pueblo dwelling southwestern Indian Tribes? Everlasting harmony with the supernatural, the universe—a goal sought by some Indians?

No matter what, Tex knew his mind had been altered. He had thoughts and words running about in his head that were not there before. He felt cleansed, experiencing warmth, a comforting feeling. Had he made a confession, was he revealed and forgiven? He seemed to know everything about those sleeping around him, even their darkest secrets. He had heard that this is what happened to the souls of the dead.

And he knew about two others, the ones who had not returned. Juan the greaser who harbored a monstrous hatred for *gringos*, killed an unknown young girl in San Francisco for no good reason, set fire to a hotel in the same city, robbed and murdered with the Joaquin Murieta gang, stole, cheated, took advantage of others whenever possible. The other, John de la Roche, a French Canadian who murdered and cheated his way into a gold fortune on the front end of his life cycle and after loosing his money, set about killing the people involved with the losses on the back of his cycle. They were evil men, assassins, deserving of punishment and he wondered if their absence was the result of their deeds.

He tried to crystallize his thoughts by asking himself questions. Did those beings without life cycles mete out justice? Did God have a cycle? Had he been judged good and returned because of some ruling? Is what's happening to me what actually takes place after death? Are the worthy returned while the hideous remain behind? And where was the dividing line between good and evil? Daly used drugs, worked as a prostitute; she had just fornicated with Pedro. Nellie was certainly no angel, an adventurer, who sought the Bad Man From Bodie. He had done plenty of sinning himself and he had broken many of the rules. But what were the rules and who made them?

The questions were too much for Tex, for any human. His mind was alive with strange new thoughts and an awareness that he could reveal his inner secrets without fear or embarrassment. He realized he knew everything about his companions and that they knew all about his private life, a fact that would have terrorized him before the abduction? Abduction? Was that the answer? Had they just been snatched away.

The settlement of Lee Vining was not far, and when the others awoke, they agreed to strike out in that direction. They came out of the hills saying nothing, fascinated, watching more and more closely the coaches, wagons, carts and other unknown kinds of wheeled-things, traveling at high speeds in both directions. There were no animals pulling the wagons. How could that be, thought Tex. They could make out people inside the conveyances, in the front, mostly, looking like teamsters without jobs. Tex asked, "How could a teamster work without a team?" But he got no answer from any of the others. They all were staring, wide-eyed.

As they approached the road, Trigo started barking at the passing vehicles. This small, yellow dog had made the trip with them. How had he changed? Did Trigo feel cleansed? What did he know about people and life that he had not known before?

Tex remembered the farewell the Houston Icehouse-gang had given him before he left for Bodie. "You-all come back now," were his friends' last words. Where were they now? He thought.

23

AT HOME THAT NIGHT, MOTHER AND I drank our wine and schemed. Both of us knew I needed a plan that would get me into Vista Oaks. Mother was good at plotting, particularly when she had a little "juice" in her system.

Two days later, dressed as an Air Force Major in the medical corps, I walked easily through the Vista Oaks gate without being challenged. I wore an official looking uniform recently tailored by a shop in Hollywood that catered to well to do military and thespians. All I had to say was, "I'm Doctor Woges from Edwards Air Force Base, assistant to Colonel Hiam Yehuda, here to see Pedro and the others." Discipline on any base is usually lax in peacetime, even in security conscious locations. I simply got into the elevator, punched the button for the fourth floor, went up, and stepped out into a corridor in front of a large room.

And there they were, all of them, sitting or flopped about, dressed in modern, casual clothes, looking nothing like the way they were described by the Lee Vining locals. I could hardly believe my luck. I was ecstatic, yet surprisingly calm

Introducing myself as Doctor Woges, I met each in turn. I felt I already knew them: Tex Garland, Sean McCarthy, Nellie Moore, Daly Storm and Pedro Olivera. They were polite, friendly, and easy to talk to. Before I could ask any questions Tex said "I got a powerful hankerin' to find out what's goin' on 'round here. It's puzzlin'. Some men in uniform—military uniform I guess— picked us up and put us in fancy wagons that went real fast. We went south, down the same trail I had taken on my way to Bodie. I know it was the same road, but it looked changed. We've been to confused to know what to do or think."

Nellie piped up, "Somebody, a doctor I think and a man in a dark suit–a real hard man took us here. They ain't told us nothin'. But, could they ever ask questions! On and on they went askin' question after question. We don't know what happened! We don't even know where we are!"

"That's what I am here for," I said, to help you understand what's happening. Let's see if we can work together and help each other."

I stayed for ten days, sitting quietly with each of them individually, listening to their stories. I slept in a spare room and ate their hospital food. I had a change of cloths in my kit and all the other necessities of life were provided by the hospital. The staff got used to seeing me around and no one seemed to question my right to be there. Getting out might pose a problem but the story came first. Hurry, finish and get out before they find me, I thought.

I was desperate to speed up the process but I knew that completeness was essential. When I was alone, trying to think or rest, the fingers of fear crept over my innards. But I took careful notes and used my recorder. I also answered their questions as best I could and we puzzled together about what they had experienced. I told them about cars, airplanes, televisions and the modern world. When I spoke of such things they sometimes acted like small children finding something for the first time; after their eyes glazed over in disbelief.

Their frankness was totally outside the norm for adults, who always concealed more than they told. They also seemed to know all about each other, a condition that was hard to accept. What would this world be like if everyone knew all about everyone else? I thought.

I learned that there were two others, evil men, Juan Olivera, the boy's father, and a French Canadian named John de la Roche. They did not return. Had some force decided to snuff out the candle of the wicked?

There was a common thread that ran through all the tales. Whatever or whoever took them had a powerful interest in life cycles. It was as if they had no beginning, no ending, no cycles of their own. None of them knew much about their abductors but all of them felt that their captors had a sincere interest in birth, maturity, aging, and death. What type of beings were they? I thought. How could they exist without cycles? How did they reproduce? I probed, searching for answers to such questions.

The strangers remembered every detail of their own lives and that of the others abducted with them but they only sensed the presence of their abductors. I pondered. Were my new friends taken for gold, for their knowledge of gold, for something related to food? Probably not. None was expert prospectors or miners and they had no food or food expertise. Then what? What kind of karma is involved here?

Difficult questions, ones that kept me awake during most nights before one possible explanation came to mind: abducted for information, knowledge, understanding of life cycles by some being that lived in perpetuity, like a computer, probably capable of repairing itself and drawing power from some unknown source. Possible, it was wild, but possible. But if that were true, how did they keep their hostages alive without aging for one hundred and thirteen years? Was time irrelevant?

There were plenty of explanations to choose from. Albert Einstein developed a mathematical formula which suggested that time travel was theoretically possible. I thought about his relativity formula: $E=MC^2$, energy equals mass times the speed of light squared. A formula relating mass, a person's, for example, to speed and energy. Given the appropriate amount of energy, mass could be moved throughout time. Sounds crazy, and I sure don't know much about science but they built the atomic bomb using that formula. Were those abducted transported on the wings of Einstein's relativity?

Or could it have something to do with electricity. Brodrick, my dear husband, was always talking about the use of electromagnetic forces in medicine. For years he had speculated that the ailments housed in the human body came from changed atoms that could be realigned electronically to harmonize with the normal healthy others. He had said it a million times in his boastful, surgeon-like way; and I could recite it from memory. "Atoms make up all human body parts. They are tiny particles of matter. Each atom has a center that contains neutrons that have no electrical charge. The center part also has protons that have a positive electrical charge. Think of protons as being like the positive terminal on a battery. Orbiting the center are electrons. They have a negative electrical charge. The electrons go flying around the nucleus much like the planets' orbit the sun. Because of their electrical charges, the protons and electrons are stimulated when bombarded with a stream of electrical energy. They can be made to move about, re-align themselves. If we learn how to control the re-alignment, we can control the form of matter. Cure illness. Stop cancer. Retard aging."

Brodrick was at least partially right. Doctors in the field of sports medicine currently employ electrical devices to speed up the healing process. Chiropractors have used similar appliances for years and there is a growing commercial body of electrically driven healing tools being peddled in specialty stores, health centers and through the mails. Could electric or electromagnetic forces be used to neutralize the aging process, placing it in remission while time passed?

Something like that might have been used to suspend the life cycles of the strangers. And maybe they weren't computer-like beings. Maybe they were people, some form of animal that had learned how to stay their life cycles. Could that be it? Could they be searching for a way to bring their cycles back? Is it possible they don't like the state they are in? Are they seeking help from us? And why wait one hundred and thirteen years before returning? And what about the comets, or what our astronomers thought were comets? Do the unanswered questions matter? I thought. No, it doesn't matter. What actually happened and what I know, is enough to blow the socks off the people in the news media.

After that ten days I had it all, the incredible histories of seven people and a dog abducted one hundred and thirteen years ago from Bodie. Only five came back. I had their fingerprints on clean white paper. I took all of their pictures, in their original cloths, individually and collectively. And I bundled up everything needed to make the story believable.

Now it's time for me to get out! I thought. They will be looking for me. I don't have a second to waste! I wish Mother were here to help. But my thoughts kept circling around to other matters. My mind kept asking, What will happen to these people when my story comes out? They are my friends now. When released, if they are released, how will they cope with their new environment, the press, the world around them, absent family, friends and familiarity? How can they be integrated into today's society? Tex could still be a cowboy, I suppose. The first wrangler to go on "forever." Pedro is young enough to learn modern ways. The ladies, one had been an entertainer, the other, well, prostitution is legal in many Nevada counties. Would she go to the Mustang Ranch? I hope not. I wish her a better fate. But what about Sean? Can he go back, be accepted, be useful? Will I be able to give these fine people a chance to regain their lives?

I now have responsibility for the future of five people, honest and open people from out of the past. Tex was so gracious. He always said, "Make yourself to home," when I arrived. And, when I left he could be counted on to say, "Talk to you later or come back—now." I could fall in love with that big handsome kid. How can I do what's best for all of them, prevent their destruction, assure their future? My decisions can kill or cure, a fact often faced by reporters everywhere.

I was resting fitfully in my small room, struggling with frightful thoughts while trying to plan my departure, steeling myself against fear much like a boxer does before stepping into the ring, when there was a soft knock on the door. It made me flinch; and the prickly fingers of fear rose in my midsection. Then the door creaked and opened slowly.

And there he was, the same man, in the same gray pinstripe, who had talked to me in the Bridgeport Jail. He looked at me, shook his head and said, "You're a mess, drunk driving, impersonating an Air Force officer, tinkering with national security. You broke your promise to stay clear of it. Now look what you have done. These people are well cared for; they are happy. Why couldn't you leave it alone? You must know we can't let you tell anything. The public isn't ready. The press would eat it up and the country would panic. That's serious stuff. Every time a kid ran off their parents would scream aliens.

"There would be chaos and who would take the blame, your government, military, F.B.I., C.I.A.? We would get all the heat. No, Frances DeQuill, this story can never be told!"

While he was talking, my eyes fell on a plastic wastebasket by the bed stand. Just as he finished, I reached down, grabbed the basket and hurled it through the door. It clattered into the corridor, making a frightful racket. Tex was there in a flash, the others were close behind. "He's trying to kill me," I screamed as Tex waded in, cowboy style. Sean followed, head down, legs and arms pumping, Irish style. Nellie and Pedro grabbed hold of a leg and held it fast. He went down, the four of them in control.

"Hold him," I shouted. I grabbed my case and ran to the elevator. On the first floor, I bolted past the reception area yelling, "Get help, there's a big fight on the fourth floor! Some unauthorized person in a suit is up there!" I was gone into the night before anyone thought to ask who I was or where I was going.

I spotted a city bus just coming to a stop at Howard Street and jumped on board, fumbling for correct change.

I got off at Colorado Boulevard in front of the Dodsworth Bar and Grill, rushed east along the seedy main boulevard of Pasadena for three blocks to Marengo Avenue. There I turned south and then turned back east to the side entrance of the Friendly Inn where I occasionally played tennis with a friend. Her name was Dee, and she worked in their business office. I ducked into an alcove that held the restrooms and a bank of six pay phones. I had used the restroom facilities and the phones in the past and knew the place well.

I can't call home, I thought. They will be covering my house and Mother's. I was seriously paranoid. But my friend, Sally Peterson, they might not know about her. Sally, the consummate computer buff, had been a friend for many years. She was single, with a short and heavy build who had no time for her appearance or men. We shared joints many times in the troubled years. Sally lived in Laguna Beach, two hours away by car. How can I get there? Gary Robertson, I thought, the tall, thin, quiet man who ran a private limousine service. He might provide the answer.

Brodrick and I had used him many times as did other affluent types in the area. Not sounding the slightest surprised, he agreed to pick me up in fifteen minutes.

I dialed Sally's number. No answer. Where was she? She was always home in the evening. Time is my enemy. I am an easy target. People who saw me running will remember. Impersonating an Air Force medical officer, a serious charge. I could be jailed, kept out of circulation, for years. I dialed again. Still no answer. Where in hell is she?

Who was that man following me and what part of government did he represent? Was he with one of the two government intelligence activities run from the Air Force Base at Belvoir, Virginia? Their existence had been kept secret for years until reporters started asking questions. One group was reportedly set-up to recover debris from space vehicles that survived re-entry to earth; the other was responsible for recovery of downed Soviet Bloc equipment. At least that's what official government sources said about the two projects.

If they catch up with me, will I just disappear, vanish, no trace, no explanation? Hiam had warned me, I thought. He had said that Bodie was a ghost town!

My hands started to shake; the realization that tomorrow might not come was almost too much. I needed to use the restroom and once there I took off as much of the military hardware and paraphernalia as possible and tossed the cap into the trash. I then dialed again. No answer. Fifteen minutes almost up. What should I do? I'll try Sally just one more time, then look for Gary.

▼▲▼

It took Roger Duvall, F.B.I. Control Coordinator, more time then he would ever admit to untangle himself from the mess that damned woman had left for him. He had been taught not to try an arrest alone but this one seemed so simple; he had her cold. The bitch tricked him, got away, leaving a thousand problems. He called Washington, the local F.B.I. office and the police. An all points bulletin was sent out for Frances DeQuill.

Duvall knew time was short. He now needed the many eyes and ears of the law enforcement community. He would coordinate the chase from the local F.B.I. office. There was already surveillance in operation at her home and her mother's place. The phones had been tapped.

He wasn't at F.B.I. control for more than five minutes when the first encouraging word came in. A police car cruising westbound on Colorado Boulevard in Pasadena had seen a woman fitting the description. The situation seemed unusual, but by the time they turned around to follow she had disappeared. They now had two cars combing the area and more on the way. There were numerous hotels, restaurants, theaters, places she could hide in the area. She couldn't be far.

He called the Pasadena police captain, demanding that he expedite the search, stressing the need for more manpower. The captain assured Roger that he was providing a maximum effort when in fact, he was not. He didn't like being pushed around by F.B.I. types and he had a particular dislike for Duvall, who was overbearing, obnoxious, a real smart-ass.

▼▲▼

A police car pulled up in front of the Friendly Inn, parked behind a Lincoln Continental with its engine running and a man sitting in front. The two officers got out and located the valet who was parking cars. They questioned him about a female Air Force Officer and were told he had been very busy and hadn't seen anyone meeting that description. They then entered the hotel, approached the desk and asked both clerks if they had seen their suspect. The clerks had seen nothing.

▼▲▼

"My God Sally, it's you. I thought you would never answer! I need your help—really need it now! Can you come get me?"

"Sure," said Sally, "You sound scared."

"You got that one right," was my answer, "Now listen."

Sally was glad for the chance to get together with Francis. And she was surprised to learn that her friend was being followed and needed to stay out of sight. "Yes I can meet you at the Martinette Hotel, the one near the airport," she said. "Of course I can loan you a raincoat."

Exciting, Sally thought. Something exciting for a change.

When I reached the door, I saw the Lincoln with Gary waiting patiently. I was startled by the empty police car parked directly behind. Where were the cops? Waiting for me? I have to chance it. I eased out the door and jumped into the back seat before Gary could get out to hold the door. "Drive, I am in a hurry! Let's get to the Airport Martinette so I won't be late meeting Brodrick."

▾▲▾

The officers soon realized the hotel was too big, too complex for a thorough search but Chip took the western corridor as Holmes went east past the empty alcove. The two officers spent about fifteen minutes questioning everyone they encountered with no positive results. Chip returned to the desk where they enlisted the help of the female clerk to check the ladies' room. She found a military cap and some other military hardware in the trash. Chip rushed out to the car and called.

Reinforcements would be on hand soon. Chip noted that the Lincoln Continental had left but it was almost forty minutes later before the overworked valet told him that he had seen a uniformed woman leave in it. He knew she must be important, he said, so he had taken down the license plate number.

"Damn," was all Duvall could say when he realized his target was on the road. A trace was run on the vehicle, and they soon found out that the car was registered in the name of Gary Robertson, Pasadena. It took another five minutes to locate his Mobilnet phone number and only a few seconds for Duvall to dial and get Gary on the line. Yes, he had taken Francis DeQuill to the Airport Martinette on Century Boulevard. Left her there a little while ago.

▾▲▾

Sally found me sitting on a chair half hiding behind a newspaper. She knew I would be in an Air Force uniform but I could tell that the sight of me still shocked her. I put the raincoat over the uniform, gave Sally the suitcase and slipped outside and into her car.

It was now a little after eleven and we heard the sirens of the five police cars converging on the Martinette as we moved away.

I quickly described what was going on and the story I wanted to tell. "Sally, someone is chasing me. I don't know who, someone from the government but if he catches me he will put me away. I'm sure of it! And my story will never get into print. I'm exhausted, can't think and can't figure out what to do. Do you have any ideas?"

Sally had a good mind and I could feel it swinging into motion.

"Do you have a transcript?"

"Yes," I responded. "And I have tape recordings, pictures, names of witnesses, everything we need to prove what I've written is real."

"Spread the information, spread it fast," Sally said, half to herself.

"But, how? There is so much material and so little time.

"Yes, you are right, it's a problem of time. And you need to tell everyone at one time—simultaneous disclosure—that's what you must have, broad-scale, simultaneous disclosure," said Sally, her mind setting a plan.

Impossible, I thought, but refrained from saying so because I didn't want to hamper Sally's creative effort.

"We can do it! Let's use technology—the simple technology I've got at my own home."

I began to feel better, feeding on Sally's enthusiasm. "Simple technology? What do you mean?"

To start with, Sally explained, we'll put it all on computer disks, making twelve copies. She was a computer expert and could type like a whirlwind. I would make a dozen copies of the tapes, the newspaper articles and the notes and other material I had gathered. "Easy, it'll be easy," she said, as we arrived at her house.

▼▲▼

Joan DeQuill was worried. Things were out of control. She had not heard from her daughter for over a week. Her strong will demanded that she do something. But what? How? Was Frances still inside Vista Oaks? Was she a

250

captive? Somehow she must find out. She had driven past Vista Oaks three times recently but had seen nothing. The unmarked car that followed her whenever she went was unnoticed.

▼▲▼

Roger Duvall had people working day and night. They had identified all the DeQuill relatives and wire tapped their homes and businesses. They had twenty-four hour surveillance on Joan and they had tapped the phones of several neighbors who were identified as friendly. They were even building a file on other friends, both new and old, checking them out. Something bad would happen if they didn't get a break soon.

▼▲▼

Where would Frances go if she left the Vista Oaks? thought Joan. Sally, her friend in Laguna, that's a real possibility, she said to herself. She looked up the number in the card file and started to dial area code 714. Then suddenly she had a horrible thought and abruptly hung up. What if they had tapped her phone, would she lead them to her daughter? "No!" Joan said out loud.

▼▲▼

Roger Duvall was puzzled. Joan DeQuill had dialed 714, then hung up. Why? Was it just an error? Where was area code 714?

▼▲▼

It took almost three days for us to complete a printable transcript. We had arranged to send hard copies of everything out via Federal Express and Sally set her computer up to transmit email copies of the transcripts just before three in the afternoon Pacific Coast time, July 11. That would make the material available just ahead of the prime-time eastern news broadcasts.

At eight that morning Sally drove me to a pay phone at the Circle K Convenience Store on Glenneyre Street. I then called a surprised Hiam Yehuda, telling him to meet me for lunch at 12:30 that afternoon, in Laguna Beach at the Surf restaurant in the Seascape Hotel on Pacific Coast Highway.

I had almost four hours to kill and I wondered what bad things could happen in those few hours? Would the phone call I had just made be traced?

Sally and I quickly returned to her place and she then made a trip downtown where there were many small shops and stores, packed together, side-by-side. I needed something suitable for my important meeting. She returned with an outfit from a boutique on Forest Street. Not a perfect fit, but it would do.

Shortly before twelve-thirty I made my way to the Seascape, finding Hiam, looking glum waiting in the lobby. The fact that he was alone was a surprise, but then my whole life was now full of surprises. We took the elevator down to the dining room and were escorted to a table set for ten in a private alcove that had been reserved by Sally. The ocean view was magnificent, I remember.

We ordered Chardonnay and got comfortable before I said, "Hiam, as you probably know I found the strangers. I have the whole story now." There was no emotion in Hiam's face as I continued. "A man, probably F.B.I, found me at the Vista Oaks Rest Home with them. Tex and the others rescued me. The press will have what I found out just before three this afternoon our time—prime-time on the east coast. I have pictures of the strangers and their fingerprints along with the names and addresses of half a dozen employees at the Vista Oaks who know them. You know about the others in Lee Vining who saw them. You helped me when I started this puzzle and now I'm giving you a chance to bail the Air Force out. There will be a reporter here in about thirty-five minutes. You can talk with him, make an official Air Force confirmation of the story.

Hiam started to interrupt, but I held up my hand. "That's not all, Hiam, I want immunity from prosecution by the Air Force, the F.B.I., the Federal Government, the Bridgeport Police, anyone who has anything to do with this incident. But most importantly, I also want a written promise from the government to take care of these people and provide training, education, housing, food, clothes, life's necessities, everything they need, until they are able to productively re-enter society and care for themselves. I don't want them to be banished to some so-called "safe house" never to be seen again, but I also won't have them paraded about like freaks. They are now my friends and I want them treated well. I have typed all that out on a paper. Here's a copy. Your official Air Force signature will be sufficient."

"I can't do that. I would need approval. We must have more time." Hiam said, his face darkening.

"Too late for delays! Here's your chance to control the story. It's up to you!" I responded.

"I better make some calls," he said.

"You have twenty five-minutes," was my answer.

I ordered a crab salad and waited impatiently for Hiam, the reporter, the F.B.I., or whoever else might show up. I was uncomfortable sitting alone at a table set for ten in my ill-fitting outfit. About thirty minutes passed before a young, short, thin-faced man with long brown hair, very thick glasses, a small frame and a dowdy, wrinkled suit showed up with a press card from the Orange County Register. He introduced himself as Jim Greenberg and he had come, skeptically, in response to an unusual phone call that morning.

I offered him a glass of wine that he accepted, and lunch that he declined. He settled himself, got out a small tape recorder and a notebook and looked over at me with a doubtful look on his face.

"I am Francis DeQuill, housewife, mother, sometimes reporter who is about to tell you a story you won't believe. Colonel Hiam Yehuda from Edwards Air Force Base is here in the hotel. I hope he will join us to confirm my story, but if not, I will give you this briefcase which contains all of the documentation you will need to confirm. This afternoon five other newspapers will receive this same information and documentation along with the news services and broadcast media. I have gone to great lengths to place the information in the hands of many. You have the unique opportunity, first hand, to make of it what you will.

At that moment Hiam Yehuda appeared with the man in the now-familiar pinstriped suit. I introduced Hiam to the reporter and then turned to the man in the suit and said, "And your name and branch of government is?"

"Roger Duvall, F.B.I.," he replied, producing an identification badge for the reporter who took down its number. "Let me add to what Mrs. DeQuill will tell you. The United States Air Force and the F.B.I. have been diligently working on case number 1376UFO-A since June 9th. The people who are involved are in our care. A complete statement from us will emanate from Washington at about three this afternoon."

While Roger was talking, Hiam slipped me the paper I had given to him. It was signed.

"What does case number 1376UFO-A relate to?" said Jim, looking straight at Hiam.

"A UFO sighting and an abduction of five, possibly seven, people," replied Hiam.

"Is the Air Force and the F.B.I. confirming this?" asked Jim.

"Yes," was the response.

In a way I suddenly felt sad—even depressed—as I watched the stir going on around me. Could this all be resolved so quickly after all I had been through? I guess I had expected more of a fight from Hiam. Now this amazing story would be published, even given credibility by the very ones who went to such measures to cover it all up. Why had they been so sure that people wouldn't be able to deal with things that seemed impossible? And why had they rolled over so quickly when I called their bluff? Had they really learned from Watergate and other cover-ups?

In time, I imagine, my five friends and their experience will be taken for granted as we discover more and more about our universe. I may never know all the new corridors this fresh knowledge will lead us down. But I do know that my life is now completely changed.

And this little hotel will never be the same either. It will now be known throughout the world as the launching pad for the bizarre story called Bodie Gone.

Notes

THIS NOVEL IS FICTION BUT IT IS ALSO packed with historical references including actual events, happenings, circumstances, experiences, concepts, places and people. The historical references are accurately placed in the time period set out in the story. Many of the historical references will be well known to the readers. Some of those that may not be so easily identified are: the gold finds on Carson Hill, near the confluence of the Quesnelle (old spelling) and the Caribou Rivers, in the Superstition Mountains and those near Bodie. Other less well known references include: Battle of Quitman Canyon, Miwok Indian attack near the American River, 1856 China Camp Tong War, Chinese escape on Rocket, Mexican oppression in Sonora, flume hanging in Columbia, Warren wagon train slaughter, killing of two Chinese by Three-Fingered Jack, capture of Joaquin Murieta, Black Bart's robbery, Lone Pine earthquake, Bodie Stock Market collapse, death of the Dutchman's wife, Bodie explosion of 1879, Louis L'amour's imposter, cock fights and badger/dog fights. The Great Comet, September 1882, including its break up into four parts, "string of pearls," was a real happening. All the UFO sightings are a part of history. They are, of course, believed by some people and debunked by others. The 1995 UFO incident in the Bridgeport Valley is based on an actual sighting that has been advanced in time to fit the story line.

Less well recognized historical concepts include *Veda Madre*, "Bad Man From Bodie" and the Indian beliefs, superstitions and folklore which are taken primarily from Chiricahua Apache faith and legend.

The descriptions and names of cities, towns, settlements, buildings, saloons, stables, mines, mills, railroads, ships, rivers, lakes, mountains, trails and other places are, for the most part, historically factual.

The novel's historical characters often interact with its fictional players and the details related to specific events sometimes deviate from history to accommodate that interaction.

The following historical characters and real people are mentioned; Mr. Anderson, Captain Armstrong, Becky Anderson, Santa Anna, Kinneth Arnold, Joan Baez, Sam Bannon, John Barclay, Martha Barclay, Black Bart, Roy Bean, Antonio Villas-Boas, W.S. Bodey (various spellings), Nick Boule, Jim Bowie, John Butterfield, Sitting Bull, White Bull, Touissant Charbonneau, Ray and Van Childs, Jesse Chisholm, Christopher Carson, William Clark, Cochise, Howard Coit, Ralph Copeland, Confucius, Charles Crocker, David Crockett, General George Custer, Mr. Denny, Rattlesnake Dick, General Greenville Dodge, George Donner, Isaiah Dorman, Jack Duncan, Albert Einstein, Leighton Finley, William G. Fargo, John Fremont, Jack Garcia, Geronimo, David Gill, Charles Goodnight, General Grant, W. M. Gwynn, Collonel Benjamin Grierson, A.S. Hallidie, James G. Hardin, John Wesley Hardin, Barney Hill, Betty Hill, Mark Hopkins, Horton, Crazy Horse, H.M. House, Callis Huntington, President Andrew Jackson, President Thomas Jefferson, Bloody Knife, Jean Laffite, Llouis L'amour, Lilly Langtry, Wan Lee, Meriwether Lewis, President Lincoln, Gabriella Linke, Oscar Link, J.G. Lohse, "Doc," Frank and Jim Manning, Thomas Mantel, James Marshall, Mike McGowan, John Muir, Joaquin Murieta, Captain Nicholas Nolan, Emperosr Norton, Richard Owens, Charley Parkurst, Phillips, Rasberry, Robinson, Joe Rouse, Andrew J. Russell, Red Rowe, Sieur de La Salle, Chief Sealth, Fray Junipero Serra, Mr. Shay, General Sherman, Sacagawea, Genrikh Silanov, John Huron Smith, Jedadiah Smith, Skoapy Smith, Leland Stanford, Dallas Staudenmire, Robert Louis Stevenson, Mr. Stokes, Louise Wanda Strentzel, John Sutter, Zac Taylor, Ben Thompson, Jon Torsteinson, Jim Travis, Mark Twain, Cabeza De Vacă, Victorio, Joseph Redford Walker, Noisy Walker, Big Foot Wallace, Jacob Walzer, Henry Wells, John Wheeler, Charles Wilkens, Chief Winnemucca, Johnny Gray Wolf, Nathaniel Wyeth, Yesler, Brigham Young.